THE CALIFORNIANS

They answered the call of the Golden State, looking for fortune, fame, a new life . . . carving out their place, taming a new and wild land.

THE BEST OF THE WEST

Celebrate the heroes of the past who staked their claim and called the West their own, challenging themselves as none have before or since.

Other Western Anthologies
Edited by Bill Pronzini and Martin H. Greenberg:

*Published by Fawcett Books

THE CALIFORNIANS

Edited by
Bill Pronzini and
Martin H. Greenberg

FAWCETT GOLD MEDAL · NEW YORK

A Fawcett Gold Medal Book
Published by Ballantine Books
Copyright © 1989 by Bill Pronzini and Martin H. Greenberg

Library of Congress Catalog Card Number: 88-92210

ISBN 0-449-13471-7

Manufactured in the United States of America

First Edition: March 1989

Acknowledgments

"Thirst," by John Prescott. Copyright © 1953 by Flying Eagle Publications, Inc. First published in *Gunsmoke*. Reprinted by permission of Scott Meredith Literary Agency, Inc., 845 Third Avenue, New York, NY 10022.

"Stagecoach Stowaway," by L. P. Holmes. Copyright © 1949 by Street & Smith Publications, Inc. First published in *Western Story Magazine*. Reprinted by permission of the author.

"The Saga of Toby Riddle," by Todhunter Ballard. Copyright © 1970 by The Western Writers of America, Inc.

"Old Tom," by Bill Pronzini. Copyright © 1970 by Zane Grey Magazine, Inc.; revised version copyright © 1988 by Bill Pronzini. First published in *Zane Grey Western Magazine*.

"The Bear Flag Mutineers," by Frank Bonham. Copyright © 1945 by Popular Publications, Inc. First published in *Star Western* under the title "Brand of the Fear Flag Mutineers." Reprinted by permission of the author.

"Farallone Bounty," by Matt Stuart. Copyright © 1946 by Street & Smith Publications, Inc. First published in *Western Story Magazine* as by L. P. Holmes. Reprinted by permission of L. P. Holmes.

"Gunslinger," by Ed Gorman. Copyright © 1988 by Ed Gorman. An original story published by permission of the author.

Contents

Introduction

The Californians is the second volume in our new series of Western fiction anthologies celebrating frontier life in various Western states. It contains stories that are not only set in California, but that fictionally recreate the many aspects of its colorful and exciting history—stories written primarily by authors past and present who have lived within its boundaries.

The thirteen tales in these pages are told through the eyes of Spanish hildagos, miners, prospectors, settlers, gamblers, law officers, outlaws, soldiers, and a most unconventional gunslinger. In them you'll visit Los Angeles under Mexican rule, Hollywood in the silent-film era, the gold camps of the Mother Lode, the vast barren expanse of Death Valley, fog-shrouded San Francisco Bay, the settlements and Indian lands near the Oregon border, the Panamint and San Bernardino mountains and the High Sierras; you'll witness firsthand the Bear Flag revolt and the Modoc Indian War; and you'll ride with the legendary Zorro on one of his swashbuckling adventures.

Subsequent volumes in the series will take you to Arizona, New Mexico, Montana, Wyoming, and other Western states large and small. In each book you'll find short Western fiction at its most entertaining and historically accurate, by such writers as Owen Wister, Jack Schaefer, Dorothy M. Johnson, Elmore Leonard, Loren D. Estleman, and Brian Garfield.

We hope you enjoy this fictional journey through the Old West, as well as the one that preceeded it—*The Texans*—and all those to follow.

—Bill Pronzini and
Martin H. Greenberg

One of California's major literary figures during the last decade of the nineteenth century and the first half of the twentieth, Gertrude Atherton was a keen observer of the people of her native state. Such collections and novels as The Californians (1898), The Splendid Idle Forties (1902), The Sophisticates (1931), and The Horn of Life (1942) are as historically accurate as they are expertly crafted. Told with her unique blend of romance and realism, "The Ears of Twenty Americans" poignantly chronicles the turbulent days of the Bear Flag rebellion from both the Mexican and American points of view.

The Ears of Twenty Americans

★★★★★★★★★★★★★★★★

Gertrude Atherton

I

"GOD of my soul! Do not speak of hope to me. Hope? For what are those three frigates, swarming with a horde of foreign bandits, creeping about our bay? For what have the persons of General Vallejo and Judge Leese been seized and imprisoned? Why does a strip of cotton, painted with a gaping bear, flaunt itself above Sonoma? Oh, abomination! Oh, execrable profanation! Mother of God, open thine ocean and suck them down! Smite them with pestilence if they put foot in our capital! Shrivel their fingers to the bone if they dethrone our Aztec Eagle and flourish their stars and stripes above our fort! O California! That thy sons and thy daughters should live to see thee plucked like a rose by the usurper! And why? Why? Not because these piratical Americans have the right to one league of our land; but because, Holy Evangelists! they want it! Our lands are rich, our harbors are fine, gold veins our valleys, therefore we must be plucked. The United States of America are mightier than Mexico, therefore they sweep down upon us with mouths wide open. Holy God! That I could choke but one with my own strong fingers. Oh!'' Doña Eustaquia paused abruptly and smote her hands together. ''O that I were a man! That the women of California were men!''

On this pregnant morning of July seventh, eighteen hundred and forty-six, all aristocratic Monterey was gathered in the sala of Doña Modeste Castro. The hostess smiled sadly. ''That is the wish of my husband,'' she said, ''for the men of our country want the Americans.''

''And why?'' asked one of the young men, flicking a particle of dust from his silken riding jacket. ''We shall then have freedom from the constant war of opposing factions. If General Castro and Governor Pico are not calling Juntas in which to denounce each other, a Carillo is pitting his ambition against an Alvarado. The Gringos will rule us lightly and bring us peace. They will not disturb our grants, and will give us rich prices for our lands—''

''Oh, fool!'' interrupted Doña Eustaquia. ''Thrice fool! A hundred years from now, Fernando Altimira, and our names will be forgotten in California. Fifty years from now and our walls will tumble upon us whilst we cook our beans in the rags that charity—American charity—has flung us! I tell you that the hour the American flag waves above the fort of Monterey is the hour of the Californians' doom. We have lived in Arcadia—ingrates that you are to complain—they will run over us like ants and sting us to death!''

''That is the prediction of my husband,'' said Doña Modeste. ''Liberty, independence, decency, honor, how long will they be his watch-words?''

''Not a day longer!'' cried Doña Eustaquia, ''for the men of California are cowards.''

''Cowards! We? No man should say that to us!'' The caballeros were on their feet, their eyes flashing, as if they faced in uniform the navy of the United States, rather than confronted, in lace ruffles and silken smallclothes, an angry scornful woman.

''Cowards!'' continued Fernando Altimira. ''Are not men flocking about General Castro at San Juan Bautista, willing to die in a cause already lost? If our towns were sacked or our women outraged would not the weakest of us fight until we died in our blood? But what is coming is for the best, Doña Eustaquia, despite your prophecy; and as we cannot help it—we, a few thousand men against a great nation—we resign ourselves because we are governed by reason instead of by passion. No one reverences our General more than Fernando Altimira. No grander man ever wore a uniform! But he is fighting in a hopeless cause, and the fewer who uphold him the less blood will flow, the sooner the struggle will finish.''

Doña Modeste covered her beautiful face and wept. Many of the women sobbed in sympathy. Bright eyes, from beneath gay rebosas or delicate mantillas, glanced approvingly at the speaker. Brown old men and women stared gloomily at the floor. But the greater number followed every motion of their master-spirit, Doña Eustaquia Ortega.

She walked rapidly up and down the long room, too excited to sit down, flinging the mantilla back as it brushed her hot cheek. She was a woman not yet forty, and very handsome, although the peachness of youth had left her face. Her features were small but sharply cut; the square chin and firm mouth had the lines of courage and violent emotions, her piercing intelligent eyes interpreted a terrible power of love and hate. But if her face was so strong as to be almost unfeminine, it was frank and kind.

Doña Eustaquia might watch with joy her bay open and engulf the hated Americans, but she would nurse back to life the undrowned bodies flung upon the shore. If she had been born a queen she would have slain in anger, but she would not have tortured. General Castro had flung his hat at her feet many times, and told her that she was born to command. Even the nervous irregularity of her step today could not affect the extreme elegance of her carriage, and she carried her small head with the imperious pride of a sovereign. She did not speak again for a moment, but as she passed the group of young men at the end of the room her eyes flashed from one languid face to another. She hated their rich breeches and embroidered jackets buttoned with silver and gold, the lace handkerchiefs knotted about their shapely throats. No man was a man who did not wear a uniform.

Don Fernando regarded her with a mischievous smile as she approached him a second time.

"I predict, also," he said, "I predict that our charming Doña Eustaquia will yet wed an American—"

"What!" she turned upon him with the fury of a lioness. "Hold thy prating tongue! I marry an American? God! I would give every league of my ranchos for a necklace made from the ears of twenty Americans. I would throw my jewels to the pigs, if I could feel here upon my neck the proof that twenty American heads looked ready to be fired from the cannon on the hill!"

Everybody in the room laughed, and the atmosphere felt lighter. Muslin gowns began to flutter, and the seal of disquiet sat less heavily upon careworn or beautiful faces. But before the respite was a moment old a young man entered hastily from the street, and throwing his hat on the floor burst into tears.

"What is it?" The words came mechanically from every one in the room.

The herald put his hand to his throat to control the swelling muscles. "Two hours ago," he said, "Commander Sloat sent one Captain William Mervine on shore to demand of our Commandante the surrender of the town. Don Mariano walked the floor, wringing his hands, until a quarter of an hour ago, when he sent word to the insolent servant of a pirate-republic that he had no authority to deliver up the capital, and bade him go to San Juan Bautista and confer with General Castro. Whereupon the American thief ordered two hundred and fifty of his men to embark in boats—do not you hear?"

A mighty cheer shook the air amidst the thunder of cannon; then another, and another.

Every lip in the room was white.

"What is that?" asked Doña Eustaquia. Her voice was hardly audible.

"They have raised the American flag upon the Customhouse," said the herald.

For a moment no one moved; then as by one impulse, and without a word, Doña Modeste Castro and her guests rose and ran through the streets to the Customhouse on the edge of the town.

In the bay were three frigates of twenty guns each. On the rocks, in the street by the Customhouse and on its corridors, was a small army of men in the naval uniform of the United

States, respectful but determined. About them and the little man who read aloud from a long roll of paper, the aristocrats joined the rabble of the town. Men with sunken eyes who had gambled all night, leaving even serape and sombrero on the gaming table; girls with painted faces staring above cheap and gaudy satins, who had danced at fandangos in the booths until dawn, then wandered about the beach, too curious over the movements of the American squadron to go to bed; shop-keepers, black and rusty of face, smoking big pipes with the air of philosophers; Indians clad in a single garment of calico, falling in a straight line from the neck; eagle-beaked old crones with black shawls over their heads; children wearing only a smock twisted about their little waists and tied in a knot behind; a few American residents, glancing triumphantly at each other; caballeros, gay in the silken attire of summer, sitting in angry disdain upon their plunging, superbly trapped horses; last of all, the elegant women in their lace mantillas and flowered rebosas, weeping and clinging to each other. Few gave ear to the reading of Sloat's proclamation.

Benicia, the daughter of Doña Eustaquia, raised her clasped hands, the tears streaming from her eyes. "Oh, these Americans! How I hate them!" she cried, a reflection of her mother's violent spirit on her sweet face.

Doña Eustaquia caught the girl's hands and flung herself upon her neck. "Ay! California! California!" she cried wildly. "My country is flung to its knees in the dirt."

A rose from the upper corridor of the Customhouse struck her daughter full in the face.

II

THE same afternoon Benicia ran into the sala where her mother was lying on a sofa, and exclaimed excitedly: "My mother! My mother! It is not so bad. The Americans are not so wicked as we have thought. The proclamation of the Commodore Sloat has been pasted on all the walls of the town and promises that our grants shall be secured to us under the new government, that we shall elect our own alcaldes, that we shall continue to worship God in our own religion, that

our priests shall be protected, that we shall have all the rights
and advantages of the American citizen—"

"Stop!" cried Doña Eustaquia, springing to her feet. Her
face still burned with the bitter experience of the morning.
"Tell me of no more lying promises! They will keep their
word! Ay, I do not doubt but they will take advantage of our
ignorance, with their Yankee sharpness! I know them! Do
not speak of them to me again. If it must be, it must; and at
least I have thee." She caught the girl in her arms, and covered the flowerlike face with passionate kisses. "My little
one! My darling! Thou lovest thy mother—better than all the
world? Tell me!"

The girl pressed her soft, red lips to the dark face which
could express such fierceness of love and hate.

"My mother! Of course I love thee. It is because I have
thee that I do not take the fate of my country to deeper heart.
So long as they do not put their ugly bayonets between us,
what difference whether the eagle or the stars wave above the
fort?"

"Ah, my child, thou hast not that love of country which is
part of my soul! But perhaps it is as well, for thou lovest thy
mother the more. Is it not so, my little one?"

"Surely, my mother; I love no one in the world but you."

Doña Eustaquia leaned back and tapped the girl's fair cheek
with her finger.

"Not even Don Fernando Altimira?"

"No, my mother."

"Nor Flujencio Hernandez? Nor Juan Perez? Nor any of
the caballeros who serenade beneath thy window?"

"I love their music, but it comes as sweetly from one throat
as from another."

Her mother gave a long sigh of relief. "And yet I would
have thee marry some day, my little one. I was happy with
thy father—thanks to God he did not live to see this day—I
was as happy, for two little years, as this poor nature of ours
can be, and I would have thee be the same. But do not hasten
to leave me alone. Thou art so young! Thine eyes have yet
the roguishness of youth; I would not see love flash it aside.
Thy mouth is like a child's; I shall shed the saddest tears of
my life the day it trembles with passion. Dear little one! Thou
hast been more than a daughter to me; thou hast been my
only companion. I have striven to impart to thee the ambition

of thy mother and the intellect of thy father. And I am proud of thee, very, very proud of thee!''

Benicia pinched her mother's chin, her mischievous eyes softening. "Ay, my mother, I have done my little best, but I never shall be you. I am afraid I love to dance through the night and flirt my breath away better than I love the intellectual conversation of the few people you think worthy to sit about you in the evenings. I am like a little butterfly sitting on the mane of a mountain lion—"

"Tush! Tush! Thou knowest more than any girl in Monterey, and I am satisfied with thee. Think of the books thou hast read, the languages thou hast learned from the Señor Hartnell. Ay, my little one, nobody but thou wouldst dare to say thou cared for nothing but dancing and flirting, although I will admit that even Ysabel Herrera could scarce rival thee at either."

"Ay, my poor Ysabel! My heart breaks every night when I say a prayer for her.'' She tightened the clasp of her arms and pressed her face close to her mother's. "Mamacita, darling," she said coaxingly, "I have a big favor to beg. Ay, an enormous one! How dare I ask it?''

"Aha! What is it? I should like to know. I thought thy tenderness was a little anxious."

"Ay, mamacita! Do not refuse me or it will break my heart. On Wednesday night Don Thomas Larkin gives a ball at his house to the officers of the American squadron. Oh, mamacita! mamacita! *darling!* do, do let me go!''

"Benicia! Thou wouldst meet those men? Válgame Dios! And thou art a child of mine!"

She flung the girl from her, and walked rapidly up and down the room, Benicia following with her little white hands outstretched. "Dearest one, I know just how you feel about it! But think a moment. They have come to stay. They will never go. We shall meet them everywhere—every night—every day. And my new gown, mamacita! The beautiful silver spangles! There is not such a gown in Monterey! Ay, I must go. And they say the Americans hop like puppies when they dance. How I shall laugh at them! And it is not once in the year that I have a chance to speak English, and none of the others girls can. And all the girls, all the girls, all the girls, will go to this ball. Oh, mamacita!''

Her mother was obliged to laugh. "Well, well I cannot

refuse you anything; you know that! Go to the ball! Ay, yi, do not smother me! As you have said—that little head can think—we must meet these insolent braggarts sooner or later. So I would not—'' her cheeks blanched suddenly, she caught her daughter's face between her hands, and bent her piercing eyes above the girl's soft depths. "Mother of God! That could not be. My child! Thou couldst never love an American! A Gringo! A Protestant! Holy Mary!''

Benicia threw back her head and gave a long laugh—the light rippling laugh of a girl who has scarcely dreamed of lovers. "I love an American? Oh, my mother! A great, big, yellow-haired bear! When I want only to laugh at their dancing! No, mamacita, when I love an American thou shalt have his ears for thy necklace.''

III

THOMAS O. Larkin, United States Consul to California until the occupation left him without duties, had invited Monterey to meet the officers of the *Savannah, Cyane,* and *Levant,* and only Doña Modeste Castro had declined. At ten o'clock the sala of his large house on the rise of the hill was thronged with robed girls in every shade and device of white, sitting demurely behind the wide shoulders of coffee-colored dowagers, also in white, and blazing with jewels. The young matrons were there, too, although they left the sala at intervals to visit the room set apart for the nurses and children; no Montereña ever left her little ones at home. The old men and the caballeros wore the black coats and white trousers which Monterey fashion dictated for evening wear; the hair of the younger men was braided with gay ribbons, and diamonds flashed in the lace of their ruffles.

The sala was on the second floor; the musicians sat on the corridor beyond the open windows and scraped their fiddles and twanged their guitars, awaiting the coming of the American officers. Before long the regular tramp of many feet turning from Alvardo Street up the little Primera del Este, facing Mr. Larkin's house, made dark eyes flash, lace and silken gowns flutter. Benicia and a group of girls were standing by Doña Eustaquia. They opened their large black fans as if to wave back the pink that had sprung to their cheeks. Only

Benicia held her head saucily high, and her large brown eyes were full of defiant sparkles.

"Why art thou so excited, Blandina?" she asked of a girl who had grasped her arm. "I feel as if the war between the United States and Mexico began tonight."

"Ay, Benicia, thou hast so gay a spirit that nothing ever frightens thee! But, Mary! How many they are! They tramp as if they would go through the stair. Ay, the poor flag! No wonder—"

"Now, do not cry over the flag any more. Ah! there is not one to compare with General Castro!"

The character of the Californian sala had changed for ever; the blue and gold of the United States had invaded it.

The officers, young and old, looked with much interest at the faces, soft, piquant, tropical, which made the effect of pansies looking inquisitively over a snowdrift. The girls returned their glances with approval, for they were as fine and manly a set of men as ever had faced death or woman. Ten minutes later California and the United States were flirting outrageously.

Mr. Larkin presented a tall officer to Benicia. That the young man was very well-looking even Benicia admitted. True, his hair was golden, but it was cut short, and bore no resemblance to the coat of a bear; his mustache and brows were brown; his gray eyes were as laughing as her own.

"I suppose you do not speak any English, señorita," he said helplessly.

"No? I spik Eenglish like the Spanish. The Spanish people no have difficult at all to learn the other langues. But Señor Hartnell he say it no is easy at all for the Eenglish to spik the French and the Spanish, so I suppose you no spik one word our langue, no?"

He gallantly repressed a smile. "Thankfully I may say that I do not, else would I not have the pleasure of hearing you speak English. Never have I heard it so charmingly spoken before."

Benicia took her skirt between the tips of her fingers and swayed her graceful body forward, as a tule bends in the wind.

"You like dip the flag of the conqueror in honey, señor. Ay! We need have one compliment for every tear that fall since your eagle stab his beak in the neck de ours."

"Ah, the loyal women of Monterey! I have no words to express my admiration for them, señorita. A thousand compliments are not worth one tear."

Benicia turned swiftly to her mother, her eyes glittering with pleasure. "Mother, you hear! You hear!" she cried in Spanish. "These Americans are not so bad, after all."

Doña Eustaquia gave the young man one of her rare smiles; it flashed over her strong dark face, until the light of youth was there once more.

"Very pretty speech," she said, with slow precision. "I thank you, Señor Russell, in the name of the women of Monterey."

"By Jove! Madam—señora—I assure you I never felt so cut up in my life as when I saw all those beautiful women crying down there by the Customhouse. I am a good American, but I would rather have thrown the flag under your feet than have seen you cry like that. And I assure you, dear señora, every man among us felt the same. As you have been good enough to thank me in the name of the women of Monterey, I, in behalf of the officers of the United States squadron, beg that you will forgive us."

Doña Eustaquia's cheek paled again, and she set her lips for a moment; then she held out her hand.

"Señor," she said, "we are conquered, but we are Californians; and although we do not bend the head, neither do we turn the back. We have invite you to our houses, and we cannot treat you like enemies. I will say with—how you say it—truth?—we did hate the thought that you come and take the country that was ours. But all is over and cannot be changed. So, it is better we are good friends than poor ones; and—and—my house is open to you, señor."

Russell was a young man of acute perceptions; moreover, he had heard of Doña Eustaquia; he divined in part the mighty effort by which good breeding and philosophy had conquered bitter resentment. He raised the little white hand to his lips.

"I would that I were twenty men, señora. Each would be your devoted servant."

"And then she have her necklace!" cried Benicia, delightedly.

"What is that?" asked Russell; but Doña Eustaquia shook her fan threateningly and turned away.

"I no tell you everything," said Benicia, "so no be too curiosa. You no dance the contradanza, no?"

"I regret to say that I do not. But this is a plain waltz; will you not give it to me?"

Benicia, disregarding the angry glances of approaching caballeros, laid her hand on the officer's shoulder, and he spun her down the room.

"Why, you no dance so bad!" she said with surprise. "I think always the Americanos dance so terreeblay."

"Who could not dance with a fairy in his arms?"

"What funny things you say. I never been called fairy before."

"You have never been interpreted." And then, in the whirl-waltz of that day, both lost their breath.

When the dance was over and they stood near Doña Eustaquia, he took the fan from Benicia's hand and waved it slowly before her. She laughed outright.

"You think I am so tired I no can fan myself?" she demanded. "How queer are these Americanos! Why, I have dance for three days and three nights and never estop."

'Señorita!"

"Sí, señor. Oh, we estop sometimes, but no for long. It was at Sonoma two months ago. At the house de General Vallejo."

"You certainly are able to fan yourself; but it is no reflection upon your muscle. It is only a custom we have."

"Then I think much better you no have the custom. You no look like a man at all when you fan like a girl."

He handed her back the fan with some choler.

"Really, señorita, you are very frank. I suppose you would have a man lie in a hammock all day and roll cigaritos."

"Much better do that than take what no is yours."

"Which no American ever did!"

"Excep' when he pulled California out the pocket de Mexico."

"And what did Mexico do first? Did she not threaten the United States with hostilities for a year, and attack a small detachment of our troops with a force of seven thousand men—"

"No make any difference what she do. Sí she do wrong, that no is excuse for you do wrong."

Two angry young people faced each other.

"You steal our country and insult our men. But they can fight, Madre de Dios! I like see General Castro take your little Commodore Sloat by the neck. He look like a little gray rat."

"Commodore Sloat is a brave and able man, Miss Ortega, and no officer in the United States Navy will hear him insulted."

"Then much better you lock up the ears."

"My dear Captain Russell! Benicia! what is the matter?"

Mr. Larkin stood before them, an amused smile on his thin intellectual face. "Come, come, have we not met tonight to dance the waltz of peace? Benicia, your most humble admirer has a favor to crave of you. I would have my countrymen learn at once the utmost grace of the Californian. Dance El Jarabe, please, and with Don Fernando Altimira."

Benicia lifted her dainty white shoulders. She was not unwilling to avenge herself upon the American by dazzling him with her grace and beauty. Her eye's swift invitation brought Don Fernando, scowling, to her side. He led her to the middle of the room, and the musicians played the stately jig.

Benicia swept one glance of defiant coquetry at Russell from beneath her curling lashes, then fixed her eyes upon the floor, not raising them again. She held her reedlike body very erect and took either side of her spangled skirt in the tips of her fingers, lifting it just enough to show the arched little feet in their embroidered stockings and satin slippers. Don Fernando crossed his hands behind him, and together they rattled their feet on the floor with dexterity and precision, whilst the girls sang the words of the dance. The officers gave genuine applause, delighted with this picturesque fragment of life on the edge of the Pacific. Don Fernando listened to their demonstrations with somber contempt on his dark handsome face; Benicia indicated her pleasure by sundry archings of her narrow brows, or coquettish curves of her red lips. Suddenly she made a deep curtsy and ran to her mother, with a long sweeping movement, like the bending and lifting of grain in the wind. As she approached Russell he took a rose from his coat and threw it at her. She caught it, thrust it carelessly in one of her thick braids, and the next moment he was at her side again.

IV

Doña Eustaquia slipped from the crowd and out of the house.
Drawing a reboso about her head she walked swiftly down
the street and across the plaza. Sounds of ribaldry came from
the lower end of the town, but the aristocratic quarter was
very quiet, and she walked unmolested to the house of General
Castro. The door was open, and she went down the long
hall to the sleeping room of Doña Modeste. There was no
response to her knock, and she pushed open the door and
entered. The room was dimly lit by the candles on the altar.
Doña Modeste was not in the big mahogany bed, for the
heavy satin coverlet was still over it. Doña Eustaquia crossed
the room to the altar and lifted in her arms the small figure
kneeling there.

"Pray no more, my friend," she said. "Our prayers have
been unheard, and thou art better in bed or with thy friends."

Doña Modeste threw herself wearily into a chair, but took
Doña Eustaquia's hand in a tight clasp. Her white skin shone
in the dim light, and with her black hair and green tragic eyes
made her look like a little witch queen, for neither suffering
nor humiliation could bend that stately head.

"Religion is my solace," she said, "my only one; for I
have not a brain of iron nor a soul of fire like thine. And,
Eustaquia, I have more cause to pray tonight."

"It is true, then, that José is in retreat? Ay, Mary!"

"My husband, deserted by all but one hundred men, is
flying southward from San Juan Bautista. I have it from the
washtub mail. That never is wrong."

"Ingrates! Traitors! But it is true, Modeste—surely, no?—
that our general will not surrender? That he will stand against
the Americans?"

"He will not yield. He would have marched upon Monterey and forced them to give him battle here but for this base
desertion. Now he will go to Los Angeles and command the
men of the South to rally about him."

"I knew that he would not kiss the boots of the Americans
like the rest of our men! Oh, the cowards! I could almost say
tonight that I like better the Americans than the men of my
own race. *They* are Castros! I shall hate their flag so long as
life is in me; but I cannot hate the brave men who fight for

it. But my pain is light to thine. They heart is wrung, and I am sorry for thee."

"My day is over. Misfortune is upon us. Even if my husband's life is spared—ay! shall I ever see him again?—his position will be taken from him, for the Americans will conquer in the end. He will be Commandante-General of the army of the Californias no longer, but—holy God!—a ranchero, a caballero! He at whose back all California has galloped! Thou knowest his restless aspiring soul, Eustaquia, his ambition, his passionate love of California. Can there be happiness for such a man humbled to the dust—no future! no hope? Ay!"—she sprang to her feet with arms uplifted, her small slender form looking twice its height as it palpitated against the shadows, "I feel the bitterness of that spirit! I know how that great heart is torn. And he is alone!" She flung herself across Doña Eustaquia's knees and burst into violent sobbing.

Doña Eustaquia laid her strong arm about her friend, but her eyes were more angry than soft. "Weep no more, Modeste," she said. "Rather, arise and curse those who have flung a great man into the dust. But comfort thyself. Who can know? Thy husband, weary with fighting, disgusted with men, may cling the closer to thee, and with thee and thy children forget the world in thy redwood forests or between the golden hills of thy ranchos."

Doña Modeste shook her head. "Thou speakest the words of kindness, but thou knowest José. Thou knowest that he would not be content to be as other men. And, ay! Eustaquia, to think that it was opposite our own dear home, our favorite home, that the American flag should first have been raised! Opposite the home of José Castro!"

"To perdition with Frémont! Why did he, of all places, select San Juan Bautista in which to hang up his American rag?"

"We never can live there again. The Gabilan Mountains would shut out the very face of the sun from my husband."

"Do not weep, my Modeste; remember thy other beautiful ranchos. Dios de mi alma!" she added with a flash of humor, "I revere San Juan Bautista for your husband's sake, but I weep not that I shall visit you there no more. Every day I think to hear that the shaking earth of that beautiful valley has opened its jaws and swallowed every hill and adobe. God grant that Frémont's hair stood up more than once. But go to bed, my friend. Look, I will put you there." As if Doña Modeste were an infant, she undressed and laid her between the linen sheets with their elaborate drawn work, then made her drink a glass of angelica, folded and laid away the satin coverlet, and left the house.

She walked up the plaza slowly, holding her head high. Monterey at that time was infested by dogs, some of them very savage. Doña Eustaquia's strong soul had little acquaintance with fear, and on her way to General Castro's house she had paid no attention to the snarling muzzles thrust against her gown. But suddenly a cadaverous creature sprang upon her with a savage yelp and would have caught her by the throat had not a heavy stick cracked its skull. A tall officer in the uniform of the United States Navy raised his cap from iron-gray hair and looked at her with blue eyes as piercing as her own.

"You will pardon me, madam," he said, "if I insist upon attending you to your door. It is not safe for a woman to walk alone in the streets of Monterey at night."

Doña Eustaquia bent her head somewhat haughtily. "I thank you much, señor, for your kind rescue. I would not like, at all, to be eaten by the dogs. But I not like to trouble you to walk with me. I go only to the house of Señor Larkin. It is there, at the end of the little street beyond the plaza."

"My dear madam, you must not deprive the United States of the pleasure of protecting California. Pray grant my humble request to walk behind you and keep off the dogs."

Her lips pressed each other, but pride put down the bitter retort.

"Walk by me, if you wish," she said graciously. "Why are you not at the house of Don Thomas Larkin?"

"I am on my way there now. Circumstances prevented my going earlier." His companion did not seem disposed to pilot the conversation, and he continued lamely, "Have you noticed, madam, that the English frigate *Collingwood* is anchored in the bay?"

"I saw it in the morning." She turned to him with sudden hope. "Have they—the English—come to help California?"

"I am afraid, dear madam, that they came to capture California at the first whisper of war between Mexico and the United States; you know that England has always cast a covetous eye upon your fair land. It is said that the English admiral stormed about the deck in a mighty rage today when he saw the American flag flying on the fort.''

"All are alike!" she exclaimed bitterly, then controlled herself. "You—do you admeer our country, señor? Have you in America something more beautiful than Monterey?"

The officer looked about him enthusiastically, glad of a change of topic, for he suspected to whom he was talking. "Madam, I have never seen anything more perfect than this beautiful town of Monterey. What a situation! What exquisite proportions! That wide curve of snow-white sand about the dark blue bay is as exact a crescent as if cut with a knife. And that semicircle of hills behind the town, with its pine and brush forest tapering down the crescent's points! Nor could anything be more picturesque than this scattered little town with its bright red tiles above the white walls of the houses and the gray walls of the yards; its quaint church surrounded by the ruins of the old presidio; its beautiful, strangely dressed women and men who make this corner of the earth resemble the pages of some romantic old picture-book—"

"Ay!" she interrupted him. "Much better you feel proud that you conquer us; for surely, señor, California shall shine like a diamond in the very center of America's crown." Then she held out her hand impulsively. "Mucho gracias, señor—pardon—thank you very much. If you love my country, señor, you must be my friend and the friend of my daughter. I am the Señora Doña Eustaquia Carillo de Ortega, and my house is there on the hill—you can see the light, no? Always we shall be glad to see you."

He doffed his cap again and bent over her hand.

"And I, John Brotherton, a humble captain in the United States Navy, do sincerely thank the most famous woman of Monterey for her gracious hospitality. And if I abuse it, lay it to the enthusiasm of the American who is not the conqueror but the conquered."

"That was very pretty—speech. When you abuse me, I put you out the door. This is the house of Don Thomas Larkin, where is the ball. You come in, no? You like I take your arm? Very well."

And so the articles of peace were signed.

V

"Yes, yes, indeed, Blandina," exclaimed Benicia, "they had no chance at all last night, for we danced until dawn, and perhaps they were afraid of Don Thomas Larkin. But we shall talk and have music tonight, and those fine new tables that came on the last ship from Boston must not be destroyed."

"Well, if you really think—" said Blandina, who always thought exactly as Benicia did. She opened a door and called: "Flujencio."

"Well, my sister?"

A dreamy-looking young man in short jacket and trousers of red silk entered the room, sombrero in one hand, a cigarito in the other.

"Flujencio, you know it is said that these 'Yankees' always 'whittle' everything. We are afraid they will spoil the furniture tonight; so tell one of the servants to cut a hundred pine slugs, and you go down to the store and buy a box of pen-knives. Then they will have plenty to amuse themselves with and will not cut the furniture."

"True! True! What a good idea! Was it Benicia's?" He gave her a glance of languid adoration. "I will buy those knives at once, before I forget it," and he tossed the sombrero on his curls and strode out of the house.

"How dost thou like the Señor Lieutenant Russell, Benicia?"

Benicia lifted her chin, but her cheeks became very pink.

"Well enough. But he is like all the Americans, very proud, and thinks too well of his hateful country. But I shall teach him how to flirt. He thinks he can, but he cannot."

"Thou canst do it, Benicia—look! look!"

Lieutenant Russell and a brother officer were sauntering slowly by and looking straight through the grated window at the beautiful girls in their gayly flowered gowns. They saluted, and the girls bent their slender necks, but dared not speak, for Doña Francesca Hernandez was in the next room and the door was open. Immediately following the American officers came Don Fernando Altimira on horseback. He scowled as he saw the erect swinging figures of the conquerors, but Benicia kissed the tips of her fingers as he flung his sombrero to the ground, and he galloped, smiling, on his way.

That night the officers of the United States squadron met the society of Monterey at the house of Don Jorje Hernandez. After the contradanza, to which they could be admiring spectators only, much to the delight of the caballeros, Benicia took the guitar presented by Flujencio, and letting her head droop a little to one side like a lily bent on its stalk by the breeze, sang the most coquettish song she knew. Her mahogany brown hair hung unconfined over her white shoulders and gown of embroidered silk with its pointed waist and full skirt. Her large brown eyes were alternately mischievous and tender, now and again lighted by a sudden flash. Her cheeks were pink; her round babylike arms curved with all the grace of the Spanish woman. As she finished the song she dropped her eyelids for a moment, then raised them slowly and looked straight at Russell.

"By Jove, Ned, you are a lucky dog!" said a brother officer. "She's the prettiest girl in the room! Why don't you fling your hat at her feet, as these ardent Californians do?"

"My cap is in the next room, but I will go over and fling myself there instead."

Russell crossed the room and sat down beside Benicia.

"I should like to hear you sing under those cypresses out on the ocean about six or eight miles from here," he said to her. "I rode down the coast yesterday. Jove! what a coast it is!"

"We will have a merienda there on some evening," said Doña Eustaquia, who sat beside her daughter. "It is very beautiful on the big rocks to watch the ocean, under the moonlight."

"A merienda?"

"A peek-neek."

"Good! You will not forget that?"

She smiled at his boyishness. "It will be at the next moon. I promise."

Benicia sang another song, and a half-dozen caballeros stood about her, regarding her with glances languid, passionate, sentimental, reproachful, determined, hopeless. Russell, leaning back in his chair, listened to the innocent thrilling voice of the girl, and watched her adorers, amused and stimulated. The Californian beauty was like no other woman he had known, and the victory would be as signal as the capture of Monterey. "More blood, perhaps," he thought, "but a victory is a poor affair unless painted in red. It will do these seething caballeros good to learn that American blood is quite as swift as Californian.''

As the song finished, the musicians began a waltz; Russell took the guitar from Benicia's hand and laid it on the floor.

"This waltz is mine, señorita," he said.

"I no know—"

"Señorita!" said Don Fernando Altimira, passionately, "the first waltz is always mine. Thou wilt not give it to the American?"

"And the next is mine!"

"And the next contradanza!"

The girl's faithful retinue protested for their rights. Russell could not understand, but he translated their glances, and bent his lips to Benicia's ear. That ear was pink and her eyes were bright with roguish triumph.

"I want this dance, dear señorita. I may go away any day. Orders may come tomorrow which will send me where I never can see you again. You can dance with these men every night of the year—"

"I give to you," said Benicia, rising hurriedly. "We must be hospitable to the stranger who comes today and leaves tomorrow," she said in Spanish to the other men. "I have plenty more dances for you."

After the dance, salads and cakes, claret and water, were brought to the women by Indian girls, who glided about the room with borrowed grace, their heads erect, the silver trays held well out. They wore bright red skirts and white smocks of fine embroidered linen, open at the throat, the sleeves very short. Their coarse hair hung in heavy braids; their bright little eyes twinkled in square faces scrubbed until they shone like copper.

"Captain," said Russell to Brotherton, as the men followed the host into the supper room, "let us buy a ranch, marry two of these stunning girls, and lie round in hammocks whilst these Western houris bring us aguardiente and soda. What an improvement on Byron and Tom Moore! It is all so unhackneyed and unexpected. In spite of Dana and Robinson I expected mud huts and whooping savages. This is Arcadia, and the women are the most elegant in America."

"Look here, Ned," said his captain, "you had better do less flirting and more thinking while you are in this odd country. Your talents will get rusty, but you can rub them up when you get home. Neither Californian men nor women are to be trifled with. This is the land of passion, not of drawing-room sentiment.''

"Perhaps I am more serious than you think. What is the matter?'' He spoke to a brother officer who had joined them and was laughing immoderately,

"Do you see those Californians grinning over there?'' The speaker beckoned to a group of officers, who joined him at once. "What job do you suppose they have put up on us? What do you suppose that mysterious table in the sala means, with its penknives and wooden sticks? I thought it was a charity bazaar. Well, it is nothing more nor less than a trick to keep us from whittling up the furniture. We are all Yankees to them, you know. Preserve my Spanish!''

The officers shouted with delight. They marched solemnly back into the sala, and seating themselves in a deep circle about the table, whittled the slugs all over the floor, much to the satisfaction of the Californians.

VI

AFTER the entertainment was over, Russell strolled about the town. The new moon was on the sky, the stars thick and bright; but dark corners were everywhere, and he kept his hand on his pistol. He found himself before the long low house of Doña Eustaquia Ortega. Not a light glimmered; the shutters were of solid wood. He walked up and down, trying to guess which was Benicia's room.

"I am growing as romantic as a Californian," he thought, "but this wonderful country pours its color all through one's nature. If I could find her window, I believe I should serenade her in true Spanish fashion. By Jove, I remember now, she said something about looking through her window at the pines on the hill. It must be at the back of the house, and how am I going to get over that great adobe wall? That gate is probably fastened with an iron bar—ah!''

He had walked to the corner of the wall surrounding the large yard behind and at both sides of Doña Eustaquia's house, and he saw, ascending a ladder, a tall figure, draped in a serape, its face concealed by the shadow of a sombrero. He drew his pistol, then laughed at himself, although not without annoyance. "A rival; and he has got ahead of me. He is going to serenade her."

The caballero seated himself uncomfortably on the tiles that roofed the wall, removed his sombrero, and Russell recognized Fernando Alitmira. A moment later the sweet thin chords of the guitar quivered in the quiet air, and a tenor, so fine that even Russell stood entranced, sang to Benicia one of the old songs of Monterey:

EL SUSPIRO

Una mirada un suspiro,
Una lagrima querida,
Es balsamo à la herida
Que abriste en mi corazón.

Por esa lagrima cara
Objeto de mi termina,
Yo te amé bella criatura
Desde que te ví llorar.

Te acuerdas de aquella noche
En que triste y abatida
Una lagrima querida
Vi de tus ojos brotar.

Although Russell was at the base of the high wall, he saw that a light flashed. The light was followed by the clapping of little hands. "Jove!" he thought, "am I really jealous? But damn that Californian!"

Altimira sang two more songs and was rewarded by the same demonstrations. As he descended the ladder and reached the open street he met Russell face to face. The two men regarded each other for a moment. The Californian's handsome face was distorted by a passionate scowl; Russell was calmer, but his brows were lowered.

Altimira flung the ladder to the ground, but fire-blooded as he was, the politeness of his race did not desert him, and his struggle with English flung oil upon his passion.

"Señor," he said, "I no know what you do it by the house of the Señorita Benicia so late in the night. I suppose you have the right to walk in the town si it please yourself."

"Have I not the same right as you—to serenade the Señorita Benicia? If I had known her room, I should have been on the wall before you."

Altimira's face flushed with triumph. "I think the Señorita Benicia no care for the English song, señor. She love the sweet words of her country: she no care for words of ice."

Russell smiled. "Our language may not be as elastic as yours, Don Fernando, but it is a good deal more sincere. And it can express as much and perhaps—"

"You love Benicia?" interrupted Altimira, fiercely.

"I admire the Señorita Ortega tremendously. But I have seen her twice only, and although we may love longer, we take more time to get there, perhaps, than you do."

"Ay! Dios de mi vida! You have the heart of rock! You chip it off in little pieces, one today, another tomorrow, and give to the woman. I, señor, I love Benicia, and I marry her. You understand? Si you take her, I cut the heart from your body. You understand?"

"I understand. We understand each other." Russell lifted his cap. The Californian took his sombrero from his head and made a long sweeping bow; and the two men parted.

VII

ON the twenty-third of July, Commodore Sloat transferred his authority to Commodore Stockton, and the new commander of the Pacific squadron organized the California Battalion of Mounted Riflemen, appointing Frémont major and Gillespie captain. He ordered them south at once to intercept Castro. On the twenty-eighth, Stockton issued a proclamation in which he asserted that Mexico was the instigator of the present difficulties, and justified the United States in seizing the Californias. He denounced Castro in violent terms as a usurper, a boasting and abusive chief, and accused him of having violated every principle of national hospitality and good faith toward Captain Frémont and his surveying party. Stockton sailed for the south the same day in the *Congress*, leaving a number of officers to Monterey and the indignation of the people.

"By Jove, I don't dare to go near Doña Eustaquia," said Russell to Brotherton. "And I'm afraid we won't have our picnic. It seems to me the Commodore need not have used such strong language about California's idol. The very people in the streets are ready to unlimb us; and as for the peppery Doña—''

"Speak more respectfully of Doña Eustaquia, young man," said the older officer, severely. "She is a very remarkable woman and not to be spoken slightingly of by young men who are in love with her daughter."

"God forbid that I should slight her, dear Captain. Never have I so respected a woman. She frightens the life out of me every time she flashes those eyes of hers. But let us go and face the enemy at once, like the brave Americans we are."

"Very well." And together they walked along Alvarado Street from the harbor, then up the hill to the house of Doña Eustaquia.

That formidable lady and her daughter were sitting on the corridor dressed in full white gowns, slowly wielding large black fans, for the night was hot. Benicia cast up her eyes expressively as she rose and curtsied to the officers, but her mother merely bent her head; nor did she extend her hand. Her face was very dark.

Brotherton went directly to the point.

"Dear Doña Eustaquia, we deeply regret that our Commodore has used such harsh language in regard to General Castro. But remember that he has been here a few days only and has had no chance to learn the many noble and valiant qualities of your General. He doubtless has been prejudiced against him by some enemy, and he adores Frémont—there is the trouble. He resents Castro's treating Frémont as an enemy before the United States had declared its intentions. But had he been correctly informed, he undoubtedly would have conceived the same admiration and respect for your brave General that is felt by every other man among us."

Doña Eustaquia looked somewhat mollified, but shook her head sternly. "Much better he took the trouble to hear true. He insult all Californians by those shemful words. All the enemies of our dear General be glad. And the poor wife! Poor my Modeste! She fold the arms and raise the head, but the heart is broken."

"Jove! I almost wish they had driven us out! Dear señora—" Russell and Benicia were walking up and down the corridor—"we have become friends, true friends, as sometimes happens—not often—between man and woman. Cease to think of me as an officer of the United States Navy, only as a man devoted to your service. I have already spent many pleasant hours with you. Let me hope that while I remain here neither Commodore Stockton nor party feeling will exclude me from many more.''

She raised her graceful hand to her chin with a gesture peculiar to her, and looked upward with a glance half sad, half bitter.

''I much appreciate your friendship, Capitan Brotherton. You give me much advice that is good for me, and tell me many things. It is like the ocean wind when you have live long in the hot valley. Yes, dear friend, I forget you are in the navy of the conqueror.''

''Mamacita,'' broke in Benicia's light voice, ''tell us now when we can have the peek-neek.''

''Tomorrow night.''

''Surely?''

''Surely, niñita.''

''Castro,'' said Russell, lifting his cap, ''peace be with thee.''

VIII

THE great masses of rock on the ocean's coast shone white in the moonlight. Through the gaunt outlying rocks, lashed apart by furious storms, boiled the ponderous breakers, tossing aloft the sparkling clouds of spray, breaking in the pools like a million silver fishes. High above the waves, growing out of the crevices of the massive rocks of the shore, were weird old cypresses, their bodies bent from the ocean as if petrified in flight before the mightier foe. On their gaunt outstretched arms and gray bodies, seamed with time, knobs like human muscles jutted; between the broken bark the red blood showed. From their angry hands, clutching at the air or doubled in imprecation, long strands of gray-green moss hung, waving and coiling, in the night wind. Only one old man was on his hands and knees as if to crawl from the field; but a comrade spurned him with his foot and wound his bony hand about the coward's neck. Another had turned his head to the enemy, pointing his index finger in scorn, although he stood alone on high.

All along the cliffs ran the ghostly army, sometimes with straining arms fighting the air, sometimes thrust blankly outward, all with life quivering in their arrested bodies, silent and scornful in their defeat. Who shall say what winter winds first beat them, what great waves first fought their deathless trunks, what young stars first shone over them? They have outstood centuries of raging storm and rending earthquake. Tradition says that until convulsion wrenched the Golden Gate apart, the San Franciscan waters rolled through the long valleys and emptied into the Bay of Monterey. But the old cypresses were on the ocean just beyond; the incoming and the outgoing of the inland ocean could not trouble them; and perhaps they will stand there until the end of time.

Down the long road by the ocean rode a gay cavalcade. The caballeros had haughtily refused to join the party, and the men wore the blue and gold of the United States. But the women wore fluttering mantillas, and their prancing high-stepping horses were trapped with embossed leather and silver. In a lumbering "wagon of the country," drawn by oxen, running on solid wheels cut from the trunks of trees, but padded with silk, rode some of the older people of the town, disapproving, but overridden by the impatient enthusiasm of Doña Eustaquia. Through the pine woods with their softly moving shadows and splendid aisles, out between the cypresses and rocky beach, wound the stately cavalcade, their voices rising above the sociable converse of the seals and the screeching of the seagulls spiking the rocks where the waves fought and foamed. The gold on the shoulders of the men flashed in the moonlight; the jewels of the women sparkled and winked. Two by two they came like a conquering army to the rescue of the cypresses. Brotherton, who rode ahead with Doña Eustaquia, half expected to see the old trees rise upright with a deep shout of welcome.

When they reached a point where the sloping rocks rose high above surf and spray, they dismounted, leaving the Indian servants to tether the horses. They climbed down the big smooth rocks and sat about in groups, although never beyond the range of older eyes, the cypresses lowering above them, the ocean tearing through the outer rocks to swirl and grumble in the pools. The moon was so bright, its light so broad and silver, they almost could imagine they saw the gorgeous mass of color in the pools below.

"You no have seaweed like that in Boston," said Benicia, who had a comprehensive way of symbolizing the world by the city from which she got many of her clothes and all of her books.

"Indeed no!" said Russell. "The other day I sat for hours watching those great bunches and strands that look like richly colored chenille. And there were stones that looked like big opals studded with vivid jewels. God of my soul, as you say, it was magnificent! I never saw such brilliant color, such delicate tints! And those great rugged defiant rocks out there, lashed by the waves! Look at that one; misty with spray one minute, bare and black the next! They look like an old castle which has been battered down with cannon. Captain, do you not feel romantic?"

"I feel that I never want to go into an art gallery again. No wonder the women of California are original."

"Benicia," said Russell, "I have tried in vain to learn a Spanish song. But teach me a Spanish phrase of endearment. All our 'darlings' and 'dearests' are too flat for California."

"Bueno; I teach you. Say after me: Mi muy querida prima. That is very sweet. Say."

"Mi muy—"

"Querida prima."

"Que— What is it in English?"

"My—very—darling—first. It no sound so pretty in English."

"It does very well. My—very—darling—first—if all these people were not about us, I should kiss you. You look exactly like a flower."

"Sí you did, Señor Impertinencio, you get that for thanks."

Russell jumped to his feet with a shout, and shook from his neck a little crab with a back like green velvet and legs like carven garnet.

"Did you put that crab on my neck, señorita?"

"Sí, señor."

A sulky silence of ten minutes ensued, during which Benicia sent little stones skipping down into the silvered pools, and Russell, again recumbent, stared at the horizon.

"Si you no can talk," she said finally, "I wish you go way

and let Don Henry Tallant come talk to me. He look like he want."

"No doubt he does; but he can stay where he is. Let me kiss your hand, Benicia, and I will forgive you."

Benicia hit his mouth lightly with the back of her hand, but he captured it and kissed it several times.

"Your mustache feels like the cat's," said she.

He flung the hand from him, but laughed in a moment. "How sentimental you are! Making love to you is like dragging a cannon uphill! Will you not at least sing me a love song? And please do not make faces in the tender parts."

Benicia tossed her spirited head, but took her guitar from its case and called to the other girls to accompany her. They withdrew from their various flirtations with audible sighs, but it was Benicia's merienda, and in a moment a dozen white hands were sweeping the long notes from the strings.

Russell moved to a lower rock, and lying at Benicia's feet looked upward. The scene was all above him—the great mass of white rocks, whiter in the moonlight; the rigid cypresses aloft; the beautiful faces, dreamy, passionate, stolid, restless, looking from the lace mantillas; the graceful arms holding the guitars; the sweet rich voices threading through the roar of the ocean like the melody in a grand recitativo; the old men and women crouching like buzzards on the stones, their sharp eyes never closing; enfolding all with an almost palpable touch, the warm voluptuous air. Now and again a bird sang a few notes, a strange sound in the night, or the soft wind murmured like the ocean's echo through the pines.

The song finished. "Benicia, I love you," whispered Russell.

"We will now eat," said Benicia. "Mamma,"—she raised her voice,—"shall I tell Raphael to bring down the supper?"

"Yes, niña."

The girl sprang lightly up the rocks, followed by Russell. The Indian servants were some distance off, and as the young people ran through a pine grove the bold officer of the United States squadron captured the Californian and kissed her on the mouth. She boxed his ears and escaped to the light.

Benicia gave her orders, Raphael and the other Indians followed her with the baskets, and spread the supper of tamales and salads, dulces and wine, on a large tablelike rock, just above the threatening spray; the girls sang each in turn, whilst the others nibbled the dainties Doña Eustaquia had provided, and the Americans wondered if it were not a vision that would disappear into the fog bearing down upon them.

A great white bank, writhing and lifting, rolling and bending, came across the ocean slowly, with majestic stealth, hiding the swinging waves on which it rode so lightly, shrouding the rocks, enfolding the men and women, wreathing the cypresses, rushing onward to the pines.

"We must go," said Doña Eustaquia, rising. "There is danger to stay. The lungs, the throat, my children. Look at the poor old cypresses."

The fog was puffing through the gaunt arms, festooning the rigid hands. It hung over the green heads, it coiled about the gray trunks. The stern defeated trees looked like the phantoms of themselves, a long silent battalion of petrified ghosts. Even Benicia's gay spirit was oppressed, and during the long ride homeward through the pine woods she had little to say to her equally silent companion.

IX

DoÑA Eustaquia seldom gave balls, but once a week she opened her salas to the more intellectual people of the town. A few Americans were ever attendant; General Vallejo often came from Sonoma to hear the latest American and Mexican news in her house; Castro rarely had been absent; Alvarado, in the days of his supremacy, could always be found there, and she was the first woman upon whom Pio Pico called when he deigned to visit Monterey. A few young people came to sit in a corner with Benicia, but they had little to say.

The night after the picnic some fifteen or twenty people were gathered about Doña Eustaquia in the large sala on the right of the hall; a few others were glancing over the Mexican papers in the little sala on the left. The room was ablaze with many candles standing, above the heads of the guests, in twisted silver candelabra, the white walls reflecting their light. The floor was bare, the furniture of stiff mahogany and horsehair, but no visitor to that quaint ugly room ever thought of looking beyond the brilliant face of Doña Eustaquia, the lovely eyes of her daughter, the intelligence and animation of the people she gathered about her. As a rule Doña Modeste Castro's proud head and strange beauty had been one of the living pictures of that historical sala, but she was not there tonight.

As Captain Brotherton and Lieutenant Russell entered, Doña Eustaquia was waging war against Mr. Larkin.

"And what hast thou to say to that proclamation of thy little American hero, thy Commodore"—she gave the word a satirical roll, impossible to transcribe—"who is heir to a conquest without blood, who struts into history as the Commander of the United States Squadron of the Pacific, holding a few hundred helpless Californians in subjection? O warlike name of Sloat! O heroic name of Stockton! O immortal Frémont, prince of strategists and tacticians, your country must be proud of you! Your newspapers will glorify you! Sometime, perhaps, you will have a little history bound in red morocco all to yourselves; whilst Castro—" she sprang to her feet and brought her open palm down violently upon the table, "Castro, the real hero of this country, the great man ready to die a thousand deaths for the liberty of the Californians, a man who was made for great deeds and born for fame, he will be left to rust and rot because we have no newspapers to glorify him, and the Gringos send what they wish to their country! Oh, profanation! That a great man should be covered from sight by an army of red ants!"

"By Jove!" said Russell, "I wish I could understand her! Doesn't she look magnificent?"

Captain Brotherton made no reply. He was watching her closely, gathering the sense of her words, full of passionate admiration for the woman. Her tall majestic figure was quivering under the lash of her fiery temper, quick to spring and strike. The red satin of her gown and the diamonds on her finely molded neck and in the dense coils of her hair grew dim before the angry brilliancy of her eyes.

The thin sensitive lips of Mr. Larkin curled with their accustomed humor, but he replied sincerely, "Yes, Castro is a hero, a great man on a small canvas—"

"And they are little men on a big canvas!" interrupted Doña Eustaquia.

Mr. Larkin laughed, but his reply was noncommittal. "Remember, they have done all that they have been called upon to do, and they have done it well. Who can say that they would not be as herioc, if opportunity offered, as they have been prudent?"

Doña Eustaquia shrugged her shoulders disdainfully, but resumed her seat. "You will not say, but you know what chance they would have with Castro in a fair fight. But what chance has even a great man, when at the head of a few renegades, against the navy of a big nation? But Frémont! Is he to cast up his eyes and draw down his mouth to the world, whilst the man who acted for the safety of his country alone, who showed foresight and wisdom, is denounced as a violator of international courtesy?"

"No," said one of the American residents who stood near, "history will right all that. Some day the world will know who was the great and who the little man."

"Some day! When we are under our stones! This swaggering Commodore Stockton adores Frémont and hates Castro. His lying proclamation will be read in his own country—"

The door opened suddenly and Don Fernando Altimira entered the room. "Have you heard?" he cried. "All the South is in arms! The Departmental Assembly has called the whole country to war, and men are flocking to the standard! Castro has sworn that he will never give up the country under his charge. Now, Mother of God! let our men drive the usurper from the country."

Even Mr. Larkin sprang to his feet in excitement. He rapidly translated the news to Brotherton and Russell.

"Ah! There will a little blood, then," said the younger officer. "It was too easy a victory to count."

Every one in the room was talking at once. Doña Eustaquia smote her hands together, then clasped and raised them aloft.

"Thanks to God!" she cried. "California has come to her senses at last!"

Altimira bent his lips to her ear. "I go to fight the Americans," he whispered.

She caught his hand between both her own and pressed it convulsively to her breast. "Go," she said, "and may God and Mary protect thee. Go, my son, and when thou returnest I will give thee Benicia. Thou art a son after my heart, a brave man and a good Catholic."

Benicia, standing near, heard the words. For the first time Russell saw the expression of careless audacity leave her face, her pink color fade.

"What is that man saying to your mother?" he demanded.

"She promise me to him when he come back; he go to join General Castro."

"Benicia!" He glanced about. Altimira had left the house. Every one was too excited to notice them. He drew her across the hall and into the little sala, deserted since the startling news had come. "Benicia," he said hurriedly, "there is no time to be lost. You are such a butterfly I hardly know whether you love me or not."

"I no am such butterfly as you think," said the girl pathetically. "I often am very gay, for that is my spirit, señor; but I cry sometimes in the night."

"Well, you are not to cry anymore, my very darling first!" He took her in his arms and kissed her, and she did not box his ears. "I may be ordered off at any moment, and what may they not do with you while I am gone? So I have a plan! Marry me tomorrow!"

"Ay! Señor!"

"Tomorrow. At your friend Blandina's house. The Hernandez like the Americans; in fact, as we all know, Tallant is in love with Blandina and the old people do not frown. They will let us marry there."

"Ay! Cielo santo! What my mother say? She kill me!"

"She will forgive you, no matter how angry she may be at first. She loves you—almost as much as I do."

The girl withdrew from his arms and walked up and down the room. Her face was very pale, and she looked older. On one side of the room hung a large black cross, heavily mounted with gold. She leaned her face against it and burst into tears. "Ay, my home! My mother!" she cried under her breath. "How I can leave you? Ay, triste de mi!" She turned suddenly to Russell, whose face was as white as her own, and put to him the question which we have not yet answered. "What is this love?" she said rapidly. "I no can understand. I never feel before. Always I laugh when men say they love me; but I never laugh again. In my heart is something that shake me like a lion shake what it go to kill, and make me no care for my mother or my God—and you are a Protestant! I have love my mother like I have love that cross; and now a man come—a stranger! a conqueror! a Protestant! an American! And he twist my heart out with his hands! But I no can help. I love you and I go."

THE next morning, Doña Eustaquia looked up from her desk as Benicia entered the room. "I am writing to Alvarado," she said. "I hope to be the first to tell him the glorious news. Ay! my child, go to thy altar and pray that the bandoleros may be driven wriggling from the land like snakes out of a burning field!"

"But, mother, I thought you had learned to like the Gringos."

"I like the Gringos well enough, but I hate their flag! Ay! I will pull it down with my own hands if Castro and Pico roll Stockton and Frémont in the dust!"

"I am sorry for that, my mother, for I am going to marry an American today."

Her mother laughed and glanced over the closely written page.

"I am going to marry the Lieutenant Russell at Blandina's house this morning."

"Ay, run, run. I must finish my letter."

Benicia left the sala and crossing her mother's room entered her own. From the stout mahogany chest she took white silk stockings and satin slippers, and sitting down on the floor put them on. Then she opened the doors of her wardrobe and looked for some moments at the many pretty frocks hanging there. She selected one of fine white lawn, half covered with deshalados, and arrayed herself. She took from the drawer of the wardrobe a mantilla of white Spanish lace, and draped it about her head and shoulders, fastening it back above one ear with a pink rose. Around her throat she clasped a string of pearls, then stood quietly in the middle of the room and looked about her. In one corner was a little brass bedstead covered with a heavy quilt of satin and lace. The pillowcases were almost as fine and elaborate as her gown. In the opposite corner was an altar with little gold candlesticks and an ivory crucifix. The walls and floor were bare but spotless. The ugly wardrobe built into the thick wall never had been empty: Doña Eustaquia's generosity to the daughter she worshipped was unbounded.

Benicia drew a long hysterical breath and went over to the window. It looked upon a large yard enclosed by the high adobe wall upon which her lovers so often had sat and sung to her. No flowers were in the garden, not even a tree. It was as smooth and clean as the floor of a ballroom. About the well in the middle were three or four Indian servants quarreling good-naturedly. The house stood on the rise of one of the crescent's horns. Benicia looked up at the dark pine woods on the hill. What days she had spent there with her mother! She whirled about suddenly and taking a large fan from the table returned to the sala.

Doña Eustaquia laughed. "Thou silly child, to dress thyself like a bride. What nonsense is this?"

"I will be a bride in an hour, my mother."

"Go! Go, with thy nonsense! I have spoiled thee! What other girl in Monterey would dare to dress herself like this at eleven in the morning? Go! And do not ruin that mantilla, for thou wilt not get another. Thou art going to Blandina's, no? Be sure thou goest no farther! I would not let thee go there alone were it not so near. And be sure thou speakest to no man in the street."

"No, mamacita, I will speak to no man in the street, but one awaits me in the house. Hasta luego." And she flitted out of the door and up the street.

XI

A few hours later Doña Eustaquia sat in the large and cooler sala with Captain Brotherton. He read Shakespeare to her whilst she fanned herself, her face aglow with intelligent pleasure. She had not broached to him the uprising in the South lest it should lead to bitter words. Although an American and a Protestant, few friends had ever stood so close to her.

He laid down the book as Russell and Benicia entered the room. Doña Eustaquia's heavy brows met.

"Thou knowest that I do not allow thee to walk with men on the street," she said in Spanish.

"But, mamacita, he is my husband. We were married this morning at Blandina's." Excitement had tuned Benicia's spirit to its accustomed pitch, and her eyes danced with mischief. Moreover, although she expected violent reproaches, she knew the tenacious strength of her mother's affection, and had faith in speedy forgiveness.

Brotherton opened his eyes, but Doña Eustaquia moved back her head impatiently. "That silly joke!" Then she smiled at her own impatience. What was Benicia but a spoiled child, and spoiled children would disobey at times. "Welcome, my son," she said to Russell, extending her hand. "We celebrate your marriage at the supper tonight, and the Captain helps us, no? my friend."

"Let us have chicken with red pepper and tomato sauce," cried Russell. "And rice with saffron; and that delightful dish with which I remonstrate all night—olives and cheese and hard-boiled eggs and red peppers all rolled up in cornmeal cakes."

"Enchiladas? You have them! Now, both you go over to the corner and talk not loud, for I wish to hear my friend read."

Russell, lifting his shoulders, did as he was bidden. Benicia, with a gay laugh, kissed her mother and flitted like a butterfly about the room, singing gay little snatches of song.

"Oh, mamacita, mamacita," she chanted. "Thou wilt not believe thou hast lost thy little daughter. Thou wilt not believe thou hast a son. Thou wilt not believe I shall sleep no more in the little brass bed—"

"Benicia, hold thy saucy tongue! Sit down!" And this Benicia finally consented to do, although smothered laughter came now and again from the corner.

Doña Eustaquia sat easily against the straight back of her chair, looking very handsome and placid as Brotherton read and expounded *As You Like It* to her. Her gown of thin black silk threw out the fine gray tones of her skin; about her neck and chest was a heavy chain of Californian gold; her dense lusterless hair was held high with a shell comb banded with gold; superb jewels weighted her little white hands; in her small ears were large hoops of gold studded with black pearls. She was perfectly contented in that hour. Her woman's vanity was at peace and her eager mind expanding.

The party about the supper table in the evening was very gay. The long room was bare, but heavy silver was beyond the glass doors of the cupboard; a servant stood behind each chair; the wines were as fine as any in America, and the favorite dishes of the Americans had been prepared. Even Brotherton, although more nervous than was usual with him, caught the contagion of the hour and touched his glass more than once to that of the woman whose overwhelming personality had more than half captured a most indifferent heart.

After supper they sat on the corridor, and Benicia sang her mocking love songs and danced El Son to the tinkling of her own guitar.

"Is she not a light hearted child?" asked her mother. "But she has her serious moments, my friend. We have been like the sisters. Every path of the pine woods we walk together, arm in arm. We ride miles on the beach and sit down on the rocks for hours and try to think what the seals say one to the other. Before you come I have friends, but no other companion; but it is good for me you come, for she think only of flirting since the Americans take Monterey. Mira! Look at her flash the eyes at Señor Russell. It is well he has the light heart like herself."

Brotherton made no reply.

"Give to me the guitar," she continued.

Benicia handed her the instrument and Doña Eustaquia swept the chords absently for a moment then sang the song of the troubadour. Her rich voice was like the rush of the wind through the pines after the light trilling of a bird, and even Russell sat enraptured. As she sang the color came into her face, alight with the fire of youth. Her low notes were voluptuous, her high notes rang with piercing sadness. As she finished, a storm of applause came from Alvarado Street, which pulsed with life but a few yards below them.

"No American woman ever sang like that," said Brotherton. He rose and walked to the end of the corridor. "But it is a part of Monterey."

"Most enchanting of mothers-in-law," said Russell, "you have made it doubly hard for us to leave you; but it grows late and my wife and I must go. Good night," and he raised her hand to his lips.

"Good night, my son."

"Mamacita, good night," and Benicia, who had fluttered into the house and found a reboso, kissed her mother, waved her hand to Brotherton, and stepped from the corridor to the street.

"Come here, señorita!" cried her mother. "No walk tonight, for I have not the wish to walk myself."

"But I go with my husband, mamma."

"Oh, no more of that joke without sense! Señor Russell, go home, that she have reason for one moment."

"But, dear Doña Eustaquia, won't you understand that we are really married?"

Doña Eustaquia's patience was at an end. She turned to Brotherton and addressed a remark to him. Russell and Benicia conferred a moment, then the young man walked rapidly down the street.

"Has he gone?" asked Doña Eustaquia. "Then let us go in the house, for the fog comes from the bay."

They went into the little sala and sat about the table. Doña Eustaquia picked up a silver dagger she used as a paper cutter and tapped a book with it.

"Ay, this will not last long," she said to Brotherton. "I much am afraid your Commodore send you to the South to fight with our men."

"I shall return," said Brotherton, absently. His eyes were fixed on the door.

"But it will not be long that you will be there, my friend. Many people are not killed in our wars. Once there was a great battle at Point Rincon, near Santa Barbara, between Castro and Carillo. Carillo have been appointed governor by Mejico, and Alvarado refuse to resign. They fight for three days, and Castro manage so well he lose only one man, and the others run away and not lose any."

Brotherton laughed. "I hope all our battles may be as bloodless," he said, and then drew a short breath.

Russell, accompanied by Don Jorje and Doña Francesca Hernandez and the priest of Monterey, entered the room.

Doña Eustaquia rose and greeted her guests with grace and hospitality.

"But I am glad to see you, my father, my friends. And you always are welcome, Señor Russell; but no more joke. Where is our Blandina? Sit down— Why, what is it?"

The priest spoke.

"I have that to tell you, Doña Eustaquia, which I fear will give you great displeasure. I hoped not to be the one to tell it. I was weak to consent, but these young people importuned me until I was weary. Doña Eustaquia, I married Benicia to the Señor Russell today."

Doña Eustaquia's head had moved forward mechanically, her eyes staring incredulously from the priest to the other members of the apprehensive group. Suddenly her apathy left her, her arm curved upward like the neck of a snake; but as she sprang upon Benicia her ferocity was that of a tiger.

"What!" she shrieked, shaking the girl violently by the shoulder. "What! ingrate! traitor! Thou hast married an American, a Protestant!"

Benicia burst into terrified sobs. Russell swung the girl from her mother's grasp and placed his arm around her.

"She is mine now," he said. "You must not touch her again."

"Yours! Yours!" screamed Doña Eustaquia, beside herself. "Oh, Mother of God!" She snatched the dagger from the table and, springing backward, plunged it into the cross.

"By that sign I curse thee," she cried. "Accursed be the man who has stolen my child! Accursed be the woman who has betrayed her mother and her country! God! God!—I implore thee, let her die in her happiest hour."

XII

ON August twelfth Commodore Hull arrived on the frigate *Warren*, from Mazatlan, and brought the first positive intelligence of the declaration of war between Mexico and the United States. Before the middle of the month news came that Castro and Pico, after gallant defense, but overwhelmed by numbers, had fled, the one to Sonora, the other to Baja California. A few days after, Stockton issued a proclamation to the effect that the flag of the United States was flying over every town in the territory of California; and Alcalde Colton announced that the rancheros were more than satisfied with the change of government.

A month later a mounted courier dashed into Monterey with a note from the Alcalde of Los Angeles, wrapped about a cigarito and hidden in his hair. The note contained the information that all the South was in arms again, and that Los Angeles was in the hands of the Californians. Russell was ordered to go with Captain Mervine, on the *Savannah*, to join Gillespie at San Pedro; Brotherton was left at Monterey with Lieutenant Maddox and a number of men to quell a threatened uprising. Later came the news of Mervine's defeat and the flight of Talbot from Santa Barbara; and by November

California was in a state of general warfare, each army receiving new recruits every day.

Doña Eustaquia, hard and stern, praying for the triumph of her people, lived alone in the old house. Benicia, praying for the return of her husband and the relenting of her mother, lived alone in her little house on the hill. Friends had interceded, but Doña Eustaquia had closed her ears. Brotherton went to her one day with the news that Lieutenant Russell was wounded.

"I must tell Benicia," he said, "but it is you who should do that."

"She betray me, my friend."

"Oh, Eustaquia, make allowance for the lightness of youth. She barely realized what she did. But she loves him now, and suffers bitterly. She should be with you."

"Ay! She suffer for another! She love a strange man—an American—better than her mother! And it is I who would die for her! Ay, you cold Americans! Never you know how a mother can love her child."

"The Americans know how to love, señora. And Benicia was thoroughly spoiled by her devoted mother. She was carried away by her wild spirits, nothing more."

"Then much better she live on them now."

Doña Eustaquia sat with her profile against the light. It looked severe and a little older, but she was very handsome in her rich black gown and the gold chain about her strong throat. Her head, as usual, was held a little back. Brotherton sat down beside her and took her hand.

"Eustaquia," he said, "no friendship between man and woman was ever deeper and stronger than ours. In spite of the anxiety and excitement of these last months we have found time to know each other very intimately. So you will forgive me if I tell you that the more a friend loves you the more he must be saddened by the terrible iron in your nature. Only the great strength of your passions has saved you from hardening into an ugly and repellent woman. You are a mother; forgive your child; remember that she, too, is about to be a mother—"

She caught his hand between both of hers with a passionate gesture. "Oh, my friend," she said, "do not too much reproach me! You never had a child, you cannot know! And remember we all are not make alike. If you are me, you act like myself. If I am you, I can forgive more easy. But I am Eustaquia Ortega, and as I am make, so I do feel now. No judge too hard, my friend, and—*infelez de mi!* do not forsake me.''

"I will never forsake you, Eustaquia." He rose suddenly. "I, too, am a lonely man, if not a hard one, and I recognize that cry of the soul's isolation.''

He left her and went up the hill to Benicia's little house, half hidden by the cypress trees that grew before it.

She was sitting in her sala working an elaborate deshalados on a baby's gown. Her face was pale, and the sparkle had gone out of it; but she held herself with all her mother's pride, and her soft eyes were deeper. She rose as Captain Brotherton entered, and took his hand in both of hers. "You are so good to come to me, and I love you for your friendship for my mother. Tell me how she is.''

"She is well, Benicia." Then he exclaimed suddenly: "Poor little girl! What a child you are—not yet seventeen.''

"In a few months, señor. Sit down. No? And I no am so young now. When we suffer we grow more than by the years; and now I go to have the baby, that make me feel very old.''

"But it is very sad to see you alone like this, without your husband or your mother. She will relent some day, Benicia, but I wish she would do it now, when you most need her.''

"Yes, I wish I am with her in the old house," said the girl, pathetically, although she winked back the tears. "Never I can be happy without her, even si *he* is here, and you know how I love him. But I have love her so long; she is—how you say it?—like she is part of me, and when she no spik to me, how I can be happy with all myself when part is gone. You understand, señor?''

"Yes, Benicia, I understand." He looked through the bending cypresses, down the hill, upon the fair town. He had no relish for the task which had brought him to her. She looked up and caught the expression of his face.

"Señor!" she cried sharply. "What you go to tell me?''

"There is a report that Ned is slightly wounded; but it is not serious. It was Altimira who did it, I believe.''

She shook from head to foot, but was calmer than he had expected. She laid the gown on a chair and stood up. "Take me to him. Si he is wound, I go to nurse him.''

"My child! You would die before you got there. I have sent

a special courier to find out the truth. If Ned is wounded, I have arranged to have him sent home immediately.''

"I wait for the courier come back, for it no is right I hurt the baby si I can help. But si he is wound so bad he no can come, then I go to him. It no is use for you to talk at all, señor, I go.''

Brotherton looked at her in wonderment. Whence had the butterfly gone? Its wings had been struck from it and a soul had flown in.

"Let me send Blandina to you," he said. "You must not be alone.''

"I am alone till he or my mother come. I no want other. I love Blandina before, but now she make me feel tired. She talk so much and no say anything. I like better be alone.''

"Poor child!" said Brotherton, bitterly, "truly do love and suffering age and isolate." He motioned with his hand to the altar in her bedroom, seen through the open door. "I have not your faith, I am afraid I have not much of any; but if I cannot pray for you, I can wish with all the strength of a man's heart that happiness will come to you yet, Benicia."

She shook her head. "I no know; I no believe much happiness come in this life. Before, I am like a fairy; but it is only because I no am *un*happy. But when the heart have wake up, señor, and the knife have gone in hard, then, after that, always, I think, we are a little sad.''

XIII

GENERAL Kearney and Lieutenant Beale walked rapidly up and down before the tents of the wretched remnant of United States troops with which the former had arrived overland in California. It was bitterly cold in spite of the fine drizzling rain. Lonely buttes studded the desert, whose palms and cacti seemed to spring from the rocks; high on one of them was the American camp. On the other side of a river flowing at the foot of the butte, the white tents of the Californians were scattered among the dark huts of the little pueblo of San Pasqual.

"Let me implore you, General," said Beale, "not to think of meeting Andres Pico. Why, your men are half starved; your few horses are broken-winded; your mules are no match

for the fresh trained mustangs of the enemy. I am afraid you
do not appreciate the Californians. They are numerous, brave,
and desperate. If you avoid them now, as Commodore Stockton wishes, and join him at San Diego, we stand a fair chance
of defeating them. But now Pico's cavalry and foot are fresh
and enthusiastic—in painful contrast to yours. And, moreover, they know every inch of the ground.''

Kearney impatiently knocked the ashes out of his pipe. He
had little regard for Stockton, and no intention of being dictated to by a truculent young lieutenant who spoke his mind
upon all occasions.

"I shall attack them at daybreak," he said curtly. "I have
one hundred and thirty good men; and has not Captain Gillespie joined me with his battalion? Never shall it be said that
I turned aside to avoid a handful of boasting Californians.
Now go and get an hour's sleep before we start."

The young officer shrugged his shoulders, saluted, and
walked down the line of tents. A man emerged from one of
them, and he recognized Russell.

"Hello, Ned," he said. "How's the arm?"

" 'Twas only a scratch. Is Altimira down there with Pico,
do you know? He is a brave fellow! I respect that man; but
we have an account to settle, and I hope it will be done on
the battlefield."

"He is with Pico, and he has done some good fighting.
Most of the Californians have. They know how to fight and
they are perfectly fearless. Kearney will find it out tomorrow.
He is mad to attack them. Why, his men are actually cadaverous. Bueno! as they say here; Stockton sent me to guide
him to San Diego. If he prefers to go through the enemy's
lines, there is nothing for me to do but to take him."

"Yes, but we may surprise them. I wish to God this imi-
tation war were over!"

"It will be real enough before you get through. Don't
worry. Well, good night. Luck to your skin."

At daybreak the little army marched down the butte, shiv-
ering with cold, wet to the skin. Those on horseback naturally
proceeded more rapidly than those mounted upon the clumsy
stubborn mules; and Captain Johnson, who led the advance
guard of twelve dragoons, found himself, when he came in
sight of the enemy's camp, some distance ahead of the main
body of Kearney's small army. To his surprise he saw that the

Californians were not only awake, but horsed and apparently awaiting him. Whether he was fired by valor or desperation at the sight is a disputed point; but he made a sudden dash down the hill and across the river, almost flinging himself upon the lances of the Californians.

Captain Moore, who was ambling down the hill on an old white horse at the head of fifty dragoons mounted on mules, spurred his beast as he witnessed the foolish charge of the advance, and arrived upon the field in time to see Johnson fall dead and to take his place. Pico, seeing that reinforcements were coming, began to retreat, followed hotly by Moore and the horsed dragoons. Suddenly, however, Fernando Altimira raised himself in his stirrups, looked back, laughed, and galloped across the field to General Pico.

"Look!" he said. "Only a few men on horses are after us. The mules are stumbling half a mile behind."

Pico wheeled about, gave the word of command, and bore down upon the Americans. Then followed a hand-to-hand conflict, the Californians lancing and using their pistols with great dexterity, the Americans doing the best they could with their rusty sabers and clubbed guns.

They were soon reinforced by Moore's dragoons and Gillespie's battalion, despite the unwilling mules; but the brutes kicked and bucked at every pistol shot and fresh cloud of smoke. The poor old horses wheezed and panted, but stood their ground when not flung out of position by the frantic mules. The officers and soldiers of the United States Army were a sorry sight, and in pointed contrast to the graceful Californians on their groomed steeds, handsomely trapped, curvetting and rearing and prancing as lightly as if on the floor of a circus. Kearney cursed his own stupidity, and Pico laughed in his face. Beale felt satisfaction and compunction in saturating the silk and silver of one fine saddle with the blood of its owner. The point of the dying man's lance pierced his face, but he noted the bleaching of Kearney's, as one dragoon after another was flung upon the sharp rocks over which his bewildered brute stumbled, or was caught and held aloft in the torturing arms of the cacti.

On the edge of the battle two men had forgotten the Aztec Eagle and the Stars and Stripes; they fought for love of a woman. Neither had had time to draw his pistol; they fought with lance and saber, thrusting and parrying. Both were skillful swordsmen, but Altimira's horse was far superior to Russell's, and he had the advantage of weapons.

"One or the other die on the rocks," said the Californian, "and si I kill you, I marry Benicia."

Russell made no reply. He struck aside the man's lance and wounded his wrist. But Altimira was too excited to feel pain. His face was quivering with passion.

It is not easy to parry a lance with a saber, and still more difficult to get close enough to wound the man who wields it. Russell rose suddenly in his stirrups, described a rapid half-circle with his weapon, brought it down midway upon the longer blade, and snapped the latter in two. Altimira gave a cry of rage, and spurring his horse sought to ride his opponent down; but Russell wheeled, and the two men simultaneously snatched their pistols from the holsters. Altimira fired first, but his hand was unsteady and his ball went through a cactus. Russell raised his pistol with firm wrist, and discharged it full in the face of the Californian.

Then he looked over the field. Moore, fatally lanced, lay under a palm, and many of his men were about him. Gillespie was wounded, Kearney had received an ugly thrust. The Californians, upon the arrival of the main body of the enemy's troops, had retreated unpursued; the mules attached to one of the American howitzers were scampering over to the opposite ranks, much to the consternation of Kearney. The sun, looking over the mountain, dissipated the gray smoke, and cast a theatrical light on the faces of the dead. Russell bent over Altimira. His head was shattered, but his death was avenged. Never had an American troop suffered a more humiliating defeat. Only six Californians lay on the field; and when the American surgeon, after attending to his own wounded, offered his services to Pico's, that indomitable general haughtily replied that he had none.

"By Jove!" said Russell to Beale that night, "you know your Californians! I am prouder than ever of having married one! That army is of the stuff of which my mother-in-law is made!"

XIV

THAT was a gay Christmas at Monterey, despite the barricades in the street. News had come of the defeat of Kearney at San Pasqual, and the Montereños, inflated with hope and pride, gave little thought to the fact that his forces were now joined with Stockton's at San Diego.

On Christmas eve light streamed from every window, bonfires flared on the hills; the streets were illuminated, and every one was abroad. The clear warm night was ablaze with fireworks; men and women were in their gala gowns; rockets shot upward amidst shrieks of delight, which mingled oddly with the rolling of drums at muster; even the children caught the enthusiasm, religious and patriotic.

"I suppose you would be glad to see even your friends driven out," said Brotherton to Doña Eustaquia, as they walked through the brilliant town toward the church: bells called them to witness the dramatic play of *The Shepherds*.

"I be glad to see the impertinent flag come down," said she, frankly, "but you can make resignation from the army, and have a little store on Alvarado Street. You can have beautiful silks and crêpes from America. I buy of you."

"Thanks," he said grimly. "You would put a dunce cap on poor America, and stand her in a corner. If I resign, Doña Eustaquia, it will be to become a ranchero, not a shopkeeper. To tell the truth, I have little desire to leave California again."

"But you were make for the fight," she said, looking up with some pride at the tall military figure, the erect head and strong features. "You not were make to lie in the hammock and horseback all day."

"But I should do a good deal else, señora. I should raise cattle with some method; and I should have a library—and a wife."

"Ah! you go to marry?"

"Some day, I hope. It would be lonely to be a ranchero without a wife."

"Truly."

"What is the matter with those women?"

A group of old women stood by the roadside. Their forms were bent, their brown faces gnarled like apples. Some were a shapeless mass of fat, others were parchment and bone; about the head and shoulders of each was a thick black shawl.

Near them stood a number of young girls clad in muslin petticoats, flowered with purple and scarlet. Bright satin shoes
were on their feet, cotton rebosas covering their pretty, pert
little heads. All were looking in one direction, whispering
and crossing themselves.

Doña Eustaquia glanced over her shoulder, then leaned
heavily on Brotherton's arm.

"It is Benicia," she said. "It is because she was cursed
and is with child that they cross themselves."

Brotherton held her arm closely and laid his hand on hers,
but he spoke sternly.

"The curse is not likely to do her any harm. You prayed
that she should die when happiest, and you have done your
best to make her wretched."

She did not reply, and they walked slowly onward. Benicia
followed, leaning on the arm of an Indian servant. Her friends
avoided her, for they bitterly resented Altimira's death. But
she gave them little regret. Since her husband could not be
with her on this Christmas eve, she wished only for recon-
ciliation with her mother. In spite of the crowd she followed
close behind Doña Eustaquia and Brotherton, holding her
head proudly, but ready to fall at the feet of the woman she
worshipped.

"My friend," said Doña Eustaquia, after a moment, "perhaps it is best that I do not forgive her. Were she happy, then
might the curse come true."

"She has enough else to make her unhappy. Besides, who
ever heard of a curse coming true? It has worked its will
already for the matter of that. You kept your child from happiness with her husband during the brief time she had him.
The bitterness of death is a small matter beside the bitterness
of life. You should be satisfied."

"You are hard, my friend."

"I see your other faults only to respect and love them."

"Does she look ill, Captain?"

"She cannot be expected to look like the old Benicia. Of
course she looks ill, and needs care."

"Look over the shoulder. Does she walk heavily?"

"Very. But as haughtily as do you."

"Talk of other things for a little while, my friend."

"Truly there is much to claim the interest tonight. This
may be an old scene to you, but it is novel and fascinating to

me. How lovely are those stately girls, half hidden by their rebosas, telling their beads as they hurry along. It is the very coquetry of religion. And those—but here we are.''

The church was handsomer without than within, for the clever old padres that built it had more taste than their successors. About the whitewashed walls of the interior were poor copies of celebrated paintings—the Passion of Christ, and an extraordinary group of nude women and grinning men representing the temptation of St. Anthony. In a glass case a beautiful figure of the Savior reclined on a stiff couch clumsily covered with costly stuffs. The Virgin was dressed much like the aristocratic ladies of Monterey, and the altar was a rainbow of tawdry colors.

But the ceremonies were interesting, and Brotherton forgot Benicia for the hour. After the mass the priest held out a small waxen image of the infant Jesus, and all approached and kissed it. Then from without came the sound of a guitar; the worshippers arose and ranged themselves against the wall; six girls dressed as shepherdesses; a man representing Lucifer; two others, a hermit and the lazy vagabond Bartola; a boy, the archangel Gabriel, entered the church. They bore banners and marched to the center of the building, then acted their drama with religious fervor.

The play began with the announcement by Gabriel of the birth of the Savior, and exhortations to repair to the manger. On the road came the temptation of Lucifer; the archangel appeared once more; a violent altercation ensued in which all took part, and finally the prince of darkness was routed. Songs and fanciful by-play, brief sermons, music, gay and solemn, diversified the strange performance. When all was over, the players were followed by an admiring crowd to the entertainment awaiting them.

"Is it not beautiful—our Los Pastores?" demanded Doña Eustaquia, looking up at Brotherton, her fine face aglow with enthusiasm. "Do not you feel the desire to be a Catholic, my friend?"

"Rather would I see two good Catholics united, dear señora," and he turned suddenly to Benicia, who also had remained in the church, almost at her mother's side.

"Mamacita!" cried Benicia.

Doña Eustaquia opened her arms and caught the girl passionately to her heart; and Brotherton left the church.

XV

THE April flowers were on the hills. Beds of gold-red poppies and silver-blue baby eyes were set like tiles amidst the dense green undergrowth beneath the pines, and on the natural lawns about the white houses. Although hope of driving forth the intruder had gone forever in January, Monterey had resumed in part her old gayety; despair had bred philosophy. But Monterey was Monterey no longer. An American alcalde with a power vested in no judge of the United States ruled over her; to add injury to insult, he had started a newspaper. The town was full of Americans; the United States was constructing a fort on the hill; above all, worse than all, the Californians were learning the value of money. Their sun was sloping to the west.

A thick India shawl hung over the window of Benicia's old room in her mother's house, shutting out the perfume of the hills. A carpet had been thrown on the floor, candles burned in the pretty gold candlesticks that had stood on the altar since Benicia's childhood. On the little brass bedstead lay Benicia, very pale and very pretty, her transparent skin faintly reflecting the pink of the satin coverlet. By the bed sat an old woman of the people. Her ragged white locks were bound about by a fillet of black silk; her face, dark as burnt umber, was seamed and lined like a withered prune; even her long broad nose was wrinkled; her dull eyes looked like mud puddles; her big underlip was pursed up as if she had been speaking mincing words, and her chin was covered with a short white stubble. Over her coarse smock and gown she wore a black cotton reboso. In her arms she held an infant, muffled in a white mantilla.

Doña Eustaquia came in and bent over the baby, her strong face alight with joy.

"Didst thou ever nurse so beautiful a baby?" she demanded.

The old woman grunted; she had heard that question before.

"See how pink and smooth it is—not red and wrinkled like other babies! How becoming is that mantilla! No, she shall not be wrapped in blankets, cap, and shawls."

"She catch cold, most likely," grunted the nurse.

"In this weather? No; it is soft as midsummer. I cannot

get cool. Ay, she looks like a rosebud lying in a fog bank!" She touched the baby's cheek with her finger, then sat on the bed, beside her daughter. "And how dost thou feel, my little one? Thou wert a baby thyself but yesterday, and thou art not much more today."

"I feel perfectly well, my mother, and—ay, Dios, so happy! Where is Edourdo?"

"Of course! Always the husband! They are all alike! Hast thou not thy mother and thy baby?"

"I adore you both, mamacita, but I want Edourdo. Where is he?"

Her mother grimaced. "I suppose it is no use to protest. Well, my little one, I think he is at this moment on the hill with Lieutenant Ord."

"Why did he not come to see me before he went out?"

"He did, my daughter, but thou wert asleep. He kissed thee and stole away."

"Where?"

"Right there on your cheek, one inch below your eye-lashes."

"When will he return?"

"Holy Mary! For dinner, surely, and that will be in an hour."

"When can I get up?"

"In another week. Thou art so well! I would not have thee draw too heavily on thy little strength. Another month and thou wilt not remember that thou hast been ill. Then we will go to the rancho, where thou and thy little one will have sun all day and no fog."

"Have I not a good husband, mamacita?"

"Yes; I love him like my own son. Had he been unkind to thee, I should have killed him with my own hands; but as he has his lips to thy little slipper, I forgive him for being an American."

"And you no longer wish for a necklace of American ears! Oh, mamma!"

Doña Eustaquia frowned, then sighed. "I do not know the American head for which I have not more like than hate, and they are welcome to their ears; but *the spirit* of that wish is in my heart yet, my child. Our country has been taken from us; we are aliens in our own land; it is the American's. They— holy God!—permit us to live here!"

"But they like us better than their own women."

"Perhaps; they are men and like what they have not had too long."

"Mamacita, I am thirsty."

"What wilt thou have? A glass of water?"

"Water has no taste."

"I know!"

Doña Eustaquia left the room and returned with an orange. "This will be cool and pleasant on so warm a day. It is just a little sour," she said; but the nurse raised her bony hand.

"Do not give her that," she said in her harsh voice. "It is too soon."

"Nonsense! The baby is two weeks old. Why, I ate fruit a week after childing. look how dry her mouth is! It will do her good."

She pared the orange and gave it to Benicia, who ate it gratefully.

"It is very good, mamita. You will spoil me always, but that is because you are so good. And one day I hope you will be as happy as your little daughter; for there are other good Americans in the world. No? mamma. I think— Mamacita!"

She sprang upward with a loud cry, the body curving rigidly; her soft brown eyes stared horribly; froth gathered about her mouth; she gasped once or twice, her body writhing from the agonized arms that strove to hold it, then fell limply down, her features relaxing.

"She is dead," said the nurse.

"Benicia!" whispered Doña Eustaquia. "Benicia!"

"You have killed her," said the old woman, as she drew the mantilla about the baby's face.

Doña Eustaquia dropped the body and moved backward from the bed. She put out her hands and went gropingly from the room to her own, and from thence to the sala. Brotherton came forward to meet her. "Eustaquia!" he cried. "My friend! *My dear!* What has happened! What—"

She raised her hand and pointed to the cross. The mark of the dagger was still there.

"Benicia!" she uttered. "The curse!" and then she fell at his feet.

*Joaquin Miller (Cincinnatus Hiner Miller, 1841–1913) was known
as the Poet of the Sierras. His years as a miner, Pony Express
rider, traveler in Mexico and Central America, and resident with
a Modoc Indian tribe in nothern California provided rich material for such volumes of poetry as* Specimens *(1868),* Pacific
Poems *(1870),* Songs of the Sierras *(1870), and* The Songs of the
Sun-Lands *(1873), and for his autobiographical novel,* My Life
Among the Modocs *(1873). "The Man-Hunt" is a self-contained
and suspenseful excerpt from the novel.*

The Man-Hunt

★★★★★★★★★★★★★★★

Joaquin Miller

ONCE across the stream, Klamat led steeply up the hill
for a time, then he would chop and cut to right and left
in a zig-zag route until we had reached the rim of a bench in
the mountain. Here he stopped and motioned the Prince to
approach, after he had looked back intently into the camp
and taken sight by some pines that stood before him.

The Prince rode up to the boy and dismounted; when he
had done so, the little fellow lifted three fingers, looked excited, and pointed down upon the old cabin. It was more than
a mile away, nearly a mile below; but the sun was pitching
directly down upon it, and all things stood out clear and large
as life.

Three men rode quickly up to the cabin, leaned from their
mules and read the inscription TO LET. The leader now dismounted, kicked open the door, and entered. It does not take
long to search a cabin, without a loft or even a bed to hide
under, and the man did not remain a great while within.

Without even taking pains to close the door, to keep out
coyotes and other things, as miners do, so that cabins may
be habitable for some wayfarer, or fortune-hunters who may

51

not have a house of their own, he hastily mounted and led the party down to the next cabin below.

The miners were evidently at breakfast, for the man leaned from his saddle and shouted two or three times before any one came out.

The door opened, and a very tall, black-bearded, hairy man came forth, and walked up before the man leaning from his mule.

What was said I do not know, but the bare-headed, hairy man pointed with his long arm up the mountain, on the other side, exactly the opposite course from the one that had been taken by the fugitives.

Here the officer said something very loud, pushed back his broad-brimmed hat, and pointed down the stream. The long-armed, bare-headed, hairy man again pointed emphatically up the mountain on the other side, and then wheeled on his heel, entered, and closed the door.

The interview had evidently not been a satisfactory one, or a friendly one to the officer, and he led his men slowly down the creek with their heads bent down intently to the trail. They did not go far. There were no fresh tracks in the way. The recent great rain had made the ground soft, and there was no mistaking the absence of the signs.

There was a consultation. Three heads in broad hats close together as they could get sitting on their mules. Now a hat would be pushed back, and a face lifted up exactly in our direction. We had sheltered behind the pines. Klamat was holding the Prince's mule's nose to keep it from braying to those below. Paquita had dismounted a little way off, behind a clump of pines, and was plucking some leaves and grasses for her pony and the pack mule to keep them still. The Doctor never seemed more stupid and helpless than now; but, at a sign from Klamat, stole out to the shelter where Paquita stood, and began to gather grasses, too, for his mule.

A poor, crooked, imitative little monkey he looked as he bent to pluck the grass; at the same time watching Paquita, as if he wished to forget that there was any graver task on hand than to pluck grass and feed the little mules.

Mules are noisy of a morning when they first set out. The utmost care was necessary now to insure silence.

Had the wind blown in our direction, or even a mule brayed below, these mules in the midst of our party would have turned their heads down hill, pointed their opera glasses sharply for a moment or two at the sounds below, and then, in spite of kicks of clubs, have brayed like trumpets, and betrayed us where we stood.

There was no excitement in the face of the Prince, not much concern. His foot played and patted in the great wooden stirrup, and shook and jingled the bells of steel on his Spanish spur, but he said nothing.

Sometimes the men below would point in this direction and then in that with their long yellow gauntlets, then they would prick and spur their mules till they spun round like tops.

When a man pricks and spurs his mule, you may be sure that he is bothered.

A Yankee would scratch his head, pull at his ear, or rub his chin; an Englishman would take snuff; a Missourian would take a chew of tobacco, and perhaps swear; but a Californian in the mountains disdains to do anything so stupid and inexpressive. He kicks and cuffs and spurs his mule.

At length the leader set his spurs in the broad hair-cinch, with the long steel points of the rowels, and rode down to the water's edge. A twig was broken there. The Doctor had done that as we crossed, to get a switch for his mule, and brought down the wrath of Klamat, expressed, however, only in frightful grimaces, signs, and the flashing of his eyes. The officer dismounted, leaned over, brushed the burs aside, took some of them up, and examined them closely.

An arm was now lifted and waved authoritatively to the two men sitting on their mules in the trail, and they instantly struck the spurs in the broad cinch, and through into the tough skins of their mules, I think, for they ambled down toward the officer at a rapid pace and—consternation! One of them threw up his head and brayed as if for life.

The Prince's mule pointed his opera glasses, set out his legs, took in a long breath, and was just about to make the forest ring, when his master sprung to the ground, caught him by the nose, and wrenched him around till he fell upon his haunches.

Here Klamat made a sign, threw the Doctor on his mule, left Paquita to take care of herself, and led off up the hill. We mounted, and followed as fast as possible; but the Prince's mule, as if in revenge, now stopped short, set out his legs, lifted his nose, and brayed till the very pine quills quivered overhead.

We could not see our pursuers now, yet we knew too well that they were climbing, fast as their strong-limbed sturdy mules would serve them, the hill that we had climbed an hour before. . . . The chances were about evenly balanced for an escape without blood. . . . When we had reached the second bench we turned to look. Soon the heads of the men were seen to shoot above the rim of the bench below, perhaps less than a mile away. No doubt they caught sight of us now, for the hand of the officer lifted, pointed in this direction, and he settled his spurs in his cinch, and led his men in pursuit.

Deliberately the Prince dismounted, set his saddle well forward, and drew the cinch as tight as possible. We all did the same; mounted then, and followed little Klamat.

We reached the summit of the ridge. Scintillations from the flashing snows of Mount Shasta shimmered through the trees, and a breath of air came across from the Klamat lakes and the Modoc land beyond, as if to welcome us from the dark, deep cañon with its leaden fringe, and lining of dark and eternal green. We had been buried in that cañon so long, we were like men who had issued from a dungeon. . . .

Klamat threw up his hand. The men had appeared on the bench below. We had evidently gained on them considerably, for here we had ten minutes rest before they broke over the mountain bench beneath. This was encouraging. . . . They dismounted now, and settled their saddles. We tightened our saddles also. This was the summit, and now came the demand for skill. . . .

The Prince was well armed. He carried his double-barrelled piece before him in the saddle-bow. The rest of us were not defenseless. The deed was more than possible.

These men wanted the Doctor: him only, so far as we knew. The Doctor was accused of murder. The officer, no doubt, had due process, and the legal authority to take him. To the Prince he was nothing much. He was no equal in physical or mental capacity. He was failing in health and in strength, and could surely be of no further possible use to us. Why should the Prince take life, or even imperil ours for his sake?

The answer, no doubt, would be very unsatisfactory to the civilized world, but it was enough for the Prince. The man needed his help. The man was almost helpless.

Now and then Klamat would turn his eyes over his shoulder, toss his head, and urge on. The eagle feathers in his black hair, as if glad to get back again in the winds of Shasta, floated and flew back at us, and we followed as if we followed a banner. A black banner, this we followed, made of the feathers of a fierce and bloody bird. Where would it lead us?

We did not taste food. We had not tasted water since sunrise, and it was now far in the afternoon. The Doctor began to sit with an unsteady motion in his saddle. The mules were beginning to bray; this time from distress, and not excess of spirits. The Prince's mule had his tongue hanging out between his teeth, and, what was worse, his ears began to flop to and fro as if they had wilted in the sun. Some mules put their tongues out through their teeth and go very well for days after; but when a mule lets his ears swing, he has lost his ambition, and is not to be depended on much longer.

A good mountain mule should not tire short of a week, but there is human nature wherever there is a bargain to be made, and there are mule jockeys as well as horse jockeys even in the mountains; and you cannot pick up good mules when you like, either for love or money. The men who followed had, no doubt, a tried and trusty stock. Things began to look critical.

The only thing that seemed unaffected was Klamat. Two or three times through the day he had stood his rifle against a pine, drew his belt a knot or two tighter, fastened his moccasin strings over, and then dashed ahead without a word. Our banner of eagle feathers still floated defiantly, and promised to lead even farther than we could follow. Closer and closer came the pursuers. We could see them striking their steel spurs in their cinches as if they would lift their tired mules along with their heels.

Once they were almost within hail; but a saddle slipped, and they lost at least ten minutes with a fractious mule that for a time concluded not to be cinched again till it had taken rest.

The sugar pines dropped their rich and delicated nuts as we rode by, from pyramid cones as long as your arm, and little foxy-looking pine squirrels with pink eyes stopped from their work of hoarding them for winter, to look or chatter at us as we hurried breathless and wearily past.

Mount Shasta still flashed down upon us through the dark rich boughs of fir and pine, but did not thrill us now.

When the body is tired, the mind is tired, too. You get surfeited with grandeur at such a time. No doubt the presence tames you somewhat, tones down the rugged points in you that would like to find expression; that would find expression in fretful words but for this greatness which shows you how small you are; but you are subdued rather than elevated.

Suddenly Klamat led off to the right as if forsaking the main summit for a spur. This seemed a bad sign. The Prince said nothing. At any other time I dare say he would have protested.

We had no time to dispute now; besides, almost any change from this toilsome and eternal run was a relief. What made things seem worse, however, this boy seemed to be leading us back again to The Forks. We were edging around at right angles with our pursuers. They could cut across if we kept on, and head us off. We were making more than a crescent; the boy was leading us right back to the men we wished to escape.

Soon he went out on a point and stopped. He beckoned us to ride up. We did so. It seemed less than half a mile to a point we had passed less than an hour since, and, as far as we could see, there was only a slight depression between. The officer and his party soon came in sight. As they did so he raised his arm. We were not unobserved.

Klamat sat down to rest, and made signs that we should dismount. I looked at the Prince to see what he would do. He swung himself to the ground, looking tired and impatient, and we all did the same. The Doctor could not keep his feet, but lay down, helpless, on the brown bed of quills from the sugar pines that clustered around and crowned the point where we had stopped to rest.

The officer and his men looked to their catenas; each drew out a pistol, revolved the cylinder, settled the powder back in the tubes by striking the ivory handles gently on the saddle pommels, saw that each nipple still held its cap, and then spurred their mules down the hillside as if to cross the depression that lay between, and head us off at once. They were almost within hail, and I thought I could hear the clean sharp click of the steel bells on their Spanish spurs as they descended and disappeared among the treetops as if going down into a sea.

Klamat had learned some comic things in camp, even though he had not learned, or pretended he had not learned, to talk. When the men had disappeared among the branches of the trees, he turned to the Prince and gravely lifted his thumb to his nose, elevated his fingers in the air, and wriggled them in the direction of the place where the officer was seen to descend.

Every moment I expected to see the muzzles of those pistols thrust up through the pines as the three men turned the brow of the hill. They did not appear, however, and as we arose to adjust our saddles after some time, I stepped to the rim of the hill and looked over to the north side. The hill was steep and rugged, with a ledge, and lined with chaparral. A white-tailed rabbit came through, sat down, and looked back into the cañon. Some quails started and flew to one side, but that was all I saw or heard.

The Doctor had to be assisted to his saddle. He was pale, and his lips were parched and swollen. Slowly now Klamat walked ahead; he, too, was tired. We had rested too long, perhaps. You cannot get an Indian to sit down when on a long and severe journey, unless compelled to, to rest others. The cold and damp creeps into the joints, and you get stiff and tenfold more tired than before. Great as the temptation is to rest, you should first finish your race, the whole day's journey, before you let your nerves relax.

Slowly as we moved, however, our pursuers did not reappear. We were still on the ridge, in spite of the sharp and eccentric turn it had taken around the head of the river.

As the sun went down, broad, blood-red banners ran up to the top of Shasta, and streamed away to the south in hues of gold; streamed and streamed as if to embrace the universe in one great union beneath one banner. Then the night came down as suddenly on the world as the swoop of an eagle.

The Doctor, who had all the afternoon kept an uncertain seat, now leaned over on his mule's mane, and had fallen, but for the Prince who was riding at his side.

Klamat came back and set his rifle against a pine. We laid the feeble man on the bed of quills, loosened the cinches as the mules and ponies let their noses droop almost to the ground, and prepared to spend the night. This was imperative. It was impossible to go farther. That would have been the death of the man we wished to save.

A severe ride in the mountains at any time is a task. Your neck is wrenched, and your limbs are weary as you leap this log or tumble and stumble your tired animal over this pile of rocks or through that sink of mud, until you are tired enough by night; but when you ride an awkward and untrained mule, when you have not sat a horse for a year, and have an old saddle that fits you like an umbrella or a barrel, you get tired, stiff-limbed, and used up in a way that is indescribable. As for poor Paquita she was literally crucified, but went about picking up quills for beds for all, and never once murmured.

The Doctor was very ill. Klamat went down the hillside and found some water to wet his lips, but this did not revive him. It was a cold evening. The autumn wind came pitching down from the Shasta, sharp and sudden. The old Frost King, who had been driven to the mountaintop in the early summer, was descending now by degrees to reclaim his original kingdom.

We unpacked the little mule and spread a bed for the suffering man, but still he shivered and shook, and we could not get him warm. We, too, were suffering from the cold. We could hardly move when we had rested a moment and let the cold drive back the perspiration, and drive the chill to the marrow.

"A fire," said the Prince.

Klamat protested against it. The sick man grew worse. Something warm would restore him.

We must have a fire. Paquita gathered up some pine knots from the hillside. A match was struck in the quills. The mules started, lifted their noses, but hardly moved as the fire sprung up like a giant full-grown, and reached for the cones of the sugar pines overhead. There was comfort and companionship in the fire. We could see each other now—our little colony of pilgrims. We looked at each other and were revived.

We had a little coffeepot, black and battered it is true, but the water boiled just the same, and as soon as if it had been silver.

This revived the Doctor. Hunger had much to do with his faintness. He now sat up and talked, in his low quiet way, looking into the fire and brushing the little mites of dust and pine quills from his shirt, as if still to retain his great respectability of dress; and by the time we all had finished our coffee, he was almost as cheerful as we had ever seen him before.

The moon came out clear and cold, and we spread our damp and dusty blankets on the quills between the pines, with the snowy front of the Shasta lifting, lifting like a bank of clouds away to the left, and the heads of many mining streams dipping away in so many wild and dubious directions that no one but our little leader, perhaps, could have found the way to the settlements without the gravest embarrassment.

Klamat had gone down the hill for water, this time leaving his rifle leaned against a pine, though not without casting a glance back over his shoulder as if to say, "Look sharp! but I will be back at once." We all were still warming ourselves by the fire, I think, though there are some sudden things you cannot just recall.

A wave of fate strikes you so strong sometimes, that you are swallowed up. Heads and ears you go under it and you see nothing, you remember nothing. It seems to take your breath.

Click! click! click! a tired mule started, snuffed, and then dropped his head, for it was over in an instant.

"Hands up, gentlemen! hands up! Don't trouble yourselves to move! There, that will do! You are the one we want. Pass in your checks!"

The Doctor hid his face in his hands, and let them take his arms without a word.

The fire had done the mischief. Klamat did not come back; at least, he did not let it be known if he did. Paquita opened her large eyes very wide, pushed back her hair, and rested her hands in her lap as she sat looking at the three strange men in elegant top boots and broad-brimmed hats.

"A pretty man you are, Mr. Prince, to run with this fellow," said the officer, "to give me this race. For a coon skin I would take you in charge, too."

Here he arose, went over, and looked at the animals in the firelight, as if looking for some cause to lay hands on the Prince, took general charge of the camp as if it were his own, lit his pipe, had one of the men make coffee, and seemed quite at home.

If the Prince uttered a word all this time I do not remember it.

"Where's your other Ingin, Prince?" said the officer, looking about and seeing but the four saddles. "Put him in the bush, or left him in the camp? Rather a good-looking piece you got here now, ain't she?" He pointed his pipe stem at Paquita.

For the first time the Prince showed color.

The officer and his men, toward midnight, spread their blankets on the other side of the fire. They were scarce of blankets, and the night was cold.

This may be the reason they all spread down together. But there is nothing that will excuse such a stupid thing in the mountains. Sleep apart. Wide apart, rods apart: never two together, unless you wish to make a broad target of yourselves where the muzzle of one gun can do the work of many.

Before lying down the men did what they could for their tired beasts; and then the officer came up to the Doctor, who still gazed and gazed into the fire, and, drawing something from his pockets that chinked like chains, said—

"Your hands!"

"He is ill," said the Prince, "very ill. I will answer for him. Iron me instead; but that man is a nervous, sensitive man that cannot bear to be chained."

The officer laughed a little and, without answering, took the Doctor's unresisting hands and linked them together with a snap that made one shudder; then, laying him back in his blankets, looked to his pistol, and saying, "Don't move! Don't you attempt to move!" he walked over to the other side of the pine-knot fire, and, pistol in hand, lay down by his companions, looking all the time across the fire at his prisoner.

The Prince arose, went and gathered up pine knots by the light of the moon, and laid them on the fire. Paquita looked inquiringly at him, and then went and did the same. When the fire loomed up, he lifted the blankets from the Doctor's feet, drew off his boots, and let the warm, cheerful fire fall on the wretched man.

The officer lay like a fox watching every move and motion, with his head on his saddle, and his nose just above the blankets. His pistol hand was at his side clutching the revolver. The other men were equally wide awake and watchful at his side.

"Lie down, Paquita," said the Prince, "lie down and rest

with your moccasins to the fire; you have had a hard and bitter day of it. I will keep the fire.''

The child obeyed. He waved his hand at me to do the same, and I was soon sound asleep.

The last I saw of the Prince before falling asleep—he was resting on his side with his hand on his head, and elbow on his blankets. In the mountains, when you spread your blankets, you put your arms—rifle or pistols—in between the blankets as carefully as if they were children. This is done, in the first place, to keep them dry, and, in the second place, to have them ready for use. They are laid close to your side. The heat of your body keeps out the damp.

I awoke soon. I was too bruised, and sore, and sick in mind and body, to sleep. There is a doleful, dreary bird that calls in this country in the night, in the most mournful tone you can imagine. It is a sort of white-headed owl; not large, but with a very hoarse and coarse note. One of these birds was calling at intervals down the gorge to the right, and another answered on the other side so faintly I could just hear it. An answer would come just as regularly as this one called, and that would sound even more doleful and dreary still, because so far and indistinct. The moon hung cold and crooked overhead, and fell in flakes through the trees like snow.

The Doctor put out his two hands, pushed back the blanket, and raised his head. He looked to the left in the gorge as if he contemplated a spring in that direction. I think that, at last, he had summoned up courage to make a desperate effort to escape.

He drew up his legs slowly, as if gathering his muscles for a leap. My heart stood still. All seemed clear. I could see the nerves of his face quiver in the moon.

He turned his head to the officer, not six feet away across the fire, and looked squarely into the ugly, sullen muzzles of three lifted pistols.

The Doctor sank back with a groan. His face was white as the moon that shone down upon it through the quills above his head.

The officer and his men exchanged glances, and lay down without a word. The Prince was possibly asleep. Still, ever and again, the doleful bird kept calling, and the woeful answer came back like an echo of sorrow across the great black cañon below.

The moon kept settling and settling to the west among the yellow stars, as broad and spangled as California lilies, and the morning was not far away.

Again the Doctor drew in his naked feet. I could see the muscles gather and contract, and I knew he was again preparing for a spring. All was still. He raised his head, and three pistol muzzles raised and met the man halfway. He crept back far down in the blankets, hid his head in the folds, and shuddered and shivered as with an ague.

Dawn was descending and settling around the head of Shasta in a splendor and a glory that words will never touch.

There are some things that are so far beyond the reach of words that it seems like desecration to attempt description. It was not the red of Pekin, not the purple of Tyre or the yellow of the Barbary coast; but merge all these, mixed and made mellow in a far and tender light—snow and sun, and sun and snow—and stars, and blue and purple skies all blended, all these in a splendid, confused, and indescribable glory, suffusing the hoary summit, centering there, gathering there, resting a moment—then radiating, going on to the sea, to broad and burning plains of the south, to the boundless forests of fir in the north, even to the mining camps of Cariboo, and you have a sunrise on the summit of Shasta.

The Prince lifted his head, rested on his elbow, rubbed his eyes as if he had surely slept, and then slowly and stiffly arose. The fire was low, almost out. He turned to gather pine knots, laid them on the fire, and turned away as if to gather more. The Doctor seemed to sleep. The officer and his men were resting, too. Perhaps they slept also.

"Click! click!"

I sprang to my feet.

"Don't trouble yourselves to move, gentlemen! Remain just where you are, gentlemen, just where you are!"

It was the Prince who spoke this time. He had approached the three heads from behind, and had the double-barrelled gun with its double handful of buck-shot levelled, as he spoke, against the tops of their heads as they lay there on their backs.

Approach a man lying down as if you meant to tread upon his scalp and pin him to the earth, and he is the most helpless of mortals. He cannot see you, he cannot turn around, he can do nothing. Here lay those men; they could see nothing but the black ugly muzzles of the double barrels. Their pistols were in their hands; they were plucky fellows, but they could not draw; they were as likely to shoot each other as an enemy or any one.

This coming upon a man when he is lying down on his back may not be the manliest way in the world, but it is the safest, certainly; and when the game is three to one, you have to take all the percent you can, or, in mountain phrase, "just pass in your checks."

"Don't trouble yourselves to move, gentlemen; don't trouble to rise!"

The Prince said this with a mockery and irony in his tone that was bitter beyond expression; as if all the poison and the venom of the cruel words and cruel treatment of the Doctor the night before had been rankling in his heart till it was ready to burst out of itself, and he now hissed it out between his teeth.

There was something in his words that told the three men that he would rather like it if they would only "trouble to move," move the least bit in the world. As if he would be particularly glad if even one of them would lift a finger, and give him even the least shadow of an excuse to blow them to the moon. They therefore "did not trouble to move."

Klamat came out here from the dark with the dawn. He approached the men like a shadow thrown by a pine from the far light, pulled down the blankets, and took the three pistols from their unresisting hands.

"You may sit up now," said the Prince, taking a seat across the fire by the side of the Doctor. "You may sit up now. You are my prisoners, but I will not handcuff you. I will give you back your arms if you obey me, and you shall return to your town.

"I will not ask you not to mention this little affair," said the Prince—raising the double barrels, as one of the men seemed to be gathering his legs under him—"I will not ask you not to mention this little affair. That is safe enough. You gents will be the last men on earth to mention it. But I give you my word that it shall never be mentioned by me, never, so long as you do not attempt to molest this man. Make the least attempt against him, or any one here, and you shall be made the laughingstock of your town."

The men looked at each other with hope. They had expected to die on the spot.

"It's your pot, Prince, take it down. You hold the papers, called us on a dead hand, you did, but this was no bluff of mine. The only mislead made was not to chain you down too, like a dog, as you deserve to be."

The Prince colored. "If you had not chained the man," he said at last, quietly, "perhaps you could have taken him with you. The only mistake you made was to chain any man at all. Chain a man that could not stand on his feet! You deserve to be shot; and if you repeat yourself, I will let Klamat scalp you where you sit."

The Indian arose with his hand on his knife. There was a fierce satisfaction on his face. He had suffered too much through the night, through the winter, through the year, to feel like trifling now. . . . He certainly looked blank amazement when, an hour later, the Prince, after discharging their arms, and emptying their catenas of ammunition, returned them all again, and turned their faces to the city, civilly, almost politely.

The men rode sadly and silently away through the trees, now and then looking back over their shoulders. The man-hunt was over.

Once the highest paid short-story writer in America, Bret Harte wrote perhaps the finest fictional accounts of the lusty and sometimes violent way of life in the mining camps and boomtowns of the great California Gold Rush. His writings cover some eighteen volumes of prose and two of poetry, and include such famous stories as "The Luck of Roaring Camp" and "The Outcasts of Poker Flat," and the memorable short novel, M'liss: An Idyll of Red Mountain (1863). Jack Hamlin, the sardonic gambler featured in the story that follows, also appears in eighteen other stories, as well as in the 1876 novel, Gabriel Conroy.

A Protege of Jack Hamlin's

★★★★★★★★★★★★★★★

Bret Harte

I

THE steamer *Silveropolis* was sharply and steadily cleaving the broad, placid shallows of the Sacramento River. A large wave like an eagre, diverging from its bow, was extending to either bank, swamping the tules and threatening to submerge the lower levees. The great boat itself—a vast but delicate structure of airy stories, hanging galleries, fragile colonnades, gilded cornices, and resplendent frescoes—was throbbing throughout its whole perilous length with the pulse of high pressure and the strong monotonous beat of a powerful piston. Floods of foam pouring from the high paddle boxes on either side and reuniting in the wake of the boat left behind a track of dazzling whiteness, over which trailed two dense black banners flung from its lofty smokestacks.

Mr. Jack Hamlin had quietly emerged from his stateroom on deck and was looking over the guards. His hands were resting lightly on his hips over the delicate curves of his white waistcoat, and he was whistling softly, possibly some air to which he had made certain card-laying passengers dance the night before. He was in comfortable case, and his soft brown eyes under their long lashes were veiled with gentle tolerance of all things. He glanced lazily along the empty hurricane deck forward; he glanced lazily down to the saloon deck below him. Far out against the guards below him leaned a young girl. Mr. Hamlin knitted his brows slightly.

He remembered her at once. She had come on board that morning with one Ned Stratton, a brother gambler, but neither a favorite nor intimate of Jack's. From certain indications in the pair, Jack had inferred that she was some foolish or reckless creature whom "Ed" had "got on a string," and was spiriting away from her friends and family. With the abstract morality of this situation Jack was not in the least concerned. For himself he did not indulge in that sort of game; the inexperience and vacillations of innocence were apt to be bothersome, and besides, a certain modest doubt of his own competency to make an original selection had always made him prefer to confine his gallantries to the wives of men of greater judgment than himself who had. But it suddenly occurred to him that he had seen Stratton quickly slip off the boat at the last landing stage. Ah! that was it; he had cast away and deserted her. It was an old story. Jack smiled. But he was not greatly amused with Stratton.

She was very pale, and seemed to be clinging to the network railing, as if to support herself, although she was gazing fixedly at the yellow glancing current below, which seemed to be sucked down and swallowed in the paddle box as the boat swept on. It certainly was a fascinating sight—this sloping rapid, hurrying on to bury itself under the crushing wheels. For a brief moment Jack saw how they would seize anything floating on that ghastly incline, whirl it round in one awful revolution of the beating paddles, and then bury it, broken and shattered out of all recognition, deep in the muddy undercurrent of the stream behind them.

She moved away presently with an odd, stiff step, chafing her gloved hands together as if they had become stiffened, too, in her rigid grasp of the railing. Jack leisurely watched her as she moved along the narrow strip of deck. She was not at all to his taste—a rather plump girl with a rustic manner and a great deal of brown hair under her straw hat. She might have looked better had she not been so haggard. When she reached the door of the saloon she paused, and then, turning suddenly, began to walk quickly back again. As she neared the spot where she had been standing her pace slackened, and when she reached the railing she seemed to relapse against it in her former helpless fashion. Jack became lazily interested. Suddenly she lifted her head and cast a quick glance around and above her. In that momentary lifting of her face Jack saw her expression. Whatever it was, his own changed instantly; the next moment there was a crash on the lower deck. It was Jack who had swung himself over the rail and dropped ten feet, to her side. But not before she had placed one foot in the meshes of the netting and had gripped the railing for a spring.

The noise of Jack's fall might have seemed to her bewildered fancy as a part of her frantic act, for she fell forward vacantly on the railing. But by this time Jack had grasped her arm as if to help himself to his feet.

"I might have killed myself by that foolin', mightn't I?" he said cheerfully.

The sound of a voice so near her seemed to recall to her dazed sense the uncompleted action his fall had arrested. She made a convulsive bound toward the railing, but Jack held her fast.

"Don't," he said in a low voice—"don't, it won't pay. It's the sickest game that ever was played by man or woman. Come here!"

He drew her toward an empty stateroom whose door was swinging on its hinges a few feet from them. She was trembling violently; he half led, half pushed her into the room, closed the door, and stood with his back against it as she dropped into a chair. She looked at him vacantly; the agitation she was undergoing inwardly had left her no sense of outward perception.

"You know Stratton would be awfully riled," continued Jack easily. "He's just stepped out to see a friend and got left by the fool boat. He'll be along by the next steamer, and you're bound to meet him in Sacramento."

Her staring eyes seemed suddenly to grasp his meaning. But to his surprise she burst out with a certain hysterical desperation, "No! no! Never! *never* again! Let me pass! I must go," and struggled to regain the door. Jack, albeit singularly relieved to know that she shared his private sentiments regarding Stratton, nevertheless resisted her. Whereat she suddenly turned white, reeled back, and sank in a dead faint in the chair.

The gambler turned, drew the key from the inside of the door, passed out, locking it behind him, and walked leisurely into the main saloon.

"Mrs. Johnson," he said gravely, addressing the steward-ess, a tall mulatto, with his usual winsome supremacy over dependents and children, "you'll oblige me if you'll corral a few smelling salts, vinaigrettes, hairpins, and violet pow-der, and unload them in deck stateroom No. 257. There's a lady—"

"A lady, Marse Hamlin?" interrupted the mulatto, with an archly significant flash of her white teeth.

"A lady," continued Jack with unabashed gravity, "in a sort of conniption fit. A relative of mine; in fact, a niece, my only sister's child. Hadn't seen each other for ten years, and it was too much for her."

The woman glanced at him with a mingling of incredulous belief but delighted obedience, hurriedly gathered a few ar-ticles from her cabin, and followed him to No. 257. The young girl was still unconscious. The stewardess applied a few restoratives with the skill of long experience, and the young girl opened her eyes. They turned vacantly from the stewardess to Jack with a look of half-recognition and half-frightened inquiry.

"Yes," said Jack, addressing the eyes, although ostenta-tiously speaking to Mrs. Johnson, "she'd only just come by steamer to 'Frisco and wasn't expecting to see me, and we dropped right into each other here on the boat. And I haven't seen her since she was so high. Sister Mary ought to have warned me by letter; but she was always a slouch at letter writing. There, that'll do, Mrs. Johnson. She's coming round; I reckon I can manage the rest. But you go now and tell the purser I want one of those inside staterooms for my niece— *my niece*, you hear—so that you can be near her and look after her."

As the stewardess turned obediently away the young girl attempted to rise, but Jack checked her.

"No," he said, almost brusquely; "you and I have some talking to do before she gets back, and we've no time for foolin'. You heard what I told her just now! Well, it's got to be as I said, you sabe. As long as you're on this boat you're my niece, and my sister Mary's child. As I haven't got any sister Mary, you don't run any risk of falling foul of her, and you ain't taking anyone's place. That settles that. Now, do you or do you not want to see that man again? Say yes, and if he's anywhere above ground I'll yank him over to you as soon as we touch shore.'' He had no idea of interfering with his colleague's amors, but he had determined to make Stratton pay for the bother their slovenly sequence had caused him. Yet he was relieved and astonished by her frantic gesture of indignation and abhorrence. ''No?'' he repeated grimly. ''Well, that settles that. Now, look here; quick, before she comes—do you want to go back home to your friends?''

But here occurred what he had dreaded most and probably thought he had escaped. She had stared at him, at the stewardess, at the walls, with abstracted, vacant, and bewildered, but always undimmed and unmoistened eyes. A sudden convulsion shook her whole frame, her blank expression broke like a shattered mirror, she threw her hands over her eyes, and fell forward with her face to the back of her chair in an outburst of tears.

Alas for Jack! with the breaking up of those sealed fountains came her speech also, at first disconnected and incoherent, and then despairing and passionate. No! she had no longer friends or home! She had lost and disgraced them! She had disgraced *herself*! There was no home for her but the grave. Why had Jack snatched her from it? Then bit by bit, she yielded up her story—a story decidedly commonplace to Jack, uninteresting, and even irritating to his fastidiousness. She was a schoolgirl (not even a convent girl, but the inmate of a Presbyterian female academy at Napa. Jack shuddered as he remembered to have once seen certain of the pupils walking with a teacher), and she lived with her married sister. She had seen Stratton while going to to-and-fro on the San Francisco boat; she had exchanged notes with him, had met him secretly, and finally consented to elope with him to Sacramento, only to discover when the boat had left the wharf the real nature of his intentions. Jack listened with infinite weariness and inward chafing. He had read all this before in cheap novelettes, in the police reports, in the Sunday papers; he had heard a street preacher declaim against it, and warn young women of the serpentlike wiles of tempters of the Stratton variety. But even now Jack failed to recognize Stratton as a serpent, or indeed anything but a blundering cheat and clown, who had left his dirty 'prentice work on his (Jack's) hands. But the girl was helpless and, it seemed, homeless, all through a certain desperation of feeling, which, in spite of her tears, he could not but respect. That momentary shadow of death had exalted her. He stroked his mustache, pulled down his white waistcoat, and let her cry, without saying anything. He did not know that this most objectionable phase of her misery was her salvation and his own.

But the stewardess would return in a moment.

"You'd better tell me what to call you," he said quietly. "I ought to know my niece's first name."

The girl caught her breath, and between two sobs said, "Sophonisba."

Jack winced. It seemed only to need this last sentimental touch to complete the idiotic situation.

"I'll call you Sophy," he said hurriedly and with an effort. "And now look here! You are going in that cabin with Mrs. Johnson where she can look after you, but I can't. So I'll have to take your word, for I'm not going to give you away before Mrs. Johnson, that you won't try that foolishness— you know what I mean—before I see you again. Can I trust you?"

With her head still bowed over the chair back, she murmured slowly somewhere from under her disheveled hair: "Yes."

"Honest Injin?" adjured Jack gravely.

"Yes."

The shuffling step of the stewardess was heard slowly approaching.

"Yes," continued Jack abruptly, slightly lifting his voice, as Mrs. Johnson opened the door—"yes, if you'd only had some of those spearmint drops of your Aunt Rachel's that she always gave you when these fits came on you'd have been all right inside of five minutes. Aunty was no slouch of a doctor, was she? Dear me, it only seems yesterday since I saw her. You were just playing round her knee like a kitten on the back porch. How time does fly! But here's Mrs. Johnson coming to take you in. Now rouse up, Sophy, and just hook yourself on to Mrs. Johnson on that side, and we'll toddle along."

The young girl put back her heavy hair, and with her face still averted submitted to be helped to her feet by the kindly stewardess. Perhaps something homely sympathetic and nurselike in the touch of the mulatto gave her assurance and confidence, for her head lapsed quite naturally against the woman's shoulder, and her face was partly hidden as she moved slowly along the deck. Jack accompanied them to the saloon and the inner stateroom door. A few passengers gathered curiously near, as much attracted by the unusual presence of Jack Hamlin in such a procession as by the girl herself.

"You'll look after her specially, Mrs. Johnson," said Jack, in unusually deliberate terms. "She's been a good deal petted at home, and my sister perhaps has rather spoilt her. She's pretty much of a child still, and you'll have to humor her. Sophy," he continued, with ostentatious playfulness, directing his voice into the dim recesses of the stateroom, "you'll just think Mrs. Johnson's your old nurse, won't you? Think it's old Katy, hey?"

To his great consternation the girl approached tremblingly from the inner shadow. The faintest and saddest of smiles for a moment played around the corners of her drawn mouth and tear-dimmed eyes as she held out her hand and said:

"God bless you for being so kind."

Jack shuddered and glanced quickly round. But luckily no one heard this crushing sentimentalism, and the next moment the door closed upon her and Mrs. Johnson.

It was past midnight, and the moon was riding high over the narrowing yellow river, when Jack again stepped out on deck. He had just left the captain's cabin, and a small social game with the officers, which had served to some extent to vaguely relieve his irritation and their pockets. He had presumably quite forgotten the incident of the afternoon, as he looked about him, and complacently took in the quiet beauty of the night.

The low banks on either side offered no break to the uninterrupted level of the landscape, through which the river seemed to wind only as a race track for the rushing boat. Every fiber of her vast but fragile bulk quivered under the goad of her powerful engines. There was no other movement but hers, no other sound but this monstrous beat and panting; the whole tranquil landscape seemed to breathe and pulsate with her; dwellers in the tules, miles away, heard and felt her as she passed, and it seemed to Jack, leaning over the railing, as if the whole river swept like a sluice through her paddle boxes.

Jack had quite unconsciously lounged before that part of the railing where the young girl had leaned a few hours ago. As he looked down upon the streaming yellow millrace below him he noticed—what neither he nor the girl had probably noticed before—that a space of the top bar of the railing was hinged, and could be lifted by withdrawing a small bolt, thus giving easy access to the guards. He was still looking at it, whistling softly, when footsteps approached.

"Jack," said a lazy voice, "how's sister Mary?"

"It's a long time since you've seen her only child, Jack, ain't it?" said a second voice; "and yet it sort o' seems to me somehow that I've seen her before."

Jack recognized the voice of two of his late companions at the card table. His whistling ceased; so also dropped every trace of color and expression from his handsome face. But he did not turn, and remained quietly gazing at the water.

"Aunt Rachel, too, must be getting on in years, Jack," continued the first speaker, halting behind Jack.

"And Mrs. Johnson does not look so much like Sophy's old nurse as she used to," remarked the second, following his example. Still Jack remained unmoved.

"You don't seem to be interested, Jack," continued the first speaker. "What are you looking at?"

Without turning his head the gambler replied, "Looking at the boat; she's booming along, just chawing up and spitting out the river ain't she? Look at that sweep of water going under her paddle wheels," he continued, unbolting the rail and lifting it to allow the two men to peer curiously over the guards as he pointed to the murderous incline beneath them; "a man wouldn't stand much show who got dropped into it. How these paddles would just snatch him bald-headed, pick him up, and slosh him round and round, and then sling him out down there in such a shape that his own father wouldn't know him."

"Yes," said the first speaker, with an ostentatious little laugh, "but all that ain't telling us how sister Mary is."

"No," said the gambler, slipping into the opening with a white and rigid face in which nothing seemed living but the eyes—"no; but it's telling you how two d—d fools who didn't know when to shut their mouths might get them shut once and forever. It's telling you what might happen to two men who tried to 'play' a man who didn't care to be 'played,'—a man who didn't care much what he did, when he did it, or how he did it, but would do what he'd set out to do—even if in doing it he went to hell with the men he sent there."

He had stepped out on the guards, beside the two men, closing the rail behind him. He had placed his hands on their shoulders; they had both gripped his arms; yet, viewed from the deck above, they seemed at that moment an amicable, even fraternal group, albeit the faces of the three were dead white in the moonlight.

"I don't think I'm so very much interested in sister Mary," said the first speaker quietly, after a pause.

"And I don't seem to think so much of Aunt Rachel as I did," said his companion.

"I thought you wouldn't," said Jack, coolly reopening the rail and stepping back again. "It all depends upon the way you look at those things. Good night."

"Good night."

The three men paused, shook each other's hands silently, and separated, Jack sauntering slowly back to his stateroom.

II

THE educational establishment of Mrs. Mix and Madame Bance, situated in the best quarter of Sacramento and patronized by the highest state officials and members of the clergy, was a pretty if not an imposing edifice. Although surrounded by a high white picket fence and entered through a heavily boarded gate, its balconies festooned with jasmine and roses, and its spotlessly draped windows as often graced with fresh, flowerlike faces, were still plainly and provokingly visible above the ostentatious spikes of the pickets. Nevertheless, Mr. Jack Hamlin, who had six months before placed his niece, Miss Sophonisba Brown, under its protecting care, felt a degree of uneasiness, even bordering on timidity, which was new to that usually self-confident man. Remembering how his first appearance had fluttered this dovecot and awakened a severe suspicion in the minds of the two principals,

he had discarded his usual fashionable attire and elegantly
fitting garments for a rough homespun suit, supposed to represent a homely agriculturist, but which had the effect of
transforming him into an adorable Strephon, infinitely more
dangerous in his rustic shepherdlike simplicity. He had also
shaved off his silken mustache for the same prudential reasons, but had only succeeded in uncovering the delicate lines
of his handsome mouth, and so absurdly reducing his apparent years that his avuncular pretensions seemed more pre-
posterous than ever; and when he had rung the bell and was
admitted by a severe Irish waiting maid, his momentary hesitation and half-humorous diffidence had such an unexpected
effect upon her that it seemed doubtful if he would be allowed
to pass beyond the vestibule.

"Shure, miss," she said in a whisper to an underteacher,
"there's wan at the dhure who calls himself 'Mister' Hamlin,
but av it is not a young lady maskeradin' in her brother's
clothes oim very much mistaken; and av it's a boy, one of
the pupil's brothers, shure ye might put a dhress on him when
you take the others out for a walk, and he'd pass for the
beauty of the whole school."

Meantime the unconscious subject of this criticism was
pacing somewhat uneasily up and down the formal reception
room into which he had been finally ushered. Its farther end
was filled by an enormous parlor organ, a number of music
books, and a cheerfully variegated globe. A large presenta-
tion Bible, an equally massive illustrated volume on the Holy
Land, a few landscapes in cold, bluish milk and water colors,
and rigid heads in crayons—the work of pupils—were presumably ornamental. An imposing mahogany sofa and what
seemed to be a disproportionate excess of chairs somewhat
coldly furnished the room. Jack had reluctantly made up his
mind that if Sophy was accompanied by anyone he would be
obliged to kiss her to keep up his assumed relationship. As
she entered the room with Miss Mix, Jack advanced and soberly saluted her on the cheek. But so positive and apparent
was the gallantry of his presence, and perhaps so suggestive
of some pastoral flirtation, that Miss Mix, to Jack's surprise,
winced perceptibly and became stony. But he was still more
surprised that the young lady herself shrank half uneasily from
his lips, and uttered a slight exclamation. It was a new experience to Mr. Hamlin.

But this somewhat mollified Miss Mix, and she slightly relaxed her austerity. She was glad to be able to give the best accounts of Miss Brown, not only as regarded her studies, but as to her conduct and deportment. Really, with the present freedom of manners and laxity of home discipline in California, it was gratifying to meet a young lady who seemed to value the importance of a proper decorum and behavior, especially toward the opposite sex. Mr. Hamlin, although her guardian, was perhaps too young to understand and appreciate this. To this inexperience she must also attribute the indiscretion of his calling during school hours and without preliminary warning. She trusted, however, that this informality could be overlooked after consultation with Madame Bance, but in the meantime, perhaps for half an hour, she must withdraw Miss Brown and return with her to the class. Mr. Hamlin could wait in this public room, reserved especially for visitors, until they returned. Or, if he cared to accompany one of the teachers in a formal inspection of the school, she added doubtfully, with a glance at Jack's distracting attractions, she would submit this also to Madame Bance.

"Thank you, thank you," returned Jack hurriedly, as a depressing vision of the fifty or sixty scholars rose before his eyes, "but I'd rather not. I mean, you know, I'd just as lief stay here *alone*. I wouldn't have called anyway, don't you see, only I had a day off—and—and—I wanted to talk with my niece on family matters."

He did not say that he had received a somewhat distressful letter from her asking him to come; a new instinct made him cautious.

Considerably relieved by Jack's unexpected abstention, which seemed to spare her pupils the distraction of his graces, Miss Mix smiled more amicably and retired with her charge. In the single glance he had exchanged with Sophy he saw that, although resigned and apparently self-controlled, she still appeared thoughtful and melancholy. She had improved in appearance and seemed more refined and less rustic in her school dress, but he was conscious of the same distinct separation of her personality (which was uninteresting to him) from the sentiment that had impelled him to visit her. She was possibly still hankering after that fellow Stratton, in spite of her protestations to the contrary; perhaps she wanted to go back to her sister, although she had declared she would die first, and had always refused to disclose her real name or give any clue by which he could have traced her relations. She would cry, of course; he almost hoped that she would not return alone; he half regretted he had come. She still held him only by a single quality of her nature—the desperation she had shown on the boat; that was something he understood and respected.

He walked discontentedly to the window and looked out; he walked discontentedly to the end of the room and stopped before the organ. It was a fine instrument; he could see that with an admiring and experienced eye. He was alone in the room; in fact, quite alone in that part of the house which was separated from the classrooms. He would disturb no one by trying it. And if he did, what then? He smiled a little recklessly, slowly pulled off his gloves, and sat down before it.

He played cautiously at first, with the soft pedal down. The instrument had never known a strong masculine hand before, having been fumbled and frivoled over by softly incompetent, feminine fingers. But presently it began to thrill under the passionate hand of its lover, and carried away by his one innocent weakness, Jack was launched upon a sea of musical reminiscences. Scraps of church music, Puritan psalms of his boyhood, dying strains from sad, forgotten operas, fragments of oratorios and symphonies, but chiefly phrases from old masses heard at the missions of San Pedro and Santa Isabel, swelled up from his loving and masterful fingers. He had finished an Agnus Dei; the formal room was pulsating with divine aspiration; the rascal's hands were resting listlessly on the keys, his brown lashes, lifted, in an effort of memory, tenderly toward the ceiling.

Suddenly, a subdued murmur of applause and a slight rustle behind him recalled him to himself again. He wheeled his chair quickly round. The two principals of the school and half a dozen teachers were standing gravely behind him, and at the open door a dozen curled and frizzled youthful heads peered in eagerly, but half restrained by their teachers. The relaxed features and apologetic attitude of Madame Bance and Miss Mix showed that Mr. Hamlin had unconsciously achieved a triumph.

He might not have been as pleased to know that his extraordinary performance had solved a difficulty, effaced his other graces, and enabled them to place him on the moral pedestal of a mere musician, to whom these eccentricities were allowable and privileged. He shared the admiration extended by the young ladies to their music teacher, which was always understood to be a sexless enthusiasm and a contagious juvenile disorder. It was also a fine advertisement for the organ. Madame Bance smiled blandly, improved the occasion by thanking Mr. Hamlin for having given the scholars a gratuitous lesson on the capabilities of the instrument, and was glad to be able to give Miss Brown a half-holiday to spend with her accomplished relative. Miss Brown was even now upstairs putting on her hat and mantle. Jack was relieved. Sophy would not attempt to cry on the street.

Nevertheless, when they reached it and the gate closed behind them, he again became uneasy. The girl's clouded face and melancholy manner were not promising. It also occurred to him that he might meet someone who knew him and thus compromise her. This was to be avoided at all hazards. He began with forced gaiety:

"Well, now, where shall we go?"

She slightly raised her tear-dimmed eyes.

"Where you please—I don't care."

"There isn't any show going on here, is there?"

He had a vague idea of a circus or menagerie—himself behind her in the shadow of the box.

"I don't know of any."

"Or any restaurant—or cake shop?"

"There's a place where the girls go to get candy on Main Street. Some of them are there now."

Jack shuddered; this was not to be thought of.

"But where do you walk?"

"Up and down Main Street."

"Where everybody can see you?" said Jack, scandalized. The girl nodded.

They walked on in silence for a few moments. Then a bright idea struck Mr. Hamlin. He suddenly remembered that in one of his many fits of impulsive generosity and largess he had given to an old Negro retainer—whose wife had nursed him through a dangerous illness—a house and lot on the river bank. He had been told that they had opened a small laundry or wash house. It occurred to him that a stroll there and a call upon "Uncle Hannibal and Aunt Chloe" combined the propriety and respectability due to the young person he was with, and the requisite secrecy and absence of publicity due to himself. He at once suggested it.

"You see she was a mighty good woman, and you ought to know her, for she was my old nurse—"

The girl glanced at him with a sudden impatience.

"Honest Injin," said Jack solemnly; "she did nurse me through my last cough. I ain't playing old family gags on you now."

"Oh, dear," burst out the girl impulsively, "I do wish you wouldn't ever play them again. I wish you wouldn't pretend to be my uncle; I wish you wouldn't make me pass for your niece. It isn't right. It's all wrong. Oh, don't you know it's all wrong, and can't come right any way? It's just killing me. I can't stand it. I'd rather you'd say what I am and how I came to you and how you pitied me."

They had luckily entered a narrow side street, and the sobs which shook the young girl's frame were unnoticed. For a few moments Jack felt a horrible conviction stealing over him, that in his present attitude toward her he was not unlike that hound Stratton, and that, however innocent his own intent, there was a sickening resemblance to the situation on the boat in the base advantage he had taken of her friendlessness. He had never told her that he was a gambler like Stratton, and that his peculiar infelix reputation among women made it impossible for him to assist her, except by stealth or the deception he had practiced, without compromising her. He who had for years faced the sneers and half-frightened opposition of the world dared not tell the truth to this girl, from whom he expected nothing and who did not interest him. He felt he was almost slinking at her side. At last he said desperately:

"But I snatched them bald-headed at the organ, Sophy, didn't I?"

"Oh, yes," said the girl, "you played beautifully and grandly. It was so good of you, too. For I think, somehow, Madame Bance had been a little suspicious of you, but that settled it. Everybody thought it was fine, and some thought it was your profession. Perhaps," she added timidly, "it is."

"I play a good deal, I reckon," said Jack, with a grim humor which did not, however, amuse him.

"I wish *I* could, and make money by it," said the girl eagerly. Jack winced, but she did not notice it as she went on hurriedly: "That's what I wanted to talk to you about. I want to leave the school and make my own living. Anywhere where people won't know me and where I can be alone and work. I shall die here among these girls—with all their talk of their friends and their—sisters—and their questions about you."

"Tell 'em to dry up," said Jack indignantly. "Take 'em to the cake shop and load 'em up with candy and ice cream. That'll stop their mouths. You've got money—you got my last remittance, didn't you?" he repeated quickly. "If you didn't here's—"; his hand was already in his pocket when she stopped him with a despairing gesture.

"Yes, yes, I got it all. I haven't touched it. I don't want it. For I can't live on you. Don't you understand—I want to work. Listen—I can draw and paint. Madame Bance says I do it well; my drawing master says I might in time take portraits and get paid for it. And even now I can retouch photographs and make colored miniatures from them. And," she stopped and glanced at Jack half timidly, "I've—done some already."

A glow of surprised relief suffused the gambler. Not so much at this astonishing revelation as at the change it seemed to effect in her. Her pale blue eyes, made paler by tears, cleared and brightened under their swollen lids like wiped steel; the lines of her depressed mouth straightened and became firm. Her voice had lost its hopeless monotone.

"There's a shop in the next street—a photographer's—where they have one of mine in their windows," she went on, reassured by Jack's unaffected interest. "It's only round the corner, if you care to see."

Jack assented; a few paces farther brought them to the corner of a narrow street, where they presently turned into a broader thoroughfare and stopped before the window of a photographer. Sophy pointed to an oval frame, containing a portrait painted on porcelain. Mr. Hamlin was startled. Inexperienced as he was, a certain artistic inclination told him it was good, although it is to be feared he would have been astonished even if it had been worse. The mere fact that this headstrong country girl, who had run away with a cur like Stratton, should be able to do anything else took him by surprise.

"I got ten dollars for that," she said hesitatingly, "and I could have got more for a larger one, but I had to do that in my room during recreation hours. If I had more time and a place where I could work—'' She stopped timidly and looked tentatively at Jack. But he was already indulging in a characteristically reckless idea of coming back after he had left Sophy, buying the miniature at an extravagant price, and ordering half a dozen more at extraordinary figures. Here, however, two passersby, stopping ostensibly to look in the window, but really attracted by the picturesque spectacle of the handsome young rustic and his schoolgirl companion, gave Jack such a fright that he hurried Sophy away again into the side street.

"There's nothing mean about that picture business," he said cheerfully; "it looks like a square kind of game," and relapsed into thoughtful silence.

At which Sophy, the ice of restraint broken, again burst into passionate appeal. If she could only go away somewhere—where she saw no one but the people who would buy her work, who knew nothing of her past nor cared to know who were her relations! She would work hard; she knew she could support herself in time. She would keep the name he had given her—it was not distinctive enough to challenge any inquiry—but nothing more. She need not assume to be his niece; he would always be her kind friend, to whom she owed everything, even her miserable life. She trusted still to his honor never to seek to know her real name, nor ever to speak to her of that man if he ever met him. It would do no good to her or to them; it might drive her, for she was not yet quite sure of herself, to do that which she had promised him never to do again.

There was no threat, impatience, or acting in her voice, but he recognized the same dull desperation he had once heard in it, and her eyes, which a moment before were quick and mobile, had become fixed and set. He had no idea of trying to penetrate the foolish secret of her name and relations; he had never had the slightest curiosity, but it struck him now that Stratton might at any time force it upon him. The only way that he could prevent it was to let it be known that, for unexpressed reasons, he would shoot Stratton "on sight." This would naturally restrict any verbal communication between them. Jack's ideas of morality were vague, but his convictions on points of honor were singularly direct and positive.

III

MEANTIME Hamlin and Sophy were passing the outskirts of the town; the open lots and cleared spaces were giving way to grassy stretches, willow copses, and groups of cottonwood and sycamore; and beyond the level of yellowing tules appeared the fringed and raised banks of the river. Half tropical-looking cottages with deep verandas—the homes of early Southern pioneers—took the place of incomplete blocks of modern houses, monotonously alike. In these sylvan surroundings Mr. Hamlin's picturesque rusticity looked less incongruous and more Arcadian; the young girl had lost some of her restraint with her confidences, and lounging together side by side, without the least consciousness of any sentiment in their words or actions, they nevertheless contrived to impress the spectator with the idea that they were a charming pair of pastoral lovers. So strong was this impression that, as they approached Aunt Chloe's laundry, a pretty rose-covered cottage with an enormous whitewashed barnlike extension in the rear, the black proprietress herself, standing at the door, called to her husband to come and look at them, and flashed her white teeth in such unqualified commendation and patronage that Mr. Hamlin, withdrawing himself from Sophy's side, instantly charged down upon them.

"If you don't slide the lid back over that grinning box of dominoes of yours and take it inside, I'll just carry Hannibal off with me," he said in a quick whisper, with a half-wicked, half-mischievous glitter in his brown eyes. "That young lady's—*a lady*—do you understand? No riffraff friend of mine, but a regular *nun*—a saint—do you hear? So you just stand back and let her take a good look round, and rest herself until she wants you." "Two black idiots, Miss Brown," he continued cheerfully in a higher voice of explanation, as Sophy approached, "who think because one of 'em used to shave me and the other saved my life they've got a right to stand at their humble cottage door and frighten horses!"

So great was Mr. Hamlin's ascendancy over his former servants that even this ingenious pleasantry was received with every sign of affection and appreciation of the humorist, and of the profound respect for his companion. Aunt Chloe showed them effusively into her parlor, a small but scrupulously neat and sweet-smelling apartment, inordinately furnished with a huge mahogany center table and chairs, and the most fragile and meretricious china and glass ornaments on the mantel. But the three jasmine-edged lattice windows opened upon a homely garden of old-fashioned herbs and flowers, and their fragrance filled the room. The cleanest and starchiest of curtains, the most dazzling and whitest of tidies and chair covers, bespoke the adjacent laundry; indeed, the whole cottage seemed to exhale the odors of lavender soap and freshly ironed linen. Yet the cottage was large for the couple and their assistants.

"Dar was two front rooms on de next flo' dat dey never used," explained Aunt Chloe; "friends allowed dat dey could let 'em to white folks, but dey had always been done kep' for Marse Hamlin, ef he ever wanted to be wid his old niggers again."

Jack looked up quickly with a brightened face, made a sign to Hannibal, and the two left the room together.

When he came through the passage a few moments later, there was a sound of laughter in the parlor. He recognized the full, round, lazy chuckle of Aunt Chloe, but there was a higher girlish ripple that he did not know. He had never heard Sophy laugh before. Nor, when he entered, had he ever seen her so animated. She was helping Chloe set the table, to that lady's intense delight at "Missy's" girlish housewifery. She was picking the berries fresh from the garden, buttering the Sally Lunn, making the tea, and arranging the details of the repast with apparently no trace of her former discontent and unhappiness in either face or manner. He dropped quietly into a chair by the window, and, with the homely scents of the garden mixing with the honest odors of Aunt Chloe's cookery, watched her with an amusement that was as pleasant and grateful as it was strange and unprecedented.

"Now, den," said Aunt Chloe to her husband, as she put the finishing touch to the repast in the plate of doughnuts as exquisitely brown and shining as Jack's eyes were at that moment, "Hannibal, you just come away, and let dem two white quality chillens have dey tea. Dey's done starved, shuah." And with an approving nod to Jack, she bundled her husband from the room.

The door closed; the young girl began to pour out the tea, but Jack remained in his seat by the window. It was a singular sensation which he did not care to disturb. It was no new thing for Mr. Hamlin to find himself at a tête-à-tête repast with the admiring and complaisant fair; there was a cabinet particulier in a certain San Francisco restaurant which had listened to their various vanities and professions of undying faith; he might have recalled certain festal rendezvous with a widow whose piety and impeccable reputation made it a moral duty for her to come to him only in disguise; it was but a few days before that he had been let privately into the palatial mansion of a high official for a midnight supper with a foolish wife. It was not strange, therefore, that he should be alone here, secretly, with a member of that indirect, loving sex. But that he should be sitting there in a cheap Negro laundry with absolutely no sentiment of any kind toward the heavy-haired, freckled-faced country schoolgirl opposite him, from whom he sought and expected nothing, and *enjoying* it without scorn of himself or his companion, to use his own expression, "got him." Presently he rose and sauntered to the table with shining eyes.

"Well, what do you think of Aunt Chloe's shebang?" he asked smilingly.

"Oh, it's so sweet and clean and homelike," said the girl quickly.

At any other time he would have winced at the last adjective. It struck him now as exactly the word.

"Would you like to live here, if you could?"

Her face brightened. She put the teapot down and gazed fixedly at Jack.

"Because you can. Look here. I spoke to Hannibal about it. You can have the two front rooms if you want to. One of 'em is big enough and light enough for a studio to do your work in. You tell that nigger what you want to put in 'em, and he's got my orders to do it. I told him about your painting; said you were the daughter of an old friend, you know. Hold on, Sophy; d—n it all, I've got to do a little gilt-edged lying; but I let you out of the niece business this time. Yes, from this moment I'm no longer your uncle. I renounce the relationship. It's hard," continued the rascal, "after all these years and considering sister Mary's feelings; but, as you seem to wish it, it must be done."

Sophy's steel-blue eyes softened. She slid her long brown hand across the table and grasped Jack's. He returned the pressure quickly and fraternally, even to that half-shamed, half-hurried evasion of emotion peculiar to all brothers. This was also a new sensation, but he liked it.

"You are too, too good, Mr. Hamlin," she said quietly.

"Yes," said Jack cheerfully, "that's what's the matter with me. It isn't natural, and if I keep it up too long it brings on my cough."

Nevertheless, they were happy in a boy and girl fashion, eating heartily, and, I fear, not always decorously; scrambling somewhat for the strawberries, and smacking their lips over the Sally Lunn. Meantime, it was arranged that Mr. Hamlin should inform Miss Mix that Sophy would leave school at the end of the term, only a few days hence, and then transfer herself to lodgings with some old family servants, where she could more easily pursue her studies in her own profession. She need not make her place of abode a secret, neither need she court publicity. She would write to Jack regularly, informing him of her progress, and he would visit her whenever he could. Jack assented gravely to the further proposition that he was to keep a strict account of all the moneys he advanced her, and that she was to repay him out of the proceeds of her first pictures. He had promised also, with a slight mental reservation, not to buy them all himself, but to trust to her success with the public. They were never to talk of what had happened before; she was to begin life anew. Of such were their confidences, spoken often together at the same moment, and with their mouths full. Only one thing troubled Jack: he had not yet told her frankly who he was and what was his reputation. He had hitherto carelessly supposed she would learn it, and in truth had cared little if she did; but it was evident from her conversation that day that by some miracle she was still in ignorance. Unable to tell her himself, he had charged Hannibal to break it to her casually after he was gone.

"You can let me down easy if you like, but you'd better make a square deal of it while you're about it. And," Jack had added cheerfully, "if she thinks after that she'd better drop me entirely, you just say that if she wishes to *stay*, you'll see that I don't ever come here again. And you keep your word about it too, you black nigger, or I'll be the first to thrash you."

Nevertheless, when Hannibal and Aunt Chloe returned to clear away the repast, they were a harmonious party; albeit

Mr. Hamlin seemed more content to watch them silently from his chair by the window, a cigar between his lips, and the pleasant distraction of the homely scents and sounds of the garden in his senses. Allusion having been made again to the morning performance of the organ, he was implored by Hannibal to diversify his talent by exercising it on an old guitar which had passed into that retainer's possession with certain clothes of his master's when they separated. Mr. Hamlin accepted it dubiously; it had twanged under his volatile fingers in more pretentious but less innocent halls. But presently he raised his tenor voice and soft brown lashes to the humble ceiling and sang.

> Way down upon the Swanee River,

discoursed Jack plaintively—

> Far, far away,
> Thar's whar my heart is turning ever,
> Thar's whar the old folks stay.

The two dusky scions of an emotional race, that had been wont to sweeten its toils and condone its wrongs with music, sat rapt and silent, swaying with Jack's voice until they could burst in upon the chorus. The jasmine vines trilled softly with the afternoon breeze; a slender yellow hammer, perhaps emulous of Jack, swung himself from an outer spray and peered curiously into the room; and a few neighbors, gathering at their doors and windows, remarked that "after all, when it came to real singing, no one could beat those d—d niggers."

The sun was slowly sinking in the rolling gold of the river when Jack and Sophy started leisurely back through the broken shafts of light and across the far-stretching shadows of the cottonwoods. In the midst of a lazy silence they were presently conscious of a distant monotonous throb, the booming of the up boat on the river. The sound came nearer—passed them, the boat itself hidden by the trees; but a trailing cloud of smoke above cast a momentary shadow upon their path. The girl looked up at Jack with a troubled face. Mr. Hamlin smiled reassuringly; but in that instant he had made up his mind that it was his moral duty to kill Mr. Edward Stratton.

IV

FOR the next two months Mr. Hamlin was professionally engaged in San Francisco and Marysville, and the transfer of Sophy from the school to her new home was effected without his supervision. From letters received by him during that interval, it seemed that the young girl had entered energetically upon her new career, and that her artistic efforts were crowned with success. There were a few Indian-ink sketches, studies made at school and expanded in her own "studio," which were eagerly bought as soon as exhibited in the photographer's window—notably by a florid and inartistic bookkeeper, an old Negro woman, a slangy stable boy, a gorgeously dressed and painted female, and the bearded second officer of a river steamboat, without hesitation and without comment. This, as Mr. Hamlin intelligently pointed out in a letter to Sophy, showed a general and diversified appreciation on the part of the public. Indeed, it emboldened her in the retouching of photographs to offer sittings to the subjects, and to undertake even large crayon copies, which had resulted in her getting so many orders that she was no longer obliged to sell her drawings, but restricted herself solely to profitable portraiture. The studio became known; even its quaint surroundings added to the popular interest, and the originality and independence of the young painter helped her to a genuine success. All this she wrote to Jack. Meantime Hannibal had assured him that he had carried out his instructions by informing "Missy" of his old master's real occupation and reputation, but that the young lady hadn't "took no notice." Certainly there was no allusion to it in her letters, nor any indication in her manner. Mr. Hamlin was greatly, and it seemed to him properly, relieved. And he looked forward with considerable satisfaction to an early visit to old Hannibal's laundry.

It must be confessed, also, that another matter, a simple affair of gallantry, was giving him an equally unusual, unexpected, and absurd annoyance, which he had never before permitted to such trivialities. In a recent visit to a fashionable watering place he had attracted the attention of what appeared to be a respectable, matter-of-fact woman, the wife of a recently elected rural senator. She was, however, singularly beautiful, and as singularly cold. It was perhaps this quality, and her evident annoyance at some unreasoning prepossession which Jack's fascinations exercised upon her, that heightened that reckless desire for risk and excitement which really made up the greater part of his gallantry. Nevertheless, as was his habit, he had treated her always with a charming unconsciousness of his own attentions, and a frankness that seemed inconsistent with any insidious approach. In fact, Mr. Hamlin seldom made love to anybody, but permitted it to be made to him with good-humored deprecation and cheerful skepticism. He had once, quite accidentally, while riding, come upon her when she had strayed from her own riding party, and had behaved with such unexpected circumspection and propriety, not to mention a certain thoughtful abstraction—it was the day he had received Sophy's letter—that she was constrained to make the first advances. This led to a later innocent rendezvous, in which Mrs. Camperly was impelled to confide to Mr. Hamlin the fact that her husband had really never understood her. Jack listened with an understanding and sympathy quickened by long experience of such confessions. If anything had ever kept him from marriage it was this evident incompatibility of the conjugal relations with a just conception of the feminine soul and its aspirations.

And so eventually this yearning for sympathy dragged Mrs. Camperly's clean skirts and rustic purity after Jack's heels into various places and various situations not so clean, rural, or innocent; made her miserably unhappy in his absence, and still more miserably happy in his presence; impelled her to lie, cheat, and bear false witness; forced her to listen with mingled shame and admiration to narrow criticism of his faults, from natures so palpably inferior to his own that her moral sense was confused and shaken; gave her two distinct lives, but so unreal and feverish that, with a recklessness equal to his own, she was at last ready to merge them both into his. For the first time in his life Mr. Hamlin found himself bored at the beginning of an affair, actually hesitated, and suddenly disappeared from San Francisco.

He turned up a few days later at Aunt Chloe's door, with various packages of presents and quite the air of a returning father of a family, to the intense delight of that lady and to Sophy's proud gratification. For he was lost in a profuse, boyish admiration of her pretty studio, and in wholesome reverence for her art and her astounding progress. They were also amused at his awe and evident alarm at the portraits of two ladies, her latest sitters, that were still on the easels, and in consideration of his half-assumed, half-real bashfulness, they turned their faces to the wall. Then his quick, observant eye detected a photograph of himself on the mantel.

"What's that?" he asked suddenly.

Sophy and Aunt Chloe exchanged meaning glances. Sophy had, as a surprise to Jack, just completed a handsome crayon portrait of himself from an old photograph furnished by Hannibal, and the picture was at that moment in the window of her former patron—the photographer.

"Oh, dat! Miss Sophy jus' put it dar fo' de lady sitters to look at to gib 'em a pleasant 'spresshion," said Aunt Chloe, chuckling.

Mr. Hamlin did not laugh, but quietly slipped the photograph into his pocket. Yet, perhaps it had not been recognized.

Then Sophy proposed to have luncheon in the studio; it was quite "Bohemian" and fashionable, and many artists did it. But to her great surprise Jack gravely objected, preferring the little parlor of Aunt Chloe, the vine-fringed windows, and the heavy respectable furniture. He thought it was profaning the studio, and then—anybody might come in. This unusual circumspection amused them, and was believed to be part of the boyish awe with which Jack regarded the models, the draperies, and the studies on the walls. Certain it was that he was much more at his ease in the parlor, and when he and Sophy were once more alone at their meal, although he ate nothing, he had regained all his old naïveté. Presently he leaned forward and placed his hand fraternally on her arm. Sophy looked up with an equally frank smile.

"You know I promised to let bygones by bygones, eh? Well, I intended it, and more—I intended to make 'em so. I told you I'd never speak to you again of that man who tried to run you off, and I intended that no one else should. Well, as he was the only one who could talk—that meant him. But the cards are out of my hands; the game's been played without me. For he's dead!"

The girl started. Mr. Hamlin's hand passed caressingly twice or thrice along her sleeve with a peculiar gentleness that seemed to magnetize her.

"Dead," he repeated slowly. "Shot in San Diego by another man, but not by me. I had him tracked as far as that, and had my eyes on him, but it wasn't my deal. But there," he added, giving her magnetized arm a gentle and final tap as if to awaken it, "he's dead, and so is the whole story. And now we'll drop it forever."

The girl's downcast eyes were fixed on the table.

"But there's my sister," she murmured.

"Did she know you went with him?" asked Jack.

"No; but she knows I ran away."

"Well, you ran away from home to study how to be an artist, don't you see? Someday she'll find out you *are one*; that settles the whole thing."

They were both quite cheerful again when Aunt Chloe returned to clear the table, especially Jack, who was in the best spirits, with preternaturally bright eyes and a somewhat rare color on his cheeks. Aunt Chloe, who had noticed that his breathing was hurried at times, watched him narrowly, and when later he slipped from the room, followed him into the passage. He was leaning against the wall. In an instant the negress was at his side.

"De Lawdy Gawd, Marse Jack, no *agin*?"

He took his handkerchief, slightly streaked with blood, from his lips and said faintly, "Yes, it came on—on the boat; but I thought the d—d thing was over. Get me out of this, quick, to some hotel, before she knows it. You can tell her I was called away. Say that—" but his breath failed him, and when Aunt Chloe caught him like a child in her strong arms he could make no resistance.

In another hour he was unconscious, with two doctors at his bedside, in the little room that had been occupied by Sophy. It was a sharp attack, but prompt attendance and skillful nursing availed; he rallied the next day, but it would be weeks, the doctors said, before he could be removed in safety. Sophy was transferred to the parlor, but spent most of her time at Jack's bedside with Aunt Chloe, or in the studio with the door open between it and the bedroom. In spite of his enforced idleness and weakness, it was again a singularly pleasant experience to Jack; it amused him to sometimes see Sophy at her work through the open door, and when sitters came—for he had insisted on her continuing her duties as before, keeping his invalid presence in the house a secret— he had all the satisfaction of a mischievous boy in rehearsing to Sophy such of the conversation as could be overheard through the closed door, and speculating on the possible wonder and chagrin of the sitters had they discovered him. Even when he was convalescent and strong enough to be helped into the parlor and garden, he preferred to remain propped up in Sophy's little bedroom. It was evident, however, that this predilection was connected with no suggestion nor reminiscence of Sophy herself. It was true that he had once asked her if it didn't make her "feel like home." The decided negative from Sophy seemed to mildly surprise him. "That's odd," he said; "now all these fixings and things," pointing to the flowers in a vase, the little hanging shelf of books, the knickknacks on the mantel shelf, and the few feminine ornaments that still remained, "look rather like home to me."

So the days slipped by, and although Mr. Hamlin was soon able to walk short distances, leaning on Sophy's arm, in the evening twilight along the river bank, he was still missed from the haunts of dissipated men. A good many people wondered, and others, chiefly of the more irrepressible sex, were singularly concerned. Apparently one of these, one sultry afternoon, stopped before the shadowed window of a photographer's; she was a handsome, well-dressed woman, yet bearing a certain countrylike simplicity that was unlike the restless smartness of the more urban promenaders who passed her. Nevertheless she had halted before Mr. Hamlin's picture, which Sophy had not yet dared to bring home and present to him, and was gazing at it with rapt and breathless attention. Suddenly she shook down her veil and entered the shop. Could the proprietor kindly tell her if that portrait was the work of a local artist?

The proprietor was both proud and pleased to say that *it was*! It was the work of a Miss Brown, a young girl student; in fact, a mere schoolgirl, one might say. He could show her others of her pictures.

Thanks. But could he tell her if this portrait was from life?

No doubt; the young lady had a studio, and he himself had sent her sitters.

And perhaps this was the portrait of one that he had sent her?

No; but she was very popular and becoming quite the fashion. Very probably this gentleman, who, he understood, was quite a public character, had heard of her, and selected her on that account.

The lady's face flushed slightly. The photographer continued. The picture was not for sale; it was only there on exhibition; in fact it was to be returned tomorrow.

To the sitter?

He couldn't say. It was to go back to the studio. Perhaps the sitter would be there.

And this studio? Could she have its address?

The man wrote a few lines on his card. Perhaps the lady would be kind enough to say that he had sent her. The lady, thanking him, partly lifted her veil to show a charming smile, and gracefully withdrew. The photographer was pleased. Miss Brown had evidently got another sitter, and from that momentary glimpse of her face, it would be a picture as beautiful and attractive as the man's. But what was the odd idea that struck him? She certainly reminded him of someone! There was the same heavy hair, only this lady's was golden, and she was older and more mature. And he remained for a moment with knitted brows musing over his counter.

Meantime the fair stranger was making her way toward the river suburb. When she reached Aunt Chloe's cottage, she paused, with the unfamiliar curiosity of a newcomer, over its quaint and incongruous exterior. She hesitated a moment also when Aunt Chloe appeared in the doorway, and, with a puzzled survey of her features, went upstairs to announce a visitor. There was the sound of hurried shutting of doors, of the moving of furniture, quick footsteps across the floor, and then a girlish laugh that startled her. She ascended the stairs breathlessly to Aunt Chloe's summons, found the negress on the landing, and knocked at a door which bore a card marked "Studio." The door opened; she entered; there were two sudden outcries that might have come from one voice.

"Sophonisba!"

"Marianne!"

"Hush."

The woman had seized Sophy by the wrist and dragged her to the window. There was a haggard look of desperation in her face akin to that which Hamlin had once seen in her sister's eyes on the boat, as she said huskily: "I did not know *you* were here. I came to see the woman who had painted Mr. Hamlin's portrait. I did not know it was *you*. Listen!

Quick! answer me one question. Tell me—I implore you—for the sake of the mother who bore us both!—tell me—is this the man for whom you left home?''

"No! No! A hundred times no!"

Then there was a silence. Mr. Hamlin from the bedroom heard no more.

An hour later, when the two women opened the studio door, pale but composed, they were met by the anxious and tearful face of Aunt Chloe.

"Lawdy Gawd, Missy—but dey done gone!—bofe of 'em!"

"Who is gone?" demanded Sophy, as the woman beside her trembled and grew paler still.

"Marse Jack and dat fool nigger, Hannibal."

"Mr. Hamlin gone?" repeated Sophy incredulously. "When? Where?"

"Jess now—on de down boat. Sudden business. Didn't like to disturb yo' and yo' friend. Said he'd write."

"But he was ill—almost helpless," gasped Sophy.

"Dat's why he took dat old nigger. Lawdy, Missy, bress yo' heart. Dey both knows aich udder, shuah! It's all right. Dar now, dar dey are; listen."

She held up her hand. A slow pulsation that might have been the dull, labored beating of their own hearts was making itself felt throughout the little cottage. It came nearer—a deep regular inspiration that seemed slowly to fill and possess the whole tranquil summer twilight. It was nearer still—was abreast of the house—passed—grew fainter—and at last died away like a deep-drawn sigh. It was the down boat that was now separating Mr. Hamlin and his protégée, even as it had once brought them together.

The first great novel of the Old West, and certainly one of the most influential ever penned, was Owen Wister's The Virginian *(1902)—a bestseller for more than ten years. Wister also wrote other memorable tales of the Wyoming range, among them the novel* Lin McLean *(1897) and many of the stories in such collections as* Red Men and White *(1896),* The Jimmyjohn Boss and Other Stories *(1900),* Members of the Family *(1911), and* When West was West *(1928). But Wyoming was not the only setting utilized by Wister for his fiction; he wrote equally well of Arizona, Texas, Idaho, Washington—and California, as evidenced by the account that follows of life, love, and justice in the far northern part of the sate.*

The Serenade at Siskiyou

★★★★★★★★★★★★★★★

Owen Wister

UNSKILLED at murder and without training in running away, one of the two Healy boys had been caught with ease soon after their crime. What they had done may be best learned in the following extract from a certain official report:

"The stage was within five miles of its destination when it was confronted by the usual apparition of a masked man levelling a double-barrelled shot-gun at the driver, and the order to 'Pull up, and throw out the express box.' The driver promptly complied. Meanwhile the guard, Buck Montgomery, who occupied a seat inside, from which he caught a glimpse of what was going on, opened fire at the robber, who dropped to his knees at the first shot, but a moment later discharged both barrels of his gun at the stage. The driver dropped from his seat to the footboard with five buckshot in his right leg near the knee, and two in his left leg; a passenger by his side also dropped with three or four buckshot in his legs. Before the guard could reload, two shots came from behind the bushes back of the exposed robber, and Buck fell to the bottom of the stage mortally wounded—shot through the back. The whole murderous sally occupied but a few seconds, and the order came to 'Drive on.' Officers and citizens quickly started in pursuit, and the next day one of the robbers, a well-known young man of that vicinity, son of a respectable farmer in Fresno County, was overtaken and arrested.''

Feeling had run high in the streets of Siskiyou when the prisoner was brought into town, and the wretch's life had come near a violent end at the hands of the mob, for Buck Montgomery had many friends. But the steadier citizens preserved the peace, and the murderer was in the prison awaiting his trial by formal law. It was now some weeks since the tragedy, and Judge Campbell sat at breakfast reading his paper.

"Why, that is excellent!" he suddenly exclaimed.

"May I ask what is excellent, judge?" inquired his wife. She had a big nose.

"They've caught the other one, Amanda. Got him last evening in a restaurant at Woodland.'' The judge read the paragraph to Mrs. Campbell, who listened severely. "And so," he concluded, "when tonight's train gets up, we'll have them both safe in jail.''

Mrs. Campbell dallied over her eggs, shaking her head. Presently she sighed. But as Amanda often did this, her husband finished his own eggs and took some more. "Poor boy!" said the lady, pensively. "Only twenty-three last 12th of October. What a cruel fate!''

Now the judge supposed she referred to the murdered man. "Yes," he said. "Vile. You've got him romantically young, my dear. I understood he was thirty-five.''

"I know his age perfectly, Judge Campbell. I made it my business to find out. And to think his brother might actually have been lynched!''

"I never knew that either. You seem to have found out all about the family, Amanda. What were they going to lynch the brother for?''

The ample lady folded her fat, middle-aged hands on the edge of the table, and eyed her husband with bland displeasure. "Judge Campbell!" she uttered, and her lips shut wide and firm. She would restrain herself, if possible.

"Well, my dear?''

"You ask me that. You pretend ignorance of that disgraceful scene. Who was it said to me right in the street that he disapproved of lynching? I ask you, judge, who was it right there at the jail—"

"Oh!" said the enlightened judge.

"—Right at the left-hand side of the door of the jail in this town of Siskiyou, who was it got that trembling boy safe inside from those yelling fiends and talked to the crowd on a barrel of number ten nails, and made those wicked men stop and go home?"

"Amanda, I believe I recognize myself."

"I should think you did, Judge Campbell. And now they've caught the other one, and he'll be up with the sheriff on tonight's train, and I suppose they'll lynch *him* now!"

"There's not the slightest danger," said the judge. "The town wants them to have a fair trial. It was natural that immediately after such an atrocious act—"

"Those poor boys had never murdered anybody before in their lives," interrupted Amanda.

"But they did murder Montgomery, you will admit."

"Oh yes!" said Mrs. Campbell, with impatience. "I saw the hole in his back. You needn't tell me all that again. If he'd thrown out the express box quicker they wouldn't have hurt a hair of his head. Wells and Fargo's messengers know that perfectly. It was his own fault. Those boys had no employment, and they only wanted money. They did not seek human blood, and you needn't tell me they did."

"They shed it, however, Amanda. Quite a lot of it. Stagedriver and a passenger too."

"Yes, you keep going back to that as if they'd all been murdered instead of only one, and you don't care about those two poor boys locked in a dungeon, and their gray-haired father down in Fresno County who never did anything wrong at all, and he sixty-one in December."

"The county isn't thinking of hanging the old gentleman," said the judge.

"That will do, Judge Campbell," said his lady, rising. "I shall say no more. Total silence for the present is best for you and best for me. Much best. I will leave you to think of your speech, which was by no means silver. Not even life with you for twenty-five years this coming 10th of July has inured me to insult. I am capable of understanding whom they think of hanging, and your speaking to me as if I did not does you little credit; for it was a mere refuge from a woman's just accusation of heartlessness which you felt, and like a man would not acknowledge; and therefore it is that I say no more but leave you to go down the street to the Ladies' Lyceum where I shall find companions with some spark of humanity in their bosoms and milk of human kindness for those whose hasty youth has plunged them in misery and delivered them to the hands of those who treat them as if they were stones and sticks full of nothing but monstrosity instead of breathing men like themselves to be shielded by brotherhood and hope and not dashed down by cruelty and despair.''

It had begun stately as a dome, with symmetry and punctuation, but the climax was untrammelled by a single comma. The orator swept from the room, put on her bonnet and shawl, and the judge, still sitting with his eggs, heard the front door close behind her. She was president of the Ladies' Reform and Literary Lyceum, and she now trod thitherward through Siskiyou.

"I think Amanda will find companions there," mused the judge. "But her notions of sympathy beat me." The judge had a small, wise blue eye, and he liked his wife more than well. She was sincerely good, and had been very courageous in their young days of poverty. She loved their son, and she loved him. Only, when she took to talking, he turned up a mental coat-collar and waited. But if the male sex did not appreciate her powers of eloquence, her sister citizens did; and Mrs. Campbell, besides presiding at the Ladies' Reform and Literary Lyceum in Siskiyou, often addressed female meetings in Ashland, Yreka, and even as far away as Tehama and Redding. She found companions this morning.

"To think of it!" they exclaimed, at her news of the capture, for none had read the paper. They had been too busy talking of the next debate, which was upon the question, "Ought we to pray for rain?" But now they instantly forgot the wide spiritual issues raised by this inquiry, and plunged into the fascinations of crime, reciting once more to each other the details of the recent tragedy. The room hired for the Lyceum was in a second story above the apothecary and book shop—a combined enterprise in Siskiyou—and was furnished with fourteen rocking chairs. Pictures of Mount Shasta and Lucretia Mott ornamented the wall, with a photograph from an old master representing Leda and the Swan. This typified the Lyceum's approval of Art, and had been presented by one of the husbands upon returning from a three days' business trip to San Francisco.

"Dear! dear!" said Mrs. Parsons, after they had all shuddered anew over the shooting and the blood. "With so much suffering in the world, how fulsome seems that gay music!" She referred to the Siskiyou brass-band, which was rehearsing the march from "Fatinitza" in an adjacent room in the building. Mrs. Parsons had large, mournful eyes, a poetic vocabulary, and wanted to be president of the Lyceum herself.

"Melody has its sphere, Gertrude," said Mrs. Campbell, in a wholesome voice. "We must not be morbid. But this I say to you, one and all: Since the men of Siskiyou refuse, it is for the women to vindicate the town's humanity, and show some sympathy for the captive who arrives tonight."

They all thought so too.

"I do not criticize," continued their president, magnanimously, "nor do I complain of any one. Each in this world has his or her mission, and the most sacred is Woman's own—to console!"

"True, true!" murmured Mrs. Slocum.

"We must do something for the prisoner, to show him we do not desert him in his hour of need," Mrs. Campbell continued.

"We'll go and meet the train!" Mrs. Slocum exclaimed, eagerly. "I've never seen a real murderer."

"A bunch of flowers for him," said Mrs. Parsons, closing her mournful eyes. "Roses." And she smiled faintly.

"Oh, lilies!" cried little Mrs. Day, with rapture. "Lilies would look *real* nice."

"Don't you think," said Miss Sissons, who had not spoken before, and sat a little apart from the close-drawn clump of talkers, "that we might send the widow some flowers, too, some time?" Miss Sissons was a pretty girl, with neat hair. She was engaged to the captain of Siskiyou's baseball nine.

"The widow?" Mrs. Campbell looked vague.

"Mrs. Montgomery, I mean—the murdered man's wife. I—I went to see if I could do anything, for she has some children; but she wouldn't see me," said Miss Sissons. "She said she couldn't talk to anybody."

"Poor thing!" said Mrs Campbell. "I dare say it was a dreadful shock to her. Yes, dear, we'll attend to her after a while. We'll have her with us right along, you know, whereas these unhappy boys may—may be—may soon meet a cruel death on the scaffold." Mrs. Campbell evaded the phrase "may be hanged" rather skillfully. To her trained oratorical sense it had seemed to lack dignity.

"So young!" said Mrs. Day.

"And both so full of promise, to be cut off!" said Mrs. Parsons.

"Why, they can't hang them both, I should think," said Miss Sissons. "I thought only one killed Mr. Montgomery."

"My dear Louise," said Mrs. Campbell, "they can do anything they want, and they will. Shall I ever forget those ruffians who wanted to lynch the first one? They'll be on the jury!"

The clump returned to their discussion of the flowers, and Miss Sissons presently mentioned she had some errands to do, and departed.

"Would that that girl had more soul!" said Mrs. Parsons.

"She has plenty of soul," replied Mrs. Campbell, "but she's under the influence of a man. Well, as I was saying, roses and lilies are too big."

"Oh, *why*?" said Mrs. Day. "They would *please* him so."

"He couldn't carry them, Mrs. Day. I've thought it all out. He'll be walked to the jail between strong men. We must have some small bokay to pin on his coat, for his hands will be shackled."

"You don't say!" cried Mrs. Slocum. "How awful! I must get to that train. I've never seen a man in shackles in my life."

So violets were selected; Mrs. Campbell brought some in the afternoon from her own borders, and Mrs. Parsons furnished a large pin. She claimed also the right to affix the decoration upon the prisoner's breast because she had suggested the idea of flowers; but the other ladies protested, and the president seemed to think that they all should draw lots. It fell to Mrs. Day.

"Now I declare!" twittered the little matron. "I do believe I'll never dare."

"You must say something to him," said Amanda; "something fitting and choice."

"Oh dear no, Mrs. Campbell. Why, I never—my gracious! Why, if I'd known I was expected—Really, I couldn't think— I'll let *you* do it!"

"We can't hash up the ceremony that way, Mrs. Day," said Amanda, severely. And as they all fell arguing, the whistle blew.

"There!" said Mrs. Slocum. "Now you've made me late, and I'll miss the shackles and everything."

She flew downstairs, and immediately the town of Siskiyou saw twelve members of the Ladies' Reform and Literary Lyceum follow her in a hasty phalanx across the square to the station. The train approached slowly up the grade, and by the time the wide smokestack of the locomotive was puffing its wood smoke in clouds along the platform, Amanda had marshalled her company there.

"Where's the gals all goin', Bill?" inquired a large citizen in boots of the ticket-agent.

"Nowheres, I guess, Abe," the agent replied. "Leastways, they 'ain't bought any tickets off me."

"Maybe they're for stealin' a ride," said Abe.

The mail and baggage cars had passed, and the women watched the smoking car that drew up opposite them. Mrs. Campbell had informed her friends that the sheriff always went in the smoker; but on this occasion, for some reason, he had brought his prisoner in the Pullman sleeper at the rear, some way down the track, and Amanda's vigilant eye suddenly caught the group, already descended and walking away. The platoon of sympathy set off, and rapidly came up with the sheriff, while Bill, Abe, the train conductor, the Pullman conductor, the engineer, and the fireman abandoned their duty, and stared, in company with the brakemen and many passengers. There was perfect silence but for the pumping of the air-brake on the engine. The sheriff, not understanding what was coming, had half drawn his pistol; but now, surrounded by universal petticoats, he pulled off his hat and grinned doubtfully. The friend with him also stood bareheaded and grinning. He was young Jim Hornbrook, the muscular betrothed of Miss Sissons. The prisoner could not remove his hat, or he would have done so. Miss Sissons, who had come to the train to meet her lover, was laughing extremely in the middle of the road.

"Take these violets," faltered Mrs. Day, and held out the bunch, backing away slightly at the same time.

"Nonsense," said Amanda, stepping forward and grasping the flowers. "The women of Siskiyou are with you," she said, "as we are with all the afflicted." Then she pinned the violets firmly to the prisoner's flannel shirt. His face, at first amazed as the sheriff's and Hornbrook's, smoothed into cunning and vanity, while Hornbrook's turned an angry red, and the sheriff stopped grinning.

"Them flowers would look better on Buck Montgomery's grave, madam," said the officer. "Maybe you'll let us pass now." They went on to the jail.

"Waal," said Abe, on the platform, "that's the most disgustin' fool thing I ever did see."

"All aboard!" said the conductor, and the long train continued its way to Portland.

The platoon, well content, dispersed homeward to supper, and Jim Hornbrook walked home with his girl.

"For Lord's sake, Louise," he said, "who started that move?"

She told him the history of the morning.

"Well," he said, "you tell Mrs. Campbell, with my respects, that she's just playing with fire. A good woman like her ought to have more sense. Those men are going to have a fair trial."

"She wouldn't listen to me, Jim, not a bit. And, do you know, she really didn't seem to feel sorry—except just for a minute—about that poor woman."

"Louise, why don't you quit her outfit?"

"Resign from the Lyceum? That's so silly of you, Jim. We're not all crazy there; and that," said Miss Sissons, demurely, "is what makes a girl like me so valuable!"

"Well, I'm not stuck on having you travel with that lot."

"They speak better English than you do, Jim dear. Don't! in the street!"

"Sho! It's dark now," said Jim. "And it's been three whole days since—" But Miss Sissons escaped inside her gate and rang the bell. "Now see here, Louise," he called after her, "when I say they're playing with fire I mean it. That woman will make trouble in this town."

"She's not afraid," said Miss Sissons. "Don't you know enough about us yet to know we can't be threatened?"

"You!" said the young man. "I wasn't thinking of you." And so they separated.

Mrs. Campbell sat opposite the judge at supper, and he saw at once from her complacent reticence that she had achieved some triumph against his principles. She chatted about topics of the day in terms that were ingeniously trite. Then a letter came from their son in Denver, and she forgot her rôle somewhat, and read the letter aloud to the judge, and wondered wistfully who in Denver attended to the boy's buttons and socks; but she made no reference whatever to Siskiyou jail or those inside it. Next morning, however, it was the judge's turn to be angry.

"Amanda," he said, over the paper again, "you had better stick to socks, and leave criminals alone."

Amanda gazed at space with a calm smile.

"And I'll tell you one thing, my dear," her husband said, more incisively, "it don't look well that I should represent the law while my wife figures" (he shook the morning paper) "as a public nuisance. And one thing more: *Look out!* For if I know this community, and I think I do, you may raise something you don't bargain for."

"I can take care of myself, judge," said Amanda, always smiling. These two never were angry both at once, and today it was the judge that sailed out of the house. Amanda pounced instantly upon the paper. The article was headed "Sweet Violets." But the editorial satire only spurred the lady to higher efforts. She proceeded to the Lyceum, and found that "Sweet Violets" had been there before her. Every woman held a copy, and the fourteen rocking chairs were swooping up and down like things in a factory. In the presence of this blizzard, Mount Shasta, Lucretia Mott, and even Leda and the Swan looked singularly serene on their wall, although on the other side of the wall the "Fatinitza" march was booming brilliantly. But Amanda quieted the storm. It was her gift to be calm when others were not, and soon the rocking chairs were merely rippling.

"The way my boys scolded me—" began Mrs. Day.

"For men I care not," said Mrs. Parsons. "But when my own sister upbraids me in a public place—" The lady's voice ceased, and she raised her mournful eyes. It seemed she had encountered her unnatural relative at the post office. Everybody had a tale similar. Siskiyou had denounced their humane act.

"Let them act ugly," said Mrs. Slocum. "We will not swerve."

"I sent roses this morning," said Mrs. Parsons.

"*Did* you, dear?" said Mrs. Day. "My lilies shall go this afternoon."

"Here is a letter from the prisoner," said Amanda, producing the treasure; and they huddled to hear it. It was very affecting. It mentioned the violets blooming beside the hard couch, and spoke of prayer.

"He had lovely hair," said Mrs. Slocum.

"*So* brown!" said Mrs. Day.

"Black, my dear, and curly."

"Light brown. I was a good deal closer, Susan—"

"Never mind about his hair," said Amanda. "We are here not to flinch. We must act. Our course is chosen, and well chosen. The prison fare is a sin, and a beefsteak goes to them both at noon from my house."

"Oh, why didn't we ever think of that before?" cried the ladies, in an ecstasy, and fell to planning a series of lunches in spite of what Siskiyou might say or do. Siskiyou did not say very much; but it looked; and the ladies waxed more enthusiastic, luxuriating in a sense of martyrdom because now the prisoners were stopped writing any more letters to them. This was doubtless a high-handed step, and it set certain pulpits preaching about love. The day set for the trial was approaching; Amanda and her flock were going. Prayer meetings were held, food and flowers for the two in jail increased in volume, and every day saw some of the Lyceum waiting below the prisoners' barred windows till the men inside would thrust a hand through and wave to them; then they would shake a handkerchief in reply, and go away thrilled to talk it over at the Lyceum. And Siskiyou looked on all the while, darker and darker.

Then finally Amanda had a great thought. Listening to "Fatinitza" one morning, she suddenly arose and visited Herr Schwartz, the bandmaster. Herr Schwartz was a wise and well-educated German. They had a lengthy conference.

"I don't pelief dot vill be very goot," said the bandmaster. But at that Aamanda talked a good deal; and the worthy

Teuton was soon bewildered, and at last gave a dubious consent, "since it would blease de ladies."

The president of the Lyceum arranged the coming event after her own heart. The voice of Woman should speak in Siskiyou. The helpless victims of male prejudice and the law of the land were to be flanked with consolation and encouragement upon the eve of their ordeal in court. In their lonely cell they were to feel that there were those outside whose hearts beat with theirs. The floral tribute was to be sumptuous, and Amanda had sent to San Francisco for pound cake. The special quality she desired could not be achieved by the Siskiyou confectioner.

Miss Sissons was not a party to this enterprise, and she told its various details to Jim Hornbrook, half in anger, half in derision. He listened without comment, and his face frightened her a little.

"Jim, what's the matter?" said she.

"Are you going to be at that circus?" he inquired.

"I thought I might just look on, you know," said Miss Sissons. "Mrs. Campbell and a brass band—"

"You'll stay in the house that night, Louise."

"Why, the ring isn't on my finger yet," laughed the girl, "the fatal promise of obedience—" But she stopped, perceiving her joke was not a good one. "Of course, Jim, if you feel that way," she finished. "Only I'm grown up, and I like reasons."

"Well—that's all right, too."

"Ho, ho! All right! Thank you, sir. Dear me!"

"Why, it ain't to please me, Louise; indeed it ain't. I can't swear everything won't be nice and all right and what a woman could be mixed up in, but—well, how should you know what men are, anyway, when they've been a good long time getting mad, and are mad all through? That's what this town is today, Louise."

"I don't know," said Miss Sissons, "and I'm sure I'd rather not know." And so she gave her promise. "But I shouldn't suppose," she added, "that the men of Siskiyou, mad or not, would forget that women are women."

Jim laughed. "Oh no," he said, "they ain't going to forget that."

The appointed day came; and the train came, several hours late, bearing the box of confectionery, addressed to the Ladies' Reform and Literary Lyceum. Bill, the ticket agent, held his lantern over it on the platform.

"That's the cake," said he.

"What cake?" Abe inquired.

Bill told him the rumor.

"Cake?" repeated Abe. "Fer them?" and he tilted his head towards the jail. "Will you say that again, friend? I ain't clear about it. *Cake*, did ye say?"

"Pound cake," said Bill. "Ordered special from San Francisco."

Now pound cake for adults is considered harmless. But it is curious how unwholesome a harmless thing can be if administered at the wrong time. The gaunt, savage-looking Californian went up to the box slowly. Then he kicked it lightly with his big boot, seeming to listen to its reverberation. Then he read the address. Then he sat down on the box to take a think. After a time he began speaking aloud. "They hold up a stage," he said, slowly. "They lay up a passenger fer a month. And they lame Bob Griffiths fer life. And then they do up Buck. Shoot a hole through his spine. And I helped bury him; fer I liked Buck." The speaker paused, and looked at the box. Then he got up. "I hain't attended their prayer meetin's," said he, "and I hain't smelt their flowers. Such perfume's liable to make me throw up. But I guess I'll hev a look at their cake."

He went to the baggage room and brought an axe. The axe descended, and a splintered slat flew across the platform. "There's a lot of cake," said Abe. The top of the packing-case crashed on the railroad track, and three new men gathered to look on. "It's fresh cake, too," remarked the destroyer. The box now fell to pieces, and the tattered paper wrapping was ripped away. "Step up, boys," said Abe, for a little crowd was there now. "Soft, ain't it?" They slung the cake about and tramped it in the grime and oil, and the boards of the box were torn apart and whirled away. There was a singular and growing impulse about all this. No one said anything; they were very quiet; yet the crowd grew quickly, as if called together by something in the air. One voice said, "Don't forgit we're all relyin' on yer serenade, Mark," and this raised a strange united laugh that broke brief and loud, and stopped, leaving the silence deeper than before. Mark and three more left, and walked toward the Lyceum. They were members of the Siskiyou band, and as they went one said that the town would see an interesting trial in the morning. Soon after they had gone the crowd moved from the station, compact and swift.

Meanwhile the Lyceum had been having disappointments. When the train was known to be late, Amanda had abandoned bestowing the cake until morning. But now a horrid thing had happened: the Siskiyou band refused its services! The rocking chairs were plying strenuously; but Amanda strode up and down in front of Mount Shasta and Lucretia Mott.

Herr Schwartz entered. "It's all right, madam," said he. "My trombone haf come back, und—"

"You'll play?" demanded the president.

"We blay for de ladies."

The rocking chairs were abandoned; the Lyceum put on its bonnet and shawl, and marshalled downstairs with the band.

"Ready," said Amanda.

"Ready," said Herr Schwartz to his musicians. "Go a leedle easy mit der Allegro, or we bust 'Fatinitza.' "

The spirited strains were lifted in Siskiyou, and the procession was soon at the jail in excellent order. They came round the corner with the trombone going as well as possible. Two jerking bodies dangled at the end of ropes, above the flare of torches. Amanda and her flock were shrieking.

"So!" exclaimed Herr Schwartz. "Dot was dose Healy boys we haf come to gif serenade." He signed to stop the music.

"No you don't," said two of the masked crowd, closing in with pistols. "You'll play fer them fellers till you're told to quit."

"Cerdainly," said the philosophical Teuton. "Only dey gif brobably very leedle attention to our Allegro."

So "Fatinitza" trumpeted on while the two on the ropes twisted, and grew still by-and-by. Then the masked men let the band go home. The Lyceum had scattered and fled long since, and many days passed before it revived again to civic usefulness, nor did its members find comfort from their men. Herr Schwartz gave a parting look at the bodies of the lynched murderers. "My!" said he, "das Ewigweibliche haf draw them apove sure enough."

Miss Sissons next day was walking and talking off her shock and excitement with her lover. "And oh, Jim," she concluded, after they had said a good many things, "you hadn't anything to do with it, had you?" The young man did not reply, and catching a certain expression on his face, she hastily exclaimed: "Never mind! I don't want to know—ever!"

So James Hornbrook kissed his sweetheart for saying that, and they continued their walk among the pleasant hills.

This brutal, gripping tale of a cowardly killer attempting to flee the law across Death Valley is so vividly drawn that you can feel the scorching heat and elemental savagery of those desert wastes. Such realism is the hallmark of John Prescott's Western novels as well, among them such successes as The Renegade *(1954);* Journey by the River, *which received a Western Writers of America Spur as Best Historical Novel of 1954; and another desert tale, in this case the Arizona desert,* Ordeal *(1958).*

Thirst

****

John Prescott

IN REAKOR'S mind the thoughts of pleasure which the sack of bank notes would give to him had begun to pale, and in their place was his consciousness of the roaring sun and of his increasing demand for water. And the vague and irritating lapses in coherent thought which the lack of water created.

He was sitting his Arabian loosely, with his head down, for he was afraid to raise his eyes for long into the awful glare of the Death Valley cauldron, or to the shimmering images of the Funeral Range still some five miles distant across the shifting sand. But occasionally he would shift his seared shoulders as gently as he could upon the plodding horse and squint backward toward the Panamints, from where pursuit might come. An unreasonable thing, though, he was sure; for it was June and no ordinary man crossed the Valley in the summer.

He did not want to think of Lawson and Cooke now, or anything that lay behind him, but the agony in his back and shoulders, the crusted streaks of salt and lather on the neck of the horse, and the slight puffing of his lips and tongue, lent an urgency to everything, and sought to turn his mind back to those things which he did not care to remember.

He had been in Darwin, Inyo County, indifferently considering some offers of day labor, when Lawson and Cooke had ridden in; and after the manner of a man who all his life had amounted to very little, and had prospects for nothing better, he was greatly flattered when the outlaws spoke to him.

His narrow, blue eyes had reflected the smallness of his being, which was not confined to his thin-shouldered stature and pinched face, and he had seen in his friendship with the pair an opportunity to raise himself above the poverty and anonymity which had been his lot.

In all his time in the mines of the Coso Range, or at the charcoal burners in the forests, there had been allotted to him only one small slice of fame. He had one time blundered upon an abundant spring of cool, fresh water in the Funeral Range across the ten-mile griddle of Death Valley; it had been purely by accident, a solitary grain of fortune in an unsuccessful attempt to find a lost mine. But he had seized upon its opportunities, brayed loudly of his find, and had always declined to give its position to any other who might be going that way. He had always hoped that there might be some profit in his knowledge.

It had happened just one day ago, but now with the pounding sun and the rising heat it seemed to him that it was in a different world. Except for the Arabian, which had belonged to Lawson, and the sack of money at the pommel, he could almost doubt that the men had ever existed. Only fragments of the last hours seemed to hold reality.

He'd known immediately that they were outlaws, and when they offered to share with him the loot from the Darwin bank in turn for his guidance to the Funeral spring, it did not surprise him or affront him. They had known their man, and he had waited a long while to put the spring to use. It was a fair price for the thwarting of pursuit.

Reakor tried to smile with the memory of those careful negotiations, but the discomfort was intense; his lips were swelling badly now and the tissue had cracked. His thirst was no longer a harassment, but a physical pain, and though he had already consumed one of the three water bottles he could not keep himself from taking a strong pull at the second one.

He drank deep but did not give any to the horse, for while its actions seemed to indicate that it was in need of some he had no interest in it other than its getting him over to the spring. It seemed strong enough for that, and since horses were alien to him anyway he would not mind the walk if it died then.

The bank haul had been easy and no trouble whatsoever. Lawson had first bought him a buckskin horse, a miserable thing when compared with the Arabians, but because it was the first Reakor had ever had, and at no cost, he could not complain. They'd waited until evening, and shortly after sundown had entered the building where a payload for the Coso mines was being kept. Except for one moment, when Reakor, in his newfound power, had shot a surprised and unarmed watchman, it had gone off well. They'd spent the rest of the night in riding for the Panamints.

There were parts of it that he could not recall too clearly. They'd ridden hard that night and it had been an effort for the buckskin to maintain the steady pace and loping stride of the Arabians, and he had occasionally drifted back alone.

During one of these moments it had occurred to him that Lawson and Cooke were going to kill him when they'd crossed the Valley to the spring. It had been just an idle thought at first, but since such a course seemed wholly logical to his mind, it took root, and when they'd descended the eastern slopes of the Panamints to the edge of the Valley, he altered the order of events.

Those events were very sharp and bright. Even with the thirst, and the sun which seemed to beat down on his head like an anvil, these things stood out.

Very clearly he could see Lawson and Cooke easing their horses down the rockslides of the slopes ahead of him. There was a small, brackish water hole down there and they had all reined up and dismounted to water the horses and to fill the bottles for the crossing of the Valley. It was all sharp and detailed.

Lawson had reached into his saddlebags and removed some yards of sacking, which he took to the water hole to soak. Reakor had wondered about that and he had thought in that moment that something was happening that he should know about, but the opportunity which fell to him had been too great to miss.

Standing slightly shielded by the rump of the buckskin he had drawn the pistol and had pumped two slugs into the broad back which faced him less than ten feet away. Lawson had fallen straight down and forward into the cleft in the rock, and as Cooke swerved from his own bags, Reakor shot him in the chest. He had then shot the buckskin and Cooke's Arabian, and though a bit remorseful, because of the money involved, he'd known it would not be good to have them wandering back up the trail, or perhaps attracting the eye of anybody going past.

These things, then, were far more clear than any other incidents, for in that moment of bloody murder he had known terror such as he had never known before; and a share of it lingered as he rode now alone across the desolation. He had always been a coward, perversely happy to stir up trouble, but never participating when it resolved in force and action, and his bravery at the robbery had been a sort of false courage engendered by the presence of the outlaws. But now he was alone with the heat, the endless burning ground and the horse that had belonged to Lawson.

For some time the Arabian had been behaving very strangely, and his natural reaction to this at first was anger, not bewilderment. He had understood in a murky way that this horse was an animal of great endurance on the desert, and had evolved from a foreign strain admirably adapted to travel in arid lands.

But now he felt that he had been deceived. He had never before brought a horse into the desert, his previous experience being with the mules of other men, and he was resentful that this one was not living up to expectations. He had been riding all the time, but presently, as the wobble seemed to increase and the whole of the neck was crusting with foam, he dismounted disgustedly and began to lead it by the bridle.

And on the ground it was a different thing. The burning ache in his back and shoulders increased in agony. The baked earth and rock, which had reflected the enormous heat into his face, now transmitted it fiercely through the thin soles of his ancient, beaten shoes, and sent it in running fires through the bones and muscles of his legs. He stumbled and jarred over the black lava outcropping and sloughed tiredly through the sand and gravel, which gave no traction; and all the while he felt the brackish, gusty breath of the Arabian issuing from its foam-encrusted mouth.

He realized soon that the energy and salt in his body were

ebbing fast. He had walked for perhaps fifteen minutes or so, and his thirst was unbearable. He was already into the second bottle, with some three miles and better yet to go, but he didn't have the strength to keep his hands from the cork. He swung it down from the saddle horn and drank until it ran in small streams from the corners of his mouth.

He was facing the horse while he did this and he saw that the animal was staring at him with an appeal which was almost haunting. He could see its strange, begging eyes, and the thick tongue which protruded grotesquely between its lips. The eyes were fixed strongly on the bottle and the water dripping from his mouth, and the tongue seemed to have a stiff, flipping motion as the eyes beseeched him.

But he would not give water to the horse. He had already been hoodwinked and it was enough of a concession that he should walk as far as he had. He laughed at it, not entirely sanely, and took another pull at the bottle for its benefit.

Then as he looked at it above the bulge of the bottle it came near to him and nudged his shoulder; it opened its lips, and made a tremendous lunge at the bottle, knocking Reakor across the rock and gravel and sending the bottle flying to the ground, where it drained quickly into the parched earth.

Reakor came slowly to his feet and cursed the horse hysterically. He was a little afraid of it because of its lunge, but that was nothing compared to the rage which clutched at him. He shrieked at the horse and then grabbed the bottle by its long strap and swung it cruelly at the horse's nose. The horse screamed and tried to rear away, but Reakor seized the bridle and struck again and again with fury until he was exhausted.

When he stopped, the exertion had left him numb and dizzy. He stared dumbly at the terrified horse and his eyes traveled beyond it, across the vast, heaving seas of lava, sand and gravel, back toward the Panamints which shook and shuddered in the waving heat. He was on a high point there and the whole of the furnace bed lay beneath his eyes. And in the ashes something moved.

It was incredible, but something stirred. There was a slight movement, far, far back, midway between the Panamints and himself. Reakor squinted, his head pounding, and refused to believe it. He held his head firmly with his hands and stared again. Surely he was wrong. It was a trick of the desert; it was a mirage. But it was not. The something moved again, and it became two things, far away, but creeping forward in his track; two men on horses. And Reakor knew that he was being followed.

The sheriff of Inyo County had not been in Darwin at the moment of the robbery and killing, but he had been nearby and had come to the scene with his deputy as soon as he was summoned. He was a medium-sized man of middle age, with an easy-going manner and a placid capability. He knew nearly everything there was to know about that part of California.

They spent a few minutes at the bank, learned that the stolen sum exceeded fifty thousand dollars, questioned the proprietor of the livery stable, who recalled the sale of a buckskin horse, listened quietly in the saloon, and before midnight took the trail for the Panamints. The sheriff knew the outlaws had a good two-hour lead.

"Because Reakor ain't in town you think he's with 'em," the deputy said, with an implied question, as they rode beneath the stars across the white expanse of the Panamint Valley.

"I think Reakor's with 'em," the sheriff said. "Hell, I know he is. Ain't just that he was seen around Darwin with them strangers, but because they could stand to have him around as long as they did. Ain't many can stand him for long. Only one reason; the spring in the Funerals."

"Lot of folks don't believe in that spring," the deputy said. "Lot of folks think Reakor was just spinnin' a tale; otherwise why wouldn't he tell others where it is?"

"Because it's the only thing he ever had and he aimed to keep it. Only thing he ever had to draw attention to himself. If he shared it with others he'd stop being different. Small men like that think strange."

"You think, then, he told 'em where it was for a share in the loot?" the deputy said.

"No, I don't think he told 'em anything like that. Reakor's not very smart, but he's cunning. He's cunning like an animal. He wouldn't tell 'em how to get there, but he'd show 'em. If he told 'em they might kill him, because then he'd be no further use to 'em. No, they need him to get across the Valley and to get the water on the other side."

For a long time they rode in silence, maintaining a steady gait in the Panamint Valley night. The trail they followed was a well-known thing to them—a way followed originally by the Panamint Indians to the water hole on the eastern slopes of the Panamint Mountains, and traveled occasionally by those whites who had the courage to cross the mountains and launch out onto the fury of the Valley.

The sheriff never doubted that this was the way which Reakor and the other two had come. The Panamint water hole was one of the very few sure supplies in the whole of the region at that time of year and he knew it would be necessary for them to stop there before setting out for the unknown spring across in the Funerals.

They talked for a while longer, a desultory conversation, and it died. They were well along the trail by then and getting into higher ground. The night was dark, there was no moon, and though the stars were big and lustrous they lent scant light once they had left the whiteness of the valley and ascended into the western spurs of the darkened hills. They traveled steadily, but slower now, resting the horses and walking afoot when the going was treacherous. It was long after sun-up when they came upon the bodies at the hole. The buzzards and coyotes had been at work and it was not a pretty sight. The deputy was a hardy man, but his stomach was sometimes weak. He nearly vomited.

"Gawd almighty," he said, with the muscles in his face drawn tight. "It always gets me when I see them eyeballs that way."

"Good food for the buzzards," the sheriff said. "I don't know why it is, but they always seem to like them eyes."

They dismounted and picked their way forward carefully. The sheriff pulled the body from the cleft of rock. It had been lying face downward and had not been moved. Only the arms and legs had been gnawed.

"This must be Lawson," he said. "They say in town he was the boss. Looks like Reakor's the boss now."

"The horses, too," the deputy said. "He got 'em proper. What a butcher! Even his own; he must've taken one of the others."

"Yes. One of the Arabians. Fine horses if used right. Fine for this kind of country. This thing had been planned fine; up to a point. They just didn't know their man as well as they thought they did."

There was a promontory of rock nearby which gave out on

the great vastness of the Valley below, and the sheriff grunted and puffed his way to the top of that and squinted through the blazing heat into the distance toward the Funerals. It was a long while before he saw what he was looking for; the figures, almost motionless, inching forward across the heated inclines of the desert.

"Maybe two miles out," he said to the deputy. "Looks like we got a long day ahead of us." He came down from the rock and inspected more carefully the ground about the bodies again. He saw the open saddle bags and the sacking near the spring and near the body of the man named Cooke. "Maybe not as long as the one ahead of Reakor," he added. "Come on, we better get at it."

They had brought three water bottles apiece and they filled these at the hole where Lawson had fallen. Then they removed the boots of the dead men, and their own, filled them with water and fastened them to the pommels of their saddles. Since the sacking of the outlaws was so convenient they did not use their own, but took what had been left for them, soaked the material in the water hole and then bound it firmly to the legs of the horses, covering the limbs from the knee joints down, and slightly over the tops of the hooves.

This done, they remounted and put their horses into the winding switchbacks to the Valley floor, the water-filled boots jogging sluggishly at the saddle horns, and their stockinged feet already hot from the contact with the stirrup leather. The sheriff never doubted that he knew what he was doing.

As soon as Reakor was certain there was no mirage back there he became solicitous of the horse. He needed that horse now. He needed that horse more than anything in the world. It was not enough any more for it just to get him to the spring; it would have to take him there and beyond to God knew where. It would be his only method of deliverance, a thing of priceless value.

Though it pained him in an unmeasured way to part with the third bottle of water he knew he had to give it to the horse. A moment ago he had smashed at the animal's nose ruthlessly, and now he was prying the stiff lips apart and forcing the neck of the bottle between them, watching jealously as the wide, dry tongue clacked about the bottle neck, and barely restraining himself from licking up the drops which dribbled from the horse's mouth. He hated the animal, but he needed it desperately.

When the water was gone he did not remount, but continued to lead it by the bridle. He had to conserve its strength in every way, he knew, and to further his own he removed his dragging gunbelt and hunting knife and secured them to the pommel beside the sack of money. He felt somehow that the horse should be grateful for these things; for the water and for his walking painfully across the ground that way, but he saw that it was not, that it was still afraid of him because of the beating. The great eyes seemed wider now, but they were full of terror and they never left him.

But still the horse was not right. Reakor had thought the water would revive it greatly, but he saw that it had not; it seemed only to have whetted its appetite for more, and there was none. Reakor had the awful and incongruously chilling feeling that he had done it all wrong, and that the horse might not even reach the spring. It seemed to be gasping more than ever now, and there was a strange sway in its walk. He did not know if it had been walking that way before or not because he had not paid it much attention, but he could tell that the legs seemed very painful, as though they were perhaps inflamed from the intense heat being conducted through the shoes and hooves and on into the legs. He felt deceived in the animal again and he wanted to yell at it, to shout at it and strike it, but he knew that would do no good. He was thinking lucidly about that now.

He talked to it. He'd never before in his life felt endearment for man or beast and he did not know how to speak sincerely in terms of affection. But he talked to the horse. He coaxed it; he tried to soothe it and to encourage it. He tried to remember some of the songs he'd heard the cowhands sing from time to time and he stumbled and mumbled over the phrases of these ballads in a giddy, sing-song voice. His mouth was very dry and swollen and some of the words would not go past his tongue.

Frequently he looked back at those who followed. Sometimes he thought he could see them and other times he was not sure. The land was so uneven and trembling; great waves of heat shook in the air and distorted everything he looked at. In that first moment of seeing them he had suffered the hallucination of thinking they were Cooke and Lawson, resurrected from the dead, and he'd nearly screamed aloud. Now that he was sure that was not so he seemed to be filled with a greater dread, for it was always the nameless and unknown which terrified him the most. It was not Lawson and Cooke, but it was someone, and that was enough.

But it was going to be all right now; he was sure of that. He was going to make it to the spring. The Funerals were only a mile or less away and already he could sense the rising incline of the ground. The going was harder and more fatiguing, if that was possible, and he could feel the added heat reflected from the rearing crags of the mountains; and the glare of the sand and gravel was intensified, so that his mouth and throat seemed filled with fire. But he was going to make it; it was in his mind, rolling and milling with the fevers of the heat and pain. He'd make it to the spring.

It was time soon to make his compass fix. He'd long flattered himself on having taken the exact location of the spring in such a manner so as never to run the risk of losing it. It was simple, really, but it was a point of pride with him. The compass was a standard miner's compass, with revolving card, an iron lid in which was placed a mirror catching the reflection of the numbers of the card. In the center of the mirror there was a slot, the shape of an arrowhead, and by sighting on a predetermined peak he got his first intersecting line.

All this revived, a little, the sense of power to know he had not failed in this. He was not far off. The peak lay impaled upon the arrowhead and the correction indicated on the card was something less than a quarter of a mile. He exulted; he shouted. He tried to sing again, but the words were too difficult to handle. He even grinned horribly at the horse, and tried to stroke its nose; but it reared in fright and he glared at it in anger.

He kept slogging forward with the bridle in his hands. He had new strength now. He would be at the spring shortly; he would be at the spring high in the rocks and when he was refreshed he would think of something. Perhaps he could create an ambush; he might be able to slink away. Perhaps they would never find him up in there.

The ground became more sharply inclined as he followed his line toward the intersection with the other. The exertion required for this final effort was staggering, sometimes caus-

ing him to reel and sway; and he had to check the compass
often to make sure he was not veering from the line.

The Arabian was wallowing in his tracks by then, and
Reakor abandoned the cajoling and pleading, removed his
belt from his trousers and lashed at the broad, white rump.
He swung the belt in wide, flailing arcs with all his strength,
but the horse seemed beyond that kind of pain, and its wavering awkward steps were not affected. He and the horse
were up in the rocks when his arm gave out, and he took the
bridle again to lead.

They went forward over the flaming granite and Reakor
was about to take another sight when the horse stopped moving. He turned on it slowly with dull rage and then he saw
the ears raise up and the head lift high. He saw the encrusted
nostrils twitching, cracking the foam and salt; he saw the dry
tongue quiver between the yellow teeth. The horse lurched
forward with eagerness; it shambled across the shelf rock and
Reakor tottered after it to the spring.

He lay on his belly on the hot rock slabs at the spring and
drank the water. He closed his eyes and luxuriated in this
ecstasy, and then he opened them and was sick all over the
rocks and himself. But the sickness was only a minor inter-
ruption, and he plunged his head into the hole again and
drank once more. He filled his hat with it and poured it over
himself, over his head and his body, and he saw how quickly
it dried on the slabs.

He lay flat down and drank the water again. He lay cheek
by jowl with the horse, who was standing spraddle-legged at
his side, and he could see how the water was drawn into the
horse as by a siphon; how the cheeks were blown and how
the foam and crust were gone from the silken nose. He saw
the open inflammation and the running sores on the lower
legs, and the curious splits in the hard bone and cartilage of
the hooves. He had not noticed these things before and he
was suddenly sorry and full of feeling for the animal. It was
a strange feeling and it was alien to him, for he had never
before felt pity for any living thing.

Presently he thought of the men in the Valley again and he
raised himself, bloated and swaying, from the spring and
pulled at the horse's bridle. But it would not raise its head;
he pulled again, but his strength was vague and indefinite and

his tugging had no force. He talked to the animal; he shouted at it. He begged, he cursed and swore, but it would not move. It spread its legs wider and stood upon them as though they were odd and unfamiliar parts of its anatomy, but it would not come away from the spring.

A small panic began in Reakor's middle and he dropped the bridle and scurried to the rim of rock which overlooked the Valley. The men were down there. They were very near, nearer than he had supposed. They were leading their horses onto the lower shelf rock and ascending toward the spring. He saw them clearly; the two men and the horses. The horses had strange-appearing legs, but it defied his imagination.

He thought of the men coming and he thought of the pistol and how he would have to kill them. He could make an ambush for them there and shoot them as they came to the spring. He watched them very carefully until they disappeared beneath a protruding shelf of rock, and then he pushed himself away from the rim.

As he turned, the horse drew its head from the spring and he saw its glazed eyes bulging unnaturally from their sockets. He saw that the belly was distended with the water and that the animal trembled in great shudders which went through it entirely and into the legs and hooves. And he saw the front legs abruptly become rubber and buckle at the knees as the horse sank down; and then it lay on the slab of rock and rolled its wide and heavy back upon the money and the pistol, dead.

Reakor refused to believe this incredible thing and he ran to the horse and jerked on the bridle. He kicked savagely at the stomach and deep chest, and he threw himself on the rock and tried vainly to reach beneath the horse's back for the gun and the sack of money.

A voice which was not his own, but was his own, was screaming vilely at the Arabian, until, in a break in the obscenities, he heard the clatter of rocks and rubble below him. Then he flung himself up and began to run. In futile, wavering strides he ran in his sole-shot shoes up the shelf of rock.

Across the scorching surface of the shelf of rock he ran with puny, senseless steps through the blazing heat of the Funeral Mountains.

L. P. Holmes began writing for the Western pulp magazines in the years following World War I and was a prolific contributor to dozens of titles until the late forties, when he began to concentrate on the production of fast-paced, hard-edged novels with a variety of authentic backgrounds. One of his historicals, Somewhere They Die, *was the recipient of a WWA Spur as Best Novel of 1955. Many of his other novels are set in California, his birthplace, among them* Delta Deputy *(1953),* Modoc, the Last Sundown *(1957), and* The Hardest Man in the Sierras *(1965). Authentic backgrounds are likewise a feature of Holmes' short fiction, as evidenced by this suspenseful tale of the Grass Valley/Nevada City region of the California Mother Lode in the year 1879.*

Stagecoach Stowaway

★★★★★★★★★★★★★★★

L. P. Holmes

I

THE southbound stage out of White Pine was being made up in the light of the chill, slowly fading stars of early morning. The six-horse team had been traced in and the hostlers were holding the bit rings of the leaders, waiting for the driver to emerge from the station of the Telegraph Stage Company and take over the reins.

The Wells Fargo treasure box had already been stowed in the depths of the boot under the driver's seat and the passengers were getting aboard. Most of these were Chinese, sleepy and sluggish after an all-night session with pai-gow or chuck-a-luck in the gambling dens of White Pine and now heading back to the mines at Grass Valley.

Driver Andy Parr came out into the silver half light of this very early dawn. With him were Steve Larkin, the shotgun

119

treasure guard, and a comely young Spanish woman with her small child, warmly blanketed, asleep in her arms.

At the stage door the woman hesitated. From the dark interior of the stage emanated gusty snores and the intermingled and unsavory odors of stale sweat and secondhand rice-wine fumes.

"Please," said the young mother in softly liquid tones. "I would ride with you, in the open."

Driver Andy Parr was gruff but kindly. "Until the sun comes up it will be powerful chilly ridin' on the box, ma'am. And you with that younker . . ."

"We are warmly wrapped, the child and I," argued the mother. "If you please . . ."

"Sure, let her ride with us, Andy," said young Steve Larkin sympathetically. "Plenty of room. I don't blame her for preferring fresh air to that layout inside. Here, ma'am, I'll hold the young un. Andy, you help her up."

So it was done, the young woman placed safely on the lofty driver's seat and her youngster returned to her arms. Andy and Steve took their places on either side of her, the driver gathering up his double handful of reins, Steve with his sawed-off shotgun across his knees.

Andy kicked off the brake and called, "Turn 'em loose!"

The hostlers stepped back and the eager, fretting team surged into their collars. The Concord stage, swaying on its heavy leather thoroughbraces, sped away into the frigid shadows of the towering black timber which blanketed all this portion of the massive western flank of the Sierra Nevadas.

This was California, 1879. The tide of golden treasure that had started with James Marshall's first discovery along the American River three decades before was still flowing out of the placer workings of the high, foaming gulches, the granite-ribbed canyons, the red-earthed flats, and the gravelly bars. Along the foothill country men were driving deep mine shafts, searching for the hidden and elusive Mother Lode, and where the lucky ones found it they tore fabulous fortunes of the precious yellow metal from the ancient matrix of porphyry and quartz.

Far out to the west and south, hidden in the mists of the great central valley and in the still more distant fogs that played along the beaches and headlands of the comberlashed shores of the Pacific Ocean, lay the teeming, turbulent, roistering cities of Sacramento and San Francisco, nurtured to hectic, lusty growth by this stream of treasure rolling down out of the fabulous mountains.

In such cities as these, men schemed, contrived, and speculated, fought, cursed, and died for gold. While throughout the diggings themselves an ominous brotherhood of deadly freebooters was taking to the lonely trails and stage roads, lying in wait with concealing mask and threatening gun to rob and pillage and kill readily and ruthlessly.

For these, the Wells Fargo treasure express box which rode in the boot of the lurching, swaying Concord stagecoaches, was the main objective, but lone wayfarers along the trails paid tribute to the dark brotherhood with their hard-earned gold and often with their lives. To combat the depredations of the stage robber, another brotherhood of brave and keen-eyed men rode the treasure express. Of these, young Steve Larkin was one of the newest members.

Full daylight found the White Pine-Nevada City stage at Bleeker's Ford. At the crossing the swift-sliding water foamed about the thrashing hoofs of the team and through the grinding wheels of the Concord. Beyond was a short flat, thickly brushed, with the road a lifting climb beyond. Under foot the flat was sandy and soft, where the rolling wheels ground deep, slowing the stage. And it was here the bandits struck.

Three of them. They appeared suddenly, masked phantoms slipping from the brush. One to the center of the road, with the gaping twin muzzles of a shotgun trained with deadly intentness, and one to either side, poised revolvers equally ready and deadly.

Andy Parr cursed softly, set his brake. Young Steve Larkin, charged with the safekeeping of the treasure box, even if his life be forfeit, started to swing his shotgun to his shoulder. Harsh command ripped from the lips of the bandit ahead.

"Drop it!"

Steve hesitated. At that distance a spray of buckshot would be deadly. But Steve was not thinking of his own safety. He was thinking of the young Spanish mother, seated there close beside him, with her sleeping babe in her cradling arms. Just as surely as a roaring shotgun blast would rip out his own life, so would it rip out theirs. Steve dropped his gun.

The bandits operated smoothly and fast. At another harsh command, Andy Parr dragged the Wells Fargo treasure box out of the boot and tumbled it heavily over the side. The startled and frightened Chinese miners were lined up beside the stage and those who had been lucky at their games of pai-gow and chuck-a-luck, relieved of their winnings. Then the dismayed Celestials were waved back into the stage.

"Drive on," came the order. "And keep going!"

Andy Parr's whip snapped, and the stage rolled on across the flat and took to the up-climbing road beyond.

Steve Larkin rode in bleak, grim-lipped silence. His first trip out as guard and he let the treasure box be taken without putting up a fight, without firing a single shot in its defense. That to have attempted such a useless fight would have un-doubtedly cost him his life and, just as surely, the lives of the young mother and her child, and perhaps that of Andy Parr, was beyond question.

But, just as surely, these were things which George Renner, the Wells Fargo District Agent at Nevada City would not con-sider at all. The only thing Renner would be concerned about was the treasure box. Renner's attitude would be that Steve Larkin had been hired to guard that treasure and see that it got safe passage from White Pine to Nevada City, regardless. And in this Steve had failed.

Andy Parr shot a stream of blackstrap tobacco juice at the spinning rim of the off front wheel and growled, "Ain't the first treasure box Wells Fargo has lost and it won't be the last. Don't feel too bad about it, boy. Had you tried to make a fight of it, everybody on this seat would have been dead by now. And I, for one, appreciate still having a whole skin."

The young Spanish mother looked at Steve's bent head with soft and understanding black eyes. "I know what you were thinking of," she murmured. "Of me and the child. Thank you!"

Which helped some, mused Steve somberly. But his thoughts reached ahead to the wrath of George Renner as the spinning wheels cut down the miles to Nevada City.

II

THE first thing Steve Larkin saw as the stage pulled up before the station in Nevada City was Kate Ashely's bright auburn head. She was standing at the door of the station, talking with her father and George Renner. Even as the stage ground to a stop, Steve saw her throw back that bright head while her laughter rang at some remark Renner had made. The bleakness in Steve's eyes deepened.

Ben Ashely and George Renner came over to the stage. "Right on time, Andy," Ashely called up. "Must have had a smooth trip."

"We were lighter from Bleeker's Ford on in," answered Andy bluntly. "They took the treasure box away from us there."

"What?" It was George Renner now. Renner was a big, slightly florid man, handsome with his mane of fair hair and sweeping mustaches. "You mean a holdup?"

"They had us dead to rights," Andy told him. "A shotgun lookin' down our throats in front. A six-shooter on each side. Wasn't a thing to do but deliver. Or," he added succinctly, "get shot to rags."

The color in Renner's face deepened and his pale blue eyes burned at Steve Larkin. "What did you do?"

Steve shrugged. "The order was to drop my gun. I dropped it."

"You weren't hired to do that," charged Renner furiously. "You were hired to bring that treasure through."

"And I didn't," said Steve. "Which means—what?"

"What do you think it means?" Under his mustache George Renner's white teeth were showing. "We don't pay wages to treasure guards to hand a box over meekly to the first sneaking bandit that comes along. You're through—now!"

"I figured that," said Steve, preparing to climb down.

The young Spanish mother dropped a hand on his arm. "I am sorry," she said gently. "But for me . . ."

Steve managed a twisted grin. "But for you I'd have been dead and so would Andy, probably. And no thanks at all from our so indignant Mister Renner. I'm glad you were along, ma'am. Good luck!"

"You hole up at my cabin, boy," Andy told him. "I want

to see you when I get back from Grass Valley. I got a few idees. Have had, for some time. Want you to listen to 'em.''

Hostlers were bringing out a fresh team to trace in. A couple of Wells Fargo men were lugging another treasure box out from the station. When it was boosted up and placed in the boot, Renner turned to one of the men.

"Round up Jim Blalock," he ordered. "He'll ride shotgun on this run, now. He's been after me for a job. Tell him he's hired."

Jim Blalock showed up by the time the fresh team was traced in. He was a short, spare intense man, who listened to Renner's directions with slightly bent head. He said nothing, just nodded, then climbed up to take the seat Steve Larkin had vacated.

Andy snapped his whip and the stage rolled away.

Steve watched it out of sight, then turned toward the station door, looking at Kitty Ashely. She had been watching him. Now she colored sharply, tossed her head, and looked away.

To Ben Ashely, George Renner said loudly, "I don't usually make a mistake in my estimate of a man's courage. Well, it doesn't take long to get rid of a coward in this game."

Steve spun around. "You just made another mistake, Renner," he gritted.

Steve got home the first punch, a winging right to Renner's mouth. It set the bigger man back on his heels, brought a gush of crimson from his lips. But Renner swiftly recovered and met Steve's rush with a savage swing to the side of the head which knocked him to his knees. Renner followed up his advantage, driving a lashing kick at Steve's face.

Steve barely got his head out of the way and Renner, thrown off balance by the missed effort, floundered a moment, long enough for Steve to regain his feet. Then, as Renner whirled back to the attack, fists swinging, Steve ducked in under the blows and dug both fists deep into Renner's body, which brought the bigger man's guard down, at which Steve nailed him with another driving right to the mouth.

Then Ben Ashely broke it up, throwing his burly bulk between them. "Enough of that—enough of that!" he roared angrily.

For Ashely knew there was far more between these two than what appeared on the surface. There was the smile of his daughter, Kate, and the favor of her flashing eyes. And if he let it go further there would be talk about it all through this town of Nevada City. A proud man, Ben Ashely wanted nothing like that.

"Enough!" he roared again. "Larkin, get out of here. George, mind your mouth in slighting a man's courage."

Steve grinned hard and whitely. "He'll mind his mouth for a while, by the look of it."

Which was true enough, for George Renner's mashed lips had already begun to swell and pout. Vain of his personal appearance, Renner was almost choking with fury. He scrubbed the back of a hand across his beaten mouth and would have charged at Steve again, if Ben Ashely had not barred his way.

Steve turned away and found himself looking at Kate Ashely. She was staring at him again, her face white, her eyes very big. Steve was all raw inside over this whole affair, for a steady job as shotgun guard could have led to bigger things, and bigger things could have led to Kate Ashely. Now everything seemed broken up and Steve spoke with bitter rashness.

"He won't be quite so pretty in your eyes for a while, Kate."

The girl did not answer. She just turned and went into the stage station.

Andy Parr's cabin stood at the south edge of town, at the mouth of a little timber gulch that came twisting in, cool and shadowy. Andy batched it there during layovers from his long tours of duty on the jouncing, swaying driver's seat of the endlessly rolling Concord stages. He was one of the best and most reliable whips in the game, a fact which his boss, Ben Ashely, knew full well.

Andy, returning from the round trip to Grass Valley, reached Nevada City late that afternoon. He turned the stage over to Toby Strang. Ahead of Toby lay the long trip deep into the mountains, and return. White Pine, North San Juan, Pedler's Flat, Camptonville, Rice Hill, China Gulch, Downieville, Sierra City. It would be two full days before Strang brought the stage back to Nevada City again, when Andy Parr would once more take over the reins to repeat the same run.

At his cabin, Andy found Steve Larkin skinning out a deer.

"Had to do something or bust," explained the young man grimly. "So I borrowed that new Henry rifle of yours, Andy, and went out after a chunk of venison."

Andy nodded. "Fine! What do you think of the gun?"

Steve's eyes gleamed. "Best I ever shot. Not much excuse for a man ever missin' with that gun."

"You'll have a chance to make good on that talk," Andy promised.

Steve flashed him a direct look. "What do you mean?"

"We'll talk about that after supper. George Renner went out on the stage with Toby Strang. What happened to Renner's face?"

"I hit it," answered Steve. "Twice. I'd have given him some more if Ben Ashely hadn't stepped in."

Andy's bearded lips twitched. "You young bucks! Never fight over a nice girl. Hard on her good name."

Steve colored and wielded his skinning knife faster.

They ate heartily of deer liver and bacon and then, as Steve began to clean up the dishes, Andy stoked up his old pipe and leaned back with a deep sigh of contentment.

"Boy," he said bluntly, "we got two things to do. One is to clear your reputation with the Wells Fargo people. The other is to make Ben Ashely's stages safe for treasure to ride in. Because if we don't, most anything can happen."

"What do you mean?"

"It's like this," said Andy. "Here and there I pick up talk. Such as Wells Fargo gettin' mighty put out over the amount of treasure they been losin' by holdup all through the diggin's. If somethin' ain't done to put a stop to it, Wells Fargo is considerin' settin' up a special treasure express of their own. If they do that, a lot of the little independent stage-line owners, like Ben Ashely, are liable to go out of business. For they make their best money haulin' Wells Fargo treasure."

"You talked to Ben about it?" asked Steve.

Andy shook his head. "Don't need to. Ben knows that jest as well as I do. He's plenty worried. These here stage bandits are gettin' more brash all the time. I heard tell of a new one operatin' up north. He jest recent pulled a job on the Oroville-Quincy run and had gall enough to leave a piece of poetry behind, pinned to a bush. He signs himself 'Black Bart.' That's jest how nervy they're gettin'. I heard tell that

Wells Fargo have lost nigh on to seventy thousand dollars in treasure to holdups since the first of the year.''

"I can't feel too sorry about that," said Steve Larkin bitterly. "I'm still trying to figure out why Renner ever hired me in the first place, with him not likin' me any better than I do him.''

Andy leaned back and blew a puff of smoke lazily toward the cabin rafters.

"If I was wantin' to get shut of another man, for good, while holdin' my own cards secret, I wouldn't ask for a better way than givin' him a job as shotgun guard. If we hadn't let that Spanish mother and her younker ride on the box with us from White Pine this mornin', you'd have been plumb out o' the picture by this time. See what I mean?''

Steve nodded slowly. "Some of it. But Renner is the Wells Fargo boss in these parts. His main interest is to see that the treasure boxes get through safe. I can figure him hatin' me, maybe, but not that much.''

Andy stabbed his pipe stem at Steve. "Boy,'' he said grimly, "you're lookin' at jest what you see in front of you. Young years are like that. It's fellers my age who get to realizin' there's two sides to a piece of paper. Now listen close. Here's what you and me are goin' to do. First off, we're goin' to play smart, jest like the bandits do. Surprise is their big ticket. The holdup has the jump, every time. He picks the time and he picks the place. You never see him until he wants to be seen, and by the time you do see him he's got the drop on you. So me, I figger the best way to fight the devil is to use his own tools.''

The oldster's eyes were gleaming. Steve said, "Go on, Andy. I'm listenin'.''

As Andy unfolded his plan, Steve's eyes began to gleam, too. They talked things over until bed time and by then had all their plans complete.

The next morning Steve Larkin went over to the stage station, a haunch of venison on his shoulder. In addition to his stage line, Ben Ashely had a little store and trading post adjoining the station. Kate Ashely ran this store for her father. Both she and her father were there when Steve walked in.

He dropped the venison on the counter. "Got a fat one

yesterday,'' he said briefly. "More than Andy can eat alone, so I thought you folks could use some.''

Ashely nodded gruffly. A successful man himself, he admired success in other men, and those who held positions of responsibility. Like George Renner. But this Steve Larkin, while a clean-cut young fellow, was not yet solidly anchored at anything.

When he first hit Nevada City Steve had gone to work for Ashely as a hostler. Then Renner had hired him as a shotgun guard, a job at which Steve had lasted but a single trip. Not because he hadn't qualified, Ashely had to admit, in all fairness. To have thrown away his own life and that of an innocent mother and her child to protect treasure he couldn't have saved anyway, would have done no good. Ashely had Andy Parr's word for it that Steve Larkin had shown good judgment and Ashely took Andy's word as being correct, even if George Renner had felt otherwise.

At the same time, Ashely had never welcomed the attention Steve Larkin had shown to Kate. A fond father, he had far more ambitious plans for the future of his attractive daughter than anything Steve Larkin could offer. And he had worried some about that, for more than once he had seen Kate's glance following this keen-eyed young fellow. So now Ben Ashely almost eagerly took up something at which Larkin had just hinted.

"Much obliged for the venison, Larkin. We'll enjoy it, Kate and me. You just said something about Andy Parr being alone. Does that mean you're leaving us?''

Steve Larkin nodded. "For a spell, anyway. Thought I'd try my hand at mining. Must be a rich gulch somewhere that nobody has stumbled on, yet. Maybe I'll find it. So I'll want an outfit. Blankets, grub, gold pan and all the rest.''

Ben Ashely began laying these required things out on the counter. He nodded to himself, pleased with the fact that he had appraised this young fellow so correctly. A likable sort, young Larkin, but foot-loose and a drifter. Definitely not the sort for Kate to grow fond of.

Kate had stood silently, listening. Now she looked at Steve, in that same grave, wide-eyed way she had the day before, after his fight with George Renner.

"What part of the diggings are you heading for, Steve?'' she asked.

Steve shrugged, grinning. "Wherever I can find that pot of gold. And when I've found it, I'm coming back after you, Kate."

She colored hotly, but far back in her pretty eyes, a soft glow shone. And she said something which jarred her father and put a frown on his face. "I hope you find it."

III

STEVE Larkin made a frugal camp in the concealment of a laurel thicket in a lonely little gulch some half mile above the White Pine–Nevada City stage road. The north side of the gulch lifted steeply to a sparsely timbered point from which a man could safely watch a considerable stretch of the road. Beyond the road the slope ran down to leap off suddenly into the depths of the canyon of the Yuba River.

Besides the outfit he had bought from Ben Ashely, Steve carried that new Henry rifle of Andy Parr's. With this across his knees, Steve spent long hours on that point above the gulch, sitting with his back to a towering pine, his eyes playing over the vast stretch of country below him.

From time to time he glimpsed travel along the stretches of road visible from his lookout; an occasional freight and supply wagon, miners on foot, trudging to and from the upper diggings. And he saw Toby Strang bring the stage whirling down from its long circle of the higher camps.

It was a peaceful world, vast, still and satisfying, and Steve Larkin luxuriated in his lonely ease. Yet the impatience of youth was upon him and he was hoping against hope when, at sundown that day, he crouched in hiding behind the upturned roots of a pine, overthrown by a past storm, and watched the incoming stage spin by. Steve's hiding place was not ten yards from the road.

Andy Parr was driving and, though he threw a glance at that down tree, he gave no other sign. So Steve slipped away and climbed back to his lonely camp. Days later he saw Andy bring the stage down from the high camps and he saw Toby Strang come heading in, then out on the same trip. And that afternoon Steve once more sought his hiding place beside the road to wait for Andy to come in, high-country bound.

This time Steve's heart leaped, for Andy threw a particularly direct glance at the down tree and a moment later deftly dropped something into the dust beside the spinning wheels of the Concord. Steve waited until the stage was fully out of sight before slipping out into the road and searching for what Andy had dropped. He recovered a small stone with a bit of paper wrapped around it. The rough scrawl on the paper read:

Pretty rich pick-up at White Pine coming out. This may be it.

The next morning Steve broke camp bright and early and trudged out weary miles, keeping well away from the road. When he camped that night he was not half a mile below White Pine.

Lying in his blankets, peering up at the stars which winked whitely beyond the crests of the timber, Steve did a lot of thinking. He had yet to fire his first shot at a man, bandit or otherwise. He wondered what his feelings would be if such a contingency came to pass. Would he hold the Henry true and surely, or would he perhaps be slow and clumsy and know the smashing bite of hostile lead himself? It was quite a question for one who had but lately reached his majority. If he failed, not only his life but that of good old Andy Parr could be lost.

Of course, there was always the chance that bandits would not strike. Maybe there was nothing to Andy Parr's suspicions, after all. Well, in the morning all these things would be answered.

Steve was up very early and kept his fire tiny as he brewed a pot of coffee and put together the balance of a frugal breakfast. Then, stamping out the last spark of his fire, he set off under the black timber, coming to a waiting halt beside the stage road. It seemed hours before he heard the patter of hoofs and the creak of the approaching stage. Here, but for one short upward pitch across the crown of a low ridge, the general run of the road was always downward. Steve was waiting just short of that upward pitch. The figures of Andy Parr and Jim Blalock loomed dark on the driver's seat of the stage. The team, moving at a spanking trot, slowed to a walk crossing the ridge.

Steve ducked into the road behind the stage, ran up to the

capacious rear luggage boot, twitched aside the leather dust cover and scrambled up and in, shoving the Henry rifle ahead of him. A moment later, breathless, his heart pounding with the excitement of what could lie ahead, Steve was curled up snugly in company with a few items of passenger luggage.

Once he was settled down, Steve began guessing what portion of the road the stage was rolling over. At first it meant nothing, but he guessed right about the long, twisting drop into the canyon to Bleeker's Ford. There was no mistaking the crossing at the ford, for there was the voice and smell of the river itself to come up to a man. Then the smooth, sandy roll across the flat beyond. Here was the spot of the other holdup and Steve was taut and alert for the first sign of interference with the stage's progress.

The road pitched upward, starting the climb up the ridge beyond. Steve relaxed. Well, it was foolish to have expected a holdup in the same place. The bandits would know, of course, that from now on, crossing the flat, the shotgun guard up above would be extra alert and ready. When they struck, no doubt, it would be at some spot far removed. For as Andy Parr had said, complete surprise was one of the bandits' strongest weapons. Maybe they wouldn't strike this trip at all. Maybe . . .

The pistol shot that sounded up ahead reached Steve's ears in the confines of the luggage boot with muffled heaviness. The stage lurched, swayed and slowed, hastily applied brake blocks squealing. The stage stopped, then rolled back down the grade for a few feet before the brake blocks took hold solidly for a complete stop.

Inside the Concord sounded the mutter of sleepy and alarmed voices, the protesting chatter of high-pitched Cantonese, the more liquid excitement of Spanish, the hard nasal growl of a down East miner. Then, from outside the stage a harsh order.

"Throw down that treasure box! Careful, or you'll get what the guard got! Hurry up! Throw down that treasure box!"

Abruptly the hammering excitement in Steve Larkin left him. A cool, steady purposefulness came over him. He pushed aside the leather boot curtain, cocked the Henry rifle, slid out of the boot and to the road below. Rifle to shoulder, he stepped past the off rear wheel.

* * *

With one swift glance, Steve saw several things. He saw Andy Parr, bent over and tugging at the treasure box, dragging it out of the fore boot of the stage. He saw the leaders of the team, swung a little to the right, dancing and chafing, nervous because of the abrupt stop and the ringing echoes of the pistol shot. But most important of all, he saw a masked figure a little wide of the off front wheel, gun trained on the laboring Andy Parr.

The Henry rifle swung in line. The bandit, glimpsing Steve at the same moment, spun to face him, venomously fast, gun stabbing level. The Henry rifle spat flame and report and a deadly accurate slug. The bandit jackknifed and fell forward on his masked face.

Steve swung the lever of the Henry forward and back, dodging past the rear of the stage, clear of the near rear wheel, and now he saw another stark picture. There was Jim Blalock, a still and crumpled figure in the dust beside the stage, where he had fallen from his seat at that first pistol shot. Just beyond him stood the second bandit, the one who had slain him without warning or mercy.

Warned by the first smashing report of the Henry rifle, this second bandit had begun warily to back away into the edge of the brush beside the road and he was almost set for the appearance of Steve Larkin. But not quite. The second slug from the Henry rifle nailed him just a breath ahead of his try for Steve. The bandit was whirling and falling as he shot and Steve felt the burn of the slug where it whipped across the top of his left forearm, just below the elbow. The impact almost tore Steve's grip from the barrel of the rifle, but he recovered swiftly, swinging the lever again, ready for another shot if necessary.

But there were no more masked figures in sight. And now Andy Parr yelled, "Steve! You all right, boy?"

Steve moved around the stage. "All right, Andy," he answered. "How many of them were there?"

"Two. They're both down?"

"Both down. They got Jim Blalock."

"Shot him down like a dog. He never had a chance."

The hard-voiced down East miner had climbed out of the stage by this time. He looked around, then turned to Steve. "Brother," he said, "you did a neat job. Where'd you come from? I didn't see you get on the stage at White Pine."

It was Andy who answered, swiftly. "He didn't. He just happened along. Out after some venison, weren't you, boy?"

"Yeah." Steve nodded grimly. "Yeah, that's right."

IV

THE stage rolled into Nevada City, carrying a grim cargo. Three dead men as well as the live passenger list. And riding beside Andy Parr was Steve Larkin, a rough bandage around his left arm. The word spread swiftly and a crowd gathered. Ben Ashely was there, and George Renner. The dead bandits were declared strangers, no one ever having seen them before.

"Boy, you get over to the cabin and take care of that arm," Andy said to Steve. "I'll get Toby Strang to take on for the Grass Valley run and then I'll be right over."

Steve, with the Henry rifle tucked under his sound arm, headed for the cabin. Ben Ashely looked after him gravely, while Renner had a strange, hot gleam in his eye.

A little later Andy Parr, Ben Ashely, and George Renner were alone in the stage station.

"Now give us the whole story, Andy," said Ashely.

Andy told it tersely.

"You mean to say that Larkin was hid out in the luggage boot?" Ashely exclaimed. "How . . . where . . ."

"It was an idee Steve and me cooked up," explained Andy. "Steve was waitin' along the road jest this side of White Pine. It was before daylight when I passed that place and Steve run up behind the stage and climbed into the boot. Nobody expected he'd be there, least of all those cussed hold-ups. So, when they jumped us, shootin' pore Jim Blalock before he had a chance, they were watchin' me, never dreamin' a man with a gun was hid out in the luggage boot. So Steve, he jest crawled out quiet and opened up on 'em."

"It was smart figuring, all right," admitted Ashely. "And as long as just us three and Steve know how it was done, it could be pulled again."

"Why not, Ben?" Andy nodded.

"If Larkin is fool enough to continue putting his neck on the line for nothing," said Renner sarcastically.

"It won't be for nothing," Ashely said crisply. "I'll pay

Steve to ride that boot. It will be worth it to me to have a few more dead bandits strewn along the roads. They'll learn to leave my stages alone. You must approve, George, for it means safe travel for your company's treasure boxes, too.''

"Just a fly-by-night trick," Renner scoffed. "It might have worked once, but that's no guarantee that it would again. I'll still use guards my own way."

"And have 'em where Jim Blalock is now?" asked Andy. Renner shrugged. "They know the risk when they hire on."

"The big thing," said Ashely, "is to keep this just to our-selves. If future holdups were to get wind of it, then Steve would be like a trapped rat in that boot."

"Trapped rat is right," said Renner. "But if you and Lar-kin want to try it, Ben, I'm willing to be convinced."

Over in Andy Parr's cabin, Steve Larkin had bared his wounded arm and was going at a washing job rather clumsily, when a light step sounded at the doorway. It was Kate Ashely, her face pale, her eyes anxious. She crossed quickly to him.

"Steve! Why didn't you tell me?" she cried.

"Doesn't amount to much. How'd you hear?"

"Dad told me. Here, let me do that. Is this the way you dig for gold, getting mixed up in another holdup?" she scolded gently.

"Just happened to be handy," explained Steve lamely. "This is mighty fine of you, Kate."

"Bosh! Hold still."

Kate's hands were light and swift and very gentle. Her bright head, bent so close over Steve, smelled of sunshine. The curve of her throat and chin was soft and golden brown. She was setting the bandages when Andy Parr came in.

"Wish I needed a mite of doctorin'," Andy teased.

Kate colored rosily as she gave the bandage a final pat. "You'll get a fine scolding, Andy Parr, if you don't see to it that Steve gives this arm a good rest."

"Hum!" growled Andy. "Anybody would think the brash young whelp was more precious than a gold mine, instead of being a darned nuisance."

"He is not a nuisance," defended Kate hotly. Then she saw the twinkle far back in Andy's eyes. Again she colored deeply. "Oh, you . . ." she exclaimed. Then she scurried away.

Andy looked after her, chuckling, but he became serious

as he turned to Steve. "Things are all set and baited, boy. Now there's that letter to write. Good thing you didn't get your right arm jimmed up. Because I'm no hand with a pen and paper."

Once again Steve Larkin held down a lonely camp in the hill timber. It had been two full weeks ago that he had left Nevada City. He had left in the very early dawn before anyone in the town was astir. He had not even had the chance to say good-by to Kate Ashely, a necessity which Andy Parr had urged upon him.

"We can't afford to have anybody trail you, boy," Andy had said. "You got to slide out without a word or sign to anyone where or when you've gone. You just got to disappear. I'll tell the lass not to worry about you. Surprise is what we got to figger on—always surprise."

The strong clean tide of youth was in Steve and his arm healed swiftly. He did not spend the time just loafing around his camp. Day after day he scouted cautiously through the hills paralleling the road between White Pine and Nevada City.

He watched the stage on its swing into the hills and back again and every time Andy was whip, Steve would be crouched behind the upturned roots of a certain storm-felled pine. But each time Andy drove by without a betraying glance. And then Steve would slip back to his hidden camp and once more go over the route he had planned, until he knew every tree, every thicket, every gulch and ridge by heart.

Always, as he traveled, he carried Andy's Henry rifle over his arm and at night around his frugal, hidden campfire he would clean and polish, clean and polish until the weapon was spotless, inside and out, and the breech block slid to the swing of the lever with faultless smoothness.

The impatience of youth was in him and he fretted for this thing to happen and be over with, one way or another. Again and again he had to shake off gloomy thoughts. Maybe the trap had not been baited as cunningly as Andy Parr thought it had; maybe the quarry had grown wary. Maybe the letter Steve had written on Andy's instructions would not bring the results calculated upon—and if it did not, why then where was his future? Steve would be back right where he had started from, and Kate Ashely would be just as far from him as she had always been.

Grimly Steve fought off these doubts and clung faithfully to Andy's instructions. And so it was that on still another day Steve crouched behind the roots of the pine tree and watched Andy swing and sway on the seat of the Concord as it came rumbling up the road from Nevada City.

The treasure guard was a man Steve had never seen before, a heavy, hulking figure with a darkly bearded face. Steve thought Andy was going to drive by as before. Then his heart leaped, for Andy flicked the barest glance his way and again something dropped in the dust by the spinning wheels of the Concord.

Steve was all caution, waiting a full half hour before stealing out into the road, recovering as before a small pebble with a note wrapped around it. Andy's awkward scrawl read:

Heavy treasure coming out. We'll gamble on this one. Juan has the horse ready. Watch this guard. There's bad color in him.

It was well after dark that night when Steve footed it softly to a solitary cabin up in a winding gulch a good mile behind White Pine. At his knock a voice called, "*Quien es*? Who is it?"

"Larkin," answered Steve. "Andy Parr sent me."

The door opened and a swarthy face looked out under a high-held lighted candle. "Come in, *señor*—come in. The horse is ready and waiting. I am Juan. It was my sister and her child who rode with you the day of the holdup. I would thank you for your kindness to her."

Steve stayed that night, and the following day and night with Juan Arguello. But before the next dawn broke, Steve was out and ready. Juan led a saddled horse up under the crisp but fading stars.

"Thees *caballo* is not much to look at, *Señor* Steve. But it is fast and sure of foot. *Vaya con Dios*—go with God, *señor*."

V

STEVE rode down to the stage road a short half mile from White Pine. There he waited, back in the timber, the Henry rifle balanced across his saddle in front of him. When the stage rumbled past it was still too dark to see it clearly, but the sound of it was all Steve needed. He swung the horse and rode with the stage, keeping even with it, but back in the timber.

Daylight came seeping down the mountains, gray and moist. Now Steve was on the course that he had so carefully worked out during the past lonely two weeks. It kept him within sight of the stage virtually all the time, yet offered enough concealment to render it unlikely that he would be seen from the road. Juan Arguello had chosen cunningly and well with this horse. The animal was a neutral bay color, agile, light-footed, quick and instantly responsive to the slightest touch of the rein.

Steve beat the stage to Bleeker's Ford and crossed the Yuba fork a good two hundred yards above the ford proper. He climbed a steep-pitched slope through stately pines and from there could look fully down onto the flat where the other two holdups had been staged. Here he dismounted, found a rest for the Henry rifle across a down log, and waited.

He watched the stage hit the ford, jounce and splash across, then roll out the length of the flat and begin the climb up the ridge beyond. Nothing happened. The world lay still and peaceful. The only movement aside from the stage that Steve saw was the deep sapphire gleam of a crested jay, caught momentarily in the morning sun, as it winged a swooping way between two tree tops. Steve went back into the saddle and rode on.

Beyond the lifting ridge above the ford, the road dipped and rose, then dipped again, crossing alternate hollow and point that looked down into the ever-deepening canyon of the Yuba River beyond. Steve's horse scrambled up and slithered down, then up again. Always, past the shifting screen of timber, Steve could see the flicker of the moving stage, see Andy Parr tooling his team along with expert hand, see the burly, dark-bearded treasure guard bulking.

Letdown began stealing over Steve Larkin. He'd been keyed up to the extreme over this plan, and now it seemed it had all been for nothing. No sign of trouble had shown. The stage was rolling on, cutting down the miles to Nevada City. It looked as though another stretch of skulking in the woods lay ahead of Steve, until Andy should call on him to make another guarding ride. It seemed that . . .

The smashing roar of a shotgun cut through Steve's gloomy and doubting thoughts. His head jerked high, and down through an open lane through the timber, he saw two things happening. The stage had ground to a halt. Up on the box, Andy Parr was struggling with the burly treasure guard. And in the road behind the stage a masked figure was in the act of driving a second charge of buckshot into the luggage boot of the Concord.

The bellow of that second shot was still reverberating when Steve left his saddle. As he swung the Henry rifle to his shoulder, he saw Andy Parr and the treasure guard, still struggling, topple off the stage on the near side. He saw the bandit with the shotgun start running forward.

The sights of the Henry rifle lay clean and true a half step ahead of that masked figure. Then the rifle's keen crack echoed and the bandit spun around and collapsed. Steve raced toward the road, swinging the lever of the Henry. He saw another masked figure, standing even with the swing horses of the team, take a step forward and throw down with a revolver. He heard the revolver *spang*.

Then this second bandit lay fairly in the sights of the Henry and when the rifle leaped in recoil, his arms flung high and he went over backward. Steve plunged ahead again, only a few yards from the road now, his heart in his throat over the fate of Andy Parr. Then he heard Andy's panting yell.

"There's one more, Steve—one more! On the other side!"

Steve saw the bandit, running now, seeking desperately the shelter of the timber below the road. It was tricky shooting and Steve knew that his third bullet had gone low, even as the Henry again slammed his shoulder in recoil. But a leg went out from under that fleeing figure and the fellow came down, floundering. His yell for mercy lifted shrilly.

"Don't shoot! Don't shoot again!"

Steve broke into the road beside the stage and saw Andy sitting astride the burly treasure guard, pushing the half-smothered fellow's face deeper into the road dust. There was a fleck of blood on the side of Andy's neck, but he was grinning triumphantly.

"This should be what we've been after, boy. Go round up that gent who's doing all the yelling. I can't wait to get to Nevada City."

Steve circled the rear of the Concord. The bandit with the bullet-crumpled leg was still yelling for mercy. Steve looked at the luggage boot as he passed. It was riddled with buckshot holes. Had he been riding there today . . .

A strange expression came into the eyes of George Renner as he watched Andy Parr's stage, trailing its banner of dust, come rumbling up to the station in Nevada City. With Renner was Ben Ashely and a spare, gray-haired, hawk-faced man but lately come to Nevada City, a man named Carson.

Ben Ashely exclaimed, "That's not Broderick, the treasure guard you sent out, George. That's Steve Larkin on the box with Andy. And there's a led horse following behind the stage."

As Andy Parr set his brake he lifted his whip in salute. "Gentlemen! A fine, bright day."

Steve Larkin dropped swiftly down from the box, the Henry rifle across his arm. The young man's eyes and lips were grim.

"There's a look about you, Steve," Ashely said doubtfully, "And with you here . . . well, you and Andy must have tricked another holdup attempt. You rode the luggage boot again?"

Steve shook his head. "No, Mr. Ashely. I didn't ride it this time. If I had, I'd be dead, now. The first thing they did was fill the boot full of buckshot. I wonder who tipped them off? I didn't and Andy didn't, and I know you didn't. Who else besides us three knew about it?"

George Renner licked his lips. "Where's Broderick?" he asked, voice hard and rasping.

"Inside," answered Andy, swinging down. "And damn well tied up. Also, three bandits, two of them very dead bandits and the other with a shot-up leg and ready to talk, forty to the minute. I think a few words can be squeezed out of your friend Broderick, too, Renner." Andy looked at the spare, hawk-faced man. "By chance, would you be a Wells

Fargo man, maybe sent up here from Sacramento because of a letter written a couple of weeks ago?''

The hawk-faced man, Carson, nodded. "By chance, I would be."

"You'll be interested," said Andy, "in all we have to tell and show you. Renner, no snake was ever able to travel without leaving a crooked track."

A wildness, a desperation had been growing in George Renner's eyes. Now he cursed and a hand, stabbing toward a pocket, came away bearing a stubby, but deadly derringer pistol. But Steve Larkin, watching closely, was also on the move. He took one swift step and the butt of the Henry rifle stabbed out and up, smashing into the side of Renner's face. The derringer went off harmlessly as Renner fell.

"Boy," said Andy admiringly, "that rifle's yours to keep. You sure get 'em with it, from either end."

They gathered in the stage station, Steve and Andy, Ben Ashely and Carson, the Wells Fargo inspector. Andy talked.

"It was always when I was carrying an extra rich treasure box that the holdups took place. I got to wondering about that. Only two people knew how much was in the box, Dan Shear at White Pine and George Renner, here. I've knowed Dan Shear a long time. He's square as they come. So it had to be Renner who was tipping off the bandits. I talked it over with Dan and he agreed that it must be Renner. Now, from what Broderick and that leg-shot bandit have told us we know this was true. Renner is head of the bandit crowd and has been pocketing the big half of the take."

Carson nodded. "I checked on that before I left Sacramento, your letter giving me the idea. I found that George Renner had on deposit in the Mercantile Bank over sixty thousand dollars, the first deposit being made only a little over a year ago. His salary in that same space of time was twenty-eight hundred dollars."

"Just to make certain," Andy went on, "after Steve and me fooled one holdup pair by having Steve hid out in the luggage boot of the stage, we kept the word of how we did it just among the four of us—Renner, Ben Ashely, Steve, and me. And on this attempt they had a man stationed to pump the luggage boot full of buckshot. Only Steve wasn't in the boot this trip. He was keepin' even with the stage on horse-

back. That"—and Andy grinned widely—"was another surprise. Maybe we won't need any more surprises to keep this
stretch of country clean of holdups, but if we do, Steve and
me will figger 'em."

Carson turned to Steve Larkin. "I know it's useless to try
and wean Andy Parr away from his job, but how about you,
young man? The company has to replace Renner. You've already demonstrated your fitness to take good care of Wells
Fargo treasure. Would you consider a permanent job in Renner's place?"

Steve gulped. This was away past his highest dream. This
could mean . . .

"Sure, he'll take it," said Andy sturdily. "And he'll make
Wells Fargo the best kind of man, Mr. Carson. I know this
boy. You can't go wrong on him."

"I wish to subscribe to that myself," put in Ashely quietly.
"Why don't you go and ask Kate's opinion, Steve?"

Steve was gone a full half hour. When he came back, Andy
and Carson and Ben Ashely were still talking. Steve had a
wide grin on his face.

"The answer, Mr. Carson, is—yes." Then he looked at
Ben Ashely who had a twinkle in his eyes. "And I got the
same answer to another question I asked Kate, Mr. Ashely."

A frequent contributor to Black Mask *and other detective pulps in the 1930s (using his mystery-fiction byline of W. T. Ballard), Todhunter Ballard began writing pulp Western stories regularly in the forties, and frontier novels in 1951 with* Two-Edged Vengeance. *His output of book-length Westerns, under his own name and such pseudonyms as John Hunter and Parker Bonner, rose to nearly fifty over the next twenty-six years. He was particularly adept at novels with California mining backgrounds, among the best of which are* Gopher Gold *(1962),* Westward the Monitors Roar *(1963), and* Gold in California!, *which was cowinner of a WWA Spur for Best Historical Novel of 1965. "The Saga of Toby Riddle" demonstrates his sure hand with a different background: the tragic Modoc Indian War.*

The Saga of Toby Riddle

★★★★★★★★★★★★★★★★

Todhunter Ballard

ON a spring day, 1862, a twelve-year-old Modoc princess, riding behind her father, came into the mining camp of Yreka in northern California. The town was so close to the Oregon line that at that time it was considered to be in the southern state.

To call the child a princess is to take a liberty with Indian custom, but women from many tribes have been so called because of their relationships with Indian leaders, and certainly Toby's family connections were as lofty as any in the Modoc nation. She was the niece of the chief called Captain Jack, who, with a handful of followers, succeeded in holding the Army of the Pacific at bay for over five months, killing more soldiers in ratio to the number of Indians involved than were killed in any other conflict of the frontier.

To a twelve-year-old who had never been far from her wickiup, a trip to Yreka should have been an exciting adventure, but for Toby it was a catastrophe. She was being taken to the mining camp to be sold or bartered, as many of the women of her race had been before her.

The Modocs at the height of their power never numbered over a few hundred members, but they were noted for their fierceness in battle and feared as the greatest horse thieves and slave traders in the Northwest.

Until the invasion of the white man into their territory they seem to have been content with hunting and fishing in their home area around Tule Lake, in the Klamath, and the rivers of its basin. But as soon as the first Modoc saw his first horse, the concept of his economy changed abruptly. He had to have horses, and he had nothing with which to trade. He stole when opportunity offered, but this was not often enough to satisfy him. So he turned to the lucrative traffic in humans.

North of Modoc country the semicivilized tribes of the Columbia basin were growing rich, trading with the Hudson's Bay Company at Vancouver, and in their advancing station they wanted slaves—a lot of slaves. Furthermore, they had the coveted horses.

The Modoc, not lacking in shrewdness, recognized the opportunity and their peculiarly favorable situation for making the most of it. South of them lived the Diggers and Piutes, groups more hapless than their neighbors, and down upon these defenseless people the Modoc raiding parties swooped, carrying them off by the hundreds. The captives were bound together in long trains and marched northward, there to be exchanged for the animals their captors considered of greater value. By the late forties some of the northern tribes owned more of these slaves than there were free members of their populations.

The discovery of gold spoiled this idyllic existence. The white man, coming in increasing numbers, spread through the California mountains, too well armed and too canny to fall victim to the Modocs, and the Modoc prosperity declined, hurried by the invaders' whiskey and diseases. Measles alone carried off half their population in one season and left the tribe so weakened that they then fell easy prey to their natural enemies, the Rogues and the Warm Springs Indians.

In this extremity they turned from capturing slaves to selling their women as prostitutes through the mining camps of Yreka and Jacksonville. It was as such a candidate that Jack's niece was mounted behind her father and brought into the cluster of straggling shacks and offered from door to door to anyone who would give four horses.

The hopeful father found the market slow. By then few miners wanted to buy a woman when they could use her for the price of a drink of whiskey. But he came finally to the cabin of Frank Riddle.

Riddle himself was little more than a boy. He had left Kentucky before his eighteenth birthday, made his way west with a wagon train, and drifted north into the Trinities in search of gold. His luck was neither better nor worse than most of his neighbors found. His placer claim yielded enough for his meager needs without much surplus.

But he was lonely. He had only seen a few white women in his three years at the mines, and he certainly had no hope of getting one of them to share his bare one-room cabin. Still, he refused the Modoc's first offer.

Something in his blue eyes, though, must have encouraged the father, and the Modocs had learned the art of trade from babyhood.

"Get down," he told the girl.

She obeyed unwillingly but made no protest when her parent stripped the thin dress, the only garment she wore, from her developing body.

Like most of her people, she was short, stocky, her legs a little too heavy for the rest of her, but she was a child, with a child's freshness. In spite of himself Frank Riddle's breath caught.

The father turned her around slowly, telling of her good points as he would in selling a horse. She was very strong, she loved to work, he said, and above all she was a virgin.

Whether that was true is debatable, since the Modoc concept of human relationships was informal and women seem to have been passed from man to man without much quibble.

The girl watched Riddle with growing attention, noting his thin face, his bearded cheeks, his light eyes. At length she smiled at him. It was the first change of expression she had shown since she entered the cabin, and it was the smile that clinched the sale. It changed her face, lighted her eyes, filling them with a promise that Riddle could not resist.

Still, he haggled. It was the custom never to pay the asking price for anything, and he finally bought the girl for three horses.

Afterward he was to tell Alfred Meacham that he got the best of the bargain because one of the horses was spavined, but Toby's father was apparently satisfied, hurrying away before the young buyer could change his mind.

Frank and his purchase stood looking at each other, hardly more than two children. The girl had little if any experience, the boy not much more. Then he picked up her dress from the corner where it had been flung and held it toward her.

"Better put it on," he said.

She knew no English and only a few of the "trade" words of the pidgin jargon used by the miners to talk to the Indians, but she needed no words to understand the gesture and to count her good fortune. There was much to be thankful for. The cabin was a shack with a sod roof, but compared with the wickiup in which she had been raised it was a palace. The Modoc homes were woven of tule reeds, more inverted baskets than buildings, and were entered only through the smoke hole at the top.

The stove was strange to her. Riddle taught her to use it. He had to teach her to boil water, to wash the tin plates, and how to cook. But once they were in the wall bunk no instruction was necessary; there was no privacy in a Modoc establishment: she had watched her parents all through her childhood.

For the next year Frank Riddle occupied himself with teaching his squaw. He taught her English and taught her to write. There is no record that he was an educated man, but he must have had some grounding, for he not only taught her well but also picked up the Modoc language from her. And this combination led directly to the part they played in the hostilities known as the Modoc War.

Toby was happy. She had a warm house, enough to eat, a man who did not drink to excess. And the following year she gave birth to a son. They named him Jefferson C. Davis Riddle. Although Frank was three thousand miles away and made no effort to return to aid the Confederacy, his sympathies were undenied.

Their years ran on, their lives unmarked, but each year the local placers returned less and less gold dust, and in 1868 they moved to the Upper Gap on the Lost River, where Riddle tried to support his family by trapping.

A year later an event occurred that would change Toby's

station and give her a love to last her life. In 1869, U. S. Grant became President, and Alfred B. Meacham was appointed superintendent of Oregon Indian Affairs. Arriving at the Klamath reservation, he was appalled by the conditions there, where Army officers where openly taking Indian women from their husbands and the women were prostituting themselves to the enlisted men in order to buy at the reservation store.

Under Meacham's administration the practice of Indian slavery was abolished and all white men were ordered to marry their squaws or to put them aside. So after nearly six years of living with her, Frank Riddle chose to marry the girl. Toby Riddle never forgot that she had Meacham to thank, and for the rest of her life she was dedicated to the superintendent.

Meacham had his troubles: with the Army—he did not like the soldiers and they did not like him—and with the Indians whom he was trying to urge to retire to the reservations and once there, to stay.

The Modocs resented being herded from their ancestral lands and more particularly objected to being confined in the same area as the Klamaths, their old enemies. Old Schonchin was senior Modoc chief, but several subchiefs commanded factional loyalties. One of these was Captain Jack, who, after an unsuccessful trial at reservation living, led his group in a breakout and simply went home.

In December, Meacham took Old Schonchin, a group of negotiators, and the Riddles as interpreters, and went after Jack. It was the first chance Toby had to serve the man who had made possible her status as a legal wife, and she argued her mentor's case like a Portia. She further repaid him by saving his life when the frustrated Indians would have killed him there.

The conference succeeded. At the end of the bickering Captain Jack agreed to lead his forty-three followers back to the reservation, where he would have remained in peace except for two things—the callous refusal of Meacham's Indian agents to keep his and the government's promises, and the continuing harassment by the Klamaths.

In earlier days when they were feared warriors of the territory the Modocs had disdained the Klamaths, stolen their horses and women, and generally reviled them. Now, with many more Klamaths than Modocs, the larger tribe delighted in returning the favors.

Finally Captain Jack's band could take it no longer, and again they fled. Once more they went back to their homes along the Lost River and at Tule Lake. Then began a two-year cold war between Jack's returnees and the settlers who had preempted the lands. The immigrants spread spine-chilling stories about Modocs, branding Jack as a drunken, bloodthirsty savage, a depraved thief and killer.

Actually, Jack's behavior showed remarkable restraint. A heavyset man in his middle forties, he had a broad, keen, intelligent face and the deeply wounded eyes of so many of the tribal chieftains. And over and over he insisted that all he wanted was to be let alone to live as his people had always lived.

Through the months, he maintained a passive resistance to both the extremists in his own band who demanded that he drive the settlers out, and to the government's pressure on him to return his people to the hated reservation.

He offered a compromise, asking that a Modoc reservation be established on the Lost River lands, the homeland, where he promised to stay. Meacham and several other prominent local men approved the idea and requested Washington to authorize it. Washington, consistent in its muddling, refused all compromises.

Then John Meacham, Alfred's brother and Indian agent on the Klamath reservation, took the decision on himself that Jack could stay on the Lost River until a different reservation was available. But the Army and the other Indian agents and the settlers would not let well enough alone.

The Army had not yet moved against the dissident Modocs because the northwest forces had been drastically depleted when General Crook, Department of the Columbia commander, departed to fight the Apache in Arizona. He was replaced by General E. R. S. Canby, a veteran of the Civil War who had commanded the Union force in the battle with Shelby's Confederates, the only battle fought in the West in that conflict.

Canby inherited a skeleton army, totally demoralized and untrustworthy. There was a single company at Klamath and no other relief within a hundred miles. Yet John Meacham's accommodation of Jack gave momentum to the train of events already running toward the final tragedy.

Egged on by the mounting panic of the settlers, the authorities decided that Jack's group must be moved back to the Klamath reservation, by force if necessary. A ragtag force was sent out, but the stupidity of the officer in charge gave the Modocs the opportunity to slip away from their tule village and retreat into a bleak badlands, the lava beds, where the black bare fissures and caves gave them hiding, and positions from which to fight. The most senseless war in American Indian history was about to begin.

The warning drumroll swept through the Lost River country. Frightened settlers hurried to find shelter with neighbors or in the town of Linkville. But Hooker Jim, a hothead in Jack's party, went out with a few men on his own, caught a few fleeing settlers, and killed them. It was enough.

The Riddles heard the news and were distressed. During the years of her marriage Toby had come to think like a white person, but she had continued her contact with her people, and the last thing she wanted to see was a war which she knew they could not win. Of equal concern to her, her idol, Meacham, was a leader of the whites.

The Army did not want trouble either, but the cries of the panicked settlers could not be ignored. And after all, Captain Jack had only a handful of followers. It should be a simple matter to round them up, carry them back to Klamath, and try the murderers before a military court.

Instead, the Indians were by now safely hidden, dug into the Stronghold of the lava beds. The soldiers found this a fearful labyrinth of broken lava flow, crazed with twisting crevices to use as trenches and pitted with shallow caves to serve the Indians as shelter and ambush. It could be easily defended. The soldiers could not penetrate it.

Southern Oregon and northern California boiled. Excitement could not have run higher if every Indian in the country had massed for attack on Washington. Yet Captain Jack had less than fifty people with him, men, women, and children.

Looking back on the Modoc War, the whole situation seems ludicrous, but at that time and place it was a very real fear to the settlers crouching in their vulnerable cabins, huddled in the miserable frontier towns, boasting in the safety of the ill-smelling saloons. It was very real to the sorry Army and to Toby and Frank Riddle; heartbreakingly real to Jack and his people, short of water and food in the evil rock jungle that was their only sanctuary, holed up with pitifully few horses and fewer guns.

With the opening skirmishes, the Army unwillingly became quartermaster corps for Jack. He surprised patrols, routed the early sorties, seized the arms and supplies thrown away by fleeing soldiers. Within a couple of weeks the Modocs had more Army guns and ammunition than they knew what to do with and food enough to sustain them through a considerable siege.

The force sent against them was an impotent, peacetime crowd of overage officers, relics of the Civil War, raw recruits straight from the boats, and men hiding in uniform to escape merited imprisonment. And they were fighting ghosts, shadows that crept from the rocky fortress, struck, and disappeared.

Jack and his handful of Indians succeeded in immobilizing the Army of the Pacific and also in paralyzing all business in the territory. He then looked again for a solution at the conference table, emerging not only as an able general but a shrewd negotiator. He almost won his goal, a separate reservation for the Modocs, preferably on the Lost River, but in the end he was defeated by the overconfidence the early victories had given his insubordinate followers, and by treachery.

The ill-fated conference had high official sponsorship. Secretary of the Interior Columbus Delano directed Alfred Meacham to head a peace commission of three men, go to the Modoc country, and with General Canby find the causes of the war, stop its spread, and perhaps move the Modocs west to the coast, where there was empty land with game and fish aplenty.

As a bad beginning Meacham refused to serve with the two chosen commissioners, and in this crisis Canby assumed command of the negotiations himself. It was a galling spectacle, the United States Government dealing with a handful of Indians as if they were a sovereign state. And throughout the series of talks the government comported itself with less honor and dignity than did the little band under siege.

Arrogantly ignoring its long history of bad faith in its dealings with the Indians, caught between conflicting and cavalier commands from Washington and dissidence among its own members, the committee alternately held out half-promises on one hand and threatened with the other. Jack's only hope lay in artful dodging, expediency, holding out until he might wear his adversaries down and wring from them an area where it was possible for his people to live.

The only rational thing the white men did was to choose Toby and Frank Riddle as interpreters between the factions. And by making her the go-between they placed the red-born girl with the white affections in a brutally frustrating position. But with the blindness of those who will not see, they blithely shrugged off what she tried to show them.

Toby Riddle, raised a savage, educated by her white husband, devoted to Meacham, was probably the only person in southern Oregon who could impartially evaluate what was happening on both sides. A girl in her early twenties, she stood before Meacham and General Canby, weighing this evaluation.

"There are men with Captain Jack who are now under an Oregon indictment for murder. You know what their chances are in a white man's court. He has won every fight with the soldiers so far, has more guns and ammunition than the tribe ever had, and Curly Headed Doctor, who ranks equal with Jack but is not as smart, has a group believing they have whipped you.

"Jack is trying to stall until you give him what he needs, and he has been lied to so often that he will not believe and surrender until he has proof that you mean what you tell him. Until then you cannot trust what any of them say. What have they to lose by holding out that they would gain by giving up?"

Meacham at least listened. He was very fond of both Riddles and trusted them, and he asked what Toby would advise.

"Let them go back to Lost River," she said. "It is not so big a place that you can't afford to give it to them. In return, make them promise to leave the ranchers alone and live in peace beside them."

General Canby was not Meacham. According to his own lights he was a reasonable man, but the indignity of treating equally with a clutch of aborigines was too demeaning, and taking advice from a squaw was quite beyond him. A nod of his head then could have averted the whole bloody, macabre blunder.

Instead, he sent two emissaries, ranchers friendly with the Modocs, with Toby again to the Stronghold, this time with an ultimatum that the time for talk was past, that the Indians must surrender or be killed.

The messengers were permitted to come into the Stronghold and deliver the order. It was not well received. Indeed the friendship was strained, the ranchers were accused of lying, and several indignant Indians wanted to kill them then and there.

Captain Jack prevented that intended murder, guarding the men with his own weapon and sending them safely back to the commission. They took with them the news that other Modocs were infiltrating the lava beds, filling out the Indian ranks.

Jack stood his ground, refusing to leave the lava beds until he was assured of a safe place to go. At one point of the discussions he offered to accept that inhospitable territory itself as his reservation.

And Canby tried. He had no authority to promise Jack what he wanted, but he did offer amnesty if the Indians would come out and promised to do his best to have the barren territory ceded to Jack in perpetuity.

Jack was understandably leery of such a bargain.

Toby carried the messages back and forth as the stalemate dragged on, as the pressure on her people increased.

Canby tightened the screws, circling the Army around the Indians, moving it in closer and closer, insisting on surrender.

The "war party" among the Indians grew more and more desperate. They maintained that if they killed General Canby and the commissioners, whom they considered the top authorities in the field, the whites would give in and go away.

Still Jack resisted them and kept to his tactic of delay.

And through the months Toby and Frank Riddle rode the monotonous, fruitless errands.

Under a nightmarelike truce individual Modocs came out of their black rock potholes and were allowed to reconnoiter freely in Canby's headquarters camp, now set on a bluff within plain view of the Stronghold; newspapermen, ministers, civilians trying to effect a breakthrough, visited the Stronghold with immunity.

And then on one of Toby's returns to Canby she brought her estimate of a deepening split in the Modoc command, a strengthening of opposition to Jack's continuing moderate course, and a direct warning. She had been told by the Modoc escorting her from the Stronghold that violence was brewing.

A tent had been put up on neutral ground, between the lava beds and the bluff, visible from both, in which the delegates were now meeting. Toby had been told, she reported, that it was no longer safe for her to go to the tent, and she had been advised to warn her friends not to go to it.

Again Canby ignored her, though she risked her life in divulging the warning, and she nearly lost it because of the favor. A minister, Dr. Eleasar Thomas, now added to the peace commission, naïvely admitted to a Modoc leader that it was Toby who had told of the new danger.

Toby was summarily summoned to the Stronghold to account for her indescretion and believed that the Modocs would kill her if she went. Yet Meacham and Canby wanted a message carried and pressed her to go. The General promised her that there would be an immediate attack on the Stronghold if any attempt were made to harm her, though it is hard to see how that would have protected her if the tribe chose to dispatch her before she could deliver the threat.

Toby Riddle bowed to Meacham's urging, took what she thought might be her final farewell of her husband and son, and with her head high rode Meacham's own horse to the rendezvous.

Her fears were not ungrounded. The Modocs surrounded her, demanded on pain of death that she reveal the name of the Indian who had warned her.

The lone girl answered with Canby's promise of attack and added that she was being watched through his binoculars, and held her breath. The ruse worked. Her tribesmen were not certain that the eyes of the glasses could not penetrate the rock behind which she was being held.

Then she claimed that she had dreamed of a plot, and even the agitator Curly Headed Doctor admitted that this was possible, for he was a religious leader who taught that spirits communicated with the living through dreams. But he was still suspicious, and it was the binocular story that saved the day for Toby. She was returned safely to the Army post.

Even with the danger that the war faction would change its mind about her, Toby Riddle continued to carry the messages, sometimes alone, sometimes accompanied by Frank. Thus far Jack's moderate line had prevailed, and in a special irony he came within an inch of winning the whole hand.

The Riddles must have felt a deep elation when at last General Canby gave them a written letter to Jack saying that if he would accept a reservation in a "warmer climate," meaning in Arizona or Indian Territory, there would be amnesty for all, even for the murderers under indictment, and what other than despair could they have felt when Jack threw the letter on the ground, saying that he could not read it and could not be sure what it said.

So again they returned empty-handed, but now with a further warning of impending tragedy. They had seen that the Indians were strengthening their Stronghold, piling rocks at strategic spots, had killed several beef, and were drying the meat in obvious preparation for a fight. Riddle guessed that they had been pushed as far as they would go and that unless they were given a reservation soon in their home country there would be violence within days.

They spoke to the wind.

The day before Good Friday a delegation came from Jack asking for one more conference of five representatives from each side to meet unarmed on the morrow. Meacham was away at the time. Dr. Thomas, the pacifist among the commissioners, prevailed in his opinion that the invitation should be accepted, and when Meacham returned in the afternoon he was confronted with the promise already made that the entire commission plus Canby and Colonel Alvan C. Gillem were going to present themselves at the tent.

Meacham sided with the Riddles. "If we go," he told Dr. Thomas, "we will not return alive."

The pacifist among the whites had his way, and in the Indian camp at the same time the champion of the conference table against the field of battle lost.

With the commissioners committed to come to them unarmed, Curly Headed Doctor found his chance to force Jack into further fighting. A meeting of all the Modocs was called after dark on Thursday night, gathering on the council ground around the cave Jack used as headquarters. Curly Headed Doctor drummed in his argument that if the five white leaders were killed the soldiers would quit, the whites would leave, the Indians would have won.

Jack denied this and announced that he favored giving up and accepting a suggested home at Yainax, an exile. But he was hooted down, grabbed, wrapped in a squaw's shawl; a squaw's headdress was forced onto his head. He was jeered at as a woman, a coward. And after all his long resisting of the urgings of the war party, Jack bowed to them. But if that was the way they were going, he said, he was their leader and lead he would. They would probably all die for it, he prophesied, but if murder was going to be done, it must be done right, planned carefully. He claimed the right to kill his opposite number, General Canby, himself.

So the plans were laid. Each white man was delegated to a particular Indian and that Indian given an assistant. The Riddles' name was raised. It was argued that they should die, too, but the vote went against that, and Scar Faced Charley, a man to be listened to, said that anyone who harmed the pair must answer to him personally.

Frank and Toby did not know this, and in any event in the heat of such a planned bloodletting the lust to kill could overwhelm any one of the conspirators.

They did not need to know the precise plans. They had read the sign, the quickening tempo among Toby's people. Again and again they had voiced their warnings. They knew what the chances were in the coming confrontation.

But they went.

Already suspect to the Modocs, the loyal Toby was now treated to the suspicion by the Reverend Thomas that she was double-dealing, in league with her kinsman, Jack.

But she went.

At the conference Toby Riddle and Frank and Meacham stood together.

Meacham was sufficiently aware of the danger to have suggested that if any treachery seemed likely the whites should promise the Indians anything they asked and get out as fast as possible. But Canby demurred. He had, he said, dealt with Indians for thirty years and had never deceived them. He would not consent to it now, to making any promise that could not be fulfilled. Meacham and L. S. Dyar, the other commissioner, surreptitiously carried derringers in their pockets. The others went unarmed.

The council was formally opened at a little before noon. Speeches were made, and then came some chilling horseplay in which an Indian tried on the coat Meacham had left on his saddle, a preview mocking what he intended to do when Meacham was killed.

Toby Riddle read the sign. There was no longer anything she could do except once more try to warn the white men, and the only way she could do that was to pretend weariness and lie prone on the ground in front of Meacham. Frank Riddle read the sign and moved quietly behind Toby's horse. Meacham tried to catch Canby's eye but could not, and so continued the farce of conference.

At twelve minutes after noon Captain Jack called for the attack, pulled a revolver from under his coat, and fired at Canby. The first shot did not fire. Canby might have run but instead sat transfixed. The second shot took him below his left eye.

One by one the other designated victims were turned on, but Indian fashion, after each was brought down there was a scramble to strip off his clothes as loot.

Canby amazingly got up and ran forty yards before he was shot again and killed. Dr. Thomas died with gentle words on his lips. Meacham ran backward, fighting to draw his derringer, tripped and fell, and was wounded by a glancing bullet that knocked him senseless. Taken for dead, he was stripped and left where he lay. Dyar ran and miraculously escaped. Frank Riddle also ran and lived.

It was done quickly. It was done by the time Toby Riddle caught her breath and her wits, saw that her idol Meacham was on the verge of being scalped, and gave him the only help she could. She raised her voice, crying aloud in her native tongue.

"The soldiers are coming. The soldiers are coming."

For the first time, the Indian girl was believed. It was not true, but the whole tribe believed it was. They ran for the safety of the Stronghold.

When finally the soldiers from the bluff raced down to the bloody field, Toby Riddle was seated beside the unconscious half-scalped body of Alfred Meacham, the only two people alive there.

And beside Meacham she stayed. When he recovered, his bald head was scarred by the scalping knife, and he took Toby, her husband, and an Indian who had attended the murder on a tour of the lyceum circuit, lecturing on the Modoc War, exhibiting the scars of his brush with death, introducing the two men, and giving to Toby Riddle the credit so long due her, acknowledging that the Modoc girl had saved his life.

Zorro, the dashing caballero, swordsman, and Robin Hood of Old California made famous by Douglas Fairbanks and Tyrone Power in film portrayals and by Guy Williams in a popular TV series, was created by Johnston McCulley in the pulp serial, "The Curse of Capistrano" (1919). It was five years before the serial appeared in book form, as The Mark of Zorro, *and yet another twenty-five years before McCulley, a prolific pulp writer, novelist, and screenwriter, would tell any more tales of "The Fox." In 1948 at the urging of pulp editor Leo Margulies, McCulley finally began a new series of Zorro stories for the magazine* West—*a series that proved to be highly popular and that lasted until the magazine's demise in the early fifties. "Zorro Draws His Blade" was the first of these new Zorro adventures, and among the most satisfying.*

Zorro Draws His Blade

****

Johnston McCulley

GAUNT and gray, with his head held high and indignation flaming in his eyes, Fray Felipe stood before the door of the chapel at Mission San Gabriel that afternoon, alone between a frenzied mob and the terrified, cringing man they sought to slay.

The strong wind whipped the fray's tattered robe around his emaciated form as his thin arms were uplifted in a gesture that demanded silence. In front of him was the seething mob—peons, natives, travelers off the highway, traders, vagabonds of the hills—all acting like maniacs as the blood lust turned them from men to beasts.

"Back!" Fray Felipe shouted in his shrill voice. "Are you mad, my sons? Would you desecrate the chapel? The man has claimed sanctuary until dawn tomorrow, and shall have it. Such is his right."

A chorus of wild cries answered him: "Give us the murderer! . . .Give us the rogue who slew Don Esteban San-chez! . . . Let us hang him!''

Fray Felipe silenced them again with a gesture. ''The man has sanctuary until dawn tomorrow. That is the law. I shall talk to him meantime and learn the truth.''

''We know the truth already, fray,'' a man called.

Fray Felipe recognized the speaker as Miguel Cortez, su-perintendente of the rancho owned by Don Carlos Martinez. He was middle aged, short and stout, and notorious for his cruelty to those who worked under him. He was the right sort of man for his employer.

For Don Carlos Martinez, despite his hidalgo blood, was a wastrel and licentious, forgetting the responsibilities of his rank and station, and received only cold and distant nods from others of gentle birth.

Two years before, Don Carlos had inherited properties on the death of his father. Because he gambled heavily, and spent huge sums in lavish entertainment whenever he visited Mon-terey, he was becoming impoverished. Men whispered that he had mortgaged his estates heavily. He left management of the rancho to Miguel Cortez, and cared little what methods Cortez used.

Now, Cortez stood out before the others and spoke to Fray Felipe.

''The halfbreed known as Juan killed Don Esteban San-chez with a skinning-knife he took from the sheep pens, where he had been working. I saw him, and caught him robbing the body, and brought him to San Gabriel. The rogue managed to escape me, and rushed here to claim sanctuary.''

The priest did not flinch. ''Which he shall have,'' Fray Felipe said, sternly.

''As you will, fray! Confess the rogue, shrive him, pray with him through the night. But at dawn he leaves sanctuary, and we hang him. And we will camp here to make sure he does not get away.''

''Enough!'' Fray Felipe shouted. ''Remain on guard if it pleases you. But act in an orderly manner, and do not dese-crate the mission.''

Men in the mob began muttering, and the crowd started breaking up into small groups. Fray Felipe watched them a moment, his mind troubled at this blood thirst and violence. Then he turned to reenter the chapel.

But he came to an abrupt stop and gave a sigh of relief at what he saw. A carriage drawn by prancing black horses was entering the mission compound. A native coachman handled the reins, and a native footman sat beside him.

In the carriage, reclining on fat silk cushions, was a young caballero dressed in resplendent attire, who brushed his nostrils with a scented handkerchief and stifled a yawn with a hand the fingers of which were adorned with jeweled rings.

This was Don Diego Vega, son and heir of Don Alejandro Vega, one of the wealthiest and most prominent men in Alta California. But the hidalgo blood which coursed his veins never seemed to set Don Diego afire. He did not join other young caballeros in their feverish adventures, but read poetry and cultivated roses, which made men decide that he was nothing but a fop and a spineless jellyfish.

The coachman shouted a warning, and the crowd parted to let the carriage through. It stopped in front of the chapel. Don Diego looked around at the crowd, turned up his nose slightly as if at an unpleasant odor, and stepped from the vehicle and upon a strip of crimson carpet the footman had been quick to spread.

"Welcome, Don Diego, my son!" Fray Felipe greeted, cordially. "What wind of good fortune blows you here?"

"I was visiting in the neighborhood, padre, paying my respects to a beautiful senorita and her estimable parents, and thought I would stop to break bread with you and spend the night in your guest house," Don Diego replied. "Usually, it is so quiet and peaceful here. But now I find a tumult that makes my head ring. What is the meaning of this riot?"

"Come into the chapel, Don Diego, and I'll explain," Fray Felipe said.

Don Diego followed him inside, and the fray closed the heavy door in the faces of the mob. Don Diego saw a barefooted, ragged man kneeling before the altar. Fray Felipe gestured toward him, and spoke to Don Diego in hushed tones.

"He is Juan, a neophyte. He would not tell me a falsehood. He says Miguel Cortez caught him and tied him to a tree beside a trail, stuffing a cloth into his mouth so he could make no outcry. Cortez took his skinning-knife from him, and waited in the brush. Don Esteban Sanchez came riding along the trail alone."

"Sanchez is a dear friend of my father's," Don Diego said.

"Your father will grieve. According to Juan, Cortez sprang out of the brush and stopped Don Esteban, pulled him from his saddle, and stabbed him to death."

"Monstrous!" Don Diego cried.

"Juan heard Cortez say, 'Now, Don Esteban, you cannot press Carlos Martinez for payment he cannot make.' Then Cortez untied Juan and made an outcry, which called workers from a field. He accused Juan of the murder and brought him to San Gabriel. That is the story. And who would believe the word of a nameless ragged halfbreed against that of Martinez' superintendente?"

"I would, for one," Don Diego said.

"Sí. And I, for another, my son. But possibly nobody else. Juan told me his story, and I believe him. It has been thought that Don Esteban held a mortgage on Martinez' estate. No doubt he hoped to seize the property and drive the notorious Martinez from the country."

"How came this Juan here?" Don Diego asked.

"He twisted away from Cortez and ran here to claim sanctuary. Cortez aroused the mob. If Juan leaves sanctuary, the mob will kill him. That is bad enough, but there is more."

"And that?" Don Diego questioned.

"I know I may speak freely to the man I christened and who confesses to me," the fray said. "Evil times have come to Alta California. Unscrupulous politicians rule the land. Favors are sold or given to friends. The missions have become wealthy through the toil and sweat of the padres and neophytes, and the politicians covet that wealth."

Don Diego nodded his head. "That is true," he admitted.

"There is strife between the missions and the political rogues. They would seize our herds and flocks, the goods in our warehouses, and turn us out. And look where I stand in this affair. If I free Juan, knowing he is innocent, it would be said we Franciscans are protecting our neophytes though they are murderers. That would arouse men against us."

"I can see that, padre."

"If I surrender Juan at dawn, it will be worse. For the natives we have converted believe they have a refuge in their faith, that it protects them from injustice. If I do not protect Juan, they will think there is no truth in our teachings, will desert the missions and return to the spiritual darkness from which they came."

"You are in a tight corner, padre," Don Diego judged.

"Juan can be saved, and I be freed of this dilemma, if the real murderer could be unmasked before dawn."

"The mob would have to be convinced of his guilt," Don Diego interrupted.

"I know one man who could accomplish it."

"And he is—?" Don Diego questioned.

"Senor Zorro. The man who rode the highway and helped the oppressed, and punished evildoers without mercy. It has been some time since he was active. He should become active again."

"Senor Zorro, the fox," Don Diego muttered, looking straight into the old fray's burning eyes. "I wonder how many men know his real identity?"

"Possibly only two, his father and his father confessor," Fray Felipe replied, smiling slightly. "What say you, my son?"

Don Diego glanced again at the altar, where the terrified Juan was imploring help. He faced Fray Felipe once more, and his reply was a whisper: "Zorro will ride tonight."

"I thank you, my son. Providence must have sent you this way today."

"I need some help. I must have a man to take a message to Bernardo, my body servant."

"Let us step outside, and I'll call a man."

They left the chapel, and Fray Felipe summoned to the one he wanted, a man he could trust.

"Ride at top speed to my father's house in Reina de los Angeles," Don Diego instructed him. "Find Bernardo, my body servant, and tell him I will spend the night here, and want him to come immediately on his fast-riding mule, fetching my heavy sleeping robe."

"I understand, senor."

"Bernardo cannot speak, having been born dumb, but he can hear and will understand. Tell him I said, 'Bring everything I need for the night.' Those exact words. Here is a bit of gold for your trouble."

The man accepted the gold, grinned, knuckled his forehead in respectful salute, and hurried away.

Bernardo reached the mission an hour after nightfall. He had been a loyal servant to Don Diego for years, and knew his secret. Being unable to speak, he could not reveal Zorro's identity even under torture, and the written word was beyond him.

Bernardo tied his mule, tucked a bundle he had brought beneath one arm, and hurried to the guest house, where Don Diego was waiting in the room assigned him. Bernardo bobbed his head and unrolled the bundle, which contained only the sleeping robe.

"You understood, Bernardo?" Don Diego asked.

Bernardo grinned, and nodded that he had.

"You brought the clothes of Zorro and his horse and hid them in some safe place near by?"

Bernardo nodded in the affirmative.

"Get my couch ready, and remain here until I return."

Don Diego strolled across the main room of the guest house to the open outside door, and looked out into the compound. Fires had been built, and men were sprawled around them. There was a sliver of moon, which would give just enough light to make moving shadows deceptive.

A sudden tumult at the gate attracted Don Diego's attention, and he saw two troopers riding through. One was Sergeant Manuel Garcia, from the barracks at Reina de los Angeles.

Don Diego drew back swiftly out of sight. As Zorro, he had clashed with Garcia often enough.

He did not fear the man, nor did he make the mistake of underestimating him.

Garcia had brains and instinct, he was a good horseman and an expert swordsman. And he had sworn long before to unmask Senor Zorro some day and stretch him lifeless on the earth with a deft thrust of his blade.

Don Diego watched the troopers dismount and tie their horses, and saw Fray Felipe welcome them and send them to the eating hut. The fray then approached the guest house and joined Don Diego in the doorway.

"They heard in Reina de los Angeles about the crime, and soldiers have come," the fray reported. "But even the Gov-

ernor's troopers dare not violate sanctuary, so Juan is safe
until dawn. The troopers will save him from the mob, but
that will not help.''

"What mean you, padre?''

"Our alcalde is on a journey. So the magistrado will come
from Reina de los Angeles in the morning to judge the case.
It will be Juan's word against that of Cortez, and the magistrado is an unscrupulous rogue and will not affront the mob
by a moment's hesitation. He will order Juan hanged forthwith, and the soldiers will carry out the sentence.''

"Then Zorro has work to do tonight. If any ask for me,
padre, say you believe I have retired.''

"I have learned that Miguel Cortez has gone to the tavern
down the highway, and that Carlos Martinez is there for the
night. Martinez has engaged a room on the patio.''

"That information saves me considerable time," Don Diego replied. "I have plans in mind.''

"Everything must be accomplished before dawn, if Juan is
to be saved and the situation cleared," Fray Felipe reminded
him. "Buenas noches, my son!''

Fray Felipe shuffled away with his hands thrust into the
sleeves of his tattered robe. Don Diego returned to his room
and closed and bolted the door. In whispers, he explained to
Bernardo what had happened and what he intended doing.

On a sheet of parchment, he scrawled a message, and
tucked it into his sash. He paced the floor for a time, thinking, then extinguished the tapers in the candelabra, so the
room would be dark and it would appear he had retired. He
opened a window in the rear of the room, and he and Bernardo dropped through it and crouched in the darkness outside the wall of the compound.

Keeping to the dark spots, they got away from the mission
and into a coulée, followed this for a short distance, and in
a mass of brush-shrouded rocks came to where Bernardo had
tethered the black horse Zorro rode. From beneath a clump
of brush, the mute pulled a roll of clothing, Zorro's attire.
Another bundle contained Zorro's blade, his pistol, powder
horn, and a pouch of bullets.

In the darkness, Don Diego Vega changed his attire and
became Zorro, dressed in black and with a black mask over
his face. Into his belt he thrust the charged pistol and the
parchment he had prepared in the guest house.

"Remain here," he instructed Bernardo. "If I am chased and reach this spot, you will know what to do."

Then Senor Zorro mounted quickly and rode away through the darkness.

He circled the mission at a distance and approached it cautiously from the opposite direction, eyes strained as he watched shadows, ears attuned to catch every sound.

The rabble around the fires were laughing and shouting, and evidently were passing wineskins around. The gate of the compound stood wide open. Zorro felt in his sash for the message he had prepared. On the parchment, he had scrawled:

The man Juan is innocent. The slayer of Don Esteban
Sanchez is known to me, and soon I shall expose him.
                                        Zorro

He rode toward the gate of the compound, approaching it slowly through the shadows. When he reached a spot where he could look through the gate, he surveyed the scene well.

Suddenly, he touched his horse with spurs. The big black sprang into action. With thundering hoofs, he dashed through the gateway and straight toward the fires and the men scattered around them.

Zorro gave a wild screech that rang out above the din and attracted the attention of all around the fires. Some men sprang to their feet, and others struggled to stand.

In a shower of gravel and dust, Zorro stopped his horse within the circle of light cast by the largest fire, so they would have a good look at him.

"Senores, atención!" he shouted. "Read this—if any of you can read." He tossed the parchment toward the nearest man. "And tell that pig of a Sergeant Garcia that Zorro is here. Perhaps the sergeant would like to capture me, and earn a fine reward."

"Zorro!" the men began shouting. "It is Zorro!"

Zorro menaced them with his pistol and backed his horse away from the fire. He held them off until he saw Sergeant Garcia lurch from one of the buildings with the trooper behind him.

"Ho, Garcia!" Zorro cried. "Glutton and wine soak! Are you able to climb into a saddle? Can you use a blade?"

"By the fiend, you need a lesson," cried Garcia, and hurried toward his horse with the trooper running after him.

Zorro rode through the gateway, but did not urge his horse to speed until he saw Garcia and the other follow through and take after him. Then, Zorro began maneuvering to keep just beyond pistol range, playing with the pursuit, knowing that the horse he bestrode could give distance easily to the mounts of the troopers.

Reaching the highway, Zorro turned toward the tavern a mile distant. This roadside inn had a reputation not of the best. It was known as a haunt of smugglers and other rogues, where dice and cards attracted some and wine others. The presence there of troopers or any other representatives of law and order was not desired.

The tavern was a long, low building built around a patio in which there was a well. It was set in a grove of huge trees and thick brush, with a winding lane leading to it from the highway. Two torches burned outside the front door.

Now that he had revealed to the pursuit that he was riding to the tavern, Zorro used his spurs and distanced the troopers. They would follow there, he knew, and being only two in number they would be cautious about entering the place because many rogues were gathered in the big main room. Nothing would delight such gentry more than to slit the throats of a couple of the Governor's troopers and leave the bodies beside the highway.

Nearing the tavern, Zorro left the lane, pulled his horse down to a walk and rode him into the depths of the grove, where he dismounted and tied the black, then hurried back to the building.

He heard the pursuit coming. But there was a sudden cessation of hoofbeats, and he knew the troopers had pulled up and were riding beneath the trees. Undoubtedly, they feared ambush, possibly thought that Senor Zorro had lured them here to their undoing.

Zorro desired their presence, for he wanted official witnesses. His one fear was that Garcia and the trooper might interrupt proceedings too soon. That was a chance he had to take, but he had taken desperate chances before. He shifted his scabbard, made sure of the pistol in his belt, and slipped noiselessly along the side of the tavern to the front door.

Glancing through a window he passed, he saw that the big

main room was half packed with men. Thieves and vagabonds they were, smugglers and possibly a few wanted murderers among them. They were drinking, playing at dice and
cards. The fat landlord was shuffling around, watching his
native servants as they poured from the wineskins and col-
lected coins.

Smoke swirled across the room from the fireplace and from
cigaritos and pipes. It blackened the strings of peppers which
dangled from the rafters, and gave new flavor to the haunches
of meat being cured. Reeking torches illuminated the place,
save where a couple of the larger gaming tables were deco-
rated with old, battered candelabra in which tapers burned.

At one of the large tables Don Carlos Martinez was sitting
on a stool, with Miguel Cortez beside him. Martinez had a
heap of coins before him, and was playing cards, while Cortez guarded his master and his gold.

Zorro ran to the door, jerked it open and entered swiftly,
slammed the door behind him and dropped the heavy bar into
place. He ran across the room to the other door, which opened
into the patio, and stopped there and turned to face those in
the room.

"Ho, senores!" he cried. "I am Zorro! Troopers pursue
me, and may be here soon."

Instant silence fell in the big room as all turned their heads
to stare at him.

"Zorro," some man muttered. "Zorro!"

"There is a reward offered for my capture, as possibly you
know," Zorro said. "Is any here mean enough, or brave
enough, to try to earn it?"

A man lurched to his feet.

"So you are Zorro, and the troopers are pursuing you,
eh?" he asked.

"Only two of them pursue."

"And do we here fear only two such scum?" He turned to
the others. "This is Zorro, who whipped a magistrado once
because he defrauded a poor peon. Are we friends with a
magistrado or with the man who whipped one?"

A chorus of howls answered that, and Zorro knew he had
nothing to fear.

He whirled and dropped the bar across the patio door, then
confronted them again. And suddenly he seemed to see Mar-

tinez and Cortez for the first time. His eyes gleamed through the slits in his mask as he strode toward them, his right hand resting on the pistol in his sash.

"Senores!" he cried to the men in the room. "Have you lost your wits? Are you trying to put nooses around your own necks?"

They shouted questions as to his meaning.

"Is it not true," Zorro asked, "that there has been an informer busy recently? Have not some friends of yours been taken, testimony given against them? Have not men been hanged, and others farmed out at hard labor?"

Growls and expressions of rage answered that. For these men had friends who had been seized by the Law recently. Such were always being arrested and punished, but now that it was called to their attention, the rogues in the tavern remembered vividly that there had been an epidemic of such seizures for some little time.

"That means a spy at work, does it not?" Zorro asked, standing back against the wall and looking directly at the table where Martinez and Cortez were sitting. "Fools! You gather here to have your fun. Wine loosens your tongues, and you talk of things which would hang you. Ears are open to catch that talk."

"Whose ears, Zorro?" somebody shouted.

"What man in this room is not one of you? There sits Don Carlos Martinez, a hidalgo, a man of broad estates, and the superintendente of his rancho beside him. They are hearing everything you say. Because they play at cards and dice with you, you are foolish enough to accept them as friends."

Exclamations of rage came from a score of throats. Some men got up from their stools and benches. They stood with feet far apart, shoulders hunched, hands working like claws, rage suffusing their faces.

And, at that moment, Zorro saw what he had been waiting to see—the faces of Sergeant Garcia and his trooper at one of the small open windows. Whatever happened now would be seen, whatever was said would be heard officially.

Don Carlos Martinez sprang to his feet with Miguel Cortez beside him. Fear showed in their faces. The ruffians before them would tear informers to pieces, torture them brutally before killing.

"Wait, senores—amigos!" Martinez shouted. "Who is this

man who makes such an accusation? Have you ever seen his face? Does he not always wear a mask?''

"If my face ever is known, my work is done," Zorro said. "Perhaps I am a man well known. Perhaps, as my own self, I am in a position to learn the moves of the soldiery, and so escape them."

The ruffians howled with delight at that, then turned toward Martinez again.

"We trust the masked man who once whipped a magistrado," their spokesman said. "We trust a man the soldiers pursue. But how do we know we can trust you, Don Carlos Martinez? What have you and your superintendente ever done to make you one of us? You are a rich hidalgo. You often go to Monterey and visit the Governor."

"Seize him!" another shouted. "Get his superintendente, too! Knives for them!"

"Wait!" Martinez shouted. "I tell you that Miguel Cortez and I are your friends. We like men of your stamp. We like to gamble and drink with you. Landlord! Bring out a fresh skin of wine. Give my friends what they want."

"He would buy you off," Zorro said.

Martinez scowled. "As for you, Senor Zorro, it will please me to cross blades and carve you," he shouted, angrily. "What does it profit you to arouse these men against me?"

"We'll attend to these rats, Zorro," the leader of the rogues shouted.

They surged forward, and Martinez and Cortez retreated to stand with their backs to the wall. Cortez got a pistol from his belt, and Martinez reached to draw blade. But they knew they could not hope for a victory against their foes. They might kill or wound two or three, and then the knives would be carving at them.

But Zorro sprang forward, and got between the two against the wall and those who would use their knives.

"Wait!" he shouted. "My friends, I have only been showing you that you are careless. Don Carlos Martinez and his man could easily have been informers. You accepted them without using any care. Let this be a lesson to you. If you value your necks, be careful in your talk hereafter when strangers are around."

"But, Zorro, you said—" the leader began.

" 'Twas but a lesson I hope you will take to heart. You have nothing to fear from Martinez and Cortez. They are one with you, as I happen to know."

"Explain!" they shouted.

"You all have heard how the rich Don Esteban Sanchez was slain today. A nameless halfbreed even now crouches in the chapel at the mission, accused of the crime. In the morning, the troopers hope to hang him. But he did not kill Don Esteban. I happen to know who did."

"Tell us!"

"Don Carlos Martinez says he is your friend. Is that true, Don Carlos?"

"It is," Martinez replied. "I would be the last to betray them."

"You will not care, then, if your friends know something of your affairs." He faced the rogues. "Senores, because Don Carlos has been a good fellow, because he likes wine and games, he has been losing his estates. Don Esteban Sanchez held a mortgage, and demanded payment."

"Enough!" Martinez cried.

"Let your friends know the truth, senor. Let them learn they have nothing to fear from you, or they may yet use their knives."

"Tell us more, Zorro," somebody shouted.

"I tell it all. Miguel Cortez today plotted well. He seized the halfbreed, tied, and gagged him. He slew Don Esteban, then untied the nameless one and shouted for help. He accused the breed of the crime and brought him to San Gabriel. But the nameless one escaped and ran to the mission and claimed sanctuary until dawn.

"By doing this, Cortez helped Don Carlos, for it will take time to settle the Sanchez estate, and by the end of that time Martinez can prepare to pay. The pair planned the murder, and Cortez executed it. Does that not make them one of you?"

Cortez' eyes were bulging at this recital of the truth, and Martinez' face had paled. Zorro glanced toward the window again, to see Sergeant Garcia and the trooper still there, interested listeners.

"How dare you say such a thing?" Martinez cried at Zorro. "With my blade, I'll split you like a goose!"

"You are with your friends, senor," Zorro pointed out.

"Possibly every man here has slain another. They will not believe that you and your superintendente are informers now—if there is truth in what I have just said."

"But how do we know it is truth?" the spokesman of the rogues demanded. "Perhaps you, Zorro, have been misinformed."

"Use the knives!" another man howled.

They surged forward again, eyes agleam and knives ready. Terror came into the face of Martinez. He threw up a hand to stop them.

"Wait!" he shouted. "It is true. It is as Zorro told you. Now you know that I am one of you, and that Cortez is, also. And any of you are welcome on my rancho whenever you care to visit. I will even show you fine hiding places, if you are pursued."

The ruffians stopped.

Some turned back to the tables in order to gulp wine.

"And, since I am one of you, I settle personal differences your way," Martinez went on. "This rogue who calls himself Zorro—were I sure he was of proper blood, I'd cross blades with him and carve out his heart."

Zorro laughed. "My blood is better than your own, Carlos Martinez," Zorro said. "I swear it!"

"A fight?" somebody cried. "Let blades ring!"

Miguel Cortez had returned his pistol to his sash, but now he drew from it a knife. Martinez whipped out his blade, and Zorro retreated a few steps swiftly and got his own from scabbard.

The rogues tossed tables and benches aside and made a cleared space in the middle of the room.

"I'll run you through," Martinez was shouting. "Then I'll tear the mask from your face and see what manner of man you were."

Zorro knew Martinez was trying to rivet his attention. From the corner of his eye, he saw the swift move Miguel Cortez made, saw the knife gleam. Zorro's left hand dropped to his own sash to jerk out his pistol. It spoke, but the ball sang past Cortez' head and struck the hard adobe wall to ricochet with a whine.

Cortez hurled the knife, which grazed Zorro's shoulder and clattered to the floor.

"Treachery," Zorro cried at the rogues. "Seize Cortez and hold him while I fight this man."

They shouted approval, rushed forward as Cortez tried to get out his pistol again, seized him, disarmed him, and held him back against the wall. Zorro tossed his useless pistol to the floor.

Blades held ready, he and Martinez met in the middle of the room.

"I'll see your blood," Martinez cried.

Martinez attacked furiously, and Zorro retreated, keeping on the defensive while he felt out his opponent. Martinez was good with a blade, but Zorro knew after those first few moments that he had nothing to fear.

He stopped retreating and stood firm, then began pressing the fighting. He heard a tumult in the patio, heard the native servants screeching in fear. Zorro glanced at the window again, to find that Sergeant Garcia and the trooper were there no longer. The front door, and the one opening into the patio, were barred inside, but the small door opening from the kitchen of the tavern was not. And through this door now stormed Sergeant Garcia and his trooper.

"Soldiers!" Zorro shouted at the rogues. "A troop of them. Save yourselves! Out the front way!"

They rushed to the door and took down the heavy bar, and many ran out into the night. But others remained, those having no particular fear of the soldiery at the moment. The door remained open.

"Grab that man Cortez," Garcia shouted to his trooper. "He is under arrest for murder. Handle him quickly! Bind him! Try to have a poor halfbreed hanged for murder, will he? And this fine gentleman, who instigated the crime, will get his deserts, also." He started toward where Martinez was fighting with Zorro.

"Back, Garcia," Zorro shouted. "This is my business. Help your trooper with your prisoner."

Martinez was making a fresh onslaught, and Zorro pretended to retreat before him, edging his way toward the open door. Too late, Sergeant Garcia understood the ruse. He could not squeeze past those flying blades and get at Zorro now. "You—Zorro!" Garcia cried. "Highwayman! There is a price on you."

"Try to collect it, senor," Zorro said.

He had stepped back to the door now, with Martinez after him and pressing the fighting. And through the ring of steel he heard the wastrel's plea.

"Do not let them hang me," begged Martinez. "If you are a hidalgo, slay me now with your blade. End my life. Do not let me die on the gallows."

Martinez attacked with fury, then, Zorro found it necessary to defend himself. The blade he sent home through Martinez' heart was in self defense. Martinez gave a sigh and collapsed in the doorway.

Before Sergeant Garcia could struggle over the body, Zorro was outside and speeding through the darkness.

He reached his horse, untied him and sprang into the saddle. The black spurned the ground with his hoofs.

Swiftly Zorro left the highway and circled, outriding the trooper Garcia sent in pursuit, while the sergeant prepared to take his prisoner back to the mission in custody. The rogues had scattered, and would not bother Garcia by going to the defense of such a man as Cortez, who blamed his crime upon another.

In time, Zorro reached the spot where Bernardo was waiting.

"All is well," he said. "Rub down the black while I change clothes. Then come with me to the mission for your mule, return here and get the horse, and be on your way before daybreak. If you are missed, I'll say I sent you back to Reina de los Angeles with a message."

He changed clothing swiftly, and they hurried to the mission carefully through the darkness. They got into the room through the window. Working swiftly, Don Diego half undressed, lit the tapers in the candelabra while Bernardo cleaned telltale dirt from his boots, then opened the door and strolled into the main room of the guest house.

There was a tumult in the compound. Somebody had brought word of what had happened in the tavern. Don Diego walked to the door and strolled toward the chapel, meeting Fray Felipe almost in front of it.

"I honor myself by being your guest for a night, padre, and you reward me with an air-splitting din," Don Diego said, yawning. "Is there nothing but turbulence in the world?"

"Thank you, my son," Fray Felipe whispered. "I am going now to give the good news to Juan. After this, his faith and that of other neophytes will be stronger."

"Let me go with you," Don Diego begged. "I want to see the expression in the man's face when he learns he has been saved. And then I will need your ministrations, padre. I was compelled to take a human life tonight."

Born in California, Bill Pronzini has published several Western stories set in his native state, among them the brief but decidedly tall tale that follows; two of his recent novels, The Hangings *and* Firewind, *also have California settings. His other Western novels include* The Gallows Land *(1983),* Starvation Camp *(1984),* Quincannon *(1985), and* The Last Days of Horse-Shy Halloran *(1987). He has also edited or coedited more than two dozen anthologies of Western short fiction.*

Old Tom

★★★★★★★★★★★★★★★

Bill Pronzini

HOWDY, boys. Mind if I was to occupy this here vacant chair? Well, thank you kindly. That's real neighborly of you.

Name's Luke Keeler, from out to Californy. Been headin' for the Dakotas kind of leisure-like the best part of two months now. Heard they was gold to be had in the Black Hills, so I just naturally packed up and took out East.

Yep, you guessed it. Prospector's what I am. Been one for nigh onto forty years now. Panned gold all over this here Western United States in my time, and down in Mexico, too.

Say, this is mighty fine whiskey. Come out of Kaintucky, I'll wager . . . Thought so. Always could tell Kaintuck whiskey when I had a taste of it. Another? Well, don't mind if I do. Man works up a thirst out on the trail this time of year. Thank you kindly.

Didn't I hear you fellas talking about bravery and friendship a while back? Thought so. You was discussin' pards, and how a real pard will side you no matter what the odds.

Well, I had me a pard like that once. A real ace he was, too. Name of Tom—Old Tom, I called him, on account of he was some along in years. He didn't like it much, but he let me do it cuz we was pals. He's gone on to his reward now,

174

rest his soul. Been gone twenty years. Only time I ever cried in my life was the day of his passing, and I ain't ashamed to admit it.

Me and Old Tom was together six—seven years back in the Gold Rush days in Californy, prospectin' for the yeller stuff in the Mother Lode. Them was rough days, boys, what with road agents and storekeepers sellin' wares so overpriced they might as well been called by the same name. Claim-jumpers, too, which was the worst of the lot by a wide margin, I'm here to tell you. If it hadn't been for Old Tom, I *wouldn't* be here, nor nowheres else neither. And that's a fact.

What happened? Well, this was back in the early spring of '50. Me and Old Tom had come up from Death Valley way, once we heard about the strike at Sutter's Mill. And everything we'd heard about it was the gospel and then some. There was so much gold around for the takin', you could of been crippled, blind, and crazy and still found enough paydirt to go into the grubstakin' business.

Old Tom and me, we found us a fine spot right off, near Mokulemne Hill. You get so you can smell the yeller stuff like it was skunkweed on a hot day. Up this canyon, it was, where a crick come spillin' down 'twixt a couple of rock walls. All nice and private, cut off from the nearest claim by half a mile of digger pine and scrub-brush. Good thing, too, for that there crick was just brimmin' with color. Found one nugget big as your fist, by golly.

Well, we filed a claim right off. Digger Claim, we called it. Built us a lean-to, set up keep, and commenced to work that stream with a sluice box and a cradle and plenty of elbow grease.

Afore a month was out, we knew we could take enough paydirt out of that crick to set us both up for some little while. And we did, too. Why, when we left the Mother Lode for Sacramento, we—

But that's another story.

As I was sayin', me and Old Tom was makin' that Digger Claim of ours pay off right well. Then one afternoon just as I was taking a shave out front of the lean-to, gettin' ready to ride over to Sonora to have our poke assayed, these three jaspers chased up out of nowheres and throwed down on me.

They was a mean-lookin' lot, I'm here to tell you. Scruffy and bearded and smellin' like they'd been rollin' in bear grease. They come off their hosses and tells me plain out that they aim to take over Digger Claim, right then and there. Want me to sign it over to 'em on a piece of paper they got. And if I don't cooperate, they says, they'll puncture my hide and stake me out and watch me bleed to death.

Now, there ain't a thing I can do. My six-shooter is hangin' on a peg inside the lean-to, and my rifle is in there, too. I'm lookin' down the barrels of three big Colts and right then I figures I'm about to meet my Maker, whether I cooperates or not.

But He decides it ain't my time, I reckon. For right then, just as them three evil-grinnin' claim-jumpers put their six-guns on cock, Old Tom shows me what a real pard he is.

He'd been prowlin' around the tall grass back of the lean-to, near the crick, and he must of heard all the commotion in camp, me yellin' foul at them three murderin' jaspers as I was. So he knowed right off I was in a peck of trouble.

Well, afore anybody knowed what was happening Old Tom comes chargin' out of the tall grass with his head down and his eyes blazin', just like a streak of blue-fire lightning. He makes straight for the nearest hard-case and before the gent can turn, Tom butts him with his head and knocks him into a patch of Scotch thistle fifteen feet away. And that's a fact, boys. Fifteen feet!

Then Old Tom pivots and gives the second jasper a kick that spins him around like a button's top and staggers him into the wall of the lean-to. Old Tom pivots again, and the third hard-case gets off a shot that grazes Tom's ear and makes him twice as mad. He lets out a bellow that shakes cones right off the pines, and latches onto that hombre's shirt collar and commences to shake him until his teeth rattles like dry bones in a box. He ain't got spit nor spunk left in him when Old Tom turns loose.

Tom's got blood in his eye by this time, and when he sees the second claim-jumper come up on his feet, he lets out another bellow and charges him. The jasper squeals and high-tails it for his hoss and vaults into leather with Old Tom breathin' on his backside like Brimstone Nick hisself. He just does manage to ride out of there afore Tom finishes him off. I've got my six-shooter by this time and I puts a couple of chunks of lead close by his ear to kind of quicken his pace.

Well, Old Tom is still fumin' and it takes me a while to

get him simmered down. When I do, we trusses up the other two jaspers, both of 'em bein' unconscious at the time, and carts 'em into Sonora and turns 'em over to the Miners' Committee, which was the law in them parts back then. There was work to be done at Digger Claim, else we'd of stayed on to watch the hangin'.

So that's the story, boys, and you'll be the first to admit that there ain't many would side his pard the way Old Tom done me, at the risk of sudden death and without no nevermind of his own hide. 'Course, that ain't the only time Tom done for me. I remember another, up by Weaverville in the Northern Mother Lode—

What's that, son? You don't think what Old Tom done to them claim-jumpers is so all-fired special? You know half a dozen men sided their pards more brave and onusual than that?

Why, hell's fire, son, didn't I tell you? Old Tom weren't no man. Rest his soul, Old Tom was the finest, bravest *mule* ever carried a pack west of the Mississippi—

Hey, where you boys goin'? No cause to shove off all bristly and jeerin' thataway . . .

Well, now, looky here at this. Them boys done left in such a hurry, none of 'em noticed there's still three—four drinks in the bottom of their bottle. Be a shame to waste good Kaintuck whiskey, even if I was a man of wasteful habits. Which I ain't.

Here's to the finest pard a man ever had, in fact or fiction. Here's to you, Old Tom. Here's to you!

Frank Bonham is another native Californian who has put his knowledge of California history to good use in his fiction. "The Bear Flag Mutineers," about a bitter and bloody confrontation between U.S. soldiers and secessionist troops in the San Bernardino Mountains during the Civil War, is one of many California-based stories he wrote for the Western pulps in the forties and early fifties. Curiously, all of his frontier novels are set in other states, primarily Arizona, Texas, and New Mexico; outstanding among these are Lost Stage Valley *(1948),* Night Raid *(1954),* Hardrock *(1958), and* Logan's Choice *(1964). Bonham was also a frequent contributor of teleplays to such TV Western shows of the fifties and sixties as* Death Valley Days *and* Tales of Wells Fargo.

The Bear Flag Mutineers

★★★★★★★★★★★★★★★

Frank Bonham

I

Shadow of the Bear Flag

TROOP security had been John Drum's credo ever since he took out his first patrol as a cavalry shavetail. He entered no gap until his scouts had signalled it safe. On bivouac, he detailed pickets before ever a saddle came down.

This he had done tonight, when D Troop of the Fourth California made dry camp at Old Woman Springs, under the blue tilts of the San Bernardino Mountains. Yet now, as the captain sat erect on his blanket, the thunder of hoofs rolled terrifyingly close, and over the dark rim of a hummock he saw horsemen pouring in a black wave. And no warning had been given . . .

The camp was awakening on a surge of panic. Corporal

Foxen was at Drum's elbow, shouting: "Boots and Saddles, sir?" He was half dressed, bugle at his lips.

Drum said: "As skirmishers," and buckled on his saber and seized his revolver in his left hand to run to where the horses were picketed. There was no time for saddling. No time for anything but a prayer and a man's stand.

First Sergeant McCullah stood near the horses, looking as stern and firmly in hand as though this were a mere falling out for reveille. Drum's courage lifted just for knowing he was here, a rock to lean on. A good man, McCullah, and a regular, like Drum himself.

"I want three squads to guard the horses," Drum said. "Two others on each flank. The rest on the line."

Somewhere the lieutenants, Mirabeau and Kelsey, were bawling their men into formation. McCullah, tunicless, with his blue trousers outside his boots and his forage cap on the back of his square head, went running through the rows of mussed blankets. His commands came back to Captain Drum, imperative as pistol shots. Three corporals ran up with their men straggling behind, pulling on clothes and buckling sabers.

The night gave up a crackle of pistol shots and a picket cried out as Captain Drum deployed his men and himself crouched behind a spiny joshua tree. Out of the formless gray-black wave materialized individual horsemen, riding back in the saddle, not on the withers, as good cavalry men ride. To the captain's surprise only a handful carried sabers. These men rode straight at the horse-holders, the others charging the line.

Drum stood beside the tree, firing his revolver with the roar of it almost lost in the din. He saw two saddles empty. A thickset man veered toward him with his saber raised. An arm of the joshua prevented his making the slash, and while he swung the horse and lifted the blade for another try, Drum's long body went in close to the horse and he sent the point of his saber up under the man's ribs. He withdrew and felt the scalding flow of blood down his arm.

Not far off he heard Sergeant McCullah yelling. McCullah had made more noise than the rest of the squadron at Gaines Mill. "*Now*, you devils! *Now*, damn you!"

He had time to glance to his left. The men were holding, green, disillusioned volunteers from the goldfields that they were. Would they understand now why he had drilled them in the sun and put them on forced marches when there was not a Secesh troop within fifteen hundred miles? Would they understand that they were soldiers, that the legends of a Bear Flag Battalion had its roots in steel?

Captain Drum's first estimate had been of a force approximating a hundred. Now he realized they were much less than that. Those who had struck his center had fallen back, badly mauled by the pistol-and-carbine-fire of his troops. They were swinging past the flanks, reaching for the safety of the night. Their force had been dissipated over a wide front instead of being hurled at one vulnerable spot.

Drum said to the bugler, "Boots and Saddles," and was the first man to catch out his horse. Confidence came to him, a readiness for anything, the stimulus any good cavalryman took from the feel of a horse between his legs. McCullah swung in beside him to relay commands.

When the troops were all in line, mounted, Corporal Neff rode up. "Lieutenant Mirabeau is missing, sir."

Drum said: "Leave two men to find and care for him."

For an hour they searched the flat, arroyo-veined face of the desert. The attackers had broken ranks and spread far and wide. D Troop returned to count losses.

Four men were dead and six wounded. Three were missing, Lieutenant Mirabeau among them. Captain Drum took the report with a frown. After the wounded had been cared for, he wrote in his journal:

> Attack was made tonight by a force of fifty horsemen, probably Bear Flaggers, intent on stealing our horses. Examination of papers on bodies shows no proof of affiliation with any Southern group. Lt. Mirabeau and two sentries are missing. Pickets had been posted but failed to give the alarm.

He was too experienced an officer to confide any suspicions in his journal. He did not set down that he had distrusted Lieutenant Mirabeau, a militia officer, from the start.

Nor did Drum add that he would have traded his whole troop for a squad of tobacco-chewing regulars such as he had led at Gaines Mill. But his reward for coming through that bloody hour alive had been to be singled out for a secret mission in California, leading a troop of inexperienced volunteers in search of the source of the Bear Flag organization, who were seeking to sever the Gold State from either the North or South, and form a Pacific Republic.

He closed the journal and lay back on his blanket, staring up at the black desert sky. By tomorrow night they would be encamped in Holcomb Valley, a mile high in the mountains. And by that time, in addition to his other troubles, he would have the nearness of a girl he had ridden away from three years ago to torment him . . .

In the morning the men broke camp sullenly. "There's a lot of complainin'," Sergeant McCullah said. "They think they've earned a day's rest." He stood with his arms crossed, displeasure written in his roughly cut features. McCullah was a man who liked alacrity. He was also a man who got it, one way or another. He was over six feet tall in his blue uniform, a good load for any horse, and not an inch of fat under his belt.

"Speak to the NCO's," John Drum told him. "There won't be a man of them reenlist next month, but by Harry they'll all be soldiers by then!"

McCullah gave the non-coms the sharp edge of his Irish tongue and D Troop moved out in column. At ten o'clock they made the gate of Van Dusen's Toll Road, an oasis of cottonwoods festooned with wild grape, its back against the barren foothills.

The eyes of Brown, the road-keeper, shone when he saw the column of ninety-odd men with six wagons. "You go through the gate with my compliments, Cap'n," he said. "Sabers and blue-coats are what this road needs."

Drum leaned against the hoary cottonwood shading the road. He drank cold water from a gourd, his eyes closed. The captain was a man just under six feet, with the erect, hipless carriage of a cavalryman. The sun had put a dark stain in his skin, and in his gray eyes were mementoes of Gaines Mill and Yellow Tavern and a dozen other places where death had been only half the horror.

"Trouble?" he asked Brown.

Brown sat on his hunkers, making marks in the dust with a stick. "About a third of the freight that starts up the road don't make it to Belleville, in the Upper Holcomb. Wells

Fargo boxes coming out with bullion from the mines have been stolen.''

"Do they bother the horses?'' Drum asked.

"They're hoss-greedy.'' Brown glanced up at him. "You want my opinion, Cap'n? Bear Flaggers! Hills are full of them. They're outfittin' troops somewhere.''

"Is that just guessing?'' Drum questioned sharply. "You couldn't mention any names or places?''

With the edge of the stick, Brown smoothed the marks he had made. He shook his head, smiling wryly. "Just guessin', Cap'n. Just guessin'.''

It was in Drum's mind that the road-keeper was afraid to say any more than he had. In things like this, men were often chary of talk. The column went on through the gate.

The toll road was a crude path hacked along steep mountainsides, now following a rocky wash, now winding along a wind-swept hogback. Through the first rank of dry hills they forged, crossing a deep canyon to mount the more rugged, timber-clad mountains that threw sharp barricades of granite two miles into the cloudless sky.

From sage brush and joshua the toll road carried them into denser stands of buckbrush, pinon and cedar. The dry, heated air of the desert was a thousand feet below them; a coolness was in the atmosphere now. By night they were in the pine country and camp was made beside a small stream that crossed a wooded flat. In the morning they crossed a heavily-timbered ridge and saw Holcomb Valley below them.

The valley formed a rough dog's-leg, a stream traversing its whole length. Drum could see the tawny scars of mine stopes and glory holes among the fragrant firs which timbered its enclosing hills. He could hear the rumble of an *arrastre* and the puff and clank of a steam engine crushing ore. Belleville, a neat pattern of log and adobe houses on the green meadow, occupied a loop of Holcomb Creek at the east end of the valley.

There was coolness and beauty and peace here, Drum saw. But for him there had been no peace for three years, and there would be none now. Not while a dark-haired girl had her fingers around his heart.

With Lieutenant Kelsey and the captain at the head, D Troop swung down through the shadowed aisles of giant trees and jogged onto the meadow. At the bank of the creek, Drum raised a gauntleted hand and said to Kelsey: "Take over, Lieutenant. I'll look up the mayor or whatever they have here and get permission to camp."

Kelsey saluted, a blond truculent young officer with long sideburns and no love for discipline. Kelsey's commission had been won through friends in the governor's office, but he had been soldiering for Drum.

Drum rode into town with no eagerness. The two letters he had received from Laurie during the last year had both been from Belleville. She might still be here, and she might not. He tried to hope that old George Owen would have packed his cobbling equipment and his daughter away to some other boom camp, but even though he knew the old wound would be reopened when he saw her, he would not have changed it.

It would be like this when he saw her, John Drum thought— both of them pleasant, smiling in the guarded way of those who hold their emotions firmly in their two hands. Both wanting each other and determined not to show it, for they had tried it before and there was no good in rehearsing all the old bitterness again.

He rode between the irregularly shaped buildings, no two of the same height or design. Men watched the upright blue figure on the sorrel horse jog past, not all with welcome in their eyes. It was a town of many interests and races, miners, *vaqueros*, and Chinamen mingling on the board sidewalks.

Drum smelled bread baking somewhere and heard the iron cry of a blacksmith's sledge as he passed a log smithy. Then everything else was forgotten when he saw the familiar, gilded boot swinging in the breeze before an unpainted adobe shop on his right. The board from which the boot swung was lettered: "G. Owen. Cobbling."

Drum dismounted. He turned from looping the reins about a pole to see Laurie standing in the doorway, tall and slender in a high-bodiced gown which fell gracefully from her waist. She put out her hands and he took them in his gloved ones, and it was not at all as he had imagined it would be. She did not smile. Her hair was a dark mass to set off the clear oval of her face, and her eyes looked at him as though she were seeing everything he had been since he had left her, as though she knew every thought he had had.

"You haven't changed," she said. "Not in three years. You're as hard and stubborn as you ever were. And as dissatisfied," she added firmly.

II

The Mayor of Hell

Drum drew off his gloves and he followed her into the shop. "You're wrong," he said. "I knew the Army was what I wanted. A man can make his plans and see them through. He can fight his enemies with their own weapons, on equal terms. It's not like Texas, Laurie."

The odor of food cooking in a back room drifted in to mix with the sour smell of leather. Dozens of pairs of boots hung from pegs in the mud wall behind a workbench.

They did not talk about Texas, nor about the plans they had built around the cattle ranch John Drum had hacked out of the *brasada* country in eight years of fighting border-loopers and wild cattle. Drum had had enemies, as any man has who succeeds where others have failed, but they had smiled at him on the street and kept out of his way, except at night, when their hungry loops and running irons ate at his herds. It was Drum's outspokenness which had finally banded the little foxes into a murderous pack.

In a slavery country it was not popular to talk abolition. Drum did. So they came for him one night, masking their hatred with a cloak of politics, and when they left, John Drum had a bullet in his shoulder, his buildings were a heap of smoking rubble, and his cattle had been run across the river into the thickets of Mexico.

That was when he grew sick of fighting in the dark. He could not justify himself by trying to kill every man he suspected of having raided him. He had not the heart to begin again, with no more prize, perhaps, than to lose it all over again. Laurie had told him he would never be satisfied to leave the fight unfinished; she would wait while he started over. But when a man has put too much of his heart into a thing, he has not enough left to begin again.

John Drum joined the Army a year before Fort Sumter. He

knew now that he would not go back to civilian life, not even if it meant losing Laurie.

Drum said: "I was sorry when I was ordered to California, Laurie. Now that I'm here I'm glad. It gives me one more chance to convince you that being an Army wife isn't much worse than being a cowman's wife."

With her hand Laurie pushed back a curl from her forehead; she let it linger there long enough for Drum to see the ring on her finger. "You're a little late this time," she said. "He's a miner. Dave Rockaway. We're going to be married next month."

Drum had felt the same coldness the night the Bear Flaggers attacked. His guard had been down, giving him no defense against the shock that struck at him. He covered it by frowning as he thrust his gloves under his belt. "You don't love him," he said.

Laurie was smiling, her quiet blue eyes amused. "Don't I? Didn't you know a woman ties a string to her heart when she gives it away?"

Drum could neither make a joke of it, nor smile at hers. "You didn't with me," he said. "You said you'd wait. I thought you meant it."

"But you wouldn't let me," Laurie protested. She looked at the ring. "He's handsome, John. And a rabid abolitionist. You'll like him."

"I imagine," Drum said dryly, as steps sounded in the back room. Old George Owen, staring over the tops of square spectacles, stood in his leather apron with a dish towel over his shoulder. He exhibited no surprise at seeing the officer. He said, "Hm! Just in time, John. We're having venison."

Drum ate with them. The talk was about the war, but Drum's mind would not let go of what Laurie had told him.

They went back to the shop. Owen sat down at his bench, looking the captain over critically. "Lost weight," he remarked. "The desert?"

Drum shrugged. "I'll put it on again up here. We'll be here some time."

The cobbler brought his sharp hook knife around the toe of a boot, slicing off the excess leather. "Copperheads?" he said.

Captain Drum looked out into the bustling street, with wagons and horses passing constantly and miners in the rough, mud-caked clothing of their trade. He said: "No.

Though there are plenty of them, too. I'm after some men who would rather set themselves up as kings of a California Republic than fight for her as a State. My information is that they have their headquarters in the San Bernardinos."

George Owen turned the boot in his hands, squinting at it. "Better keep your eyes open," he warned. "Maybe just a little thing like this boot here will tell you something you want to know."

The remark rang oddly in the shop. Drum looked at the boot, which was a thoroughly worn black one badly stirrup-marked, but otherwise not unusual. "Meaning anything in particular?" he asked, somehow a bit annoyed.

Owen again began to trim. "Meaning that nobody will tell you much if he does know anything. We all know the Bear Flaggers are thick hereabouts. But nobody knows but what the man that shoes his horse is one, so we don't talk about 'em much. They do a lot of night work."

It was Drum's impression that Owen had meant something more specific than that, but the boot told him nothing. "Do you have a mayor?" Drum asked.

"You want Matt Harrower," George Owen said. He spat some tacks into his hand and began to pound with staccato bursts of the hammer. "Harrower sells mining supplies up the street."

Laurie went to the door with him; John Drum held her hand. It was a little stiff; it was not quite his, he knew, and knowing that hurt. "Then all I can offer you is my congratulations," he said. "But I'll be hoping this miner of yours goes booming off to some other camp."

Laurie said quietly: "If he does, I'll go with him."

Mayor Matt Harrower held forth in a large, barny sort of a store on the corner across from the tree in the road. The place was a conglomerate of every kind of implement a gold miner could conceivably employ to entice gold from the earthrocker and pan and pick-axe; bottles of *aqua regia* and iron rings to be sunk in concrete *arrastres*. A red door in the rear was lettered: *Explosives. Keep out.*

Harrower sat on a toolbox prying at his teeth with a gold toothpick. The mayor was a short, square-bodied man with a wide mouth like a bear-trap. He wore a corduroy jacket and corduroy pants tucked into lace boots.

He gave the officer a silent, assaying stare, then kept his eyes on him while he wiped the metal toothpick and replaced it in a tiny case.

"Well?" he said.

Drum said: "I'm Captain Drum, commanding D Troop of the Fourth California. My orders are to encamp here until further notice. To make it official, I'd like to get your permission to camp on the meadow."

Harrower strolled to the door and gazed off across the rolling green meadow at the lines of tents going up. "Somebody tell you we needed help?" he asked.

"We didn't need to be told," Drum replied. "Belleville is notorious as a rendezvous for a lot of unwholesome elements."

Harrower smiled, showing him a line of wide-set teeth. "Well, some of the boys like to stir up a tempest in a teapot. Nothing serious. The boys at the mines are too busy to worry about politics."

"I don't suppose you would care to mention names?"

Harrower, not losing his smile, said, "I don't know that I would."

He was a man, Drum saw, who kept his guard up; a man who might know much, but would tell nothing deliberately.

"I'll need some lumber for a few temporary buildings," he said. "Is there a mill nearby?"

"There's the Mormon's Mill," the mayor told him, "run by Mormon Dowling. Don't let the name fool you, though. The Saints threw him out before they went back to Utah. Mormon will have a drink with you and take a chaw, then rob you on his lumber."

It was Drum's impression that Mayor Harrower's eyes, when he left the store, contained more of distrust than of friendliness; and more of concern than of casualness.

III

Mormon's Mill

When he reached camp it was noon. The tents, a colony of dun pyramids on the light green grass, were all up and the stakes and poles were being dressed. Sergeant McCullah said,

"These parlor pioneers will be the finish of me, Captain. It's a gypsy camp this bivouac looks like."

"Any more complaining?" Drum asked.

The Sergeant did not answer at first. "Yes, sir; some," he admitted after a moment. "I can't enforce an order without a fist behind it. With all respect to Lieutenant Kelsey, sir, he ain't much better than the men. I believe he has given Corporal Neff permission to bring you some grievance."

Drum's face did not change, but there was faint amusement in his eyes. "Send him to my tent," he said.

McCullah had had the captain's tent, larger than the rest, erected under a lone pine near the stream, at the end of the troop street. Lieutenant Kelsey's tent stood between it and that of the ranking non-com. Kelsey was sitting in the shade before his tent, writing a letter. He had his blouse off and his collar undone. When he saw the captain, he came to attention and made his salute.

"I don't think I heard Retreat sounded, Lieutenant," Drum said.

Kelsey's blue eyes could not mask his pique. He looked very young and very resentful. "No, sir," he said. "But a blouse gets hot."

"The uniform is dress until after Retreat," Drum said. And then: "I have sent for Corporal Neff. I understand he has something on his mind."

Kelsey scowlingly got into his blue coat. It was in his face that he was finding soldiering under Captain Drum different from squiring the daughters of militia officers about the capital.

Corporal Neff appeared, a lanky, red-headed soldier with an aggressive chin and a small mouth made for cynicism. He wore the yellow chevrons on his sleeves without dignity.

Drum gave him at ease. "What's on your mind, Corporal?" he said.

Neff crossed his arms. He said: "Well, sir—most of us is plumb tired of soldierin'. It's all spit and polish, and hard work. On top of that, we ain't been paid in two months. What we want is our pay and a day or two off to spend it."

"You'll get it," Drum said quietly.

Neff's brows raised a trifle in surprise. But he saw the loophole in the statement and frowned. "Yes," he said, "but when?"

"Just as soon as the pay-train gets through. While you wait, you'll continue to get Sundays off when there is no urgent reason to work. In the meantime, there will be drill every day, including today. I think some dismounted work wouldn't hurt anyone."

Neff's fists worked. "I don't know," he said, "how the boys is going to take it."

The captain shrugged. "There will be discipline for anyone who finds the work tedious. Pass the word along, Corporal—and do it now."

When he had left, Drum spoke to Lieutenant Kelsey. "I'll leave McCullah to drill the men," he said. "Take five men and ride to the mines. Get a gathering together here and there and see how many recruits you can bring back."

Kelsey's fair skin, already sunburned and peeling, went redder, so that his sideburns and eyebrows stood out sharply. He pressed his lips together, then, without a word, turned on his heel and went to saddle.

After lunch, Drum rode down the valley toward the saw-mill. All the confidence he had spoken was not in him. These men he commanded were a stubborn, tired and rebellious group of disillusioned volunteers, but their demand for pay was, of course, legitimate. However, until the paymaster's train came up from Fort Yuma, on the Colorado, there was not a penny to pay them. He was using government scrip himself for supplies and until the money came through there was nothing to do but keep them busy; busy men had not the time to grouse.

For a slightly different reason, Drum kept himself busy. He didn't like the intrigues that his job pointed at, and he didn't like inactivity. And he didn't like to think of Laurie, who had made it plain enough that any love that had been between them before had been buried long ago.

The Holcomb Creek trail carried him three miles west, the valley funnelling down until it was a deep, ferned slot with slender stands of second-growth bull-pine standing back from the edge of the creek. Where a rutted log-trail descended from the mountain, the trail became a road, passing through sharply fragrant mottes of manzanita and buckbrush. Over the tinkling voices of the creek Captain Drum picked out other sounds: a muley-saw's protesting whine and the roar of a waterfall.

He came through the trees onto a bench where a sawmill and a handful of other log buildings stood in the slanting rays of the sun. A flume of whipsawn logs carried the creekwater from where Drum sat his pony to the top of a penstock about fifty feet high. Green water gushed from a gate in the bottom of the penstock to turn a ponderous undershot wheel. Drum watched two men with brown, bare backs feeding logs into the saw.

A voice near him said: "Looking for someone, soldier?" It was a girl's voice. A voice with humor and warmth.

The girl lay on a great gray stone set in the hill, her chin resting on her linked fingers. Drum could see her upper body, slender as a young animal's. He could see her hair, bright gold, with a shining wash of copper. He had to stare for a moment; it was like seeing a scarlet tanager flash though the top branches of the sombre trees on a gray afternoon. She raised herself on her elbows.

Drum said: "Why yes. I'm looking for Mormon Dowling."

"Pop's in the office," the girl said. She slid down the rock and stood beside the trail, slim and brown-legged, with a wild, wanton sort of beauty. "I'm Selena Dowling. I'll take you inside."

Drum dismounted, introduced himself, and they walked to the mill. The girl smiled up at him. "What's the matter?" she said. "Are we fighting the war down here, now?"

"No," Drum answered soberly. "We're just making sure we don't have to."

Selena Dowling looked at him, from boots to forage cap, her eyes frankly admiring. "You Army men," she said. "Vain as peacocks! You had that uniform tailored, didn't you?"

Drum smiled. "The Army way, Miss Dowling, is to give a man a uniform and then tailor *him* to fit it."

They went up six steps to the sawing floor. Here the cry of the muley saw set Drum's nerves on edge, while the air was filled with floating particles of sawdust. The smell of hot pitch was a pleasant tang. They went into an office where a bearlike man sat at a desk counting yellow-backs. He scowled and shoved the money into a drawer.

"Seleny," he said, "don't be comin' in here without knocking. I've told you that."

The girl said, "Company, Pop. This is Captain Drum."

The Mormon looked at him without standing. He was a massive-shouldered, black-browed man with his vices written on his face. A preacher would have called it a face without a soul. Drum was not concerned with souls, but he could find no mercy for an antagonist in Mormon Dowling's small eyes or heavy-lipped mouth.

"What is it you want?" the Mormon said.

Drum gave him a slip of paper on which he had written the amount and description of the lumber he would need. With a stubby finger Dowling dug in his ear. "Is this cash?" he said.

Drum said: "Scrip. It will be redeemed within a few weeks."

The Mormon's eyes wandered up to his face. "I sell for cash."

Drum's jaw set. "This time you sell for scrip," he said. "I'll take the mill over if I have to."

Dowling made a mock gesture of assent, smiling one-sidedly. "Write out your scrip," he said.

Drum endorsed the draft and laid it on the desk. He said: "Another thing. I'm looking for some of my men who deserted a few days ago. Have you seen any other troopers recently?"

He saw a glance pass between the mill owner and his daughter, and he saw the Mormon's dark eyes barricade. But the girl said: "Three men?"

An electric eagerness went through the captain. "Yes. An officer and two privates," he said. "When were they through?"

Selena went on, blithely, while her father pulled his brows down in disapproval. "Yesterday. They stopped and asked directions to Bear Valley." Her eyes sparkled. "A good-looking officer, Captain. Tall and dark; hadn't shaved, or he'd have been downright handsome."

"He was in too much of a hurry to shave. Deserters usually are. Did you show him the way?"

"I took them up to Marcos Pass Lookout. That's only about two miles south, but it's straight up all the way."

Drum addressed his next remark to the Mormon. "I'd like

to ride up there for a look around. Can you spare a man as a guide?''

''I know the trails better than any of the loggers,'' Selena said. ''I'll take you up.''

''You'll stay here,'' said the Mormon curtly.

''There might be trouble,'' Drum agreed. ''They're probably clear to San Bernardino by now; but just in case—''

Selena opened the door, admitting the shriek of the saw and freshened odors of sawdust and pitch. ''I'll saddle my pony,'' she called back.

Mormon Dowling shoved the scrip roughly in the drawer. His face showed anger, yet a rueful sort of amusement, too, ''Damned little vixen,'' he said. ''Wild as a catamount. But I reckon she can take keer of herself as well as any man.''

They followed the log road for a mile, crossing a meadow blocked with fresh pine stumps that stood like stakes. The light mountain air carried the ring of axes from the still wooded section. Selena led across a creek and they started up the mountain trail. She had changed to denim pants, and she rode as easily as any cowhand.

Two miles, she had said. Most of it was along shelving ledges and slippery, tilted carpets of pine needles. They reached the Lookout, a high saddle in the timber, where the wind combed the treetops with a soft, secret music and the vista was of blue ranges to the south, and then a great void where the valley lay, and farther still the pinkish bulk of San Gorgonio thrusting frostily into the sky.

''That notch is the Pass,'' Selena said, pointing. ''Bear Valley is eight miles from here.'' The wind's fingers were in her hair, and her eyes were bits of the sky's own blue. Many men might love her, Drum thought, but no man would ever own her. She was too wild; freedom was the very pulse of her.

Then his reflections were scattered, as something struck the rock beside him with a sharp, explosive sound. Drum had heard this sound before; thus he was rolling his spurs and driving against Selena's horse an instant before the crack of the rifle invaded the forest stillness.

IV

Revolt in the Mountains

He sent the girl's pony clattering down the trail. He drew his carbine and swung from the saddle, giving the horse a single command. The animal lay down and remained rigidly still, while Drum sprawled in the space between head and chest and laid his rifle-barrel across the sorrel's neck.

The scent of burned powder came to him. He noted the direction of the wind, and after this it was not difficult to locate the sniper. Directly before him, a hundred feet away, was a pile of moss-blackened boulders. Into a notch of this natural battlement he saw a gun-muzzle thrust; a dark head rose behind it.

Drum knew the angry thoughts that would be in that treacherous head: disgust at having muffed the rifle shot, and at having now to resort to a pistol. He got the face behind the gun in the notch of his battle-sights. He did not hurry the shot; the advantage now was his, and he would make it count. Steadily he took up trigger-slack; just before the hammer fell another ball thudded against the earth and spat dirt over him. The dark head rose higher, studying, and Drum felt his own weapon thrust against his shoulder.

Selena, crouching behind a manzanita, cried out excitedly: "You got him!"

Drum said: "Stay where you are!" He changed swiftly to his .44. The sniper's revolver clattered down the rocks. There was no sign of the man, now, and though the cavalryman waited several minutes, no other gunmen showed themselves.

Drum circled the rocks and saw the body lying crumpled in a cleft of the boulders. He was not surprised to find that the sniper wore the blue and yellow of the cavalry. Going closer, he discovered that it was Gorton, one of the deserters.

A high flame of eagerness mounted through him. If Gorton had been posted as sentry, Mirabeau and the other trooper would not be far off. It was Drum's thought that at this moment he was not more than a mile from the mountain rendezvous of the Bear Flag Battalion. Yet he did not dare go farther, if only for the sake of the girl. If there were any considerable organization to be reckoned with, it would not be moved far or fast before tomorrow.

He went back to the girl. "I'll take you back," he said. "The rest may be here before long."

She let him help her to the saddle, and he noticed that there was no pallor or trembling in her. She held his hand for a moment. "I like you, Captain," she said, in her frank, open way. "I have never liked very many men."

Caught without an answer, Drum felt color flame into his face. He made himself busy for a moment with her latigo. "I suspect the reverse can't be said," he remarked. "I am sure many men have liked you. A rifle ball seems to be the way to your heart."

Selena laughed. "A gruesome way to put it," she said.

They rode back. Not far from the sawmill she let him pull in beside her. She gave him a direct, earnest glance. "Have you ever lived in a place like this?" she asked. "I mean, without anyone to talk to except a man who can't see beyond his cash drawer, and a crew of loggers without much space between the eyes?"

"I've lived in army camps," Drum replied. "They aren't always what the recruiting sergeants tell you."

Selena's face showed an inner eagerness. "An army camp would be like heaven compared to this," she told him. "A woman isn't young forever. And she can get old in a hurry. I remember my mother used to tell me that and I saw it work out, in her case. We followed Pop around to logging camps and mining camps and wild-horse trapping outfits. She married young. I guess she never went to a dance in her life. She died when I was twelve. I made a promise when she died, Captain: That I would see some of the world besides the back woods. I still mean to keep it."

Drum looked at her, sensing the ferment within her, the pressure of youth seeking an outlet. "You will, Selena," he said. "You haven't the kind of spirit they can tie down. And when you get out you'll have enough men around you to start an army of your own."

Selena stopped her pony under the branches of a black oak, facing him with eyes that had a challenge. "I don't want an army," she said. "Just the man I pick. Do you want to kiss me, Captain?"

Drum did. Not because he loved her, because he was too close to the hoyden spirit, the impulsive heart of her, to be concerned with anything so complex as love. She was a coquette, and it would have been the same with any man she took a fancy to; but it did not render her lips any less warm when Drum drew her toward him and brought her body tight against his.

They were both breathless after he released her. All the hunger of his love for Laurie had gone into that kiss; but when it was all over he knew that hunger had not been satisfied even for a moment, for Laurie's lips had been between them.

When he left her at the Mormon's Mill, she watched him remount with a high color along her cheekbones. "You'll be back, Captain," she said.

Drum hesitated. "Yes," he said finally. "I'll be back." If only with a posse for the deserters, he thought. He didn't know how well his desire for her would wear after he was out of her sight . . .

It was after nightfall when he returned to camp. First Sergeant McCullah was waiting at his tent with a cigarette in his lips which he threw down and tromped out as the captain dismounted. Drum had noticed the strange lack of activity about the camp. McCullah's stony face told him there was trouble.

"Where are the men?" Drum asked him.

McCullah's jaw muscles worked. "In town, sir," he said. "I took roll call an hour ago and there's twenty-four missing. Lieutenant Kelsey ain't back yet. I told them there would be company punishment for any that left camp."

Drum struck his gloved hands together. He began to smile. "Do you reckon two old-army men are as good as twenty-four volunteers, McCullah?" he said.

When McCullah grinned, it was like ice breaking up; his dark skin folded into many wrinkles and his eyes and his even teeth flashed. "I'll saddle and be right with you, Captain," he said.

Belleville possessed many saloons, but only one Hollow Log. An immense section of pine log, a door cut in the heart of it, made a woody halo about the entrance. Inside, yellowing pine boughs framed every door and window. The light came from lamps roosting about the rims of horizontally suspended wagon wheels.

Drum and the sergeant stood in the doorway. The bar of

the Hollow Log was a solid rank of blue. Here and there at gaming tables sat a trooper or two; a few more men of the Fourth California moved about the dancing area in back, with the bar girls. Mayor Matt Harrower, his bear-trap mouth full of laughter, had his arms about the shoulders of Corporal Neff and Corporal Foxen, the bugler.

Drum said to the first sergeant, "Bring Foxen over here."

McCullah spoke to the bugler, who reared back and swore in his face. The mayor made pacifying gestures with his hands, but Sergeant McCullah stepped up to Foxen and brought his fist up, almost gently, under his jaw. He caught the sagging body and half carried it to the door. Matt Harrower came along. No one but a few men at the bar had seen it happen.

Foxen looked angry and undecided when he saw the captain. Harrower tucked his thumbs in his vest pockets. "Aren't you being a little hard on the boys, Captain?" he said. "A little likker lubricates the joints."

"It also disgraces the uniform and leaves the camp unprotected," said Drum flatly. "Sound Assembly, Corporal."

Foxen, his eyes rebellious, unslung the bugle and blew the call, the sharp brassy sounds cleaving the mix of saloon noises. Every man in the saloon, and a dozen spangled beauties, stared at the quartet by the door.

Drum said: "You've got five minutes to finish your drinking and fall in by the pine tree." As he turned to go, he heard Corporal Neff's voice.

"Maybe we ain't finished, Captain. What about that?"

What Neff did, the captain knew, would be a pattern for the conduct of the rest. He walked down the bar and stopped before him.

"Well, if you're sure you aren't ready," he said, "we might as well settle it right now. Peel off, mister."

He removed his own saber, revolver, and tunic and laid them on the bar. The red-head, moving with jerky eagerness, followed suit. He faced the captain, his fists knotted, but still hanging at his sides. To Drum, there was a fantastic side to it: the War Department would have demanded his commission in an hour if his brawling with an enlisted man in a saloon were ever reported. But the portent of this moment went deeper than the customs of the service. The valley was a serpent that wanted only a touch to come to life. While it lay dormant, Drum could lay his traps. Once aroused, it would be too late. A challenge like Neff's could be the impetus to wake the sleeping fangs.

Neff stepped in fast, driving for the captain's face. Drum tilted his head and the fist slipped past; he gave Neff a short jab to the stomach. The corporal grunted, backing away. Drum did not follow him. He counted on the enlisted man's temper matching his hair; an angry opponent was always a floundering one.

With some discretion, Corporal Neff advanced again, keeping his guard up this time. Drum feinted at his stomach, and when the big, freckled fists dropped he found Neff's nose with a stinging left. Now the corporal was bleeding and hurt and filled with rage. He moved in without caution, swinging savage roundhouse blows.

Captain Drum took them on his shoulders, his forearms. He let the trooper swing until he was winded, now and then slashing short and hard through an opening. Neff slowed down; his breath labored through swollen lips. And then Drum went to work.

A cracking blow over the eye stunned the man and stood him up like a target. Drum threw a hard one against his jaw, following it instantly with a driving blow to the mouth which sent Neff stumbling down the bar. Drum followed, hooking, jabbing, cutting the horsey face until the blood splattered as he landed each telling blow. There was a stricken look in the corporal's face now. He was finished, but he could not fall. Drum sank a fist in his stomach that doubled him up, then slugged him on the jaw. Neff went down, a clean blue pattern against the tawny sawdust.

Drum put on his tunic and walked out without a glance back. And as he went, carrying his equipment, he heard them following him.

V

Gold Camp Recruits

In the morning a courier from Fort Yuma rode in on a gaunt-looking mount. Drum read the letter he carried and was relieved to learn that the government pay-train would make rendezvous with them in Bear Valley in two days. But at the same time he was worried. They were too close to the Bear Flaggers' hide-out. There was small chance of cutting sign on the rebels before the rendezvous, unless Mirabeau's trail led him to their stronghold. He was deciding how many men he could afford to take with him when Lieutenant Kelsey appeared with a group of six miners. The officer seemed crestfallen.

"Recruits, Captain," Kelsey announced. "I covered most of the diggings, but we don't seem to be popular."

Drum swore them in and sent them off in charge of a non-com to draw equipment. Then he called back one of the men to whom he had given the oath. "Did you say your man was Rockaway?" he asked.

The man grinned. He was a young fellow with blond hair and friendly brown eyes, a jaw like a saddle-horn and a big man's fists. He nodded. "I got tired of shoveling gold out of the hills while other men are shoveling trenches. Think we'll see any action?"

"Liable to," Drum said. Then he said: "You're engaged to Laurie Owen, aren't you?"

Rockaway grinned. "That's right. You must have liked the Army, Captain, to have given her up."

"So she told you," Drum said. "This puts us both in an embarrassing position, Rockaway. I don't make a secret of the fact that I'd still marry Laurie if she'd have me. Perhaps I should have you transferred to Pennsylvania!"

Rockaway shrugged. "I joined up to fight. But if you transfer me, I don't think it will be for revenge."

Drum walked toward the quartermaster's tent with him. "If you know these hills," he said, "I can put you to work right away. I found proof yesterday that two men who deserted in the desert are hiding near Bear Valley. We're taking their trail this morning."

"I've spent ten years up here," Rockaway said. "I can take you to every cave and canyon big enough to hide a jack-rabbit."

John Drum watched him join the men getting outfitted. A well set-up lad, he thought, with the makings of a good soldier. He sighed. It would have pleased him to have been able to suspect Dave Rockaway of sedition. Admiration was the last thing he wanted to feel for a rival.

While he was waiting for the detail to form, Laurie Owen

came rattling down the creek road in a buggy. She stopped by his tent. She was smiling, but he saw soberness behind her eyes.

"So you've stolen my fiancé," she said. "I didn't think you'd misuse your power this way, John."

"I tried to talk him out of it," Drum told her. "Now that he's in, I won't have to worry about running into him when I go courting. I thought you'd give him back his ring for joining, though. I remember once before when you did that to a man."

His irony did not disconcert her. "This was patriotism," she said. "The other time it was—running away." Then she changed the subject, indicating a pile of boots in the space behind the seat. "I'm taking these down to the Mormon's. Those loggers go through a pair of soles in a month. If you have any to be repaired, I'll pick them up on the way back."

Drum chuckled. "I may have a few pairs, at that." He noticed a high black knee-boot on the top of the pile, and his smile faded. "That's a cavalry boot," he said sharply. "Does that go to the sawmill?"

Laurie said quietly: "That's the real reason I stopped here. Look at it."

Drum picked up the boot, which had seen hard wear but had thick, new soles. He glanced inside, near the top, and what he saw made his heart strike his ribs. The boot was marked: *Anthony R. Mirabeau, Lt. 4th Calif. Cav.*

"Dad tried to tell you the other day," Laurie said. "He used to talk Union all the time, until a couple of fires were started in the shop at night that cost us six months' profit. We knew it would be a bullet the next time."

She looked at the heap of mended boots. "Those don't all belong to loggers. The Mormon sends up a half-dozen pairs a week. He's only got fifteen men on his payroll. Most of the boots are miners'. Someone is drilling troops in these hills. And I think the Mormon knows who—and where."

"You don't think it's Mormon Dowling?"

"Dad and I think that Matt Harrower is the kingpin. It would logically be a man who knows all the undercurrents he has to reckon with. And that would mean the mayor."

Drum stood there with the boot in his hand, thinking that as small a thing as this could make or break a revolution; that if he could follow this clue down to its source, he could destroy the Bear Flag movement before it went any farther. But if Mirabeau got his troops out of the San Bernardinos and began to prey on the stage and freight lines from Los Angeles, a hundred other secret organizations would rush to join him. And then, with the supply line two thousand miles long, across the Seven Deserts of the Territory, it might be too late to beat out the flames of revolt.

He threw the boot back into the buggy. "I'll take a few men and deliver these for you," he said. "I don't like to spoil a good customer, but we may be throwing some business in the way of the undertaker before we're through."

He had the boots loaded onto a pack animal. With fifteen men, he started for the sawmill. He had picked his men, McCullah and the best rifle shots in the troop, for if there were a battle it would likely be a forest skirmish where sabers would be almost useless.

They rode down the river, feeling the coolness and moisture of the air on their skin. Some distance short of the mill, Drum called a halt. He looked at the faces of the men; they were surly and stubborn, but deeper than that he saw the beginnings of confidence in themselves and their weapons. They would never believe that the endless drilling they had undergone had made something like soldiers out of them, but when they came face to face with slaughter and exhaustion, they would stand up like men, and marvel at their own courage.

"I'll go on alone," Drum told McCullah. "If the Mormon sees a gang like this he may fight on general principles. I don't know how many men we have to reckon with, but if I can get inside, I may be able to find out what we want to know without a scrap. Give me five minutes, then attack."

He jogged boldly into the mill yard, between piles of fresh-sawn planks. The undershot wheel sent up its creaking and the saw screamed monotonously, just as though there were nothing to differentiate this mill from any other. As he dismounted, he saw the Mormon standing on the sawing floor. The mill owner stood at the top of the steps, and Drum stopped a step below him. In the Mormon's piggish eyes could be read anything—warning, or anger, or native sullenness.

"The lumber goes out tomorrow," he said. "That what you came for?"

Selena came to stand behind her father. The same tension was in her face that filled the sawmill. The four men at the saw-table had stopped to watch.

Drum said: "It appears we'll be here longer than I thought. My instructions are to put up permanent barracks. It will mean a big order. Suppose we go inside and talk prices."

Selena's eyes were saying, *No!* But her attitude was casual as she stood there with one hand on her hip.

"We can talk about it here," the Mormon said.

Drum spoke impatiently. "We'll both lose our voices if we try to shout over that saw any longer."

Mormon Dowling's bulky shoulders moved carelessly; then he turned and led the way toward the office.

Selena Dowling walked beside the trooper. "Are you crazy?" she whispered. "Mirabeau is in there. He came back last night. He'll kill you."

Drum said: "Get out of here. There may be shooting."

The Mormon passed through the door first and just before Drum entered the room Selena's slender body thrust itself in front of him. Thus the lean, dark man in cavalry blues who sat behind the desk held his fire for an instant. Mirabeau had just shaved; his jaws were still shining from the touch of the razor, and his small mustache was a clean, black line. Suave and cynical and dangerous—that was Mirabeau.

Drum's gun was already out, but he was not prepared for the pair who leaped upon him from either side of the door.

He went down loosely, feeling the brutal impact of a gun-barrel against his head, Selena's scream hammering against his ears.

He had a memory of many men moving through the room, of shots and angry cries. Then there was silence, until the shock of icy water brought him back to consciousness.

McCullah had loosened his collar, was holding a dipper of water near his face while he tried to sit up. John Drum drank some of the water before he said: "Outflanked, McCullah. They got away?"

"The Mormon, Mirabeau and two others," answered the Sergeant. "They made it across the flume before we realized what was happening. Their horses were tethered in the brush. We dropped three of the loggers."

Full recollection came back to Drum, like a fist around his heart. He said: "The girl?"

The Sergeant closed one eye and made a clucking sound. "Game as a catamount. She dived out the window when the shooting started and waited for us. She took the boys on up the hill after them. What trails she don't know, Rockaway may."

But when the troopers returned, it was without encouragement. Drum left two men at the mill to stand watch. Selena Dowling stayed with them, confident that the Mormon and his cronies would not return.

As they started off, Dave Rockaway looked back once. "Plucky little devil," he said. "Knows these hills better than I do. And ain't afraid to ride 'em."

Looking at him, Drum had a thought that was not entirely scrupulous. Perhaps Rockaway's interest in her could be helped along a little—a few passes, sentry duty at the mill, and the like . . .

VI

Rebel King

It was near sundown when they returned, but Laurie was still there with the buggy. Drum drove her back to town. She was full of curiosity about the skirmish at the sawmill, but her questions did not come until they were rattling up the road. Drum felt her gaze on him as he drove.

"There's a cut on your forehead," she remarked. "Was there a fight?"

Drum told her about it. "Aren't you interested in how Dave Rockaway came out?" he asked. He was smiling, and the color spread out quickly on her cheeks.

She said tartly: "Of course! I supposed he was all right, or you'd have said so."

"He's fine," Drum told her. "He spent most of the afternoon riding around with Selena Dowling. They seem to hit it off pretty well. But then, any man would get along with Selena."

Laurie made an almost imperceptible sniffing sound. "You know, you didn't have to drive me back to town, if there was anything else you'd rather be doing."

Drum said: "I'm going in on business. This boot thing of

yours has begun to work into something big. I'm going to talk to Harrower."

He left her at the shop and walked into the early night, full of optimism. Of one thing he was sure: Laurie had taken Dave Rockaway on the rebound. Whether or not her loyalty would make her go on with the marriage was another matter . . .

Matt Harrower's living quarters were behind the shop where he sold mining equipment. When there was no answer to Drum's knock, no gleam of light in the dark building, the cavalryman walked down an alley and approached the store from the rear. He held a match to the window and could make out the foggy outlines of a table, a chair and a cot. But it was the stout, steel-banded trunk in one corner that held Drum's interest.

A stout brass padlock on the door blocked entrance that way, and Drum inspected the casing of the window. It was the usual wood-and-adobe proposition: a frame of one-inch lumber mortared into the opening with mud plaster. Drum went to work with a knife. Ten minutes was all he required to scrape away enough mud to loosen the whole casing. He crawled into the room.

Now, as he stood in the small room, sorting the impressions that came to him, sounds reached him; the room was dark and cold as a cellar, smelling of stale coffee and dirty linen. Drum lighted a candle.

The trunk was locked. He brought an eight-pound maul from the front and smashed the hasp loose. Then he went swiftly through the trunk, finding nothing but clothing and a few old books.

Drum remembered now the red door in the main room, the one with the sign reading: *Explosives. Keep out.*

It took longer to break into this compartment. After he had smashed the padlock to pieces, Drum stood and listened. Only dim sounds from the saloon, a faint singing and the muted clatter of glassware, came to him. He went inside and shut the door, then carefully struck a match. At the same instant, his breath caught.

The cubicle was only a blind. Along the walls were ranged kegs of black powder and coils of fuse. In the center of the dirt floor was an open trapdoor with stairs leading away into blackness. As he stood there, Drum heard a sound.

Just a whisper, the faintest tinkle of a spurrowel, but Drum knew that nothing moves so lightly as Death. The cellar opening was suddenly a doorway to hell. Men were down there: he didn't know how many; there was a way, possibly, to tell. He extinguished the candle and rolled a powder keg to the top of the stairs; with a shove he sent it thundering down into blackness, then followed swiftly after it.

A man shouted profanely. Someone cried out, and there was the room-trapped sound of a shot. Silence came then, until a man said cautiously: "Matt?" It was the nasal voice of Corporal Neff.

"Right here," Mayor Matt Harrower growled. "I think he slipped on the stairs. The light went out and down he come. Reckon I got him."

Rusty metal scraped, and across the blackness drove the startling beam of a hurricane lantern. Drum saw the two men staring down at the splintered keg. A table stood behind them, and there were maps on the wall, as well as a flag showing a brown bear on a white background. Drum stepped from the stairway into the room.

"All right, boys," he announced quietly. "The Army's moving in now."

Neff dropped the hood of the lantern and reached for his gun just as darkness rushed into the cellar. Drum fired once and moved quickly from the spot. There was no sign from the corporal; not until a Colt blasted into the blackness, and then Neff and Harrower began to move frantically. Drum knew the rush would be for the stairs. He sent a shot where he reckoned the red-head would be; in the brief flash he saw him break stride and twist spasmodically, trying to claw at his back.

He heard Harrower plunging up the stairs. When he moved to follow him, four shots came in staccato from the top. Drum heard the door of the dynamite room bang open. He ascended cautiously. The store was soundless when he gained the top. He went out into the alley, but there was no trace of Harrower, no sign that the gunfight had been heard by other ears. Drum knew the futility of trying to scare up a posse to hunt his man down. It would be better to scour the cellar stronghold now and form his own posse later.

Neff was dying when he returned to place the lamp on the table. He was breathing in a snoring fashion, his mouth streaming blood. Horror was no novelty to Drum; he ignored the dying man while he made a quick inspection of the room.

On the wall were colored maps of various sections of the State, showing in red all the stage and freight trails. Black stars along these routes could have meant anything; Drum's notion was that they indicated vulnerable points to be struck when the Bear Flaggers were ready. In a wooden box against the wall he found the correspondence of the Bear Flag outfit. As he riffled through it, he realized that all the tangled life-lines of the organization, from San Diego to the Oregon border, had their source in this cellar.

The letters were all addressed to "Mayor Matt Harrower." Many were terse, ungrammatical scrawls: "We got twenty-five men drilling now. Carbine for each and six sabers for outfit. Talking about combining with the Santa Barbara outfit. Would this be all right?"

In another receptacle, a tin strong-box, were onion-skin letterpress copies of organization rosters. A glance showed Drum that the Bear Flag Battalion numbered something over a thousand. Who knew how many other thousands would be drawn to this wild-eyed core, like filings to a magnet, when the rebels took the field? Drum paid special attention to the Holcomb Valley roster. He counted seventy-six names, including those of Mormon Dowling and Lieutenant Mirabeau.

With his search completed, he noticed a much-folded sheet of yellow paper lying on the table where the two men had sat. He read it, scanning again the words that the courier from Fort Yuma had brought him. Neat, traditional phrases that had the force of a thousand bugles: *Government pay-train consisting of one officer and twelve enlisted men . . . proceed to a point known as Marble Rock . . . to make contact not later than July 26 . . .*

July 26! The detail bringing the gold would be somewhere on the Green Canyon trail, now, riding into whatever ambush the Mormon and Mirabeau had prepared for them. Drum had carried the dispatch with him, intending to destroy it. He had not had time, however, because the Mormon had removed it from his pocket while he was unconscious.

An hour ago there had been no hurry to make contact with the train. A four hour's ride in the morning would have brought them to Marble Rock, at the head of Green Canyon. Now it was clear that they must ride like fools to head off Mirabeau's party.

VII

Boots and Saddles!

It was an hour before Drum made it back to camp. He awoke Sergeant McCullah and Lieutenant Kelsey and ordered them both to his tent in fifteen minutes. He gave Foxen, the bugler, the order for Boots and Saddles. Foxen gave him an incredulous stare, as if wondering whether this martinet did not know that a night detail, with the men in their present rebellious mood, might be the last pound of pressure to cause an explosion.

In his tent, Drum showed Kelsey and McCullah what he had brought from Harrower's cellar. "It's the real thing, this time," he said. "Matt Harrower jerks the wires for all of California. He's jerked them this time to intercept our paytrain in Green Canyon. If they reach them before we do, we've lost doubly—they've got gold to operate on and we've lost whatever chance we still have to hold D Troop together."

Kelsey's still sleepy eyes were sardonic. "Does the captain think any of the men will re-enlist?" he asked.

Drum regarded Kelsey carefully, noting the bored manner, the petulant mouth. "You're very young, Lieutenant," he said. "Very young and very inexperienced." He said, as if changing the subject: "Have you ever seen a man decapitated by a saber?"

Kelsey's eyes flinched.

Drum drew his sword and turned the bright blade in his hands. "Sometime tonight or tomorrow morning you'll see how one of these looks when it's running with blood. If you're lucky, you'll learn how it feels when it passes through bone. If you're not, you'll learn the other lesson. You and the rest of my pea-green command will find out about horror and fear.

"Dying men make ghastly sounds; they get under your horse's feet and scream when they are stepped on. But you keep on swinging, because you're fighting for your life. You've forgotten all about strategy and plans of attack, but you fight like a madman, cutting your way through a wall of flesh, and when you break through you realize, suddenly, that you've carried out your plan. The enemy is yours. Do you know why you've succeeded, even after you forgot everything but how much you wanted to live?''

Kelsey only stared, his jaw hanging.

"Because a man you hated made you drill in the sun," Drum continued relentlessly. "Because he woke you up on a score of nights and made you ride around officering resentful troopers. He made you take so many imaginary enemies that when you came up against a real one you did it automatically."

Suddenly Drum smiled, a little pityingly. The lieutenant's face was waxy. He said, "I'm sorry if I've been crude, Mister Kelsey. But I want you to know what you're going into. And I want to hear you swear at your men and threaten them and saber the first who turns back. Afterwards, I'll join you in praising them."

Kelsey said, "Yes, sir," and went outside, forgetting to salute. They heard him pause on the walk, getting a deep breath of cool air.

Drum had a pint of brandy in his portmanteau. He poured two inches in a tin cup and handed it to First Sergeant McCullah. "Gaines Mill, Sergeant," he said.

"Gaines Mill," the Irishman said. They drank the brandy. "And don't worry abut the men," McCullah said. "No outfit that can complain so much can be too short on fight."

D Troop formed resentfully on the drill field, sabers clanking, horses snorting in the crisp mountain air. Drum sat his horse, his commands coming with a hard ring. He watched the men swing into the saddle. They faced him in silence, their faces lighter patches along the dark line. There was hate in those faces, but in a few hours there would be so much fear in them that they would have no room for hate. Then they would either hold, because he had made them strong, or they would break, because he had failed.

His voice went sharply through the night. "Right by twos— ho!"

The going was swift on the meadows, but when they swung up the Marcos Pass trail caution was the order. He sent Rockaway and a non-com ahead to smell out traps. About midnight a cold slice of moon rose over the hills to filter a wan light through the trees. The pines stood starkly menacing as they worked upward toward Marcos Pass. It was cold; the men had their tunics buttoned high and their gauntlets pulled up over their cuffs.

They halted for a ten-minute break in the high gap known as Marcos Pass. Below them, Bear Valley was a dark, echoing void, full of the whisper of moving waters. Miles to the right a notch in the chain of timbered peaks showed where Green Canyon cut toward the desert, a two days' ride west.

A pre-dawn grayness was in the east by the time they reached the valley floor. Rockaway came back with the other scout from Marble Rock. He gave his report with subdued excitement.

"We raised 'em in the canyon below the rock," he announced. "There's lights along both sides of the canyon where they're smoking. They haven't been soldiering long enough to learn about giving away their position."

"Any chance for a frontal attack?" Drum asked him.

Rockaway shook his head, making a sketch in the dirt. "The canyon is straight up and down. They're deployed along a hundred-foot front. If we attack on this side of the canyon we'll run into cross-fire from the other side. I'd advise sending a detail across to the other side to strike at the same time we hit them. It's chancy, though."

Drum said: "That's the way the Eighteenth did it at Hunt's Ferry. Does fighting come natural to you?"

Rockaway grinned. "I fought the Kaws under Major Hastings for two years. That was six years ago."

"You got out before the war, though."

Rockaway said, "You bet. I didn't mind the fighting so much. But I hate the spit and polish, and fifteen dollars a month isn't much for working like a pit mule."

In the gloom, Drum looked at him. This man hated the Army, and yet he had joined again. He had given up Laurie, perhaps, and his stake in a gold boom that couldn't last forever, to risk his life. It made it a little painful to think of his own reason for joining . . .

Near the head of Green Canyon, Drum split his command. He said to Lieutenant Kelsey, "Take your men across here and time it to attack in a half hour. The bugle will be the signal. Allow yourself some leeway, in case the pay-train should come through sooner. And watch out for traps. Mirabeau is no fool.''

Drum took his command along the narrow mountain trail on the precipitous north wall of Green Canyon. The river brawled in the grayness far below, sending up its moist coolness. Suddenly Rockaway spoke to Drum.

''They're directly below us, Captain.''

Drum picked out the skirmish line that Rockaway's finger indicated, perhaps a quarter-mile below them in the rocky bed of the canyon. There was little to indicate where the Bear Flaggers lay, except an occasional movement of man or horse. The animals were tethered back in the pines on the steep hillside; the ambuscaders had their positions in a fringe of willows along the river road.

The situation was ideal—mounted troops against dismounted. Drum's pulse quickened. He consulted his watch. Twenty minutes since he had left Kelsey. If they could remain undiscovered until Kelsey had had time to take up his position, they could crush Mirabeau's force with one stroke.

Sergeant McCullah rode along the line, talking to the tight-lipped noncoms. He gave them nothing but irony and censure, but the men he spoke to somehow sat a little straighter after it. McCullah stopped near the captain to scan the canyon, as the first spears of daylight struck the tops of the trees. He stared, his body rigid.

''Captain!'' he said. ''Look there!''

Drum's first warning was the tinkle of a harness bell. Then he saw what the sergeant had indicated—a little line of pack-animals and a dozen blue-coated troopers riding into the ambush . . .

Now there was no time to wait for Kelsey, no time for anything but shouting the charge and plunging down the slope at the head of the line. Foxen pulled in beside him; halfway down Drum gave him the signal to sound the charge for Kelsey—if Kelsey could possibly be within a mile of the battlefield.

Below them, startled men were pouring out of the willows and running for their mounts. The horse-holders fought the excited ponies while the rebels tried to mount. And now rifle fire broke from the trees across the river. Over there other men were leaving their carefully selected vantage points to mount and meet Drum's charge.

Among the miscellany of miner's rigs and nondescript attire one uniform stood out—Mirabeau's, as he whipped his men into formation. Across the river another skirmish line was forming, the Mormon's voice coming hoarsely. There would be no surprise now, no quick victory. Every foot they won would be at a cost.

Drum glanced along the surging, sliding line to each side of him. The men of D Troop were too busy avoiding falls to worry about what lay ahead. But as they hit the flat above the road the Bear Flaggers came out in a wide spearhead, and sabers came up with one impulse.

They tangled, the blue tide and the patchwork; but it was the blue that plunged on. The men were yelling, sabers bloody, tasting the strong brandy of victory. Anxiety struck at Drum. It had been too easy; the line had given way in the middle like a rotten cord. And there was still no sign of Kelsey's detail. They were badly outnumbered, and suddenly he saw Mirabeau's strategy. It would not have worked, with Lieutenant Kelsey as a diverting force. But Kelsey was not there. Drum was confronting the Mormon and his band, splashing across the river to tangle with them, and he was flanked on each end by the two segments of Mirabeau's broken line.

He shouted at McCullah: "Deploy three squads in the rocks to hold Mirabeau! I'll take the Mormon."

He met the Mormon's forty-man thrust with twenty sabers. Drum picked out the bearish man's red plaid shirt and met him in mid-river, half-standing in the stirrups with his saber out across the head of his mount. There was no sureness in the way Mormon Dowling charged him, waving his sword like a flag. The blade came down like a guillotine at the top of Drum's head.

It was the easiest parry of all. Drum's blade tipped up and slipped the force of the Mormon's stroke. His saber came down again, finding the soft flesh under his opponent's collarbone. The blade sank in to the hilt, so that the force of Drum's charge hurled his victim from the saddle.

As he wheeled now to pick out another, he saw things that made him proud of these rebellious parade-ground soldiers of his. They were not throwing away an inch. They were dug in like bulldogs, sabering, swearing, emptying their pistols with their left hands, as he had taught them to do. But they were falling, too, borne down by superior numbers.

Back in the willows, McCullah and his men were on their knees, mangling Mirabeau's troopers with their accurate fire. They had tried a rush and been thrown back. Now they were packing in closer for a charge that must succeed by sheer weight and daring.

Drum saw it coming. He wished there were some way he could tell these men that he was proud of them—that at last they were the soldiers he had tried to make of them, and that they were not being slaughtered because of any fault of theirs. A laggard officer who had, perhaps, deliberately delayed his charge, was responsible for that.

He heard McCullah roar a fire order, and knew as he turned back to meet a rebel's charge that Mirabeau was coming through. And then he heard another voice—a high-pitched voice without much confidence in it, but stiffened, somehow, with determination. Kelsey was here. Kelsey, who had thought to fight the war in the drawing rooms of Sacramento, was throwing his men against Mirabeau's!

Mirabeau swerved, confused, and First Sergeant McCullah called up the horse-holders and remounted his men. He struck at the dark-faced deserter from the left flank, so that Kelsey was able to draw off half his platoon to go to Drum's aid. The blond lieutenant had blood on him. He had lost his forage cap. His tunic was ripped open and he went into the mass with a slaughter-house swing.

Matt Harrower was the first of the rebels to turn back, a man who liked to fight in the dark with the odds on his side. Drum levelled his revolver and picked him out of the saddle as he hit the road.

There was nothing now to keep the Bear Flaggers' courage from leaking away except a thing called *esprit de corps*, and the rebels had not been taught the meaning of that phrase. They broke. They tried to escape, and the men of the Fourth California cut them down or took them prisoner. But when they started back up the canyon with the pay-train in tow, only twenty men went with them as prisoners.

* * *

In the coolness of the late afternoon Drum dismissed the men on the drill field. They were tired and half-sick with the things they had seen. But he liked the way they held their ranks until he released them. There was respect in it, for him and for themselves. Lieutenant Kelsey came to his tent after the surgeon had taken care of his wound. Kelsey looked sheepish.

"I don't believe we need to worry about the men any more, Captain," he said. "They've started wrangling about which platoon accounted for the most Bear Flaggers. I heard Corporal Foxen promise that his platoon would bag two men for the Second's one, next time they go out."

First Sergeant McCullah was there, helping with the report. He said to Kelsey: "That's right, sir. They started gambling as soon as they got their pay. They're old soldiers, now." It was the first time McCullah had used the "sir" with Lieutenant Kelsey.

Passes were issued that night, and Drum rode into Belleville with Dave Rockaway. Just short of the town the Owen buggy came down the road in a swirl of dust, with Laurie on the seat. She stopped, Rockaway and Drum dismounting beside the buggy. They looked at her.

Laurie jumped down. She seemed completely oblivious of Rockaway. She took John Drum's hands and looked at him with relief and resentment. "The least you could do would be to let me know you were all right!" she told him. "Your men have been coming in for an hour."

"I've been pretty busy," Drum said. "Of course I wasn't sure whether it mattered much to you anyway."

Laurie did not seem to think it was funny. Then Dave Rockaway spoke.

"Hello, Laurie," he said. "I thought you'd be glad to know I was all right, too."

Laurie released Drum's hands. She said: "Oh!" and then stopped, without the words to go on.

Rockaway smiled. "I think maybe we went into this kind of sudden," he said. "Naturally I won't hold you to your promise, if you want to change your mind."

Drum watched the girl, enjoying her discomfiture. "I guess nobody's got to decide anything right now," he said. "Rockaway, suppose you ride down to the sawmill and see about that lumber."

Rockaway saluted. He said, "Yes, sir. Maybe I'd better

scout around a little to be sure there aren't any more Bear Flaggers running loose, too. I know where I can get a guide.''

''It might be a good idea,'' Drum told him.

He had dinner in the little room behind the shoe shop. Afterwards, he and Laurie walked up the creek and sat on the bank to watch the sunset. Laurie was very quiet. It was plain that she had something deep and troubling on her mind.

''I've been thinking about us and the Army, John,'' she said at last. ''I suppose I wouldn't mind being an Army wife so much, if that's what you want. After it's all over—''

''After it's over,'' Drum interrupted her, ''we're going back to Texas, Laurie. We're going to pry that ranch back out of the *brasada* and dare them to put us off. And I have a notion we'll still be there, twenty years from now.''

Laurie did not ask what had changed his mind. Men made up their own minds, and women made the best of it. But it was in the smile deep in her eyes that sometimes a woman could turn her man's mind in just about the direction she wanted . . .

Matt Stuart is the most prominent of three pseudonyms used by L. P. Holmes for his Western novels and short stories (the other two being Dave Hardin and Perry Westwood). More than a dozen of Holmes's fifty-plus novels appeared under the Stuart name, notably Gun Law at Vermilion *(1947),* Bonanza Gulch *(1949),* Deep Hills *(1954), and* The Lonely Law *(1957). As with his earlier story in this volume, "Farallone Bounty" has an authentic and evocatively drawn background: pirate menace on foggy San Francisco Bay and the Farallone Islands in the 1870s.*

Farallone Bounty

★★★★★★★★★★★★★★★

Matt Stuart

I

THERE were three of them and they were growing surly, for they had bet their cards neither wisely nor well. Sheldon watched them closely as they pushed back from the gaming table and drifted with growling reluctance to the door. He hooked a thumb in his vest pocket and, beneath his palm and spread fingers, could feel the comforting bulk of his gold-mounted derringer. These burly fellows from the foothill "diggings" were unpredictable and it never hurt to be on the alert.

But they went out and slammed the stateroom door behind them and Sheldon relaxed and yawned hugely. It had been a long session, all the way from Sacramento, for the miners had accosted him for a game even before the *Washoe* had cast off her mooring hawsers for the down-river run to San Francisco.

A man of medium size, with slightly aquiline and more than passably handsome features, Abner Sheldon had in his eyes that somewhat remote, slightly sardonic, and completely cynical look of one of the gambling fraternity.

Sheldon had played fairly enough. He could, if occasion warranted, flip as dexterous and as shady a card as the next, but such tactics were never necessary with these poke-heavy miners, avid for a run for their money. In fact, mused Sheldon virtuously, he had given the fellows a far fairer deal than they would have gotten in any of the dives or gambling hells in San Francisco.

The air in his stateroom was close and heavy, charged with tobacco smoke, through which the light of the ship's lamp shone murkily. Sheldon yawned again. What he needed was a turn or two about deck.

Even as he rose from his chair, from above sounded the hoarse mutter of the *Washoe*'s whistle. Fog, no doubt. Sheldon quickened his movements at the thought of it. Cool, moist, clean, and tangy with the breath of the ocean. A relief after the heat and dryness of the upper valley country.

He sought the lower deck and went far forward, past the mounded piles of cargo until he was out on the very prow of the river steamer. Dusk was settling in, along with the fog. The *Washoe* was beating down from the upper bay and was beginning to roll slightly in the long ground swell that came in on the making tide through the Golden Gate.

Lighting a cheroot, Sheldon buttoned his long, dark coat snugly and welcomed the chill brush of the fog against his cheeks. At intervals the *Washoe*'s whistle grumbled and growled and, as she beat closer to the waterfront and more congested shipping lanes, she was answered in kind by other craft, feeling their way through the murk.

They came out of the mounded cargo shadows with a rush. The same three men. They had Sheldon trapped, there on the narrowing deck above the *Washoe*'s forefoot. He had no time to get a hand inside his tightly buttoned coat and reach the derringer in his vest pocket. Wiry and quick though he was, his strength was no match for the burly power of three of them. A hard forearm locked across his throat, jerked back wickedly, shutting off any cry for help and nearly dislocating his neck. His arms were seized, pulled back just as harshly. And hands began delving his pockets under the muttered order: "Get his poke! It'll be mostly ours, anyway."

They found it, in the deep right-hand pocket of his coat. Then a clubbing fist crashed into the side of his head, half stunning him. The port rail was against the small of his back and he was bent over it. Then he was over and gone, into the black, cold waters of the bay.

He went far down, came up slowly, struggling and swimming instinctively. A series of concussions thundered in his ears, beat at his tortured lungs. The flailing buckets of the *Washoe*'s paddle wheel! He clawed desperately at the water, trying to drag himself clear. That churning wheel would make mincemeat of a man, beat him to sodden pulp. It passed, so close to Sheldon's staring, streaming eyes the beaten spray stung his face like leaden pellets. Then the foaming wake had him, tossing him violently, rolling him over and over.

He got his head clear finally, choking and gasping. Panic was in him and he sent out a desperate cry for help. But even as it broke from his lips the thunder of the *Washoe*'s whistle roared hoarsely, blanketing all lesser sounds. Another billow of the wake rolled over his head.

When he came up again he was far gone. That long coat, his other clothes, sodden and cramping, were pulling him down. The chill, his fading strength were against him. He thought he saw the bulk of something looming above him but he couldn't be sure. It didn't matter, for the hungry waters began closing over his head for a last time. . . .

He was being shaken like a rat in the jaws of a terrier. Constriction was about his middle and his forehead was bumping and scraping against salt-encrusted deck planking.

"Not yet, Nella lass," a deep voice growled. "We got to get the water out of him before we can get the coffee in. Once more, Tobe!"

Again Sheldon was lifted at the waist, so that he was jackknifed, his legs and feet dragging limply, his face bumping those hard deck planks. He was jerked and shaken, up and down. Bay water came out of him, out of his lungs, his throat, raw and salt and scalding. He coughed, strangled, coughed and coughed. Finally he was dropped to the deck and a voice said: "I reckon that drained him."

It seemed he could never stop coughing, but he did, finally, as the terrible pressure in his lungs and throat eased. Then there was hot coffee trickling between his lips and he managed to gulp down a mouthful or two. "He's making it," the deep voice growled. "We'll take him below, now."

He was taken through a narrow hatchway and down a ladder, none too gently, tossed on a bunk, with the light of a grimy little ship's lamp blinding his eyes. After his sodden clothes were stripped from him, he was rolled into dry blankets and laid again on a bunk. There were two men, the older one bearded and with great, shaggy eyebrows. The younger, burly as a bull, said disgustedly: "Look at these fancy clothes, Cap'n Hoxie. We picked up a gambler, a damned card sharp. He probably pulled his crooked tricks to rob some poor devil on the *Washoe* and got thrown overside for it. Just a damned gambler!"

"Ay, Tobe," answered the older man. "But a forlorn and helpless human being. I'm glad we heard his cry and that your pass with the boat hook had the luck to tangle in his coat." He pressed a flask to Sheldon's lips and said gruffly, but not unkindly: "Drink deep, friend. It will drive out the chill."

The hot, raw bite of the whiskey helped enormously. "Where am I?" mumbled Sheldon weakly.

"Aboard the sloop *Sea Lark*. Cap'n Hoxie Martin. That's me. Tobe, you'll be telling Nella she can bring on her coffee jug again, and then you'd best take the wheel. Blinker hasn't the nose for fog and the feel of the currents that you have."

Tobe went up the ladder, growling to himself. "Just a damned gambler. Why couldn't it have been a man? We're goin' to need help if Gascoyne's gang gets any more funny ideas . . ."

The girl came down the ladder so swiftly and lithely Sheldon hardly realized she was present until she was standing beside the bunk, holding out a steaming mug of coffee, which Cap'n Hoxie spiked heavily with his flask before handing it to Sheldon, who had regained enough strength to prop himself up on one elbow while he drank.

The girl was looking at him curiously, out of cool, clear, sea-green eyes. She was dressed in the sea garb of a man, heavy and warm, yet even in these shapeless garments there was a slim, fine grace about her. Her hair, glistening with fine beads of fog, gleamed like dull bronze under the lamp.

"Who is he, father?" she asked.

"A gambler, by his clothes, so Tobe says," answered Cap'n Hoxie Martin. "He must have fallen overside from the *Washoe*."

"Oh," murmured the girl, nodding ever so slightly. "A gambler."

Something in the way she said it sent the blood burning across Sheldon's face, though there was no sane reason why he should have cared a hoot, either way. "Sheldon is the name. Abner Sheldon. I played with three miners. The game was square," he defended. "They lost, and later saw their chance to rob me and throw me over the side."

He knew it sounded weak and not too convincing.

"You'll dry his clothes in the galley, Nella," said Cap'n Hoxie.

The girl gathered up the dripping garments and went up the ladder lightly. Cap'n Hoxie, about to follow her, paused with one foot on the lower step. "Every man to his own trade," he rumbled. " 'Tis a matter of taste, I reckon. But we've had plenty of trouble lately with a bunch of pirates and we could have wished Providence had seen fit to send us a man stout enough to help us."

Sheldon, left alone, stared around at the tiny fo'c'sle. There were four bunks, two port, two starboard. His was the lower starboard. The *Sea Lark*, not a very big craft apparently, was lifting and falling with the feel of the open sea.

The whiskey he had taken was biting deep, now, and the movement of the sloop soothing. The chill and shock were passing. He was warm under the blankets—and incredibly weary. He slept.

II

THE *Sea Lark* was lifting and falling in a wide, long rhythm that told of big waters. Cap'n Hoxie and Tobe were again beside Abner Sheldon and it was Cap'n Hoxie who had shaken him awake.

"You'll be feeling better?" he asked.

Sheldon blinked and nodded. "Much. Quite normal, in fact."

"You'll be feeling better yet with a feed of Nella's hot food. And then you'll be lending us a hand with the egg gathering."

"Egg gathering?" Sheldon stared, wondering if he was hearing right.

"Ay, the egg gathering. You'll need warmer clothes than you came to us in. You'll find these oversize, no doubt, but they'll do. Look sharp. We want to be in with the first light."

The clothes were oversize, plenty. But they were thick and warm and Sheldon managed. In clumping sea boots he followed Cap'n Hoxie up the ladder. Behind him he heard Tobe grumbling: "A damned gambler. He'll never do."

The *Sea Lark* was at anchor, riding out long, open sea swells. The fog pressed closely in on all sides, faintly gray with the promise of dawn.

The girl was in the tiny galley and she handed Sheldon a mug of coffee and a big bowl of steaming hot sea chowder of some sort. It was savory and filling and Sheldon found himself ravenous for it. Yet he did not wolf it and the girl watched with that same clear-eyed, impersonal way.

"Best get it stowed," she said. "Father is an impatient man."

Cap'n Hoxie came clumping up. "We'll take both dories," he told the girl. "You and I to the one, Tobe and Sheldon to the other. Blinker will stay aboard and he's had his orders about what to do should any of the Gascoyne's thieving, murderous pack show up. We'll be leaving, now."

The dories looked like the merest cockle shells, lifting and falling, there in the graying light beside the *Sea Lark*. Their bows were stacked with tarp-covered gear.

The burly Tobe dropped into one, took the oars. "All right, gambler," he called up to Sheldon. "Down you come. We'll see if you can play a man's hand for a change."

Sheldon gauged the swing of the little craft, dropped into the stern. Instantly Tobe bent at his oars, following the other dory, which Cap'n Hoxie was already driving into the gray smother toward the sound of those breakers.

The *Sea Lark* vanished in the fog, the thunder of the breakers came closer. Sheldon wondered how any man could keep his bearings in this ghostly gray, moisture-laden world. Those breakers—Tobe was driving the dory straight into them, it seemed. The man was either mad, or entirely sure of himself. And this egg business? How did it make sense?

The thunder of the breakers was deafening and their foaming turbulence was tossing the dory like a chip. But Tobe rowed on with powerful strokes, his chin on his shoulder.

Sheldon gripped the gunwales of the dory, sure that utter destruction lay just ahead. Still Tobe drove on.

The foaming, black bulk of rocks lifted and lifted above them. Sheldon wanted to yell at Tobe, curse him for a madman. But he locked back the words with set teeth, remembering the seaman's slurs and sneers.

Then they were in a funnel of rock and rushing, roaring water. The rocks seemed to suck them into a giant maw, as though to devour men and dory at one gulp. Then, abruptly, they were in a little, rock-walled basin, where the water rose and fell in endless agitation, but with the destructive fury of the breakers locked outside. Tobe gave a final surge on the oars and to Sheldon's amazement, he found the dory sliding up alongside the one that held Cap'n Hoxie and the girl.

Cap'n Hoxie was already unloading hamperlike boxes on a dripping, rocky shelf and Tobe began doing the same. "Hand 'em up—hand 'em up," he called to Sheldon.

The boxes unloaded, the dory secured, Tobe pushed a stout, leather-woven basket of cavernous size at Sheldon. "Gather them in that," he instructed. "And see that you don't break any. A broken egg on the Farallones is worth nothing on a breakfast plate on Market Street. Come on!"

They went up and over wet, slimy rocks, Sheldon panting and slipping and floundering as he tried to keep Tobe's burly figure in sight through the fog. Here they were high above the thunder of the breakers and here a new sound met Sheldon's ears.

A wild, shrill crying, a squawking, hissing, scolding crying. And movement, in the growing, pale, misty light. Movement, as though every cliff and ledge, every point and slope were alive, shifting and slithering. Then Sheldon understood.

Sea fowl. Thousands of them, solid ranks upright and heavy on short, clumsy legs, a confusion of two colors which seemed black and white. They flowed like waves of water away from Tobe and Sheldon, pouring out over the ledges to drop into the open sea.

Tobe turned and waited. "Mostly murre," he said. "And the only kind of eggs we're wanting, this trip. This kind."

He held one in his hand. It was light enough now to mark size, shape and color. They were large, queerly pointed, blue-green in color, spotted and splotched with darker markings.

"Fast as you fill your basket, take 'em down and put them in the hampers. Then come back for more. Move sharp!"

There was no difficulty in finding the eggs. They were everywhere, in every nook and cranny, balanced on seemingly impossible slopes and ledges. And now Sheldon understood that definitely pointed shape. These eggs would not roll. When his unpracticed hands started several down a rock slant, they did not roll, merely spun around to a stop. Nature, it seemed to Abner Sheldon, planned with incredible cunning.

The air was rank with mingled odors. Strongest was the raw, ammonialike stench of the guano, the fishy breath of these thousands of sea fowl, the smell of seaweed, of salt, of cold, wet, lonely rocks.

The basket filled fast, and Sheldon toiled back and forth, filling it and emptying it. Cap'n Hoxie and the girl were working the rocks to the north of the dories, he and Tobe to the south. Several times Sheldon met the girl or Cap'n Hoxie at the hampers, but they did not speak, so neither did he. They were hurrying, rushing against some sort of deadline, it seemed.

It was hard work. Sheldon was drenched in sweat, as well as fog and sea water. His legs and back and arms ached. But there was no let-up. His pride would not let him. Just a gambler. Tobe sneered when he said the word. The girl spoke it with an inflection more punishing still.

"See if you can play a man's hand," Tobe had said. He'd show them—show them all. He owed them much, for they had, beyond all question, saved his life. But he owed himself something, too. Which was to prove to them, and to himself, that he could play a man's hand. But another thought set him laughing, a little wild and crazy. He, Abner Sheldon, who had prided himself on his immaculate dress, his poise, his supple, deft hands—yes, he, Abner Sheldon, floundering about on these fog and wind-swept Farallone rocks, slimy and stinking from sea fowl rookeries, busy at, of all things, gathering eggs! It was enough to make the gods laugh, let alone himself. . . .

Then the girl was hurrying toward them, calling, urgency in her voice.

III

CAP'N Hoxie had slipped and fallen, down there by the dories. His left arm was broken, between wrist and elbow. So did Abner Sheldon swiftly diagnose, and tell them.

"How would you know?" growled Tobe.

"I studied once, as a doctor," Sheldon explained.

Cap'n Hoxie, his face gray and drawn with pain, said: "Tobe, you'll be taking Nella to the *Sea Lark*. Then you'll come back for Sheldon and me."

"No!" cried the girl. "You're to take father first, Tobe."

"That," said Sheldon, "would be the wisest. I'll bring the second dory. I can handle a pair of oars."

"You'd get lost," sneered Tobe.

"No," said the girl, "he won't. For I'll be with him."

Most of the hampers had been filled with eggs. Sheldon labored with Tobe, loading them into the dories. Cap'n Hoxie called anxiously to Sheldon: "It's heavy going, clearing the breakers. At the oars . . . you're sure, Sheldon?"

"I'm sure. You lead, we'll follow."

Tobe nosed toward the funnel of streaming rock and churning water, feeling for an out surge to carry through on. He caught it and the dory darted out.

Sheldon gripped his oars, squared himself. The girl, in the stern, was facing him. And now she smiled at him, gravely and with warm friendliness.

Sheldon nosed the dory around, up toward the funnel. A surge of water churned in and the dory lifted and lifted. As the out run started, Sheldon was bending to the oars with all his strength. They shot out toward the open sea, toward the narrow gap through the breakers.

The out run slowed and dwindled as it met the next incoming swell. Here, Sheldon knew, was the big test. He had to hold what he had gained, not let the incoming swell carry him back too far. He felt the power of it gripping and sucking at the dory and he fought it with lashing oars and straining muscles. He fought it doggedly and savagely. The dory seemed to be hanging motionless, walled in by roaring, foaming chaos.

The drag of the waters reached a peak, fell swiftly off. Then the dory was surging ahead once more, aided by the new out run. Sheldon used every inch of it, fought off the suction of another swell, and then was clear. The voice of the girl came to him, through the thunder of waters. "Well done! Oh, well done!"

The bellow of the breakers faded and dulled and the fog swallowed them up. Nella, her head high, almost as though she was keening the wind, guided Sheldon's efforts with little motions of her hands. Sheldon heard her swift little cry of consternation as a new sound came through the gray smother—the hollow, thin wailing of a conch horn, in short, sharp blasts. Right after that came the whipping, shattered echoes of gunfire.

"Gascoyne," said the girl, her face set with strain. "Father was afraid of this."

"Why? What for?" panted Sheldon.

"I have seen a dollar apiece paid for such eggs as these in San Francisco. It's easier to pirate them, than to risk going through the breakers and gathering them as we did. At least, that's Gascoyne's way. We must hurry! Father—the *Sea Lark* . . ."

Sheldon bent to the oars with all his strength. He had the queer feeling of heading nowhere and getting nowhere, in that gray smother of fog. Yet the girl, poised high and alert before him, was definite in her gestures of direction.

The dory, loaded with egg hampers, was heavy. The oar grips were hard and briny under Sheldon's soft, uncalloused palms and fingers. Even before he forced the dory entirely past the breakers, his hands were burning. Fighting on this way, he knew the blisters were building up rapidly.

The girl gave another swift little cry and, twisting his head to follow the direction of her gaze, Sheldon glimpsed the dark, shadowy bulk of another boat. It wasn't Cap'n Hoxie and Tobe, for there were more than two men in it. There were nearer half a dozen.

Darting a hand into a little compartment under the stern seat of the dory, Nella brought it away gripping a heavy old Colt revolver. She pointed it at that other boat threateningly. But she did not shoot, even though there was a hoarse yell of discovery and the other craft spun around under the lash of two pair of oars and came plunging toward the dory.

"Keep off!" cried the girl. "Keep off, or I'll shoot!"

Her voice sounded thin and futile under the fog and over

the growl and swell of the restless sea. Her answer was a gloating curse and the other boat came smashing on.

Sheldon understood. Nella did not want to shoot. It was the feminine in her recoiling from the act, until too late, perhaps.

"Give me that gun!" Sheldon rapped.

He let go of an oar, reached out and up to take the gun from the girl's reluctant fingers. "Get low!" he ordered sharply.

Sheldon centered on the bulk of the boat and its occupants, let drive. The report was hollow and thumping, across the water. A man howled, fell to thrashing about in the other boat. Sheldon shot again and one of the oarsmen collapsed. Laying the gun on the bottom of the dory between his feet, Sheldon bent to his oars again.

He gained a little, and the pirate boat grew dim and misty in the fog. Curses came from it, and then gunfire. A bullet gouged splinters from the dory gunwale. Another splashed a gout of water. Sheldon, jaw set, muscles straining, put everything he had into the bending oars.

A yell came in out of the fog. "Nella—Nella girl!" It was Cap'n Hoxie's voice.

"Don't answer yet!" panted Sheldon. "First thing we've got to do is get clear of that other boat."

The girl nodded, her eyes big and dark with strain.

The pirate boat seemed reluctant to close in again. A thickening swirl of fog came in, hiding it altogether and Sheldon bore down savagely on his oars to make the most of the interval.

The conch horn was moaning again, not far away now, and off to port.

"The *Sea Lark*!" cried Nella. "Over there!"

Sheldon beat toward the sound and abruptly the bulk of the little sloop lifted above them. "Blinker!" called the girl. "Blinker!"

"Right here, lass—right here! Pass up that painter."

Nella scrambled past Sheldon, tossed up the end of the rope and Blinker made it fast. The drift swung the dory close under the lee of the sloop and the girl and Sheldon climbed aboard.

"Father?" asked the girl. "And Tobe?"

Blinker shrugged, picked up the conch horn and sent its

mournful but penetrating blast echoing. For a moment, straining ears could only pick up the whisper of water, the drone of the wind. Then they heard the unmistakable creak of oars and the other dory came whipping in out of the fog, driven by Tobe's powerful, expert strokes.

"Father!" cried Nella. And Sheldon heard Cap'n Hoxie's rumbling curse of relief.

Sheldon pulled on ropes that Tobe and Blinker told him to pull on. The rough, brine-soaked lines cut into his raw, cramped palms. But he stayed with it until the anchor was up, the sails set and drawing and the *Sea Lark*, with Tobe at the wheel, sliding away on the port tack.

Sheldon sought Cap'n Hoxie and the girl, found them in the little cabin aft of the galley. The girl was stripping off her father's shirt. The broken arm was swelling, coloring up.

"The job," said Sheldon crisply, "will hurt. But not nearly so much as it would several hours from now. Let's get at it. I'll need something for splints, plenty of cloth strips for bandage. A big drink of whiskey for the captain will help."

Blinker came and watched, talking to try to take Cap'n Hoxie's mind off the pain as much as possible.

"They came up in their small boat—Gascoyne's crowd. Thought they'd find the *Sea Lark* with nobody aboard. I put a few shots over their heads and they got back into the fog, fast. Then I kept giving you the conch horn signal. How many eggs, Cap'n?"

Cap'n Hoxie's face was gray and beaded with cold sweat, but he answered through set teeth. "Better'n a hundred dozen, I figure. More'n a thousand dollars riding in those two dories towing astern. We ain't inside the heads with 'em yet, though. Keep a sharp lookout, Blinker—and don't shoot over the heads of those pirates, next time."

IV

THE arm was set finally, and Cap'n Hoxie resting on his bunk. The girl, a strange light in her eyes, touched Sheldon's arm. She had seen bloodstains on some of the bandages Sheldon had worked with.

"Come!" she ordered.

She took him into the galley and went to work gently on his blistered, raw, bleeding palms. Her eyes and smile were very soft. "They would be clumsy with cards, now," she murmured. "But they were strong and sure in setting father's arm. Doctor—or gambler, Abner Sheldon?"

Sheldon was uncomfortable under her scrutiny, and a little annoyed. He could hardly explain how he had forgotten the one thing, to take up lesser purpose. Perhaps because he had not finished his medical studies when the call of gold came and he joined the mad rush across plain and mountain to the land of El Dorado. And the cards had an insidious charm and paid well, when you knew how. It had been one of those things.

"I have forgotten much," he defended. "It is a long road."

"What has been once learned may be learned again. And no road is too long if traveled with good purpose."

A man could not waver, under the impelling scrutiny of those clear, sea-green eyes. He was either one thing or the other.

"I would need help . . . encouragement," said Abner Sheldon, a trifle desperately. "Inspiration, too."

Nella colored slightly, but her eyes did not waver. "You would have it," she said.

Back aft, Tobe yelled a warning. They hurried on deck. Cap'n Hoxie came out, too, cradling his injured arm with his sound one. Off on the starboard beam, ghostly in the fog, loomed another craft, larger than the *Sea Lark*.

"Gascoyne, all right," growled Cap'n Hoxie. "'Tis the *Kiskadee*. Blinker, fetch the rifles. Tobe, hold the *Lark* as she runs. But be quick for the chance to come about and get across her bow. On the starboard tack we'll have the heels of her."

The *Kiskadee* bore closer. She also was sloop-rigged. With lessening distance, it was possible to distinguish more detail. Nearly a dozen men crowded her port rail, with a dark and burly figure spread-legged at her wheel, bawling hoarse orders.

"He means to close and board us," rumbled Cap'n Hoxie. "Gascoyne, the pirating whelp! That's him at the wheel. Nella, you'll be going below. Blinker, try a shot!"

The girl did not move. Blinker tried a shot, high and wild,

plainly knowing little of the use of weapons. A yell of hoarse mockery came from the *Kiskadee*.

"You wasted lead, man—you wasted it," cried Cap'n Hoxie. "Try again, at Gascoyne himself. This arm of mine . . ."

"Let me," said Abner Sheldon. "I've handled arms."

He caught up a rifle, bracing himself against the lift and fall of the deck beneath him. It would be very difficult. He took a long time, with the *Kiskadee* driving ever closer. But the swing of sights and target blended finally, although the line was somewhat low. The gun snarled and Cap'n Hoxie let go a great roar of delight.

"You did it, lad—you did it! He's down! Gascoyne's down! You cut a leg from under him. And he's lost the wheel. The *Kiskadee* . . . she's falling away. Now, Tobe—now! Bring the *Lark* about!"

Sure enough, that burly dark figure at the *Kiskadee*'s wheel was down on the deck, flopping and floundering. And the wheel was spinning free, the *Kiskadee*'s sails were slatting and she was losing weigh, near to broaching.

Under Tobe's deft touch, the *Sea Lark* came about, her boom swinging, sheets snapping taut. She leaned into the starboard tack and fled like a frightened deer. She cut across the *Kiskadee*'s bow with only short yards to spare, and Cap'n Hoxie cried: "That whips them—that whips them! They'll never catch us, now!"

Some gun shots came across the widening gap, but the *Kiskadee* was still rolling wildly, her rudder kicking. The lead flew far and harmlessly, and the *Sea Lark* darted away into the protecting fog.

Inside the heads the fog was breaking and sunlight coming through. Whitecaps creamed the bay. Gulls soared and dipped. The *Sea Lark* foamed along.

Abner Sheldon had fashioned a sling for Cap'n Hoxie's arm and the latter was at ease enough to puff at his blackened pipe.

"There'll be a share coming to you, of course," said Cap'n Hoxie. "You did well, lad—very well indeed. I dislike seeing you leave us."

Nella was standing at her father's elbow, watching Abner

Sheldon, waiting as though listening for some yearned-for echo.

Sheldon stared at his puffed and swollen hands. "They had grown weak and soft," he murmured. "And of no use to anyone. They must be made strong again, and cunning in a way that counts. There will be much studying to be done, between trips. But . . . when do we sail again, Cap'n Hoxie?"

Sheldon was looking at the girl now, and smiling. And her smile came back, warm and full. For she had heard that yearned-for echo, and it was good!

Mark Twain (Samuel Langhorne Clemens) mined some of the same rich California Gold Rush lore and background as Bret Harte, in such classic stories as "The Notorious Jumping Frog of Calaveras County" and such story segments as "Buck Fanshaw's Funeral" and "Millionaires" from Roughing It *(1872), his autobiographical account of his days in California and other parts of the Western frontier. These works, like those penned by Harte and Owen Wister, helped shape both the modern Western story and the enduring Western myth.*

Millionaires

★★★★★★★★★★★★★★★

Mark Twain

I NOW come to a curious episode—the most curious, I think, that had yet accented my slothful, valueless, heedless career. Out of a hillside toward the upper end of the town, projected a wall of reddish-looking quartz croppings, the exposed comb of a silver-bearing ledge that extended deep down into the earth, of course. It was owned by a company entitled the "Wide West." There was a shaft sixty or seventy feet deep on the under side of the croppings, and everybody was acquainted with the rock that came from it—and tolerably rich rock it was, too, but nothing extraordinary. I will remark here, that although to the inexperienced stranger all the quartz of a particular "district" looks about alike, an old resident of the camp can take a glance at a mixed pile of rock, separate the fragments and tell you which mine each came from, as easily as a confectioner can separate and classify the various kinds and qualities of candy in a mixed heap of the article.

All at once the town was thrown into a state of extraordinary excitement. In mining parlance the Wide West had "struck it rich!" Everybody went to see the new developments, and for some days there was such a crowd of people about the Wide West shaft that a stranger would have supposed there was a mass-meeting in session there. No other topic was discussed but the rich strike, and nobody thought or dreamed about anything else. Every man brought away a specimen, ground it up in a hand-mortar, washed it out in his horn spoon, and glared speechless upon the marvelous result. It was not hard rock, but black, decomposed stuff which could be crumbled in the hand like a baked potato, and when spread out on a paper exhibited a thick sprinkling of gold and particles of "native" silver. Higbie brought a handful to the cabin, and when he had washed it out his amazement was beyond description. Wide West stock soared skyward. It was said that repeated offers had been made for it at a thousand dollars a foot, and promptly refused. We have all had the "blues"—the mere skyblues—but mine were indigo, now—because I did not own in the Wide West. The world seemed hollow to me, and existence a grief. I lost my appetite, and ceased to take an interest in anything. Still I had to stay, and listen to other people's rejoicings, because I had no money to get out of the camp with.

The Wide West company put a stop to the carrying away of "specimens," and well they might, for every handful of the ore was worth a sum of some consequence. To show the exceeding value of the ore, I will remark that a sixteen-hundred-pounds parcel of it was sold, just as it lay, at the mouth of the shaft, at *one dollar a pound*; and the man who bought it "packed" it on mules a hundred and fifty or two hundred miles, over the mountains, to San Francisco, satisfied that it would yield at a rate that would richly compensate him for his trouble. The Wide West people also commanded their foreman to refuse any but their own operatives permission to enter the mine at any time or for any purpose. I kept up my "blue" meditations and Higbie kept up a deal of thinking, too, but of a different sort. He puzzled over the "rock," examined it with a glass, inspected it in different lights and from different points of view, and after each experiment delivered himself, in soliloquy, of one and the same unvarying opinion in the same unvarying formula:

"It is *not* Wide West rock!"

He said once or twice that he meant to have a look into the Wide West shaft if he got shot for it. I was wretched, and did not care whether he got a look into it or not. He failed that

day, and tried again at night; failed again; got up at dawn
and tried, and failed again. Then he lay in ambush in the
sage-brush hour after hour, waiting for the two or three hands
to adjourn to the shade of a boulder for dinner; made a start
once, but was premature—one of the men came back for
something; tried it again, but when almost at the mouth of
the shaft, another of the men rose up from behind the boulder
as if to reconnoitre, and he dropped on the ground and lay
quiet; presently he crawled on his hands and knees to the
mouth of the shaft, gave a quick glance around, then seized
the rope and slid down the shaft. He disappeared in the gloom
of a ''side drift'' just as a head appeared in the mouth of the
shaft and somebody shouted ''Hello!''—which he did not answer. He was not disturbed any more. An hour later he entered the cabin, hot, red, and ready to burst with smothered
excitement, and exclaimed in a stage whisper:

''I knew it! We are rich! IT'S A BLIND LEAD!''

I thought the very earth reeled under me. Doubt—
conviction—doubt again—exultation—hope, amazement, belief, unbelief—every emotion imaginable swept in wild
procession through my heart and brain, and I could not speak
a word. After a moment or two of this mental fury, I shook
myself to rights, and said:

''Say it again!''

''It's a blind lead!''

''Cal, let's—let's burn the house—or kill somebody! Let's
get out where there's room to hurrah! But what is the use? It
is a hundred times too good to be true.''

''It's a blind lead for a million!—hanging wall—foot wall—
clay casings—everything complete!'' He swung his hat and
gave three cheers, and I cast doubt to the winds and chimed
in with a will. For I was worth a million dollars, and did not
care ''whether school kept or not!''

But perhaps I ought to explain. A ''blind lead'' is a lead
or ledge that does not ''crop out'' above the surface. A miner
does not know where to look for such leads, but they are
often stumbled upon by accident in the course of driving a
tunnel or sinking a shaft. Higbie knew the Wide West rock
perfectly well, and the more he had examined the new developments the more he was satisfied that the ore could not
have come from the Wide West vein. And so had it occurred
to him alone, of all the camp, that there was a blind lead

down in the shaft, and that even the Wide West people themselves did not suspect it. He was right. When he went down the shaft, he found that the blind lead held its independent way through the Wide West vein, cutting it diagonally, and that it was inclosed in its own well-defined casing-rocks and clay. Hence it was public property. Both leads being perfectly well defined, it was easy for any miner to see which one belonged to the Wide West and which did not.

We thought it well to have a strong friend, and therefore we brought the foreman of the Wide West to our cabin that night and revealed the great surprise to him. Higbie said:

"We are going to take possession of this blind lead, record it and establish ownership, and then forbid the Wide West company to take out any more of the rock. You cannot help your company in this matter—nobody can help them. I will go into the shaft with you and prove to your entire satisfaction that it *is* a blind lead. Now we propose to take you in with us, and claim the blind lead in our three names. What do you say?"

What could a man say who had an opportunity to simply stretch forth his hand and take possession of a fortune without risk of any kind and without wronging any one or attaching the least taint of dishonor to his name? He could only say, "Agreed."

The notice was put up that night, and duly spread upon the recorder's books before ten o'clock. We claimed two hundred feet each—six hundred feet in all—the smallest and compactest organization in the district, and the easiest to manage.

No one can be so thoughtless as to suppose that we slept that night. Higbie and I went to bed at midnight, but it was only to lie broad awake and think, dream, scheme. The floorless, tumble-down cabin was a palace, the ragged gray blankets silk, the furniture rosewood and mahogany. Each new splendor that burst out of my visions of the future whirled me bodily over in bed or jerked me to a sitting posture just as if an electric battery had been applied to me. We shot fragments of conversation back and forth at each other. Once Higbie said:

"When are you going home—to the States?"

"Tomorrow!"—with an evolution or two, ending with a sitting position. "Well—no—but next month, at furthest."

"We'll go in the same steamer."

"Agreed."

A pause.

"Steamer of the 10th?"

"Yes. No, the 1st."

"All right."

Another pause.

"Where are you going to live?" said Higbie.

"San Francisco."

"That's me!"

Pause.

"Too high—too much climbing"—from Higbie.

"What is?"

"I was thinking of Russian Hill—building a house up there."

"Too much climbing? Sha'n't you keep a carriage?"

"Of course. I forgot that."

Pause.

"Cal, what kind of a house are you going to build?"

"I was thinking about that. Three-story and an attic."

"But what *kind*?"

"Well, I don't hardly know. Brick, I suppose."

"Brick—bosh."

"Why? What is your idea?"

"Brown-stone front—French plate-glass—billiard-room off the dining-room—statuary and paintings—shrubbery and two-acre grass-plat—greenhouse—iron dog on the front stoop—gray horses—landau, and a coachman with a bug on his hat!"

"By George!"

A long pause.

"Cal, when are you going to Europe?"

"Well—I hadn't thought of that. When are you?"

"In the spring."

"Going to be gone all summer?"

"All summer! I shall remain there three years."

"No—but are you in earnest?"

"Indeed I am."

"I will go along, too."

"Why, of course you will."

"What part of Europe shall you go to?"

"All parts. France, England, Germany—Spain, Italy, Switzerland, Syria, Greece, Palestine, Arabia, Persia, Egypt—all over—everywhere."

"I'm agreed."

"All right."

"Won't it be a swell trip!"

"We'll spend forty or fifty thousand dollars trying to make it one, anyway."

Another long pause.

"Higbie, we owe the butcher six dollars, and he has been threatening to stop our—"

"Hang the butcher!"

"Amen."

And so it went on. By three o'clock we found it was no use, and so we got up and played cribbage and smoked pipes till sunrise. It was my week to cook. I always hated cooking—now, I abhorred it.

The news was all over town. The former excitement was great—this one was greater still. I walked the streets serene and happy. Higbie said the foreman had been offered two hundred thousand dollars for his third of the mine. I said I would like to see myself selling for any such price. My ideas were lofty. My figure was a million. Still, I honestly believe that if I had been offered it, it would have had no other effect than to make me hold off for more.

I found abundant enjoyment in being rich. A man offered me a three-hundred-dollar horse, and wanted to take my simple, unindorsed note for it. That brought the most realizing sense I had yet had that I was actually rich, beyond shadow of doubt. It was followed by numerous other evidences of a similar nature—among which I may mention the fact of the butcher leaving us a double supply of meat and saying nothing about money.

By the laws of the district, the "locators" or claimants of a ledge were obliged to do a fair and reasonable amount of work on their new property within ten days after the date of the location, or the property was forfeited, and anybody could go and seize it that chose. So we determined to go to work the next day. About the middle of the afternoon, as I was coming out of the post-office, I met a Mr. Gardiner, who told me that Capt. John Nye was lying dangerously ill at his place (the "Nine-Mile Ranch"), and that he and his wife were not able to give him nearly as much care and attention as his case demanded. I said if he would wait for me a moment, I would go down and help in the sick-room. I ran to the cabin to tell

Higbie. He was not there, but I left a note on the table for him, and a few minutes later I left town in Gardiner's wagon.

Captain Nye was very ill indeed, with spasmodic rheumatism. But the old gentleman was himself—which is to say, he was kind-hearted and agreeable when comfortable, but a singularly violent wildcat when things did not go well. He would be smiling along pleasantly enough, when a sudden spasm of his disease would take him and he would go out of his smile into a perfect fury. He would groan and wail and howl with the anguish, and fill up the odd chinks with the most elaborate profanity that strong convictions and a fine fancy could contrive. With fair opportunity he could swear very well and handle his adjectives with considerable judgment; but when the spasm was on him it was painful to listen to him, he was so awkward. However, I had seen him nurse a sick man himself and put up patiently with the inconveniences of the situation, and consequently I was willing that he should have full license now that his own turn had come. He could not disturb me, with all his raving and ranting, for my mind had work on hand, and it labored on diligently, night and day, whether my hands were idle or employed. I was altering and amending the plans for my house, and thinking over the propriety of having the billiard-room in the attic, instead of on the same floor with the dining-room; also, I was trying to decide between green and blue for the upholstery of the drawing-room, for, although my preference was blue, I feared it was a color that would be too easily damaged by dust and sunlight; likewise while I was content to put the coachman in a modest livery, I was uncertain about a footman—I needed one, and was even resolved to have one, but wished he could properly appear and perform his functions out of livery, for I somewhat dreaded so much show; and yet, inasmuch as my late grandfather had had a coachman and such things, but no liveries, I felt rather drawn to beat him—or beat his ghost, at any rate; I was also systematizing the European trip, and managed to get it all laid out, as to route and length of time to be devoted to it—everything, with one exception—namely, whether to cross the desert from Cairo to Jerusalem per camel, or go by sea to Beirut, and thence down through the country per caravan. Meantime I was writing to the friends at home every day, instructing them concerning all my plans and intentions, and directing them to look up a handsome homestead for my mother and agree upon a price for it against my coming, and also directing them to sell my share of the Tennessee land and tender the proceeds to the widows' and orphans' fund of the typographical union of which I had long been a member in good standing. [This Tennessee land had been in the possession of the family many years, and promised to confer high fortune upon us some day; it still promises it, but in a less violent way.]

When I had been nursing the captain nine days he was somewhat better, but very feeble. During the afternoon we lifted him into a chair and gave him an alcoholic vapor bath, and then set about putting him on the bed again. We had to be exceedingly careful, for the least jar produced pain. Gardiner had his shoulders and I his legs; in an unfortunate moment I stumbled and the patient fell heavily on the bed in an agony of torture. I never heard a man swear so in my life. He raved like a maniac, and tried to snatch a revolver from the table—but I got it. He ordered me out of the house, and swore a world of oaths that he would kill me wherever he caught me when he got on his feet again. It was simply a passing fury, and meant nothing. I knew he would forget it in an hour, and maybe be sorry for it, too; but it angered me a little, at the moment. So much so, indeed, that I determined to go back to Esmeralda. I thought he was able to get along alone, now, since he was on the war-path. I took supper, and as soon as the moon rose, began my nine-mile journey, on foot. Even millionaires needed no horses, in those days, for a mere nine-mile jaunt without baggage.

As I "raised the hill" overlooking the town, it lacked fifteen minutes of twelve. I glanced at the hill over beyond the cañon, and in the bright moonlight saw what appeared to be about half the population of the village massed on and around the Wide West croppings. My heart gave an exulting bound, and I said to myself, "They have made a new strike tonight—and struck it richer than ever, no doubt." I started over there, but gave it up. I said the "strike" would keep, and I had climbed hills enough for one night. I went on down through the town, and as I was passing a little German bakery, a woman ran out and begged me to come in and help her. She said her husband had a fit. I went in, and judged she was right—he appeared to have a hundred of them, compressed into one. Two Germans were there, trying to hold him, and

not making much of a success of it. I ran up the street half a
block or so and routed out a sleeping doctor, brought him
down half dressed, and we four wrestled with the maniac, and
doctored, drenched and bled him, for more than an hour, and
the poor German woman did the crying. He grew quiet, now,
and the doctor and I withdrew and left him to his friends.

It was a little after one o'clock. As I entered the cabin
door, tired but jolly, the dingy light of a tallow candle revealed Higbie, sitting by the pine table gazing stupidly at my
note, which he held in his fingers, and looking pale, old, and
haggard. I halted, and looked at him. He looked at me, stol-
idly. I said:

"Higbie, what—what is it?"

"We're ruined—we didn't do the work—THE BLIND LEAD'S
RELOCATED!"

It was enough. I sat down sick, grieved—broken-hearted,
indeed. A minute before, I was rich and brimful of vanity; I
was a pauper now, and very meek. We sat still an hour, busy
with thought, busy with vain and useless self-upbraidings,
busy with "Why *didn't* I do this, and why *didn't* I do that,"
but neither spoke a word. Then we dropped into mutual ex-
planations, and the mystery was cleared away. It came out
that Higbie had depended on me, as I had on him, and as
both of us had on the foreman. The folly of it! It was the first
time that ever staid and steadfast Higbie had left an important
matter to chance or failed to be true to his full share of a
responsibility.

But he had never seen my note till this moment, and this
moment was the first time he had been in the cabin since the
day he had seen me last. He, also, had left a note for me, on
that same fatal afternoon—had ridden up on horseback, and
looked through the window, and being in a hurry and not
seeing me, had tossed the note into the cabin through a broken pane. Here it was, on the floor, where it had remained
undisturbed for nine days:

> Don't fail to do the work before the ten days expire. W.
> has passed through and given me notice. I am to join him
> at Mono Lake, and we shall go on from there tonight. He
> says he will find it this time, sure.
>
> CAL.

"W." meant Whiteman, of course. That thrice accursed "cement"!

That was the way of it. An old miner, like Higbie, could no more withstand the fascination of a mysterious mining excitement like this "cement" foolishness, than he could refrain from eating when he was famishing. Higbie had been dreaming about the marvelous cement for months; and now, against his better judgment, he had gone off and "taken the chances" on my keeping secure a mine worth a million undiscovered cement veins. They had not been followed this time. His riding out of town in broad daylight was such a commonplace thing to do that it had not attracted any attention. He said they prosecuted their search in the vastnesses of the mountains during nine days, without success; they could not find the cement. Then a ghastly fear came over him that something might have happened to prevent the doing of the necessary work to hold the blind lead (though indeed he thought such a thing hardly possible) and forthwith he started home with all speed. He would have reached Esmeralda in time, but his horse broke down and he had to walk a great part of the distance. And so it happened that as he came into Esmeralda by one road, I entered it by another. His was the superior energy, however, for he went straight to the Wide West, instead of turning aside as I had done—and he arrived there about five or ten minutes too late! The "notice" was already up, the "relocation" of our mine completed beyond recall, and the crowd rapidly dispersing. He learned some facts before he left the ground. The foreman had not been seen about the streets since the night we had located the mine—a telegram had called him to California on a matter of life and death, it was said. At any rate he had done no work and the watchful eyes of the community were taking note of the fact. At midnight of this woeful tenth day, the ledge would be "relocatable," and by eleven o'clock the hill was black with men prepared to do the relocating. That was the crowd I had seen when I fancied a new "strike" had been made— idiot that I was. [We three had the same right to relocate the lead that other people had, provided we were quick enough.] As midnight was announced, fourteen men, duly armed and ready to back their proceedings, put up their "notice" and proclaimed their ownership of the blind lead, under the new name of the "Johnson." But A. D. Allen, our partner (the foreman), put in a sudden appearance about that time, with a cocked revolver in his hand, and said his name must be added to the list, or he would "thin out the Johnson company some." He was a manly, splendid, determined fellow, and known to be as good as his word, and therefore a compromise was effected. They put in his name for a hundred feet, reserving to themselves the customary two hundred feet each. Such was the history of the night's events, as Higbie gathered from a friend on the way home.

Higbie and I cleared out on a new mining excitement the next morning, glad to get away from the scene of our sufferings, and after a month or two of hardship and disappointment, returned to Esmeralda once more. Then we learned that the Wide West and the Johnson companies had consolidated; that the stock, thus united, comprised five thousand feet, or shares; that the foreman, apprehending tiresome litigation, and considering such a huge concern unwieldy, had sold his hundred feet for ninety thousand dollars in gold and gone home to the States to enjoy it. If the stock was worth such a gallant figure, with five thousand shares in the corporation, it makes me dizzy to think what it would have been worth with only our original six hundred in it. It was the difference between six hundred men owning a house and five thousand owning it. We would have been millionaires if we had only worked with pick and spade one little day on our property and so secured our ownership!

It reads like a wild fancy sketch, but the evidence of many witnesses, and likewise that of the official records of Esmeralda District, is easily obtainable in proof that it is a true history. I can always have it to say that I was absolutely and unquestionably worth a million dollars, once, for ten days.

A year ago my esteemed and in every way estimable old millionaire partner, Higbie, wrote me from an obscure little mining-camp in California that after nine or ten years of buffetings and hard striving, he was at last in a position where he could command twenty-five hundred dollars, and said he meant to go into the fruit business in a modest way. How such a thought would have insulted him the night we lay in our cabin planning European trips and brown-stone houses on Russian Hill!

*Ed Gorman is one of the best of the newer writers in both the mystery/detective and Western fields. He has published three Western novels to date, two about a lawman turned bounty hunter named Guild—*Guild *(1987) and* Death Ground *(1988)—and a nonseries book,* Graves' Retreat *(1989). He has also edited two excellent Western anthologies,* The Silver Spur Anthology of Western Fiction *and* Westeryear, *both published in 1988. "Gunslinger" is the highly unusual tale of a man on a mission of vengeance in the days when Hollywood film-making was in its infancy.*

Gunslinger

★★★★★★★★★★★★★★★

Ed Gorman

HE reaches Los Angeles three days early, a scrawny forty-eight-year-old man in a three-piece black Cheviot suit made of wool and far too hot for the desertlike climate here. He chews without pause on stick after stick of White's Yucatan gum. He carries, tucked in his trousers beneath his vest, a Navy Colt that belonged to his father, a farmer from Morgan County, Missouri.

As he steps down from the train, a Negro porter accidentally bumping into him and tipping his red cap in apology, he takes one more look at the newspaper he has been reading for the last one hundred miles of his journey, the prime headline of which details President Teddy Roosevelt's hunting trip to the Badlands, the secondary headline being concerned with the annexation by Los Angeles of San Pedro and Wilmington, thereby giving the city a harbor. But it is the third headline that holds his interest: DIRECTOR THOMAS INCE, NOW RECOVERED FROM HEART TROUBLE, STARTS NEW PICTURE THURSDAY WITH HIS FAMOUS WESTERN STAR REX SWANSON.

Today was Monday.

* * *

He finds a rooming house two blocks from a bar called The
Waterhole, which is where most of the cowboys hang out.
Because real ranches in the west have fallen on hard times,
the cowboys had little choice but to drift to Los Angeles to
become extras and stunt riders and trick shooters in the silent
movie industry. Now there is a whole colony, a whole sub-
culture of them out here, and they are much given to drink
and even more given to violence. So he must be careful
around them, very careful.

In the street below his room runs a trolley car, its tingling
bell the friendliest sound in this arid city of 'dobe buildings
for the poor and unimaginable mansions for the rich. It is
said, at least back in Missouri, that at least once a day a Los
Angeles police officer draws down on a man and kills him.
He has no reason to doubt this as he falls asleep on the cot
in the hot shabby room with its flowered vase lamp, the ker-
osene flame flickering into the dusk as his exhausted snoring
begins.

In the morning he goes down the hall, waits till a Mexican
woman comes out of the bathroom smelling sweetly of perfume, and then goes in and bathes and puts on the things he
bought just before leaving Morgan County. A bank teller,
he is not particularly familiar with real Western attire, but he
knew it would be a mistake to buy his things new. That would
mark him as a dude for certain. He had found a livery up in
the northern edge of the county that had some old clothes in
the back, which he bought for $1.50 total.

Now, looking at himself in the mirror, trying to be as objective as he can, he sees that he does not look so bad. Not
so bad at all. The graying hair helps. Not shaving helps. And
he's always been capable of a certain blue evil eye (as are
most of the men in his family). Then there are the clothes.
The dusty brown Stetson creased cowhand-style. The faded
denim shirt. The Levi's with patches in knee and butt. The
black Texas boots.

For the first time he loses some of his fear.

For the first time there is within him excitement.

In his room, before leaving, he writes a quick letter.

Dear Mother,

By the time you read this, you will know what I have done. I apologize for the pain and humiliation my action will cause you but I'm sure you will understand why I had to do this.

If it were not for the man I will kill Thursday, you would have had a husband all these years, and I a father.

I will write you one more letter before Thursday.

Your loving son,
Todd

The next two days . . .

In the Los Angeles of the movie cowboy extra, there are certain key places to go for work. On Sunset Boulevard there is a horse barn where you wait like farmhands to be picked for a day's work; then there are a few studio backlots where you can stand in the baking sun all day waiting for somebody already hired to keel over and need to be replaced; and then there is Universal's slave-galley arrangement where extras are literally herded into a big cage to wait to be called. Five dollars a day is the pay, which for some men is five times what they were getting back in the blizzard country of Montana and Wyoming and Utah.

It is into this world he slips now, making the rounds, trying to get himself hired as an extra. If he does not get on Ince's set Thursday, if he does not get that close, then he will be unable to do what he has waited most of his life to do.

He is accepted. Or at least none of the other cowboys question him. They talk in their rough boozy way of doing stunt work—something called the "Running W" or the even more frightening "Dead Man's Fall" are particularly popular topics—and they gossip about the movie stars themselves. Which sweet young virginal types can actually be had by just about anybody who has taken a bath in the past month. Which so-called he-men are actually prancing nancies afraid to even get close to a horse.

All this fascinates and frightens him. He wants to be back home in Morgan County, Missouri.

All that keeps him going is his memory of his father. The pennies on Father's eyes during the wake. The waxen look in the coffin. The smell of funeral flowers. His mother weeping, weeping.

The Navy Colt burns in his waistband. Burns . . .

Late on Wednesday, near the corral on the Miller Brothers 101 Ranch where Ince makes his two-reelers, a fat bald casting director in jodhpurs comes over and says, "You five men there. Can you be here at sunup?"

He has traveled fifteen hundred miles and forty-one years for this moment.

Dear Mother,

I never told you about where I saw him first, in the nickelodeon six years ago. He used a different name, of course, but I've seen so many photographs of him that even with his dyed hair and new mustache I knew it was him. I see now that his whole so-called "murder" was nothing more than a ruse to let him escape justice. He is not dead; he's alive out here . . .

He is very popular, of course, especially with the ladies, just as he was back there. He is also celebrated as a movie hero. But we know differently, don't we? If Father hadn't been riding back from the state capital that day on the train . . .

In the morning I go out to the Miller ranch where the picture is to be shot.

It will not be the only thing being shot . . .

Say hello to Aunt Eunice for me and think of me when you're making mince meat pie next Thanksgiving.

I think of your smile, Mother. I think of it all the time.

Your loving son,
Todd

All he can liken it to was his six-month stint in the army (six months only because of what the post doctor called his "nervous condition")—hundreds of extras milling around for a big scene in which a railroad car is to be held up and then robbers and good citizens alike are attacked by an entire tribe of savage Indians. It is in this way that the robber will become a hero—he will be forced to save the lives of the very passengers whom he was robbing.

The trolley car ran late. He did not sleep well. He urinates a lot. He paces a lot. He mooches two pre-rolls from a Texas cowhand who keeps talking about what a nancy the casting director in the jodhpurs is. The smoke, as always, makes him cough. But it helps calm him. The "nervous condition" being something he's always suffered from.

For two hours, waiting for the casting director to call him, he wanders the ranch, looks at the rope corral, the ranch house, the two hundred yards of train track meant to simulate miles of train track. There's even a replica of the engine from the Great Northern standing there. Everything is hot, dusty. He urinates a lot.

Around ten he sees Rex Swanson.

Rex is taller than he expected and more handsome. Dressed in a white Stetson, white western shirt with blue pearl buttons, white sheepskin vest and matching chaps, and enough rouge and lipstick to make him look womanly. Rex has just arrived, being dispatched from the back of a limousine long enough to house thirty people. He is instantly surrounded and in the tone of everybody about him there is a note of supplication.

Please Rex this.

Please Rex that.

Please Rex.

Rex *please*.

Just before lunch he sees his chance.

He has drifted over to a small stage where a painted backdrop depicts the interior of a railroad car.

It is here that Rex, in character, holds up the rich passengers, a kerchief over his face, twin silver Peacemakers shining in his hands. He demands their money, gold, jewelry.

A camera rolls; an always-angry director shouts obscenities through a megaphone. Everybody, particularly the casting director, looks nervous.

His father knocking a baseball to him. His father bouncing him on his knee. His father driving the three of them—how good it felt to be the-three-of-them, mother son father—in the buggy to Sunday church. Then his father happening to be on the train that day/so waxen in the coffin/pennies on his eyes

He moves now.

Past the director who is already shouting at him.

Past the actors who play the passengers.

Right up to Rex himself.

"You killed my father," he hears himself say, jerking the Navy Colt from his wasitband. "Thirty-seven years ago in Morgan County, Missouri!"

Rex, frantic, shouts to somebody. "Lenny! My God, it's that lunatic who's been writing me letters all these years!"

"But I know who you really are. You're really Jesse!" he says, fear gone once again, pure excitement now.

Rex—now it's his turn to be the supplicant—says, "I'm an actor from New Jersey. I only play Jesse James in these pictures! I only *play* him!"

But he has come a long ways, fifteen hundred miles and forty-one years, for this moment.

He starts firing.

It takes him three bullets, but he gets it done, he does what Robert Ford only supposedly did. He kills Jesse James.

Then he turns to answer the fire of the cowboys who are now shooting at him.

He smiles. The way that special breed of men in the nickelodians always do.

The gunslingers.

About the Editors

Bill Pronzini has written numerous western short stories and such novels of the Old West as *Starvation Camp* and *The Gallows Land*. He lives in Sonoma, California.

Martin H. Greenberg has compiled over 200 anthologies, including westerns, science fiction, and mysteries. He lives in Green Bay, Wisconsin.

THE BEST OF
THE WEST

BY BILL PRONZINI AND
MARTIN H. GREENBERG